The Coronavirus Effect

Story

JUANITA TISCHENDORF

ALSO, BY JUANITA TISCHENDORF

Three Little Girls (Murder in Rochester, NY)
Based on a True Story

Circle of Seven
Fiction – Thriller

Love Will Find A Way
Fiction – Romance

Playground In My Mind
Fiction - Thriller/Suspense

All The Missing Pieces
Fiction – Thriller/Suspense

Body Of Evidence
Fiction - Thriller/Suspense

Do not Look Back
Fiction – Thriller/Suspense

The Selfie
Nonfiction – How To

Mastering Childhood To Womanhood
Five book series
Nonfiction – How To

Over My Head
Nonfiction - Biography

An Unfair Advantage
Nonfiction – Biography

The Madman The Marathoner
Nonfiction – Biography

COPYRIGHT

Preface

It is different now. No longer can we jump into the car and run to the store to pick up something and know it will still be there. That was our welcome to the year 2020!

Other than being a numerically auspicious date, it was to be a fresh new decade, with the election of a new president. Only disbeliefs at the beginning of the year would have us wish Earth had a reset button.

From the beginning of the 21st century, so much happened. It was enough to put us on alert, but we still felt in control of our destiny.

There was the computer flaw, the so-called "Millennium Bug," that led to the Y2K (Year 2000) scare. When complex computer programs were first written in the 1960s, engineers used a two-digit code for the year, leaving out the "19." As the year 2000 approached, many believed that the systems would not interpret the "00" correctly, therefore causing a major glitch in the system, but we survived.

We were concerned with the US led war in Afghanistan that had begun on October 7, 2001, called the Operation Enduring Freedom. What started the conflict was on September 11, 2001, there was the attack on American soil that killed nearly 3,000 people. The concept of an invasion of the United States seemed impossible. The United States has only been physically invaded once during the War of 1812, once during the Mexican American War in the late 1800s, and once during World War II in 1940, yet we survived.

So, here we are again faced with a war, a viral war that threatens our way of life and has taken away most of what we cherish.

The schools have been closed for months. No longer can you get up and go out to a movie, or even out to dinner. The shelves in stores no longer carry everything or have choices you can make. Instead we put on our masks and hope for the best as we make our way out for groceries.

What will not happen is the 2020 Summer Olympics in Tokyo, so far, the release of many new movies unless there is a roundabout way to make them. There will not be the August 13, 2020, New York Yankees, and the Chicago White Sox game in the middle of a corn field in Dyersville, Iowa, to play a special "Field of Dreams" at a newly constructed ballpark. Nor will you be able to go to the stadiums to see your favorite baseball games, football games or basketball games played. You will have to watch them on television.

What will they say in the history books about COVID-19? Will it be mentioned as a footnote somewhere within the major events that reshaped our lives? The COVID-19 pandemic puts every other event of this century to shame. It is a plague so deadly it killed more people in a single year than all the natural causes combined. Before it is contained, it will change the life of people all over planet earth beyond recognition.

I am sure they will not mention all the 'should of, would ofs' that the story entailed. COVID-19 is our Noah's Ark and what the world looked like before it came, will never return. We are leaning toward a new way of life and we need to be prepared.

Chapter 1

Elise is excited. She has been picked to do the travel guide on Hubei Province. When it was first announced that they wanted someone to prepare a travel guide to this part of China, she could hardly contain her enthusiasm as she sat waiting for her boss to ask for a volunteer. As soon as he said, "Is anyone interested?" Elise's hand flew up. She twisted and turned her body to see who was to be her competition, but hers was the only hand up.

Elise's boss, Mr. Robinson was old school, and she knew he had a problem with her mixed heritage. From his receding gray hair line, squinty eyes, and shiny pink skin, he was and acted like a thoroughbred, unaware of how his manner and ways could be taken inappropriately. She had sat in this room with the other writers, feeling as though he only saw an empty chair as he scanned the room and handed out assignments. This time she prayed it would be different as she wanted this assignment more than anything she had ever wanted before.

"Okay, Elise, the job is yours."

"Huh," Elise said stupidly, sure she had not heard him right.

"I said, the job is yours." She watched Mr. Robinson walked over to her and hand her the folder that contained details for the assignment.

Elise cleared her throat and looked directly at him. "Thank you, Mr. Robinson. You will not regret it."

Elise hardly got the words out of her mouth before Mr. Robinson announced the next job and enthusiastic writers' hands shot up around the room. She watched in silence as they competed for what they envisioned as the top assignments. A tour guidebook for Italy, or one for France. Whatever did they think had not been said before.

Elise was anxious, wishing the assignments to end so that she could check out the details for the project. Finally, the last assignment was announced, assigned and all-around chairs were being pushed back as her co-workers prepared to leave the room.

She was out of her chair and first to the door, making her escape. Who knew, maybe someone did not like their assignment and was right now asking Mr. Robinson to switch with someone. She was not waiting around to find out. No one was taking this from her.

"Elise! Elise McKenna, slow down. What were you thinking?"

It was Melissa Gilbert. From the first day she joined the company, it was Melissa who helped her settle in. She could never understand her interest. Melissa was the star pupil of the company. She wrote the best travel guides and had even written a book. That and her striking good looks and personality made it easy for her to be noticed in a good way. Now as Elise turned to see Melissa's flaming long red hair and sincere smile that not only appeared on her lips, but shone in her eyes, she stopped.

"Hi Melissa."

"Hi, yourself. Why did you take that assignment?"

"It is a godsend for me." They walk side by side making a path through the group that is heading in the same direction.

"I do not know if I told you this or not, but my great-great grandmother was born and raised in Wuhan, China."

Melissa's mouth dropped. "Get out of here…"

From that reaction alone is why Melissa was her best friend. There was not a prejudice bone in her body, nor did she hide her feelings. "It is true. I know it is hard to tell that I have Chinese blood in me. I know most people know I am of mixed race, but it never dawns on them that the other part might be Chinese."

Melissa lays a finger next to her mouth. "Well, it cannot be half." She laughs as she grabs Elise's arm and walks down the hallway with her in tow. "I know your mother is white and your father, black, so..."

"True, but my mother's mother was Chinese."

Melissa squeezes her arm. "You are full of surprises Elise McKenna. Just full of them."

They arrive at Elise's desk and before parting ways, Melissa adds, "I will stop by after work and we will go out for a drink to celebrate our new assignments."

"Fabulous. Sounds like a plan."

Melissa turned, her hair splaying as she gingerly perambulated down the hall. As she pass by the desks of her coworkers, they wave or call out a greeting. Everyone loved Melissa. And they should. She was the one who stood up for a coworker when something adverse was said about them. She was the one who would willingly help if you were having problems getting your guide in on time. No matter what was happening, Melissa was there for anyone who needed help or just a friendly, hello. There was no doubt, Melissa loved people.

Elise was the last person to doubt that. When she had started at SCILICET Tours, she had arrived on the scene all excited, but her reception by her coworkers was brutal.

Being African American, this was not a new experience for her, though in truth most people would have to spend some time to figure out her nationality. But first impressions can be a nightmare to overcome. But Elise always tried.

Elise was the first to admit she has extreme emotional responses, both when happy and angry. When she found out she was accepted to her first choice for college, she threw her head back, long brown curls flying, raised those slender arms toward the sky and immediately broke into dance moves as she sang 'Do not Stop Believin' and threw her long slender legs all over the room. And one day, when someone stole a parking space she had been waiting for, Elise followed that man all the way into the store, shaking her finger and calling him rude and several other terms.

A heart shaped face, curly dark brown long hair, trim body from years of ballet lessons should have been enough attraction for a good first impression. That and her small mouth with full lips and wide expressive eyes should have sealed the deal.

She was the first woman of color to join the staff, so she gave them the benefit of the doubt, trying hard to fit in. But nothing worked. Not a smile, an offer to assist...nothing. And then she met Melissa Gilbert. The woman swooped in and saved her. It was Melissa that helped her learn how to check her temper and spread the smile around.

Melissa was the real thing. She had told Elise that people had a thing about redheads that she had to overcome before she could fit in. Once she overcame that stigma, they found her to be friendly and optimistic and that drew people towards her. She never had to try after that as she genuinely gave positive comments and was happy to help anyone in need. In a way, Melissa felt that the red hair stigma allowed her to get away with truly expressing her feelings and thoughts without appearing fake.

Melissa liked her from the moment they met because Melissa liked everyone. Only Melissa saw something genuine and interesting in Elise and she made it her mission to become her best friend. She succeeded. That in turn helped her coworkers become interested in her too. Elise hated to think what would have happened if Melissa had not taken the lead. She probably would have been on the street looking for another job and it would not fit her as well as this one did.

Seated in her office, Elise finally takes the time to check out the details of her assignment. She looks it over, smiling. For so long she has wanted to visit this remote area 7,285 miles away from Rochester, New York, but travel cost alone would run close to two thousand dollars for just the flight. That was out of her budget.

She lean back in her chair slowly turning the sheets of paper that outline the project. She is to leave for Wuhan on Sunday, November 2, 2019 and complete the assignment for return on Sunday, November 22. That gave her a total of 20 days in Wuhan.

When she was growing up, her Grandmother Chen would tell her stories of how it was living in what is now Wuhan, China back before the region evolved into an important port on the middle reaches of the Yangtze River, and the cities of Hanyang, Hankou and Wuchang were united into the city of Wuhan in 1926. Grandmother Chen had passed before the change happened so the Wuhan, she visited now would be different, but the history would still live on.

As Elise reads further, she sees that she will be arriving and leaving from Wuhan. She is to spend five days there, giving her plenty of time to get to know the region and its people. Knowing her granddaughter is finally going to her birthplace, would have given her Grandmother Chen such joy and she plans to make the most of it.

"Elise, it is like paradise." Grandmother Chen would say. "There are ancient sites and relics, imposing imperial palaces, and amazing natural wonders. It would take years to see it all but there are some that you cannot pass up like the Yangtze River and Hans River."

Elise leans back in her chair wondering how they came up with the name Wuhan. She turns on her computer and googles it. She reads through several sites before finding what she wanted.

"Oh," Elise, said aloud as she read, "Wuhan is the base and it got its name from its three parts—Wuchang, Hankou, and Hanyang—commonly called the Three Towns of Wuhan. Putting the three names together 'Wu' from the first city and 'Han' from the other two. The three former cities face each other across the rivers and are linked by bridges, including one of the first modern bridges in China, known as the 'First Bridge'."

Elise was enthralled as she continued reading about Wuhan. "There are so many lakes and so many mountains to explore with its sub-tropical climate in Hubei."

"So where is Hubei" she asked herself, searching on the name.

"Ah, it is where Wuhan is. Hubei province." She liked the sound of it as it rolled softly off her tongue."

Grandmother Chen had told Elise that though she was born in Wuhan it was easy for her to settle in Rochester because of the similarity of weather and seasons.

Growing up Elise had often heard her mother tell how hard it had been for her father to adjust to Rochester weather as he was born and raised in Chesterfield, Virginia where the winters were milder and the summers much hotter. But her mother would say that love does conquer all because they did fall in love and he agreed to settle in Rochester. His parents, wanting to be close to the grandchildren followed and Rochester became home.

So, though Elise had not been to Wuhan, physically, she had mentally. Over the years listening to the stories she had developed a mental picture of wonder and fascination and wanted to share this with the world. It may be why she became a travel guide writer in the first place. It may be what shaped her future.

Elise leans forward and looks through the information in the folder. This was going to be her step up to the head of the class. She would not only write and illustrate the best travel guide, but maybe, just maybe write a book. Elise was on cloud nine as she gathered up her belongings and left to join her coworkers at the local bar.

The two-story red painted brick building with its imposing oversized neon letters over the entrance is of a style that speaks to its having been there for a long time. Voted "Best Neighborhood Bar" and "Best Happy Hour" by City Newspaper's 'Best of Rochester' Awards in 2015 Lux Lounge is an alternative bar like what you would find in a city like Portland or NYC.

Elise likes the LUX because it has benches and a hammock out back for the clientele to use when the inside became too overcrowded. Whereas Melissa who loved to socialize, likes that the atmosphere is very laid-back and conducive for conversation. It has appeal for those who like to play board games or sit in front of a toasty fire during the winter months and listen to the juke box.

When Elise enters the LUX, it takes a few minutes for her eyes to adjust, then she scans the area for her friends.

"Over here Elise." She sees Melissa waving before she hears her call out to her. Elise squeezes through the crowd excusing herself until she makes it over to the table to join her friends. Earlier, she began preparing herself for the remarks that she knows will follow. It begins the minute she grabs a glass and starts pouring herself a beer. "I cannot believe you took that assignment."

She had her response ready. "Yes, well, someone had to."

There were several other comments coming, and she handled them easily without giving any personal details. She was direct and after several minutes the attention turned to discuss other assignments, handed out that morning. In most cases, the writers were happy with their job and only a few wished they had been given something different.

It was no matter to Elise who enjoyed listening to the banter going on and having a private conversation with Melissa. "Thanks Melissa."

"For what?"

"For not telling them why I wanted the assignment."

Melissa made a pouty face. "You thought I would tell them your personal business."

Elise smiled, "No, I guess I knew you would not, but still, thank you for being you."

Melissa leaned over and hugged Elise. "No thanks needed."

After consuming two pitchers of beer there is no need for another as the coworkers need to get home and put the final changes on their previous assignments. This way they can start fresh in the morning on their new projects.

It is like a domino effect. One decides to depart and immediately others follow. There is a rustle of chairs as one by one they get ready to leave. Some stand and finish off the last of their drinks, while others wave or hug before departing. As for Elise she walks out, arm in arm with Melissa, parting when they reach Melissa's car. "See you in the morning."

Elise gives Melissa a hug and walks down the street to climb into her car. She takes a minute to just breathe. She has been so excited about her project that she is sure her pulse is racing. Finally, she pulls out of her parking space and drives straight home. When she pulls into her space, she rushes inside the building and fidgets with the lock on her apartment, before she is finally able to step across the threshold, put her things down, then reach into her purse and pull out her cell.

"Guess what mom."

"Well, hello to you daughter."

Elise can tell by her voice her mother is moving about with the cell phone tucked on her shoulder to keep it to her ear so she can continue what she is doing and listen to her at the same time.

They are more like best friends then mother and daughter since they have spent a lot of time alone together since her father became famous with his best seller. Elise loves her father, but her mother is the center of her universe and she shares everything with her.

She knows her so well and she knows at this moment her mother is tucking her hair behind her ear so it does not block her view as she lowers her head and Elise can already imagine her stopping what she is doing with stunned surprise when she blurts out her news.

"Mom, I am going to Wuhan."

Complete silence on the other end. Then the sound of a phone dropping, a minute of body movements and finally her mother's voice, shaking with excitement.

"You are kidding, you are, aren't you?"

"Noooo. It is true. My next assignment is a travel guide on Wuhan, or more specifically, Hubei Province."

Elise gives her a minute to let it sink in and then she is unstoppable. "Oh Elise, you are so lucky. How long will you be gone?"

"Three weeks, mom. But the reason I am calling is I want to get your advice on what I should see and do."

"Oh, my, it is been so long, but Ezhou City. It is the birthplace of China's Pure Land Buddhism. Oh yes, and the Liangzi Lake." She pauses a moment, then adds, "Qiongtai Palace on Wudang Mountain is breathtaking…"

Elise is writing as her mother speaks. "What about cities. I can check out the sights, but which cities should I visit."

"Ezhou, Xiangyag City, Shiyan and of course Wuhan."

"I will be staying five days in Wuhan so I should be able to see a lot there."

"You know what your grandmother would say?"

"Yes, that it would take a lifetime to see it all."

Her mother laughs and Elise knows she is nodding her head and her hair is coming out from behind her ears as she does so. "I wish you could come with me mother."

"I wish I could too. If it were not on short notice I could… Is it short notice?"

"No, not really. I leave on November 1, two weeks from now."

There is silence on the line and Elise knows her mother is checking her calendar and biting her lip. "I wish I could, but for me that is too soon to cancel my appointments and get ready. I do not want to leave your grandfather alone either. But promise you will call me before you go, and I will call you if I think of anything else." She pauses and Elise knows what she is about to say. "Daughter, I miss our long lunches."

"I know, mom. You have been quite busy at the hospital and me, well this job is particularly important to me and I need to make a good impression. But I will be calling regularly anyway, to pick your brain for details. I can promise you that."

"I love you Elise. And Elise your grandmother was always so proud of you. Now, knowing you are going to her native land she would be beside herself."

"Thanks mom. I love you too."

Chapter 2

It is always the same in the office at the beginning of the next travel guide assignments, everyone busy working on trying to make the best travel guide ever written. Each night she calls her mother and refreshes the information she has heard all her life. The two of them laugh and plan out every minute of her three weeks there. Her mother also gives her advice on what she should take with her.

Each day when they talk, it brings back the memories of listening to her grandmother as she spoke about her home in China. Elise stares off in the distance, recalling a time before her grandmother was sick. Her grandmother would come in to say goodnight to her and sit in the chair next to her bed and tell her stories about her childhood and family. It sounded like a fairytale as she weaved a picture of the many lakes and rivers to swim in and how they watched the petals fall from the trees with the light shining through them and making them appear mystical while pretending they were getting married. This was the personal side of the area that would not be in travel guides but would make for a good book.

Elise remembers laughing as her grandmother told her about snacks, she would eat that she would see as creepy and how she felt when she first saw the great wall. She loved rickshaw rides and cycling through the countryside and swimming and watching shadow puppetry. "And you cannot imagine," she would say, "how exciting it is to see a giant panda free and in the wild".

At that moment Elise's had a memory jog. Her grandmother told her how she loved to explore the caves and see the bats hanging from the top of the caves and making a squeaking noise when they were disturbed. Yes, she would say, she loved her home, her siblings and they had many adventures together.

Elise made a note on her pad. Must visit the caves.

Back then she thought she would have more conversations with her grandmother but then she started forgetting. The day her mother took her to the doctors was the day her grandmother's life changed forever. She had been the one to store the memories and share them and now, that was over. Her stories were told like she was reliving the moment, and Elise could not grasp what not remembering would do to her.

The change happened rapidly as each day her grandmother was more confused than the day before. Elise would go to see her and find her grandmother sitting peacefully within another realm that Elise only sometimes can reach through and have her grandmother back. Then, when Elise tries to refresh her memory, her grandmother would snap at her. Her calm sweet grandmother was replaced by a frustrated and angry person she barely knew.

When her grandmother finally had to be under constant care, Elise went with her mother to take her to the local, 'A Place for Mom', feeling a deep loss and sad that they could not care for her themselves. Each time they visited her, which was often in the beginning, Elise and her mother felt contentedness, pride, and joy if she remembered them. Each meaningful connection at first raised hope, but then they learned to just enjoy the moment.

On many of their visits, she would see other patients all alone and having no one come to visit them. It hurt her dearly and the experience made Elise want to do something, so she started volunteering to visit with other patients with Alzheimer's. At first it felt virtuous, but then she made the mistake with one of the patients to ask her to tell her about her daughter. The woman said she did not have a daughter.

Elise had been there long enough to have learned all there was about the two ladies they had assigned for her to visit and she did know better, but stupidly held up a photo of the woman's daughter and said. "Is not this your daughter?"

The woman's face went bright red and deep crevices appeared on her forehead as her eyes filled with tears. In a low voice she quietly said that yes, that was her daughter. She could tell the woman was embarrassed by her forgetfulness and Elise was sorry she had made such a blunder. She could have said, "That is OK. I forget things like that, too," but she did not even think to say that.

Elise made similar mistakes when visiting her beloved grandmother. One day her grandmother told her, she had talked to her father the previous evening. Elise's great grandfather had been deceased for more than 50 years. Again, she was inconsiderate and told her grandmother that her father was dead. She would never forget that hurt and confused expression on her face.

It was Elise's mother who saved her that time by chirping in, "I talk to him often myself." The hurt expression immediately went away, and they continued pleasantly safe conversations during the rest of their visit.

One day on their way home Elise told her mother she did not want to visit her grandmother anymore. She said, "She does not even know who I am and gets terribly angry sometimes. Then, sometimes I forget and say things that hurt her. It's difficult trying to do and say the right thing."

Her mother was quiet, then said, "Well, Elise have you ever experienced memory or judgment problems, or been afraid of something?"

"Yes."

"Well what if you also had to give up most or all of your favorite activities too. It would be perfectly normal to be depressed or anxious and wander away from a possibly threatening situation or to strike out at someone we think is trying to hurt us."

"Think of having to wake in a building you have never been in before that is full of furniture and items you do not recognize. Then, have complete strangers enter your room and talk to you as if you have known them their entire lives. Have these strangers tell you they are your daughter and grandchild. The entire time you will be wondering what in the world is going on."

"So, whether we go or not go to visit, she sees no connection to us and our lives."

"Well, yes, but she does have her moments and then it is worth it."

All Elise could do was nod.

There were tears in Elise's eyes as she sat cross legged on the couch thinking about all of this, then wiping her eyes she got back to outlining an itinerary. By the time she turned in for the night, she knew she was going to have a lot more than just a travel guide when she finished gathering information and pictures.

Elise got up and started getting ready to turn in for the night. As she stared at herself in the mirror, she thought about her father and smiled. She would experience China on her own and her mother would add the intimate details, but her father would be the one to help her turn it all into a book.

The next morning Elise woke up late and had to hurry to get to work on time. She stopped at Starbucks for a coffee and then headed for the office. When she got off the elevator, she could see everyone was busily putting together their agendas. Not wanting to interrupt she smiled when she caught someone's eye and hurried to her desk to work on her outline.

It was always the same. Each of them would get the assignment and then needed to prepare and turn in their agendas the next morning to the person at the outer office, assigned to them for their project. In this case hers would be going to the Wuhan office where she would be allocated a guide who would take her schema and any notes she prepared and create a full itinerary for her trip.

While she waited for a response back, Elise busied herself with packing and spending time with her mother who was as excited as she over the upcoming trip. At work she picked the brains of her coworkers who had done travel guides that took them out of the States. This would be Elise's first time for a major travel assignment. Most of her previous travel guides were local places so she relished any advice she could get. Finally, she received a response back from the Wuhan office.

The moment she opened the email, it all became real. It was really happening. She, Elise was about to journey to China on an adventure of a lifetime.

That it would be in many ways.

Chapter 2

Elise was excited. After reviewing the itinerary, she was happy to learn they accepted her agenda in total and she could not wait to share the news with her mother. Anxiously she called her mother at work.

"Dr. Sonya McKenna's office, how can I help you."

"Hi, this is Elise. Is my mother available?"

"Hang on, I will check." In a few, Elise heard her mother's voice.

"Hi sweetheart. Is everything all right?"

"Yes, I just wanted to invite you to dinner. Her mother being a doctor clocked long hours and it was not always easy for her to be flexible.

"What time were you thinking."

"Whatever works for you."

"Then, yes, I can make a 6:00 dinner with my daughter."

"Thanks mom. I will come by and pick you up."

That taken care of, Elise went over the final draft of her previous travel guide writeup and carried it to her boss, Mr. Robinson's office for final approval.

As usual he was on the phone and she had to wait to see him. His secretary asked if she could get her a cup of coffee, but Elise declined, not wanting to lose her spot for seeing him. She only had to wait a few minutes before he buzzed his secretary, and she was shown into his office.

"Ah, Ms. McKenna. What do you have for me?"

She never knew for sure if he was trying to be funny or did this to everyone. He knew they were to turn in their assignments today so her being there should not be a surprise. Elise ignored the question and walked over to his desk and handed him the folder.

"Please, take a seat Ms. McKenna."

As usual, no matter how well she felt she had done, she tensed up when she had to hand her assignment over. She sat on the edge of her seat, nervously waiting.

It was Mr. Robinson's habit to read the descriptions aloud, in the writer's presence, so after opening the folder, he begins. His voice usually so commanding and take-charge changes when he reads, making the written words sound so exciting. There is a volume or depth, even at times an accent. He makes the words jump off the page as he reads them.

"Scilicet tours presents a trip to remember." He pauses and stands up behind his desk. From experience Elise knows it is his nature to read and pace around the room, so she watches, quietly as he continues.

"Join us on our famous Lake Ontario tours. The Great Lakes of North America are lakes Superior, Michigan, Huron, Erie, and Ontario. They represent a series of interconnected freshwater lakes in the upper mid-east region of North America and are the largest group of freshwater lakes on the earth. They are second-largest by total volume with Lake Ontario being the smallest in size, but the most interesting as it connects to Toronto and Niagara-on-the-Lake. The popularity of Lake Ontario is its islands, beaches, wildlife, and waterfront trails, offering something for everyone."

Mr. Robinson pauses, taking in the picture of families enjoying the trails and beaches. She has even included shots of wildlife. He says nothing as he begins reading again.

"You will leave on Sunday to travel around Lake Ontario on this exclusive tour with a friend. The tour begins at 7:30 in the morning when you head to Prince Edward County, taking the 401 east from Toronto. Breakfast will be served at the Tucson Cooking Institute, at 10:30 am where you will be attending a cooking class with none other than the world renown Chef Odell Baskerville who will provide you with professional kitchen basics in preparing your own breakfast. From there we will tour the Prince Edward County wineries. After an afternoon of sampling different wines you will be taken to the Picton Harbor Inn where you will have time to freshen up in you room and be taken to the East and Main Bistro featuring local food and wine. It will be a fulfilled day and after a good night sleep we leave for the American side of Lake Ontario. You will be taken to Rochester, NY via the Thousand Islands Bridge, Route 81 south to Route 90 west. Here we will travel through the Finger Lakes for a tour of wineries before going to The Ellwanger Estate B&B on Mount Hope Ave. After a homemade breakfast at the B&B you will be taken to the George Eastman House museum of photograph and film and have lunch at Java's before picking up your bikes and cycling along the Genesee Riverway Trail which goes through the city to the Lake. After a good day of biking you will return to the B&B and prepare for dinner at Hogan's Hideaway on Park Avenue. This will end your three-day tour."

Mr. Robinson lets out a 'hmmm' then stares a moment out his office window before continuing. By now, Elise is sitting on the edge of her seat. She cannot see his face, so she does not know if he is enjoying her descriptive presentation or thinking she has overdone it again. Since too much verbiage was his usual complaint.

Silence permeates the room. Elise dare not speak and Mr. Robinson seems entranced as his mouth moves as if silently repeating what he has read. After torturous silence, he looks up and finally his eyes find hers.

Elise sits paralyzed to the spot, the menacing aura holding her in a tightening grip. She could feel her pulse beating in her ears, blocking out all other sound except the breath that was raggedly moving in and out of her mouth. This moment was crucial as it was not too late for him to pull the plug on her new assignment. Nothing else mattered beyond the words he would speak at this moment.

"This is good, Elise. I sensed you were getting better and this proves it. You are ready for a major assignment and I am glad you volunteered for one."

"Ah, thank you." she mumbled, barely able to form the words. "I mean, thank you very much," she added.

Elise allowed herself to breathe as she continued eye contact with her boss. His expression told her he was waiting for her to leave so she stood feeling like she should curtsy or something, but she did not. Instead she turned and headed for the door.

Just before she crossed the threshold, she could not help herself and she turned back around to say, "Thank you. I will live up to your expectations." She then turn back around, smiling as she left his office.

Once at her desk Elise enthusiastically signed off on her completed project, then took care of some follow-up calls that came in while she was in Mr. Robinson's office. She also took the time to download the translation app onto her phone, along with the instruction manual that she could examine later. That, she did not want to forget to do.

Elise stood up and stretched, then sat back down and said a prayer before going to her Hotmail account. Earlier that week she had prepared an email requesting information on modern day China. She had sent it out to contacts she knew had recently visited China to get a personal view and suggestions of places of interest. Though she had a lot of history from her grandmother, she had nothing on what it was like now. Thinking ahead she knew that much of what her mother shared may not be pertinent today and the travel agent assigned to her in China, might only head her toward the major tourist attractions.

She was beaming. She had received several responses back.

Elise wanted to open them but saw one from the travel agency in China. She opened it. "Hoping you are prepared for your trip. Attached is your itinerary, flight details and hotel arrangements. No car has been assigned, but kindly let us know if you would like one. Our agent will be taking you everywhere you wish to go."

She printed out the attachments.

Elise next opened the first of several detailed information she had requested. She smiled, hoping her guide would be flexible and allow her to make changes to the itinerary.

It was long and informative; just what she had hoped for and she leaned forward, elbows on her desk and face just inches from the screen. This one was from a writer friend of her dads and using careful examples he conjured a scene that vividly described his experience in China. Elise was taken away as she could visualize the places, smell, and taste the food and hear the sounds that surrounded him.

So enthralled with what she was reading, she had not seen Melissa approaching so when she felt a tap on her shoulder, she caught her breath in a startled gasp.

Melissa laughed at Elise's surprised expression and then composed herself. "Sorry Elise. Did not mean to scare you, but it is five o'clock."

"Oh no. I lost track of time. Elise frantically started shoving papers into her briefcase.

"Slow down, Elise, do not rush. I will wait while you get ready."

"No, it is not that. I cannot go out with you guys tonight."

"And why is that?"

"Oh, Melissa, I am so sorry. I should have told you earlier. I am taking my mother out to dinner tonight, so I will not be joining you and the gang at Lux."

Melissa put on her most pouty look; her lower lip pushed out way too far to be attractive but working for her. "Come on Elise. You can come for one drink at least."

Elise stood up and continued gathering her things before turning toward her friend, giving her a sympathetic hug. "Cannot. It is a special night."

"What! Did I miss your birthday…?" Elise could see the wheels turning. "Is it your mother's birthday?"

"Stop. It is neither. It is just that she is anxious to see my itinerary for Wuhan. We are going to be just two gals on the town tonight sharing a meal and talking about the past that is about to become real for me. You can understand Melissa. Can't you?"

"Yes, I understand even if I do not like it. So, okay, I will give your regards to everyone and see you at work tomorrow." Elise watched as Melissa sashayed down the hall before she turned back to check her area. She picked up a brochure she wanted to take with her and after a final check, she turned off her computer and mouse. As she stepped out of her compartment, she grabbed her purse, swung it over her shoulder, along with her briefcase.

As she rushed down the hallway, the strap of her briefcase caught on the corner of one of the short wall panels. "Damn," she said, leaning down and repositioning the straps on her shoulder, then placing a hand over the side of her purse so that it was all held tight against her. "Okay, Let's try that again," she said, talking to herself as she hurries the rest of the way without incident.

The elevator arrives quickly. Elise stepped in, her mind going a mile a minute. It does not seem possible, but in a few days, she will be on her way to Wuhan, China. A shiver of excitement courses through her body.

In her possession is her assignment folder, tickets, and details on the trip. The assignment begins on November 1, 2019 and ends on November 22, so she has 20 days to gather information for her guidebook.

When the elevator stops, Elise steps out on the ground floor, her mind still going over the plans for her trip as she makes her way to her car.

Her flight will take 1 day and 15 hours to Wuhan, the absolute longest she has been on a plane. She has checked the logistics and is aware there is 12 hours difference in time which means leaving November 1st, she will arrive on November 2nd at almost 10 pm. In her adrenaline level state, she tells herself that is not too late to do something that evening.

Finally, Elise reaches her car and slides her purse and briefcase off her shoulder and holds them both by the strap as she runs her finger across the raised bars on the handle of her car. She hears the sound as it unlocks and opens the door, tossing her purse and briefcase into the passenger seat before she climbs in behind the wheel.

"Hello Cher," she says, using the name she has given her Toyota CH-r. It was not until recently she realized how important it was for her to have a car that was not only new, but also a model that was just coming out for the first time. First it was the Chrysler, PT-Cruiser that she cried over when it died. And now, she had the CH-r. With all her updated features this car won her heart.

Elise pressed the brake pedal and the start button, then put on her seatbelt. She pressed the switch and watched as the side mirrors unfolded, then, backed out of her parking space to head toward her mother's house.

Usually there would be the work traffic to deal with but being late she pretty much had the road to herself. She found the expressway traffic flowing just as well and she made it in record time from her work downtown to West Irondequoit. She decides not to take the Portland exit since she will have to deal with the hospital traffic.

Her mother, Sonya, known to most as Dr. McKenna, is on staff there and has warned her many times to take an alternate route or sit at the light waiting as the cars exit and enter the ramp garage. Hearing that so often, Elise usually takes St. Paul Blvd, which is closer to her mother's, but Portland takes her almost directly to her apartment. When she finally pulls into her mother's driveway, she sees Sonya sitting on the porch, waiting.

Elise opens the passenger window and laughing says, "Mom, come on. I can see you are in a hurry." Sonya smiles as she descends her front steps and walks down the sidewalk to her daughter's car. She reaches for the door handled, then stops and turns back toward the house.

"Mom, what is it?"

"Nothing. I will be right back."

It is not like her to be forgetful so Elise figures it must be something else. She giggles thinking it may be that her mother needs to go to the bathroom before they take off.

In minutes she is back out the door and hurrying to the car.

"All set?"

"Yes."

"Forgot something?"

"Do not ask."

They have reservations at the Pasta Villa on Ridge Road East, a place they have gone to for years and never tire of the food. They have the best homemade Italian food this side of Italy. The building has a homey atmosphere and aside from the large sign over the front porch of this ranch style home, it looks like a quaint house with its long front porch and beautiful flowers.

"So, mom, what did you forget."

"You are not going to let it go are you."

"No."

Sonya hesitates a bit then finally admits, "Well, I was waiting quite a while and when I saw you drive up, I got a little excited and, and..."

"And, what?"

"Peed my pants a little."

Elise cannot hold it in and starts giggling making her mother even more embarrassed. "Sorry, sorry."

Sonya does not respond at first but then very calmly, slowly, a smile spreads across her face intensifying until she is laughing along with her daughter.

"It is, kind of funny."

They had been standing at the entrance only a short while when the host takes them to their table. The minute they are seated they start talking about Elise's trip with Sonya sharing more tidbits she had found in some of her grandmother's papers stored in the attic. Elise shares what she has learned from the responses to her emails.

"Mom, would not grandmother be surprised to learn that Wuhan is the capital city of Hubei province and is the largest city in Hubei."

Sonya, who has a mouth full of pasta, nods. She chews and takes a swallow of her water before adding.

"It would be even more surprising to her to learn about the super trains and that the population has gone from one million during her lifetime there to over 11 million. That would blow her mind."

As soon as she said it, Sonya regretted it. Her mother's mind... Mother and daughter look at each other, each thinking the same thing and feeling embarrassed, but then slowly, they cannot help but smile over the accidental pun that has slipped out.

As predictable, the meal is amazing, and the conversation cannot be exceled as Mom and daughter start catching up on what was going on in their life's. That conversation does not take long as they try to keep in touch every day. Then with the meal over and the tab delivered, Sonya and Elise bicker over who should pay. Elise wins out and they walk out arm and arm together. On the drive home, Sonya says, "Elise, I want you to be careful over there. They have different ways then us Americans."

"Don't worry, mom. I will not be totally alone. Remember, I will have a guide and they will be taking me around so they will keep me in check."

"Sure," her mother says with sarcasm dripping off her words. "Taking you around, good. Keeping you in check...Yeah, right."

Elise smiles as she pulls into her mother's driveway. Her parents had taken an old three-story colonial house and turned it into a showpiece inside and out. It had not happened overnight, but her mother was always saying, "It was the best two years of our life." Her father, then a struggling author, had more time on his hands to work on the house and spend with his wife. Now, her parents were still close and very much in love, but their time together was short with his book promotional tours and her long hours at the hospital. They were always saying, "The time will come when we will be able to sit back and enjoy each other's company again."

Elise hugs her mother and says. "I wish I could come in, but I am exhausted."

"I know, dear. And I have an early call at the hospital."

They say their goodnights and Elise drives home. Once through the door of her apartment, she drops her purse and briefcase on the side table and heads to the back where she strips out of the clothes she has been in all day. She brushes her hair, and while brushing her teeth turns on the shower.

Even with the vent, the room is steamy when she steps in, allowing the hot water and steam to relax her before stepping out and drying off. She concentrates on emptying her mind but gives up as she steps into her pajama bottoms and slips her arms through the short sleeve top. When she finally climbs into her bed, she closes her eyes, but her mind keeps spinning until finally she falls asleep.

Elise is awakened suddenly. She sits up staring around the room in the thralls of a nightmare. When her heart stops racing, she tries to remember what scared her, but it was gone so she laid back down and slept peacefully until the alarm went off.

The next few days, Elise spend as much time as she could with Melissa and her coworkers who constantly insisted, she had to be crazy to want her assignment.

"Come on Melissa," Elise would say, "this is where my grandmother was born and raised. I have an attachment to this place."

"Sure, but it is not your grandmothers, Wuhan. You are going to be in a city where there is so much smog you cannot see a foot in front of you, and, oh yes, you will not have to worry about falling because you will be walking amid 10 million people." She grabs me by the shoulders and puts her face close to mind as she shares the details.

Elise cannot help but giggle. "It is not that bad Mel. Not every person in the area will be walking around at the same time and, besides, if you were given an assignment in New York City, you would jump at it and be in the same situation."

Mel frowns thoughtfully. "At least I can understand what they are saying about me," she retorts as she puts her arm through mine and drags me along beside her.

They gingerly argue back and forth, but not seriously since Elise accepts her friend's opinion because she knows it's that she cares, and Melissa accepts Elise's determination because she does understand.

Then there is Sonya who is at first all for the trip, but the closer it comes, the more she backs off. Sonya begins to worry, telling her daughter that she had a premonition that scared her.

"Come on mother, you cannot be serious."

"Elise, you know I do not believe in foreseeing the future, but this was so real."

"Because it is about me. I will be safe. It is not like I will be there alone wandering around. Remember I will have a guide with me at all times." Mischievously she adds, "Well, except when I am sleeping."

Each day during their phone conversations, Sonya would confront Elise with proof that she should not snuff at her premonitions. Each day Elise would smile, give her a hug, and try to ease her fears. She must understand that it is too late for her to change her mind now. Even if she could, she would not.

Chapter 3

November 1st finally arrives and Elise being an early riser by nature, has no trouble getting ready for her 6 o'clock a.m. flight. She has studied the flight itinerary so many times she could recite it from memory. The plane would take off from the Greater Rochester International Airport at 6:15 a.m. and land at Dulles International Airport at 7:33 a.m. where she has a 49-minute layover before departing at 8:22 a.m. for Newark. They arrive at Newark Liberty International Airport at 9:53 a.m. After a 2-hour 2-minute layover they depart at 1:35 p.m. for the lengthy flight to Beijing Capital International Airport.

But that is not the end of the layovers as she has a 5 hour and 55 minute layover in Beijing before she boards for the last time at 7:30 p.m. for a 2 hour, 20 minute flight to Wuhan, arriving at Wuhan Tianhe International Airport at 9:50 p.m.

It is annoying that she will spend 8 hours and 6 minutes in layover time, but she tries to look on the bright side. She can read and do a little airport sightseeing or maybe study the language of Wuhan. She has downloaded the app along with a language training program which has Standard Mandarin Chinese. She knows a little Mandarin from her grandmother, but not enough to get around on her own.

The thought that this trip would take one day, and fifteen hours blew her mind. Once up there harnessed to a seat, there was not much to do but sleep. She should be well rested when she finally reaches her destination.

Not one to wait till the last minute, Elise is packed and ready when the Uber driver arrives. She stands on the front porch waiting in the cool morning air watching the driver pull into a space near the front door. He parks the car and walks up the sidewalk until he is at the bottom of the stairs.

"Madam, my name is Henry. Can I help you with your luggage?"

"Thank you, Henry. I am Elise."

After the brief introduction they manage the luggage in one trip and soon she is seated in the back seat starting the first leg of her exciting voyage.

One of the things Elise has learned to appreciate in Rochester, New York, is the traffic… there usually is not any. She has been in several cities and sat in bumper to bumper traffic with travelers who seem to take it for granted since it happens every day. That would drive Elise crazy. She appreciates the fact that the time from place to place in Rochester is minimal and less stressful.

It is smooth sailing from her apartment to the airport and once Henry pulls up, at the Delta gate, he gets out and helps her unload her luggage.

"Thank you, Henry. It is been nice riding with you." She says as she hands him a tip.

"You are welcome, Miss Elise."

When she turns, a porter casually asks, "Can I help you with your luggage."

"Sure. Thank you."

They step into the revolving door and slowly walk around in the revolving door entrance until the opening is at the lobby. Elise steps through and while she adjusts the straps on her shoulder the porter stands beside her. "Oh, we are so lucky, she says."

"What, Madam?"

"Sorry, this will be a mass of people causing quite a hassle at other airports, but not here."

"You are right. It is usually quite manageable," he response as they continue to the counter where he stops and Elise thanks him, giving him a tip. "Thank you, miss.

Elise is met with silence inside the airport and takes it all in knowing that this would not be the case at the other airports along the way. She strolls up to the counter of Delta and is immediately greeted by a smiling attendant.

Elise reaches into her purse and takes out her ID and her flight information. She could have printed out her boarding pass at home, but this gives her something to do. While the airline attendant prepares her tickets, they chat about her destination.

"Is this your first time to China."

"It is, it is."

"I see your final destination is Wuhan…I have not heard of it before?"

"I know. Most people have not', but it is the birthplace of my grandmother and I have always wanted to visit. When the opportunity came, I took it."

"That is nice. My family is from Italy and I have always wanted to go there."

"You should."

At this point the attendant has completed the processing of her ticket and tagged her luggage, placing it on the conveyor belt. "You are all taken care of Miss McKenna. Have a safe trip.

"Thank you. I will."

Elise goes to the security check in, weaving through the line with three other passengers. She places her belongings on the conveyor belt and soon she is in the millimeter wave machine. Elise had read up on this replacement to the full body scanner, so she knew what to expect. She stands still as the twin vertical arrays of extremely high-frequency transmitters circle her body to create a three-dimensional image. The transmitters emit beams of radio frequency energy, which bounce off sub–clothing surfaces but will expose any hidden items.

When she gets the okay, she steps out and picks up her belongings off the conveyor belt. She is on her way, whispering to herself, "Millimeter wave machine, it sounds so futuristic."

Elise makes her way to the nearest screen and locates her flight. She checks the gate number she will be leaving from and then heading in that direction, she is interrupted by a familiar sound. She turns her head and sees a woman hurrying across the tiled floor in high heels. Why would anyone wear high heels to catch a plane, she wonders. It seems so ridiculous to her as she turns her head forward, adjust the straps of her carry-ons and walks silently in her sneakers to the gate.

It is like walking through a ghost town. Outside of the airport personnel, and the high-heeled lady she is alone. When she turns down the corridor, she sees the gold tree sculpture and then the Clock of the Nations.

She pauses, feeling a little sad. When the Clock of the Nations was unveiled at Midtown Plaza's opening on April 10, 1962, a crowd of 5,000 cheered as Mayor Henry Gillette and former mayor Peter Barry cut the ribbon to unveil the Clock of the Nations, the centerpiece of the new Midtown Plaza in Rochester. The clock was made by artist Dale Clark who was a former Lockheed Aircraft engineer turned artist. Now, it has been over 10 years since visitors took final photos inside Midtown, before the plaza's doors were locked one last time, never to open again. The clock was moved to what was supposed to be a temporary location beyond security checkpoints at Greater Rochester International Airport. Its puppets still twirl to tinny folk songs. But the centerpiece of Rochester's groundbreaking downtown mall now is out of sight to all but travelers in and out of the airport. It was the spot where people would say, "Meet me under the Midtown clock". Now it sits with its little doors closed until the hour when the designated door will open, and the little characters will dance and twirl with no one paying attention.

Nothing is open on the concourse, so Elise continues her way to the gate. This is a relatively small airport that has gone through transformation to enhance the terminal. They added a high-tech smart facility to serve the business and economic customers and a canopy covered walkway as well. The only purpose for that is to give the building a grandeur affect. It obviously is not done to attract the locals as much as to impress the outside world.

When Elise reaches the waiting area for her flight, she takes a seat near the entrance doorway and pulls out her book. She still enjoys a book over the kindle. She gets a thrill out of turning a page and being able to tell just how many more pages exist before she reaches the end. Plus, she likes using her fancy book marker. She bought it at a quaint shop when she visited New York City with her book club members. Every time she uses it, she remembers that trip and how much fun they had.

Elise has barely settled in when they start calling the passengers to board. With her nose in the book she had not realized that more people have joined her at the gate. The waiting area is full, and passengers are lining up. Elise stands up and slides her purse off her shoulder so she can retrieve her ticket and boarding pass. Once she has them in her hand, she puts the shoulder strap on and comfortably adjusts her carryon before joining the other passengers.

For the first time she takes a good look at her boarding pass. A frown appears on her face. She looks again, thinking it had to be a mistake. She had been conversing with the attendant so she might have made a mistake. Elise tries to remain calm as she holds tightly onto her boarding pass.

The gate agent begins by greeting the passengers and starts calling the boarding order.

"Will those who need assistance or additional time to board, including families with car seats or strollers, please board now."

That seems to be a small group and in short order the boarding agent begins, "Will all Delta One customers; First Class customers and Diamond Medallion members board now."

Hesitantly Elise moves to the front, then stands back, allowing the other passengers in this group to board first; just in case her first class status is a mistake. When it is her turn and she hands the agent her boarding pass, the agent smiles and says, "Enjoy your flight."

As she goes down the jetway her mind is reeling. Her company has never sent her on assignment and given her first class status.... never. This not being one of the so-called 'glamour' assignments which might warrant first class makes her think it is a mistake. But it does not matter now as she picks up her pace and walks down the jetway feeling like someone special.

Once on the plane she breathes much easier as she walks down the aisle, but then she hears a voice behind her. She freezes thinking, 'Oh, no, I have been found out'.

"Miss, may I see your boarding pass." Hesitantly Elise holds it out, ready to explain it is not her fault. She feels the heat rising in her body and her breathing quicken and then the miracle continues.

"Here, let me help you with that bag." The flight attendant steps forward and places her bag over the seat that appears on her ticket. She is to sit in first class. Hallelujah! She almost says it aloud.

Instead she smiles and says, "Thank you," before taking her first-class seat near the window.

"Can I get you something to drink?"

Elise glances around the cabin and notices for the first time that most of the first-class passengers are already being served drinks.

"Can I have a cup of coffee?"

"Sure."

In minutes, the flight attendant returns. She lowers Elise's tray and places the coffee on it, along with two packs of sugar and a creamer. "Thank you."

This is amazing. While passengers walk down the aisle pass her seat, she feels so élite. She could get use to this, but she better not. The mix up will not happen again; of that she can be sure.

Settled in the comfortable seat, she looks at her ticket. She has one hour and eighteen minutes to enjoy the luxury of first class on this leg of her journey. She plans to savor every minute as she sits back and relaxes. As always happens, the motion of the plane lulls her to sleep and once they are airborne her eyes start to close. The flight attendant stops to ask if she would like a blanket and a pillow. "Yes, thank you." No one has taken the seat next to her so Elise has plenty of room to stretch out as she leans back and quickly drifts off to sleep.

When she wakes it is to the sound of the pilot's voice announcing descent. Elise has slept through the first leg of her trip and feels refresh. She notices the coffee has been removed so she puts her seat and tray in the upright position, then stares out the window as the plane slowly drops below the cloud cover and Dulles International Airport comes into view. Even though she knows it, she looks at her ticket to confirm her short layover before changing planes. Listening carefully to the announcements of the connecting flights and their gates, Elise writes hers down. It is not written in stone because at this airport gate assignments tend to change. But at least she will be heading in the right direction once they debark.

Elise is familiar with this airport, having flown here several times to visit an old college friend. She has not done so recently. Matter of fact, she has not even called Sandra in a while. Sandra had been a pistol in school, always coming up with ways to infuriate the professor. One time during an English class the professor wrote on the whiteboard, 'William Shakespeare (1564-1616),' and when he stepped back, Sandra said, "Ah, the professor knows Shakespeare's real phone number."

That was so Sandra. You never knew what she would do next, but you could count on it being something outlandish, but never criminal. Elise makes a mental note to call Sandra at the first chance she gets. Sandra would get a kick out of her heading to China. She often told her, "Elise, you may be stuck to the ground here, but I see movement in your future..."

It was time to get off the plane, so Elise stood and not waiting for assistance, opened the bin above her seat to retrieve her things. She stepped into the aisle and moved ahead to the exit, doing the smile thing and 'thank you' thing to the attendants and the pilot before she makes her way down the jetway.

Stepping on the carpeted terminal she is not surprised to see it is bustling with activity. Elise takes a moment to adjust her carry-ons then enters the flow of passengers moving in many directions. Unlike Rochester where you have an escalator and foot traffic only to get to your gate, here there are multiple assisting methods of transport beyond the escalator. There are moving walkways and automated trains to take passengers between the terminals. They provide quick movement to the midfield gates for domestic and international departing flights and domestic arriving flights. With the crowd of people everywhere it behooves one to know which way to go once in the airport.

Since Elise does not have long before her next flight, she uses every automated method she can find. She tries her best to be courteous and understanding which is hard; especially when a man, in a business suit, acts like a jack ass, almost pushing her down as he tries to enter the walkway before her.

There are occasional slow-moving passengers, but that does not bother her. It is that frantically pushing man, who seems to be going in the same direction that drives her to the brink of insanity. She wants to turn and yell at him, but refrains. When she arrives at her gate there is just enough time to breathe deeply and slow down her heartbeat before pulling out her boarding pass.

Again, she is boarding with the first-class passengers, this time without hesitation. After that marathon to the gate she has no resistance left if they tell her the ticket is mismarked, so be it.

Only that does not happen. When the plane takes off on time, she is seated in first class again. She allows the attendant to put her carryon in the overhead bin, but she keeps her purse near her. Elise looks at her ticket. They will be in the air for one hour and thirty-one minutes, landing at the Newark International Airport.

"Can I get you something to drink?"

Elise raises her eyes and smiles. "Yes, please. May I have a glass of orange juice."

"Would you like me to bring you a cup of coffee, too."

"No, just the orange juice."

In a matter of minutes, she has her orange juice and drinks it down quickly. Then Elise adjusts her seat, squirms into a comfortable position, and easily falls asleep, not hearing or seeing the flight attendant who stands over her, about to ask if she would like a blanket and a pillow. Not wanting to disturb her, the flight attendant lays them on the empty seat next to Elise.

This time she feels a slight touch on her shoulder that wakes her. "Sorry, miss. It is time to leave the plane."

Elise sits up straight, wipes her hand over her eyes and is wide awake. She has always been able to do that. In bed, she just hops out when the alarm goes off. Now she says, "Thank you," and stands, stretching her body. She slides her purse strap over her shoulder and sees that her carryon has already been retrieved and sits on the empty seat next to her. She adjust that on her shoulder and steps into the aisle. Soon she is off the plane and on her way to where she will catch her next flight.

Elise does not worry about making it to her departure gate this time because she knows there are only three terminals. Her flight takes off from Terminal B.

Even though she is on an international flight, she does not have to show her passport or go through customs here. The official customs and immigration control will be once she lands in China. So, since she has a good two hours to kill, she paces herself. She will find the location of the gate first, then can decide if she wants to get something to eat.

Heading in the same direction Elise is surrounded by other passengers going the same way. As she walks, she hears different languages being spoken and wonders what they are saying and where they are going. Are they on their way back home, or just beginning their trip? Everyone seems friendly and smile as they pass her on the moving walkways. In between, Elise moves into the center area, then back on the walkways when the center area becomes too crowded.

When she arrives at the escalators, she decides to take the stairs. It feels good to get a little exercise knowing that on the final leg of her trip she will be in the air for over thirteen hours.

Soon she sees her gate listed on the signs hanging from the ceiling and knows she is close. Elise moves off to the side to walk at a slower pace, so she will not hinder other passengers.

She stops at a purse shop, thinking she might get one for her mother. She sees the price and walks back out. When she comes to a souvenirs and gift shop she enters and buys a pack of gum. She makes one more stop at a bookstore where she looks over the titles and reads the flaps on several books that interest her but buys nothing before proceeding to her gate.

When she arrives, Elise stops and surveys the area. There are passengers everywhere, standing in the walkway, seated in the chairs and even some seated on the floor. The first empty seat she sees, she hurries toward it noticing there are no personnel at the entrance to the plane yet.

If only she had known that first class passengers had their own special lounge. Never having flown first class, she was not privy to that information.

She sits in what she sees as a prime seat as there is an open charger near. Elise takes out her phone and connects it to the charging station and while connected, she places a call to her mother.

Her mother has set her ringtone for Elise to "You Can't Lose Me" by Faith Hill and before the first two words come out, she opens the line.

"Hello mother."

"Hello daughter. Where are you?"

"I am at the Newark airport. It has been smooth sailing all the way."

"Oh, Elise that is great. So where to now."

"My next flight is to Beijing, and mom, guess what?"

"What daughter."

"I do not know if it is a mistake, but I have been flying first class all the way."

Silence on the other line. "Oh, Elise, have you checked to see if it is a mistake. Those tickets are expensive, and you do not want to end up with a bill for the difference.

"Why would they charge me. They made the mistake…if it is a mistake. Frankly since it has been on both flights, it might not be."

"Well, okay, but don't be surprise…"

"Don't worry mother. They won't put me in jail."

The two chat a bit longer, then Elise says her goodbyes. Now she can read her book, so she takes it out of her carryon and opens to the page with the bookmarker. She pauses for a moment to watch the passengers making their way to their gates or sitting and talking with their fellow passengers. The man seated across from her is bouncing a little girl on his knee and she has the cutest laugh. Every time she laughs, it makes Elise smile. Slowly she looks away and watches two passengers leaning against a pillar and all but climbing into each other's skin. For some reason it does not seem obnoxious, but kind of sweet. Elise wishes she had someone in her life. Her job is fulfilling, but she wishes she had a man to love. She wondered why that had not happen for her yet. She sighs and turns her eyes to the words on the page.

The announcement for boarding her flight comes over the intercom and Elise gathers up her belongings, putting her phone and cord into her purse. While she was busy snooping on passengers, the flight personnel had arrived at the gate and taken their places. After several announcements they begin calling the passengers in the same order Elise has heard before and after checking her boarding pass, she does not hesitate to step in the first-class line for boarding. Soon she is walking down the jetway to the airplane.

The minute she steps through the doorway she is astounded. This is a huge, luxurious plane. Trying not to look shellshock she shows her pass to the flight attendant who walks her to her first-class seat.

Elise moves forward and cannot help thinking this is sheer luxury. Before her are wide, oversized seats and when she slides into her plush seat, she sees a large, high-definition TV screen with a multitude of entertainment options along with Bose headphones. There is also a list of a few dozen movies to choose from.

Already it is apparent that flying domestic first class was an entirely different experience for her, but. international first-class was about to put that encounter to shame.

When the flight attendant opens the half door to her first-class accommodations, Elise sees that it is the size of a room. There are hidden orange glowing lights around the top of the ceiling where her carryon and purse can be stored. Under the storage area is a bay of three windows and situated under the center one is a small table with various toiletries for her personal convenience. There is also room for storage if she needs it.

Elise looks at the back wall to her unit and sees little amber pot lights built in and two standard light sconces above, which she assumes are for reading.

The flight attendant informs her she will be back after dinner to help her make the bed.

Elise sits dramatically on the recliner and suppresses a giggle. It is so extravagant she thinks as she puts her purse on the side table and takes out the inflight book. The first thing she sees is a menu for the flight. For starters there is

Camboaola, Chaumes, Manchego and Fresh seasonal fruit. Elise chuckles thinking she does not know what any of the first items are, but she is sure she will like them.

The main courses offered are stir-fried prawns with conch steamed rice and mixed vegetables or grilled beef tenderloin, rosemary roast kipfler potatoes and mixed vegetables, or braised chicken and chestnut egg fried rice, pak choy and black mushrooms. Finally, for the vegetarian there is truffle porcini mushrooms and ravioli with Parmesan cream sauce. Then for dessert they offered a cheese and fruit plate, a morello chocolate mousse cake with raspberry coulis. As if that is not enough there are snacks offered throughout the flight including wontons with kailan in noodle soup, Joe Shanghai crab dumplings served with dark vinegar and ginger, chicken tikke with mint yogurt sauce and ice cream. There is also a wine and premium liquor list presented at the start of the flight.

When she is alone, she does some exploring and finds there are several power outlets so she can charge her phone and her laptop. A flight attendant comes to offer her a pre-departure drink, but Elise asks only for water. When she returns, she hands Elise a warm hot towel. Again, Elise must control herself as her mind flashes a picture of everyone washing their faces and armpits. Feeling herself about to lose it she turns to look out the window. She raises the towel and covers her face, so the attendant does not see her facial reaction.

Once they are in the air, the attendant returns, removes the towel and informs Elise there is a bar with olives, crackers, cheese, and fruit located at the front of the plane for her perusal. She then asks what she would like for dinner. Elise gives her the choices and watches as the attendant leans over and releases her tray, large enough to be a table for one. She places a white tablecloth over it and lays a cloth napkin to the side. She steps back and smiles. Elise suppresses a giggle. When she returns later, it is with her meal on a china plate and with real silverware. To this she adds a cup and saucer, along with a glass of water. When she brings Elise's dessert choice, she brings along with her a stemmed wine glass.

Once dinner is over and evening approaches, the attendant asks if she would like to use the restroom. Elise says "Yes, thank you" and the attendant waits while she retrieves her toiletries then follows the attendant.

The attendant walks in with her and retrieves a fluffy white bath towel, a hand towel, and places them on the side of the marble sink. She hangs a white cozy robe on the back of the door and then excuses herself.

It is quite roomy and there is a good size shower as well. Elise welcomes the feel of the water as she spends time washing her hair and body before stepping out and putting on slippers that have been placed near the shower. She brushes her teeth and dries her hair before finally opening the door, steam pouring out behind her.

Not every seat is taken in first class, making it seem even more exclusive as she glances around the cabin to take in her fellow travelers. Across the aisle sits a heavyset, very tall man from the height of his head over the headrest. Even though the seats are well spaced, his knees almost reach the back of the seat in front of him. His head is as bald as a billiard ball, reflecting the light coming from the pot lights above him. His bulk does not afford a glance at the passenger next to him, but by the way he leans in to speak, she can assume they are traveling together.

As she takes in the area, further ahead she can view the back of a woman who has the shiniest black hair she has ever seen. It is like a silk sheet gracefully moving every time she turns her head. Elise absentmindedly tugs on one of her curls, wishing her hair were smooth and easy to manage.

Her eyes travel next to the man in the seat just before the seats across from her. She starts to smile, but something about the way he stares at her freezes her face and she must quickly lower her gaze. That puts an end to her survey.

When she returns to her sleeping pod it is now a full reclining bed with a top and bottom sheet, a duvet, and a nice thick pillow. All the amber lights as well as the reading lights are on, making it seem safe and inviting. She closes the half door and climbs in the bed. She then searches and finds the lever to raise the head so that she can comfortably watch television.

The flight attendant asks several times if she would like something more to drink and Elise polishes off three glasses of water and several glasses of wine before finally declining.

Elise continues watching the movie until her eyelids get heavy, then lowers the bed. She turns off the television and reaches behind her head to fluff the pillow and immediately falls sound to sleep.

There being a twelve-hour time difference between Rochester and Wuhan and not being a worldly traveler, Elise is confused when she opens her eyes. She reaches for her cell on the side table and sees that it has adjusted to the time change. It is too early to rise so she tries to fall back to sleep. She manages an off and on doze for a while, but finally gives up and heads to the bathroom with her carryon and flight bag in tow. She manages to keep her eyes facing forward and not glancing into the other passengers' private space. When she comes out of the bathroom she feels refreshed with a change of clothes and hygienically clean, ready to face a new day.

This time when she reaches her pod, she removes the bedding and places it on the side of the table before putting the recliner into an upright position. She puts on the headset and turns on the television to hear the morning news.

Elise is settled in when she hears other passengers waking. She watches as while waiting their turn in the bathrooms they fold up their sheets and blankets to hand to the flight attendants as they move down the aisle.

"Miss?"

Elise has been engrossed in the news and had not heard the flight attendant, so she had tapped her on the shoulder.

It gave Elise a fright as she quickly turned her head toward the aisle. Seeing the flight attendant, she relaxed. "Yes. What is it?"

"Your bedding miss. Can I get that out of your way?"

"Thank you." Elise gathers the bedding, the robe and slippers and passes them to the flight attendant who adds them to the large bag she is carrying.

Even though she slept well, Elise begins to feel drowsy, and slightly disoriented. She knows from talking with friends who have flown overseas, that she is experiencing jet lag.

When breakfast is served, she plays with her food only taking a few bites. The flight attendant notices and asks if anything is wrong. "No, its fine, I just…"

"How you feel?" Elise nods.

"That is normal. It happens all the time. It is the time zone changes."

"So, what should I do?"

"Your body will adjust. Jet lag is temporary, and most people recover fully within a few days. In the meantime, all you can do is try and rest."

Elise thanks her, then taking her advice, leans back and allows herself to drift off and on for the rest of the morning.

When lunch is served, she is famished and eats everything. She feels much better and manages to concentrate on her book and read a few more pages.

When the announcement comes from the pilot that they are about to land at Beijing Capital International Airport, Elise checks her Fitbit and sees that the flight is on time. It is now 1:35 p.m., Beijing time.

Her trip is almost over now. Elise sits up and watches out the window as the jet lands in Beijing. When the jet is stationary, she stands in her pod and gathers her belongings. She will have almost six hours here before her last flight takes off for Wuhan,

After entering the airport just as she suspects it is congested with passengers. Elise, along with her fellow passengers, are taken to the security check point where they are be required to present their passports and some, their immigration cards. The line moves slowly and once they make it through customs, they still must go through re-checking security. Elise is asked for her transfer document and she hands it over with her passport.

The attendant peers at her after looking at the passport and then flips the page and puts an inked passport stamp on the next blank page. She has successfully passed through customs and is now allowed to head toward the gates.

As soon as Elise is through the checkpoints, she goes directly toward the gate where her next flight is scheduled to take off. It is only three o'clock, but this is a big and busy airport and once she feels sure of where she needs to be, she will be more comfortable. She checks the flight board and sees that her flight has not appeared in the listing yet since it is not due to take off until 7:30 that evening.

As Elise makes her way to the waiting area, it dawns on her she has lost a day. She left on Sunday morning and now it is Monday evening. It feels weird in a way, she thinks, as she walks toward the waiting area.

Almost there, she stops and enters a shop where she purchases a sandwich, a bottle of water and chips. Elise is happy that the salesperson speaks English, though she has downloaded the translator app onto her phone.

Everyone seems to be in a hurry. She manage to find a seat in the waiting area where again passengers are seated on the floor, window ledges and standing, leaning against pillars. She stands, keeping an eye on the seating area and when a passenger gets up, she makes a beeline for the seat. Once seated, she eats her sandwich and entertains herself by watching the people as they scurry down the aisles.

So many different nationalities pass by, talking to each other in their own language and making a sort of orchestrated combination of sounds. What does not seem to change much is their attire. Most are dressed in similar fashion with the occasional traditional Chinese or other foreign attire. Elise smiles, reminding herself that here she is the foreigner.

Her lunch finished, she does not chance getting up to throw the trash away, instead stuffs it into her purse and pulls out her book. One more glance around and then Elise is lost in the pages of her book.

The hours pass quickly and before she knows it, they are calling the boarding arrangements. Since she will be among the first passengers, Elise relinquishes her seat and stands, stretching, before carefully squeezing her way towards the jetway.

With so many passengers waiting to board the flight, Elise is amazed at how efficiently the boarding is handled. Before she knows it, she is comfortably seated with a drink in hand, watching the stream of passengers pass by on their way to coach.

Orchestrated well, the boarding and flight progresses without delay and in a little over two hours they are landing in Wuhan.

She did not expect her reaction. Exhilarated to the point her breath is sporadic, Elise tries to calm herself while the jet taxies to the gate. It does not feel real. She is in Wuhan, the home of her ancestors. "I'm here grandmother, I'm really here," she says silently.

Elise takes a few deep breaths. To quiet down she needs to focus on something else, so she pulls out her itinerary. Her eyes scan to the bottom and sees that it says that she will be met at the airport and driven to her hotel from there.

"No need to worry," she whispers. "Someone will be there for sure."

She is in the home of her ancestors and her mind is already making plans that she hopes her guide will accept and be open to. This is a trip of a lifetime and it may never come again so she is going to enjoy every single minute of it.

It is hard to be patient as she leaves the jet. She responds to the flight attendant and pilot who wish her a safe and wonderful time in Wuhan. Then she is finally in the airport and making her way through the gate walkway to the waiting area for visitors, her eyes darting left and right until she sees the sign with her name on it. It is being held by a tall man and at first the sign covers his face. When it is lowered, she pauses a moment to wipe the admiring expression off her face.

As Elise smiles in his direction, she reminds herself that this is a business trip and if she knew anything, business and romance did not work well together. She takes a deep breath as she adjusts her skirt that has twisted to the side, then raises her arm to pat wisps of hair into place, before signaling in the direction of the handsome man holding the sign.

When he sees Elise he smiles, his white teeth sparkling in the light coming through the window and when she is near he says, "Welcome to Hubei our landlocked province of the People's Republic of China, and part of the Central China region."

Elise expects him to click his heels and salute, but it is just his way of extending a little humor to relax her; or at least that is the impression she gets from the laughter that follows.

Finding her voice and wanting to impress she says, "The north of the lake, in direct translation."

It pleases him. She can see it on his face. "Yes, that refers to Hubei's position north of Dongting Lake."

Taking it a step further she adds, "So, we are here in Wuhan the provincial capital, that is the major transportation hub…"

"Also, the political, cultural, and economic hub of central China." he adds.

While his lips move, Elise is trying not to think of him as handsome and tan. She will be spending a lot of time with this charming man and what she wants is for them to be friends and enthused about only what matters which is this assignment. "Okay, enough banter." She holds out her hand. "Hello, I am Elise McKenna."

"I am Bai Zhao, your guide. It is good to finally meet you and to know you have brushed up on the area."

Elise falls in step with him as he starts walking through the airport to luggage claim. As they stand waiting for her bags, he glances at his watch and see that it is almost ten in the evening. Elise watches him as he checks the time but decides this is a good time to tell him her plan.

Bai is silent, listening to her and when she finishes, he says, "A woman after my own heart."

"What?"

"Well, if I were coming to Wuhan to do a travel guide, I would want to start in the same way. Therefore, I do what I do and not be a guide for vacationers. They get off the plane and want to go to the hotel, eat and sleep away the day." He turns and gives her one of his enchanting smiles.

"Thanks Bai, thanks for that. I slept most of the time on the plane, so I am not tired." That is not entirely true, but she cannot sleep now because she is too excited. She pauses to lean over the conveyor belt. "Here comes my luggage."

Bai is right beside her. He grabs one bag and Elise, the other. Soon they are making their way through the airport and out to the curb where he has parked the car. It is sleek and black, just what she would expect a serious person to drive. Elise walks with him to the back of the vehicle and waits while he puts her luggage inside, then walks to the passenger side to hold the door for Elise.

Elise slides into the passenger seat and reaches back for her seatbelt when she freezes. Fear flows through her body making her limbs weak. If she had been standing, she would have collapsed. Elise had raised her eyes and stared out the window trying to compose herself and there he is. That man from the plane is standing on the sidewalk staring back at her or is it her imagination. She blinks and he is gone. Just as quick as the feeling came, it went with the vision.

Elise grabs the strap of her seatbelt and tugs it across pushing until she hears it snap into position. She turns to watch Bai as he climbs behind the wheel and starts the car. "Okay," he says as he straps himself in. "As you requested, we are on our way to Luojia Mountain."

Chapter 4

It is late, it is dark, but Bai seems to understand her entreaty to not just climb off the plane and head for bed. He drives to the airport exit and Elise sees a sea of cars. "There are more than a billion cars on our planet, and they are all here in front of us. What, did something happen," Elise asks innocently.

"What do you mean."

"All this traffic."

Bai laughs and even his laugh is sexy. "No. Driving in China is either utterly terrifying, or amazingly awesome depending on your state of mind and attitude."

"At least you have right lane driving and the English translations on signage."

"And" Bai says, "If you could see the roads they are generally in great shape - especially the interstates."

They continue on the road and Elise cannot believe what she witnesses. "Bai, that man is just weaving in and out with no regard to his fellow drivers. Oh, where's a cop when you need one."

Again, Bai laughs. "It is called herd mentality. You see the beauty of traffic in Wuhan is that people adopted their driving styles from the way they ride bikes. It is every man for themselves, compromise and courtesy be damned. I have seen people start using oncoming lanes to pass slow moving traffic. I agree it is crazy, but you get used to it."

As he explains, Elise watches as a car going the same way as they are, skirts over to the ongoing traffic lane that is barely moving and soon the cars in front sway away. Right there in front of her eyes, a car has managed to make an entirely new lane. All she can say is, "It is crazy. It is like a game of chicken."

"It is a game of chicken. That is why I say, this can be terrifying and curse-worthy, or you can have fun with it. It is all in your attitude."

"Well at least they stay on the road... Oh, did you see that!"

Up ahead a car is driving on the sideway to get around the car ahead of him.

"Do not worry, pedestrians always have an eye out for traffic," he laughs. "Even if they are in their own driveways."

"I'd use Uber. That is what I would do. I would not drive in this mess."

"Oh, my friend, I think you are braver than you suppose. All you need to do is be vigilant and attentive. Driving in China makes you an unbelievable good driver because you learn to expect random, crazy behaviors."

Elise grins. "So, what happens when you get into an accident."

"Well, if you get in an accident as a foreigner, it is your fault regardless. A friend of mine was stopped at a red light, another car rear-ended him. It was his fault...for being in the country. Had he not been there, the accident would not have happened. So when you are driving you must be alert and look out for yourself or face the consequences."

"Hmmm," is all Elise can master.

As they make their way Elise tries to relax. After all Bai is proving to be an excellent driver, weaving through the traffic until he is where he needs to be. That is amazing, but more amazing is he can talk and drive in this congestion. "I am sure you have read up on the area so you know that Luojia is located in the central part of Wuchang, Wuhan City, and on the southwest shore of East Lake, so let me tell you something you might not know.

At that instance Elise sits up straighter and turns slightly to take in his profile. It is like he is reading her mind. She was about to ask him if he had any information other than that published version on the web that he could share with her. Then she grins. But of course, he knows she wants the untold version. He is a travel guide after all.

Bai begins, "Well Ms. McKenna, Mount Luojia is part of a chain of mountains and Putuo Mountain and Luojia Mountain, are located at the eastern part. These mountains are one of the Four Holy Buddhist Mountains and are full of mystic caves. Legend has it that it was the place where Bodhisattva Guanyin practiced Buddhism, but truth of that is still out."

Pausing for effect he continues, slowly. "Let me set the scene first. Luojia Mountain is part of over a dozen hills and Luojia is a stressed structure, making it and the surrounding area subject to earthquakes." Bai turns his head slightly to look at Elise. He sees that she is listening closely to his story.

"Well, as the story goes, that before the beginning of the world there were two opposite forces. Yin was the female element, representing softness, darkness, and the earth; Yang was the male element, representing hardness, light, and the heavens. Though the two forces were opposites, they were still dependent on each other to maintain the harmony of the universe. Originally, the Yin and Yang were contained in an egg from which the deity Pangu eventually emerged."

Bai pauses, then continues. "Pangu lived for 18,000 years, growing bigger and filling the space between the earth and sky. Then, Pangu died, and his body formed the world and lives deep inside Luojia mountain."

Elise, being a writer always has her recorder out and running from the minute she awakes. Now, if this had not been her habit, she would have been so engrossed she would have missed the tale and would have asked him to repeat it. When Bai turns his head to look at her again, he sees she has been recording him and smiles, thinking this is going to be a good experience for them both.

During the rest of the drive, Bai is silent, watching the road while Elise stares at the scenery outside her window. Tall impressive buildings are everywhere with trees and bushes dotting the landscape and lots of streetlights illuminate what seems like millions of people making their way on foot or on bikes. To Elise it looks like the traffic you might find after a parade or sports event...not an everyday occurrence.

She persists taking it all in and views the moment it suddenly changes to fewer lights, less people. She feels the change in altitude as they make their way to higher ground. Her body tingles with anticipation knowing that soon she will be standing where her grandmother and other ancestors stood so many years ago. Her anticipatory excitement builds when Bai stops the car. "We are here. Wait while I get the lights out of the trunk.

"You've thought of everything."

Bai does not answer as he busies himself getting out the flashlights. When he turns, he holds one out to Elise saying, "The Wicked Lasers were touted as the world's brightest and most powerful flashlight with a whopping 4,100 lumens." He is smiles. "Here is hoping they are right." This is the first chance he has had to test them. He hands one to Elise. "Shall we go."

Together they walk up to the top of Mount Luojia, the flashlights blazing a path that could be seen from space. When they are at the top, she moves forward and looks down. It takes her breath away and her heart bursts with pride at the beauty of her family's homeland. Down below is Hubei province.

Bai stands beside her understanding the need for silence. Though he has seen it before, it never gets old. But that is not all that excites him. When Elise told him, she wanted to go straight to Luojia Mountain and find a spot where they could see most of the area of Hubei province he was impressed. But even more, he liked it when she said, "I want to do this first because this would be like my summary spot for the guidebook.

While Bai was admiring her, Elise was captivated by the vision before her. She now knows without a doubt that this will be the best travel guide of all time.

"Okay, Bai, tell me what I see."

"First, let me explain something so that you get the full picture. Cities use to pop up in complete disorder. Some were for defensible sites on a hill or island or near resources or routes. Then cities grew around places where people worked since they needed to eat sleep, and worship. But around the 20th century, things changed. Cities started to happen on purpose." He pauses for a moment.

"So, let us jump to now: after human beings started putting their minds toward designing cities using high tech materials, sensor networks, new science, and better data. Cities started getting more environmentally sound, more fun, and more beautiful. And just in time, because today more human beings live in cities than not."

"It is beautiful. It is like a beautiful painting."

Bai nodded. "In order to appreciate the places we visit you need to think about the old and the new so that you capture the spirit of the area. That way you can write with a deeper understanding."

Elise nods, liking the way he has prefaced it.

"Okay, let me identify what you see below." Bai magically moves his light like a pointer. "That is Donghu Lake, also known as East Lake. It is a large freshwater lake within the city limits of Wuhan, China, and the largest or the second largest urban lake in China." He adds, "Of course it is a high spot for tourist visits."

Elise moves her flashlight in the same direction as Bai's, listening as he continues. "That is Yichang, a prefecture-level city in western Hubei province. Yichang is the second largest city in the province after the capital, Wuhan."

Their lights blaze over the area and when Bai turns his body his light follows. "Over there is Shiyan. It is in the northwest of Hubei Province, the upper reach of the Han River. It borders Xiangfan City in the east. Then there is Xiangyang city, also a prefecture-level city in northwestern Hubei and the second largest city in Hubei by population."

With very slight movement of his light, Bai manages to bring life to the areas below. "Finally," he says pointing out the direction, "we have Ezhou city. Ezhou lies in the east of Hubei Province, on the south bank of the middle reaches of the Yangtze River." Of course, the actual places are far away, but the view from this height seems to take away the distance, making it possible to visualize.

She keeps her light in line with his and it is like they are gods and this beam, is their sun. Elise smiles.

"Okay, Elise, close your eyes." Without hesitation she follows his instructions and allows him to position her body, to face the direction he wants.

"Keep your eyes close." Slowly Bai begins to speak, his voice melodiously telling a tale. "As I said earlier, the city of Wuhan is the capital of Hubei province and Wuhan and China have a rich history that dates back over 3,500 years. The region evolved into an important port because of its location on the Yangtze River, and the cities of Hanyang, Hankou and Wuchang were united into the city of Wuhan in 1926. Modern-day Wuhan is known as 'China's Thoroughfare' as it is a major transportation hub, with dozens of railways, roads and expressways passing through the city and connecting to other major cities. Not only is the city known for its progressions, but Wuhan is 3,280 square miles in size. What you will see is its miles of moonlight-hued matrix of light. Roads will look brighter because while other cities around the world use LEDs to save money and add splashes of color and emphasis, Wuhan does more than show what is happening right in front of you. It uses lights to tell you something about the entire city." Bai moves her body one more time, turning off their lights as he does so. He says, "Now, open your eyes."

Elise almost topples over from the beauty below. It is like a futuristic vision of a place that goes on and on. It takes her breath away.

"This is just a preview Elise. You cannot see this when you are down below, but you will remember what it was like from above when later we are up close really seeing the areas and possibly uncovering secrets."

Standing there, listening to Bai, is comforting. She feels as though she is a part of all that she views, and she totally understands his way of showing it to her. Elise turns to gaze at Bai and is glad it is dark, so he does not witness the full impact of her admiration.

Bai turns on his light and Elise follows suit. There he stands with his black hair glistening in the glow of their flashlights, turning from side to side giving her several views of his profile. Yes, he is handsome from all angles, but more importantly she can sense he knows his business and is proud of the place he calls home. He is going to be the perfect guide for her as he understands her desire to know more than just the facade of the area.

"Are you ready to go?"

"No, but I guess we must. This has been fantastic. It has been one of my most memorable experiences, ever."

They make their way down the mountain and Elise is happy. She is happy she has this incredible man as her guide and happy to be here. This will be one of those adventures you pray will never end.

If only she could have apperceived. This will mark the beginning of the end. This will be the last sane thought she would have before her life takes a dangerous turn.

Chapter 5

Elise is beginning to feel the first signs of jet lag as they make their way back to the SUV, but she is not ready to call it a night. "Well, that is enough sightseeing for today. What say we go back, and we can have a quick drink before I check in."

Bai has been busy observing the woman next to him. Elise is stunning in an elegant way. He likes how she stands so straight and tall and how her neck is long and graceful. Yet even knowing her for such a short time, he senses there is an inner fire that portrays a whole different personality. He sensed that back at the mountain. He has been a guide to many types of people and has a good judgement of character. Bai is sure that spending time with Elise will be pleasurable.

Elise turns to face Bai and he watches her long curly brown hair bounce into action giving her a playful appearance. And those brown eyes staring at him seem to penetrate to his soul. At that moment he senses there is a lot of power in her 5' 4" fame of slenderness and long legs and there is something else. He cannot quite put his finger on it, but there is something more to envisage and discover and it piques his interest even more.

"Bai?" He has been deep in thought and does not hear her at first.

"Bai. Where are you?"

Finally, the sound of her voice penetrates his mind. "Sorry, Elise. "What did you say?"

"Not say, ask, if you would like to have a drink before you leave. That is if you are not too tired."

"Yes, that will be great. And, no, I am not too tired. I was just thinking."

"Thinking about what."

"Nothing in particular, just random thoughts." He smiles at her.

They are at the car and Bai helps her in. Once seated she pulls her seat belt slowly across her lap as she leans her head back on the headrest. It has been a long journey, starting with the flight from Rochester to going to Luojia Mountain. Even though she slept on the plane, her body lets her know she has not fully recovered. Soon she will no longer be able to fight sleep.

While Bai concentrates on driving, Elise takes in his profile again, now noticing the stubble around his mouth that outlines his full lips. His hair that he wears in a longish style curls up on the ends and there where loose curls falling over his forehead. As if sensing he is being stared at, Bai turns, and her attention is drawn to his surprising hazel eyes.

He is quite tall, too. Elise recalls reading somewhere that the Northern and Northeastern Chinese are substantially taller than their southern cousins. In the Beijing areas, the native Hans appears to have male and female approximately 3 to 6 inches taller than their southern compatriots. so, Bai's height which she gauges at a little over 6 foot is quite normal in this area of the country.

Elise knows she likes him. Usually it takes a lot of time learning everything about a person before she makes even that decision. This is the exception. Not only does she like him, she feels comfortable around him. He has displayed all the unique features she likes in a man and since he is to be her guide for the next few weeks, she will have time to really get to know him.

Elise turns to stare out the window as they draw closer to the city. As marvelous as the view driving toward the mountain had been, the return view is its equal. With a bounty of high-class skyscrapers and ancient architectures, Wuhan's skyline is breathtaking. The streets, the building, the lights, the river are major attractions as phosphorus moonlight adds to the glow of the majestic view. There are rows of towering skyscrapers stretched before her, their windows alight from within. A half-moon hovers at the fringes of the luminous cityscape, where the red blinking lights of distant radio towers twinkle in the night. Lights glitter everywhere just like stars dropping to the earth.

Elise is absorbed in the captivating view when she hears Bai say, "Look ahead, Elise. That is the hotel where you will be staying.

She has seen the pictures of the hotel online, but the beauty of the building complex, is more fabulous under the yellow lights at night. Piercing the sky is this tower of yellow lights with white glistening pyramid shapes surrounding the very top of it. Those same shapes emerge on the levels below the tower's structure seeming to encase the tower and expand outward. Though not as tall, the red illuminating circular building with a diamond design has equal appeal. This is the Wanda Wuhan Movie Park Entertainment building. "This is spectacular, Bai."

Bai briefly turns toward Elise and smiles then concentrates on maneuvering the SUV into a parking space in front of the hotel. Before they can make a movement, the passenger side door is opened and a bellhop says, "Welcome to Wanda Reign," as he holds out his hand to help Elise out of the vehicle.

Elise gingerly undoes her seatbelt. She then swivels on the seat and steps down with the aid of the proffered hand. She beams and then turns toward Bai who is now standing by the driver's side. "I will wait for you in the lobby."

It is like she has entered a fairy tale as the bellhop guides her to the lobby of this magnificent structure. From her research she would learn that the hotel is centrally located in an upscale neighborhood of Wuhan, sitting on the edge of the East Lake. Elise has stayed in many hotels during her career writing travel guides, but none can compare to this, nor will this assignment match any she has done before. It is going to be the highlight of her five-year career and she is confident it will be the most enjoyable.

As soon as they enter, a man, dressed dapperly in a black tailored suit smiles at her, his teeth as white as the shirt he wears. Unlike Bai, he is on the short side and quite thick through the middle, making his jacket pouch out a bit. There is not a clue of the color of his hair as there is none, and his eyebrows seem to have faded as well, but he has one of those faces that draws you in. He makes her feel comfy.

He nods and introduces himself. "My name is Jeffries. He is to be her concierge." Elise nods. The name does not fit him but once again doing her homework pays off. It is common for hotel workers to choose names easier for the foreigners to pronounce and relate to.

Jeffries walks a step in front of her, guiding her on a leisurely stroll through the lobby. Elise's eyes go every which way. From the marbled-walls, gold-framed pictures, stunning chandeliers and a jaw-dropping view of Wuhan's peaceful scenery, every inch of it is grand in its unique blending of European glamour and Asian elegance. She is about to experience firsthand a seven-star hotel ideal of royal treatment.

Too soon they arrive at the reception area and the concierge stands slightly back allowing Elise to approach the desk. "Good evening, Miss."

"Good evening." Elise reaches in her purse and pulls out an embossed envelope, from which she carefully removes the black and gold reservation card she received in the mail.

The woman behind the desk reaches out and gracefully accepts the card and smiles. Then, she lowers her eyes. Elise stands watching her graceful movements, unable to see what she is doing. When she gazes at Elise, she once again gifts her with a smile before she hands her a matching, holder in a gold embossed casing and says, "Ms. McKenna. Here is your pass card. I hope you enjoy your stay with us."

"Thank you. I will."

When Elise turns Jeffries is already beside her. He bows and Elise follows his lead, floating across the marble floors to the elevator. Jeffries presses the button and the doors immediately open. He waves her inside and then follows. Elise tries to hold in her praise of the interior as he presses the button for her floor.

So far, Elise is spoken to in English and she does not need to use her translator. As the elevator ascends Jeffries informs her of the hotel amenities and a little about its history. When the elevator door opens, Elise again must suppress sounds of admiration as he leads her down the wide hall through elaborately embroidered Chinese motifs, carved frames, and elegant furnishing until reaching her room.

Jeffries pauses at the side of the door and says, "May I," as he reaches for the pass card and smiling, Elise hands it to him.

While Jeffries unlocks the door, Elise reaches in her purse and when Jeffries turns around, he extends his arm toward the doorway. "There you are, miss."

"Thank you, Jeffries," she says as she places a generous tip in his hand.

Then with a smile and a nod, Jeffries turns and makes his way back down the hall.

Once inside the room, Elise hurries to the bathroom to take a quick check. She runs her fingers through her hair then opens her luggage that has mysteriously appeared in her room. She dresses up what she has been wearing all day by adding a necklace, earrings, and a jacket. Then, she removes her sneakers and replaces them with a pair of heels. She does it quickly knowing there is not enough time to pamper herself yet. She swings her purse over her shoulder, checks to make sure she has the passkey in her purse and then hurries back down to the lobby.

Taking deep breaths to calm herself, she scans the area and sees Bai. He sees her at the same time and starts walking towards her. When their eyes meet, he grins lifts his left arm and she slips her arm through his. Anyone seeing them would not know they had only recently met.

There was not much that Elise can recall about the rest of the evening. After two glasses of wine, jet lag and sheer exhaustion force her to call it a night. "I am sorry, Bai, but I must get some sleep."

"Yes, I understand. You must be exhausted." They walk arm in arm, back to the lobby, only this time Elise is using him to keep herself upright. Bai senses this and instead of just taking her into the lobby, he walks her to the elevator before saying "Sleep tight Elise. I will meet you here around seven. If it is okay with you, I want to get an early start."

Elise nods and mumbles, "Good night. See you in the morning." When the elevator doors open, she wobbles in, using the sides of the opening for support. With her arm at her side, she bends her hand and gives Bai a little wave before the elevator doors close.

Elise, alone in the elevator, steps backwards until she feels the wall behind her. There she remains until the elevators stops and the doors open.

At first, she has trouble making her mind connect to her body and it is just before the elevator starts to close, she manages to step out of the opening and into the hallway.

She leans down and takes off her heels. It helps some and she manages to sway down the aisle until reaching the door to her room. She is so busy concentrating on finding her pass card, she does not see the man standing off to the side in the hallway, gaping at her.

Finally, she gets the door to her room open and steps over the threshold, barely able to stand on her own. In her last moment of consciousness, she remembers Jeffries informing her that if she wants a wakeup call, she only needs to say, Wanda wake me and give her the time. Elise says the words, manages to lock the door and walk forward until her legs meet the edge of the bed. Her body flops forward. All thought leaves her as she passes out.

Something wakes her. Elise stares above her and sees light in the room framing the coffered ceiling with a yellow glow and a fancy chandelier above the bed. Her eyes travel across the room and fall on end tables on either side of a sofa with fancy lamps. As her gaze travels closer, they see what looks to be a Panda doll and she remembers brushing it off the bed before she passed out.

Frantically, she pushes her torso up and glances around the room. This scares her even more. She does not recognize anything. All around is luxury. From soft grey carpet, to the strategically placed grey leather recliner before the best window view ever. Comfortably tucked into the chair is a towel shaped into an elephant. She relaxes. Slowly her mind starts to work, just when she hears a voice say, "Are you awake Ms. McKenna?"

Elise responds, saying "Yes, Wanda…wherever you are," she whispers at the end. She is in her hotel room and the light streaming in through the windows announces it is morning.

Elise looks down at herself as she sits on the edge of the bed, fully clothed, remembering. "Oh, my god, I need to meet Bai this morning."

Elise picks up her cell and looks at the time. "Oh my god, oh my god…" This is not like her at all, she thinks as she tries to slide her body backward off the bed, her knees bend down on something and she turns to see what it is. There is a silk covered settee at the base of the bed with bolo pillows. She straightens her legs and slides over the settee until she is off the bed that she never climbed into and hurries into the bathroom. She has less than a half hour to shower and get dress if she is to meet Bai at seven.

Not wasting a minute, she rushes into the bathroom, doing two things at once as she takes her toothbrush loaded with toothpaste into the shower to brush her teeth while she bathes. When she steps out, she grabs a towel with one hand and the other grasps the bottle of mouthwash. She swishes and wipes her body dry before spitting out the liquid.

A quick check in the mirror forces her to pause and put on her face, brush her hair and apply deodorant before hurrying into the front room where she cannot thank the blessings of the gods this hotel thinks of everything. Her clothes are hung, just like her toiletries were displayed on the bathroom counter.

Finally, she has herself all together. She puts on her Fitbit and checks the time. She allows herself to breathe. She is going to make it.

Elise picks up her purse and makes sure her pass card, and recorder are in it. She walks over to the side of the bed and grabs her cell and puts it into the purse. One last mental check and she is ready.

Outside her room, she adjust her clothes as she makes her way to the elevator. After pressing the button, she senses someone is staring at her, but when she turns, she sees no one.

Chapter 6

Elise checks her Fitbit and sees it is Tuesday, November 3, 2020 at exactly seven o'clock. When the elevator doors open the first thing she sees, is Bai in silhouette from the light streaming in from the window. He has his back to her, and Elise decides to take advantage of it by sneaking up behind him, but he turns before she reaches him.

"Ah, ha, thought you could sneak up on me, huh?"

"I did, I did."

"First lesson of the day is that I have eyes in the back of my head. Second lesson is that we need to have a good breakfast before we start our day."

Elise nods in agreement. She had not realized she was hungry until he mentioned food. She turns to the left, but Bai reaches out and taps her shoulder. "This way madam." Then he guides her out of the hotel.

They start walking down Donghu Road a short distance and they are in a local area with lots of food vendors. Elise stares up at Bai with a frown on her face.

"Listen, Elise, you have to have the whole experience." She knows he is right and resignedly follows him into the throng of people. When Elise pulls his arm to halt him in front of a stand offering American breakfast fare, he shakes his head and moves on. Instead he stops at several vendors and ends up with her helping him carry fried bread sticks (you tiao), fried rice buns (mian wo), steamed dumplings with minced meat, bean pies (dou pi), hot-and-dry noodles, rice noodles with beef, sautéed noodles with minced meat (zha jiang mian), bean stripes (dou si), wontons, and sweet dumplings (tang yuan). Elise thinks she is going to throw up, but she does not. It is not bad at all, and besides, she is starving. The vendors, at Bai's request has given them small portions of each dish so that it looks like a smorgasbord of tastes. Elise tries everything and out of the corner of her eye, she can see Bai is waiting to hear her opinion. When she finally finishes the last bite, she turns toward him. "It is not bad, but after eating this heavy fare, I have to get up and walk."

And that is what they do. Their next stop is Han Street and Bai fills her in on the history. "Han Street runs along the south bank of the Chu River. And there are roughly 200 businesses located on the street. Han Street, along with the Chu River which you will see, were developed as a project of the Phase 1 of Wuhan Central Cultural Zone. Earlier this year Chinese authorities blew up part of a dam in eastern Anhui province to relieve flood pressure, as heavy rains continued to swell rivers across parts of the country. The project marked the launching of the Dadong River Ecological Water Network in Wuhan and celebrates the centennial of the Xinhai Revolution which took place in 1911."

As they wander down Han Street, they pass Madame Tussauds and Elise stops. "I want to go in there, if that is okay with you." Bai hesitates before telling Elise that it is nice but small, so crowding is a problem. He looks at Elise and laughs, "Okay, but remember I warned you.

Inside it is crowded as they maneuver their way around viewing approximately 40 wax figures of famous Chinese and non-Chinese personalities. It gets worse when they hear screaming kids and people talking loudly on cell phones. "Okay, I have seen enough. Let us get out of here."

"Told you…"

Back out on the street, Bai asks if she is hungry and surprisingly she is, so he stops at a food stall and gets two Doupi, He hands one to Elise and explains that it is considered a popular snack food and it is made out of sticky rice combined with beef, egg, mushrooms and beans and wrapped in a coating of soy skin then fried . Elise likes it.

Bai guides her to the best shopping stores as they make their way to the Hubei Museum of Art. He explains that this is a landmark building with high-grade art exhibitions, and it has ten exhibition halls. As they enter, she can tell Bai knows something he is not sharing. "What is it?"

"Just wait. You'll see."

She soon finds out as he leads her to a craft art exhibition on the intangible cultural heritages of Wuhan. The exhibits includes Han Embroidery works, paper cuttings, wood carvings, bamboo carving lacquers, dough modellings, hand laminating, and much more. The handcraft masters present their skills on the site. In her memo of things to see she had mentioned that, if possible, she would like to see some local craft.

Elise enjoys it immensely.

It is getting late and Bai starts walking back, then stops in front of the Han Show Theater. It is time for their performance. Elise takes in the amazing, spectacular show with acrobatics, high diving, jet skis, and more. The stage itself is remarkable and the effects from their billion-dollar screens on giant robotic arms is super cool. He guides Elise to their seats, and he watches Elise become captivated with the performances on stage. He does not speak until it is over, and they are on their way back toward her hotel. "So, Elise, did you enjoy the show.?"

"Oh, yes," Elise pauses then says, "Absolutely loved the show! It was Cirque du Soleil meets Olympic diving with a twist of jet skis and water jet packs. That will be covered in my travel brochure." She laughs and adds. "I wonder if I should mention if you sit in the first 5 rows of the C section area, you will get wet. You should have mentioned that."

Bai breaks out in laughter. "Remember. The full experience. Besides, it was only a little water…

Elise pushes her body into Bai's side in response.

"If you are not too tired, I would like to take you to one more spot before we call it a day."

"I am game. Let's go."

Bai takes Elise back to get the car. They climb in and after sliding behind the wheel, he turns and looks at her.

72

Elise is glowing and Bai at that moment has an urge to touch her. He reaches a hand over and places it on top of her hand. When Elise turns, she smiles and leaves her hand under his. Bai removes his hand and starts the car.

"So, where are we going."

Before he answers, Elise knows what he will say. "You will have to wait; it is a surprise."

Chapter 7

She grins and leans back on her seat, listening and recording as Bai asks her questions about the day. He wanted to know her every thought and impression and Elise was eager to share. They drive for a little over thirty minutes before he stops the car.

"Here we are."

Elise has spent her time speaking to Bai's profile and alternately taking in the scenery beyond her window. Now, she turns to the front. Her mouth drops open and her eyes grow wide. Before her she can see a large grassy circle of pink and yellow flowers surrounded by a cement border and behind them is a low brick wall with Wuhan Botanical Gardens written in Chinese and English.

Elise's eyes are drawn further back to the building beyond that holds as much appeal as the foreground. It has the pagoda design over the front entrance bordered in white and beyond that sits a beautiful Chinese structure with a pagoda like front entrance. She is so engrossed she barely hears Bai explain that the locals call it the WBG and that they are now in the eastern part of the city, on a peninsula in the East Lake.

From the minute they climb out of the car and enter the building she is enthralled. There are wall waterfalls, exotically carved bridges and a pagoda that is seated on the bridge with green lights highlighting the background of trees and buildings, but the pagoda itself has tiny yellow lights outlining it and turning the pagoda into a dramatic display. The image is doubled by reflections in the water.

Bai, knowing she has her recorder on continues his recitation. He explains that the WBG is not only a botanical garden but also one of three research-oriented botanical gardens in China and it opened to the public in 1958.

"WBG now boasts more than 10,000 plant species and varieties and has 16 specialty gardens. There is a kiwifruit garden the aquatic plant garden the wild fruit garden, the rare and endangered plant garden, and the medicinal herb garden."

"What about these beautiful flowers."

"Ah, yes," he adds fumbling through the brochure he pulls out of his pocket. "There is a collection of more than 4000 species of flora."

They walk around and Elise tries to take it all in, only her feet are not cooperating. As though reading her mind, Bai says, "I think we should call it a night and get back to the city. I have a full day planned tomorrow so we will be heading out early again." He grabs her hand to help her down the ramp at the edge of the bridge but does not release it right away.

When they are seated in the car, he asks, "So what do you think."

"It is a huge garden. The greenhouse is spectacular, and all the structures and lights give it more depth. I loved the rose garden and the ponds of water lily." Elise turns to the front as she fastens her seatbelt. "I loved it all, really, every inch of it."

Bai beams as he starts the car.

Back at the hotel, Bai and Elise sit down to a quiet meal in the hotel restaurant. Bai orders a bottle of champagne. "Oh, Bai, you do not have to do that." She adds, "Besides, my agency will not pay for it..."

Bai interrupts her. "I do not expect them to. It is my treat. It is my way of saying thank you for a wonderful day. I cannot tell you how interesting it is to see my country through your eyes."

Elise is speechless; something she rarely feels as she concentrates on the food. When they finish eating, Bai offers a toast before they drink the most delicious champagne she has ever had. As they sit there staring out at the wonderful scenery through the hotel window, Elise wonders if this is what her father experiences on his book tours. If so, the next time he invites her to join him, she is going to say, yes.

The rest of the week is a whirlwind of activity. They begin touring Wudang Mountain, also called Taihe Mountain. It borders Xiangfan city in the east, Shiyan city in the west, Shennongjia Forestry District in the south, and Danjiangkou reservoir in the north. It is named after Wudang Chuan, one of the current martial arts in China.

The following morning, they travel by cable car to the highest peak in Wudang Mountain - Tianzhu Peak. Taihe Palace is here, situated between the Tianzhu Peak and the Golden Hall. Bai tells Elise, "It has been said that you are not visiting Wudang Mountain unless you ascend to Taihe Mountain. Here they enjoy hiking up to Golden Palace also known as Jin Ding or Peace of Harmony.

Standing on the peak, Elise has a panoramic view of the vast and sacred Wudang Mountain and its hidden temples.

Next Bai takes her to the Palace of Harmony that has an impressive sea of clouds, lush forests, and rocks before taking a cable car down to Xiaoyao Valley also known as Carefree Valley.

They go to see Yuxu Palace of Heavenly Upper Emperor, explaining yuxu refers to the dwelling of the Jade Emperor. It has all the lines and beauty of Chinese architect and Bai explains that it is an architectural complex having its cities one enclosing another. Waile City, Lile City and Zijin City. He points out the two palace walls, and two pavilions housing tablets.

Next, they visit Yuanhe Temple. There Elise sees a concentration of statues and utensils for sacrifice, most of which are gold copper and the best-preserved wood carving called True Warrior Grand Emperor Statue. All of this is explained to her as she takes in the beauty. Bai catches her off guard when he adds, "In the past, it served as a prison to punish those Taoist priests who broke Taoism rules."

"You are kidding. It is too beautiful to be a prison."

Bai smiles and shrugs his shoulders.

They check out Yuzhen palace also called Loess City. It is notable for its golden copper Zhangsanfeng statue of the founder of Wudang Sect.

Then it is on to the Xuanyue Gate, a four-post structure with what appears to be diminishing pagoda roofs. Once stepping through it they are on the way to Taoism Mecca.

There is so much architecture to view as they take in Mozhen Jing, known as Chunyang Palace. Then the Three Temples of Qiongtai that is composed of Bai Yu Gui Tai, middle temple Zi Yue Qiong Tai and lower temple Yu Yue Xiao Tai.

Elise feels confident she has seen everything, until Bai takes her next to the Golden Hall, located on the main peak Tianzhu Peak of Wudang Mountain. This is a large golden copper hall with unventilated structural parts and has the golden copper statue of Heavenly Upper Emperor enshrined. The structure is breathtaking with large golden cranes on either side of the entrance and ornate figures across the top of the two pagoda rooflines. It sparkles in the daylight.

Then it is on to Taizi Po, also called Fuzhen Temple. It sits beside the main road for ascending the mountain. From here, Bai pauses and tells Elise to look down. From the temple she can see the Golden Hall at a different angle.

For the average person, all of this would flow into one another, but for Elise with her interest based in her heritage and her desire to produce the best travel guide for her company, there is a high interest in everything around her.

The Zixiao Palace Bai tells her was where Taoist rites are observed and it is the only wooden structure with double eaves. Clay statues of a dragon and a tiger are guarding the Longhu Hall with a hundred staircases leading to the main hall.

It is fascinating to Elise that most of the Palaces have two names. This is the case again at Nanyan Palace also known as Zixiaoyan. It takes its name from the location of facing the north. Its Nanyan Stone Hall sits on a cliff, its structure made of heavy stones.

Each structure has its draw and Longtou Xiang amazes her with its vivid carvings of the two twisting dragons swallowing a fire ball.

Five Dragons Palace at the foot of the Five Dragons Peaks, west side of Tianzhu Peak of Wudang Mountain is one of the earliest architectures of Wudang Mountain. When they visit Chaotian Palace Bai has her look down where she can see Nanyan Palace from a different viewpoint. Then he directs her to look up and there is Tianzhu Peak. "During the rainy season, waterfalls splash like the Milky Way, while in winter, it looks like a white silk hanging skyward."

That ended their tour of the mountain and on Friday Bai takes Elise to the Hubei Provincial Museum. From one exquisite item of bronze, jade, and lacquer work, they move on to the porcelain and the colorful paintings. Then with a snack in hand they enjoy a performance of chime bells, stone chimes and other ancient instruments. The music is relaxing as well as entertaining.

"Elise, that is the last of the places and things I want to show you here in Wuhan. But is there anywhere else in Wuhan you want to go?"

Without hesitation Elise says, "Yes, back to Mount Luojia."

"You got it."

Chapter 8

Bai drives them back to Mount Luojia where they had gone on her first day in Wuhan. Only this time they hike through the lush, mountainous countryside to the mouth of a vast cave.

It is hot outside but when they reach the mouth of the cave the temperature drops. Inside it is dark and dank and at first Elise hesitates, but this is what it is all about. She wants to explore the unexplored as well as the highpoints of this beautiful country.

They advance further into the cave and out of the corner of her eye she sees movement. Not one to be frightened, being in an unfamiliar place, fear becomes a tangible, living force that creeps over her like some hungry beast, and for an instant she is immobilized.

"What is it," Bai ask, reaching out to her. Elise stares ahead and turns around to look behind, but there is nothing and she says. "Nothing. It is nothing."

Together they move slowly, adjusting to the darkness and taking it all in. There is still light coming from the entrance, but it is darker the further they go. Elise checks to make sure her recorder is on and starts to pull out her flashlight but decides against it. She keeps a random whisper going as they proceed explaining every thought and feel as they go deeper into the cave.

Beneath her feet the surface seems to change. "Bai, what is this we are stepping on?" Not waiting for his response, Elise kneels to get a closer look.

There is a change in Bai's voice as he replies, "It is layers of bat dung…" He pauses in mid-sentence, but he need not explain why as Elise sees what appears to be thousands of winged black dots crowding the cavern walls. The last word she hears is Bai yelling, "Run."

It is too late. Her mind is busy working on telling the recorder what she sees, and his word does not register. By the time Elise's mind translates the meaning there is nothing she can do. She hears the fluttering sound above her and peers above to see a colony of bats.

This time it is clear when Bai says, "Please, Elise, hurry."

Only she does not. "Stop Bai, they are not going to hurt us. I did an article on bats once and know that they will always try to avoid contact with humans and other animals."

"But rabies, Elise...have you heard of rabies?"

"Yes, but the incidence of rabies in bat populations is less than one percent and bats do not bite unless they are provoked." Bai pauses and Elise can tell he believes her, but remains at a distance, watching as she records.

Elise reaches into her pocket and pulls out what looks like a pen but is a small light. She wants to see the wings better. "I cannot remember ever seeing bats up this close and I am not going to let this opportunity get away from me." She turns on the pen light and shines it above.

The wings are fascinating, appearing like arms and hands with greatly elongated fingers, and a very thin membrane webbing stretching between the long skinny finger bones. She keeps her light focused so that as she speaks, she outlines one bat that is now flying above her.

The light attracts the bat confusing it as he tries to get out of the path of her light. But it is not just the one bat that is frighten as heightened movement of the bat fascinates her as she continues to record.

"Come on Elise. That is enough. Please."

Elise cannot help herself as she starts laughing so hard, she cannot stop and can barely put one foot in front of the other. "It is okay Bai. They are not interested in us, I promise."

"I do not care. Please, come on." By now he is standing at the mouth of the cave with the light framing his body. His face is in shadows, but she imagines from the sound of his voice it is crimped up in disgust, or maybe fright.

"Okay, Bai, I am coming."

Moving swiftly, she catches up with Bai and they make their way out of the cave without incident. At least, so she thought. When they step out of the cave Elise sees that they have bat droppings on their legs and arms. It covers their jackets and is in their hair.

"Whoa," Elise says in disgust as they shed their jackets and use them to wipe off their legs and hair.

"Yeah, we are a mess, and we stink too."

Still Elise cannot help laughing as she tries to say, "Oh, were you scared…"

Bai does not answer, just pushes his body against her playfully as they get to the car. Before climbing in they take their jackets and shoes off and put them on the rubber mat in the back of the SUV.

That ended the day of touring and Bai takes her back to the hotel to clean up. He drops her off at the front and says, "I am going home to shower and change."

"What about by coat and shoes."

"Do not worry. I will clean them and bring them back with me. It should take me a couple of hours."

Elise tries to avoid eyes as she hurries to the elevator. Once inside, she stands in the center, not allowing her body to touch anything and does the same when she reaches the door to her room. She gingerly reaches into her purse and pulls out her pass card.

Once inside she locks the door and hurries into the bathroom to strip naked and climb into the shower. She stays in there for a long time, washing her hair several times and doing the same all over her body until she finally feels clean again.

The bathroom is foggy when she finally climbs out, so she uses one of the towels to wipe off the mirror. Checking her Fitbit, she sees that she has plenty of time before Bai is to return so she slows down and enjoys the comfort of her surroundings. She picks up a brochure and takes it with her to the chair and smiles when she reads if she has any laundry to put it in the cloth bag hanging on the hook in the bathroom.

Elise gets up, locates the bag, and fills it with her dirty laundry. She sits it beside the door so that she will not forget to take it out with her. Then she begins getting out fresh clothes to put on.

Finally, she is ready, figuring if Bai has not returned there is much to enjoy at the hotel until he does arrive. So, once she reaches the lobby and not seeing him, she explores on her own and when she makes her way back to the lobby Bai is there.

Before she knows it is happening, he leans in and kisses her on the cheek. Elise does not know what to think as she smiles at him and when he is not looking, gently lays her hand on her cheek. They spent the day exploring the shopping areas and other attractions near the hotel and polish off several locally made cuisines at street vendors before sitting down to enjoy a glass of wine together.

That night as they sit eating dinner at the hotel, they randomly chat about the many places they have visited. When they finish with dinner, Bai asks her to walk with him to his car where he hands her cleaned shoes and jacket. "They smell much better, too," he adds.

"Thank you, Bai."

"You are welcome."

They walk back into the hotel lobby and Bai motions her to take a seat on one of the couches that sits off to the side. "Elise, we are going to travel to Shiyan tomorrow morning which is the farthest point in our agenda. We will not be able to comfortably make it back so you will need to pack an overnight bag."

"Okay. That's fine with me." Not knowing what else to say, she adds, "I guess I will see you in the morning."

"Sleep well, Elise."

She watches him as he leaves and then goes up to her room. That evening she sits before her laptop putting into words what her eyes have seen. She starts making sense of all she has recorded thus far, but pauses in the midst, thinking of her great-grandmother who she called bak hoo. She remembers the stories of her early life in Wuhan. Chinese imperial history always seemed so distant, so ancient but not anymore. Elise leans back remembering those childhood stories that she feels closer to now.

Once when she complained about her shoes being too tight her bak hoo had said, "Elise, when I lived in Wuhan, I wore cloth shoes that were called one-thousand-layered shoes. There were 100 stitches per square inch of the sole which helped them to be water-proof, but they were not extremely comfortable."

Elise closed her eyes and recall the people they passed during her tours with Bai and thinks she has seen this style of shoe on the feet of several Chinese people as well as the clothing of weaved silk cloth, colored with dyes, that led to the creation of the silk shoes that had replaced the straw shoes of the past.

Something as minor as shoes has made a visual connection between her and the family history.

She opens her eyes. A smile plays at the corner of her mouth as she sits up straight in front of her laptop. What she has seen and remembered she captures in words on her computer.

Chapter 9

On Saturday, November 7 Elise wakes up refreshed and anxious to get the day started. Her curly hair is tousled, and she takes a hand to push strands back off her face as she stretches her arms up over her head while turning to the side. Her eyes take in the scenic stretch of picturesque Wuhan visible through her hotel window and the view has a calming effect.

Just like all the days before, today would be filled with first times. It will be her first-time visiting Shiyan and her first-time riding on a high-speed train. What could be more thrilling. Elise had done her research. Today they would be traveling at the unbelievable speed of 200 mph, making a 250-mile trip in less than 2 hours. How do you wrap your head around that, she wonders. It is futuristical and the reality both chills and thrills her.

As she climbs out of the bed and out of habits, smooths the covers, her legs lean against the side as she peers at her Fitbit. It makes her aware that she needs to think of a parting gift for Bai.

During a conversation she had with her mother, Elise is aware of symbols of Chinese superstitions and that conversation replays in her head.

She had asked her mother what type of gift she might give to the person assigned to her during her time in China. Her mother had chuckled and said, "Give me a minute while

I try to remember it all. That's a tricky question and it's not to be taken lightly."

"Remember all of what."

"I know you have done a lot of research for your trip, but even you would not think to check out superstitions."

Elise nodded. It had not crossed her mind.

"Okay, here goes. First, clocks are a symbol of time running out so nothing showing time. Then there are sharp objects. They symbolize wanting to cut off your relationship with them. Do not give a gift of four. The number 4 in Chinese sounds like their word for death. That is why there is no floor four in some buildings and hotels."

Sonya presses her lips together tightly. "Oh yes, not that you would do it anyway, but shoes are a sign of evil."

Elise stares pensively at her mother. "Come on, shoes are evil?"

"Yes. It is because shoes sounds exactly like their word for bad luck or evil. Plus, shoes are something that you step on, and are thus not good gifts." Sonya giggles. "You must avoid shoes at all costs."

"Anything else."

"Yes. Handkerchiefs. Handkerchiefs are something given at the end of a funeral, so it symbolizes you are saying goodbye forever. You know, severing all ties. And then there are pears. Not all fruit, just pears are taboo."

Elise gives her mother a puzzled expression.

"You see, the Chinese word for pears sounds the same as the word for leaving or parting so giving pears is frowned upon."

"You have to be kidding."

Again, Sonya chuckles as she touches her daughter's cheek. "I kid you not." She then goes on. "Cut flowers are generally presents for funerals, so do not give them as a gift; yellow chrysanthemums and any white flowers, which represent death. And anything that is black or white as well. There is another reason, but I cannot remember it right now." Sonya adds, "Oh yes, now red however, is believed to be a festive and fortunate color, so anything red is always a great option.

"Then there are umbrellas. They see a gift of an umbrella as a sign the relationship with them has fallen apart."

"Anything else."

"There are probably much more, but the only other one I can recall are mirrors. They attract ghosts."

By the end of her list, Elise is laughing. She laughs because to her it sounds weird and entertaining, but Sonya stops her. "It is not funny, my daughter. We have our quirks as well. Every time you see something as a strange custom, remind yourself of ours."

"Like what."

"Like the number 13."

That is all she needed to say to bring Elise around.

Only now, Elise is running out of time as she heads into the bathroom to prepare for the day. While in the shower she goes through the items she should pack for their trip to Shiyan. Except for her hygiene items, she did most of the packing before turning in for the night. Only now she thought of a few other things, or rather, she hears her mother's voice in her head.

"Make sure you have a good nightie, change of underwear, extra shorts or slacks, just in case. Same with the shirt in case you spill."

How could she survive without her mother, Elise wonders as she places her cosmetic bag in the overnighter and then hears her mother's voice once again. "And, daughter, do not forget a wrap in case it is cold and an extra pair of shoes in case you need them." She adds those to her bag and one more thing that she herself thinks of. A nice dress and shoes in case they eat out somewhere special.

Finally, Elise is ready and leaves the hotel room feeling prepared as she makes her way to the elevator, her purse and electronic bag over her shoulder and the wheeled overnighter in tow.

As she stands waiting for the elevator she wonders where everyone is. She has not seen a person on the floor since arriving, but then, she has been leaving quite early and returning quite late. When the elevator arrives, Elise tugs the overnighter up close to her body before stepping in.

As the elevator descends, Elise's whole body is one mass of energy as she anticipates what she knows will be a magical day of new experiences. When the elevator door opens, and she steps into the lobby the fantasy continues. Even after seeing it five days it still takes her breath away and she stands, taking it all in until her eyes fall on Bai who stands ready and waiting.

Jeffries comes out of nowhere. "Miss, can I help you with that?"

"Oh, no, Jeffries, I got it. But thank you." He nods and turns away and soon is out of sight. Elise walks over to Bai.

They do not leave immediately. Instead, they eat breakfast at the hotel and throughout the meal they talk about their upcoming trip. Just to be sure, Bai asks, "Do you have your recorder on?"

"What do you think?" Elise smiles coquettishly.

"Okay, let me give you some details to start. Shiyan is in the northwest of Hubei Province, which is the upper reach of the Han River. We will begin our tour at the Wudang Mountain." While he talks, Elise senses a touch of excitement in his voice. She knows he has been there before, so it must be knowing he will be showing it to her for the first time. It gives her body a tingle. She mentally tells herself to calm. Even she gets excited when she can share something with interest to someone who is interested in hearing and seeing it. That is all it is.

"Elise, my company has a branch in Shiyan so we will be met by a local guide at the train station and he will take us to the hotel in Wudangshan to drop off our bags before our tour. He will stay with us and take us around.

"What do you mean by 'stay with us'?"

"Oh, he'll stay with us at the hotel since he lives outside Shiyan and it will be easier for him."

Bai takes a bite of food before adding, "That way we get an early start each morning. As I mentioned before, we need to stay in Shiyan for 5 days since it will be our start point to tour not only Shiyan, but Xiangyang, Suizhou, Jingmen and Xiaogan."

Elise nods to let Bai know she is listening. This morning she has opted for the traditional American fare of eggs, bacon, and toast and until she started eating, she had not realized how much she had missed this breakfast staple. She has a feeling she may not have it again, so she enjoys every bite. Even though Bai has assured her they will have American food, she has a feeling it might not taste the same in the small towns they will be visiting.

"Done?" Bai asks

"Yes. Done and ready to go."

Elise looks around as she stands, and Bai walks over beside her. "What is it."

"Nothing, really. Just that I am going to miss this luxury."

"Yes, I know, but Tao, that is our guide, says the hotel in Shiyan is nice."

They walk side by side through the restaurant to the front door of the hotel where, to her surprise, Bai's SUV sits waiting for them. Seeing the astonished expression on her face, Bai says, "When I arrived and told them I was waiting for you they confiscated my keys and told me they would take care of my vehicle."

"But you are not staying here."

"Right, but I am paying for the stay and get some of the amenities…"

Elise smiles at him as she climbs in and fastens her seat belt. That explains it. She knew her company would not dish out such extravagance as flying first class and staying in this luxurious hotel. It is Bai's travel agency that has not only arranged the accommodations but is paying the bill as well. So, now knowing this she must come up with the perfect thank you gift.

Bai checks to make sure she is ready and then they are on their way for her first high speed train ride.

It is a short distance from the hotel that they drive to the station. Once there, Bai parks the car and they climb out, meeting at the back to gather their bags. Bai reaches in and grabs his bag, then leans in to grab hers while Elise stands waiting. She observes as Bai situates his bag over his shoulder and then places her wheeled carryon at his side.

"What are you doing?" She asks.

"Getting our bags."

"I am very capable of carrying mine, you know."

"No one said you were not; it is just as easy for me to carry them."

"Ah…" Elise starts but, stumbles forward causing Bai to reach out quickly to grab her arm, making the bags slide off his shoulders as he does so.

Elise stands with her mouth agape gawking at the station. She heard Bai telling her earlier that Wuhan is in the middle of China and it is a major junction point for China's railway lines so there would be many trains shuttling between the city. But she cannot remember him saying anything about the station building."

Elise cannot talk at that moment. The train station itself resembles a flying crane. "The station…" she manages finally to get out.

"Yeah, it is mind-blowing. Four major architect firms designed the station. The design was inspired by the yellow crane, the symbol of Wuhan City. Look at the roof line Elise. It is designed to resemble the crane's wings."

They are now standing amongst a crowd of people waiting to board the train. Bai has already purchased their tickets. "Since we will not be going in the building, let me tell you a little about it. It consists of nine separated parts, symbolizing China's nine provinces, plus a central thoroughfare."

"So much thought put into it," She replies, while thinking of their small, unimpressive Rochester station.

"Yes, there has been. It is reputed to be the world's most beautiful railway station. It has one underground floor and three above ground floors."

"And so many trains." Elise was thinking there would only be one. "And so many people."

"Come on." Bai gives Elise a little shove and she starts walking forward. He explains that this is more like a transportation mecca. There are floors from bottom to top sequentially containing the subway platform, arrival hall, platforms, and waiting hall. In addition, 9 pairs of regular trains are operated daily to serve passengers travelling between Wuhan and Shiyan. Plus, the city bus stop and long-distance bus station are situated at the east square of the station while the west square is a recreation and green belt area."

"I cannot believe it."

"Believe it. There are 14 pairs of high-speed trains in service for passengers travelling from Wuhan to Shiyan or from Shiyan to Wuhan and it takes a little over 2 hours to finish a running distance of around 400 kilometers which is equal to 250 miles."

They move slowly with the crowd to board the sleek train sporting a maroon top and shiny grey sides that sits in front of them and even with this massive crowd, the boarding is handled quickly and efficiently. At that moment, Elise is impressed by everything she sees and is experiencing.

As soon as they are on board Bai guides her to their seats and in no time, they are on their way, leaving the station and beginning her next adventure.

As they start out, the areas they pass seem abandoned without buildings or pathways in view. She looks out the window and observes wires above and across the tracks. Bored with that view she turns her attention to the interior. It is like the best lounging chair she has ever sat in and with the large windows that fill the full side of the car it feels light and airy inside.

Elise cannot help but smile as she looks around the car at its shiny wood paneling and glass door separators between the different cars. A tv is viewable from all seats and the ride is smooth as they travel at some points high above the city streets and then back down. Inside the temperature is perfect, not to cold or too hot.

Elise looks above and notices there are separate open shelf areas where Bai has placed their luggage. Several passengers are dozing, and others walk through the glass door entrances that are unlocked so you can move easily between the cars. In their area there is one seat on one side and two on the other side of the aisle and all are in red leather. There are connected headrests that feel like pillows making it comfortable enough to catch a few winks. Elise believes this is the most amazing transportation ever.

To give Elise the total experience, Bai guides her on a tour, explaining as they go. "If you take a high-speed train with 8 carriages, the dining car is in the fifth carriage. For a high-speed train with 16 carriages, the dining cars are in the fifth and thirteenth carriage." We are on a 16 carriage." They pass through several cars and Elise notices that there are some with twice the seats as are in their car and the seats are black, but they look as comfortable and spacious as the ones they are seated in. Seeing Elise notice the change, Bai says, "We are in first class seats."

Elise just nods. They step into the dining car where the décor totally changes. There are bench like seating for two on either side of a table, draped in a white tablecloth with a glass topping over the fabric to keep it clean.

They find a seat and order tea since they have already eaten. Elise glances at Bai. "No one is pushy. From entering the train to moving between the cars it is total politeness."

"Yes, it is. Is it not like that in America?"

"N-o-o-o. Everyone is in too much of a hurry to think of the other guy."

They finish their tea in silence, each in their own thoughts until it is time to go back to their seats. Bai walks behind Elise, talking this time about the travel guide who will be waiting for them at the station. Elise finds it easier to relate to his voice with him behind her. Once she has taken in the area, she finds she sometimes just stares at him and his words seem to be coming out of a tunnel.

They are almost to their seats when Elise sees him. She stops short. Bai runs into her and instinctively reaches out to keep her from falling.

"It is him… she whispers," her back against Bai's chest.

"Who, Elise?"

"That man. The one just entering the car ahead of us."

Bai gently pushes her to an upright position and moves beside her so he can get a look at the man.

"Where do you know him from?"

"The plane, outside in front of the airport, and now here."

Bai is silent for a moment and then says confidently. "It is just a coincidence. He is traveling through the country just like you are and arriving when you did maybe put him on a similar schedule."

"But look at him."

Bai stares at the man. He has the stocky build of a rugby player. Solid and strong. He towers over the other passengers and Bai guess him to be over six feet. As he peers ahead, Bai notices that one eye and eyebrow seems lower, the eye barely open and his cheekbones above his mustache protrude out in lengthy puffs. Unlike his mustache, his beard, reaching down to his chest, is sparsely populated with hair. He whispers in Elise's ear, "He is kind of scary. I would not want to meet him in a dark alley." He pauses and then says, "Come on, Let us go to our seats."

They must pass right by him. Bai steps back behind her and when she is right beside the man, she feels his body bump into her; at least that is what she thinks.

Back at their seats, Elise realizes she has been holding her breath and she lets it out. She half listens as Bai tells her more about the guide who will be joining them. She can tell he is trying to distract her from thinking about the strange man.

The train comes to a stop and an announcement comes over the speaker. "Shiyan Station." It is spoken in several different languages, including English. Bai stands and retrieves their luggage and Elise says nothing, allowing him to carry it all. When it is their turn to disembark, she tries to forget about the man, forcing herself to not turn around. Soon they are standing on the platform and Bai is scanning the area. "Ah, there he is Elise. Come."

Elise continues to concentrate on what is in front of her. It takes all her effort as she feels the hair bristling on the back of her neck thinking he is behind her. It is like she fears he is trying to sneak up on her and she finds herself hurrying to keep directly beside Bai.

Soon Bai stops and the man in front of him smiles widely. "Hi, my friend," the stranger says before turning towards Elise. "Hello Miss McKenna. I am Tai Chen, your guide."

Tai Chen wears his hair bone straight and long, with the top layer pulled back and held in a ponytail band. He has one of those faces that seems to be smiling even when he is not. He is handsome and personable. Bai told Elise while they were on the train that he met Tao when they were training for their Certified Travel Agent (CTA).

Bai hugs Tai and then steps back. "Here," Tai says, "Let me help you with those bags."

As they head for the parking area, Tai imparts, "I hope to make your experience here as memorable as Bai has made it for you in Wuhan." Elise likes him instantly. He, like most of the people she sees rushing about, is dressed in the Chinese fashion, adorned with a loose-fitted tunic over white pants. Elise notices, women also wear tunics but in a longer variation reaching just above their shoes. The men tunics reach their knees. Even though it is a warm day, the tunics have long loose-fitting sleeves. Bai and Elise stand out in our more American attire, but that does not bother her or their new friend, Tao.

Tao takes them back to his SUV that is like the one that Bai drives. He puts their luggage in the back while Elise climbs in, allowing Bai to sit in front. Once Tao is behind the wheel, he says, "We are going to the hotel first to drop off your bags before we begin the tour. If you would like, you can freshen up a bit."

Elise responds. "Sounds good to me."

The rest of the ride, Elise is quiet listening as Tao and Bai catch up with each other. Soon they are pulling up in front of the Wudangshan Jianguo Hotel in Shiyan. Though not as chic as Wuhan's, more northern style, once inside,

Elise finds it has charm and the view fantastic as it is located at the foot of the Wudangshan Mountain.

Tao turns to face her. "Elise, this is a 5-star hotel catering to local tourists but because of its location, there are few English-speaking staff. You have Bai, but you can also use Google translate. The Wi-Fi works quite well so you should not have any problem and there is a shopping district close by with a number of places to eat." Tao informs them that he has upgraded them to a suite."

Elise smiles as she nods in appreciation.

"Tomorrow we will be doing a lot of hiking so make sure you wear some good hiking shoes." He turns to look at Elise.

"What? You don't think I plan on wearing heels, do you?" He can tell by her tone she knows he is kidding so he adds, "You know, you Americans…."

"Oh, yes, one more thing. Unfortunately, many Chinese smoke and few bother to stick to the rules. If you end up with a room that smells of smoke, tell me and I will ask for a change to another room."

In the hotel Elise and Bai show their credentials and are given pass cards. They walk together to the elevator and Elise cannot help wondering how this is going to work. She can tell by Bai's face he is wondering as well. When they arrive at their floor, they walk silently up the hall and Elise stands aside while Bai uses the passkey. They step into the room and all their doubts are removed. This is a true suite. It is very roomy, and she can see it not only has two bedrooms, but also two baths as well. "I will take the one on the left," Elise says. With the door open she can see it has a beautiful yellow décor.

"Great. I will take that one," Bai says pointing across the living room area. Elise takes her bag and goes into her room. There she quickly puts her things away and then heads for the bathroom to check her face and hair. She then changes into appropriate clothes for the day. When she enters the living room, Bai and Tao are waiting for her.

"Shall   we   go?"

"Yes. I am ready."

Elise, who knows some southwestern mandarin, is not familiar with the dialect that Tao and Bai whisper as they make their way to the lobby.

She is enjoying the atmosphere of this hotel that is fitting for the area. When they are at the front door, she asks Bai, "What language were you two conversing in?"

"Oh, it was a little, Jianghuai Mandarin, Gan, and Xiang. You will hear one of these languages throughout this area and it was a way of brushing up on my dialect skills.

Tao starts to say something, pauses and then he asks, "Is everything okay?"

"Yes, everything is fine," Elise says.

"If it is not, tell me. I could get you separate rooms at the Double Tree by Hilton, which is cheaper and mainly English is spoken, but Bai thought you would prefer a more Chinese environment. And the suite was all they had."

"Tao, it is fine."

"So why the serious expression?"

Bai speaks for Elise this time and says, in Mandarin, "She was wondering what language we were speaking earlier, is all. Elise knows a little Mandarin, but that is it."

"Oh, my fault," Tao says. "I was showing off for Bai and as usual, he surprises me by understanding the dialect variations."

That settled the three are on their way

As they drive to their destination, Tao in excellent English explains, "I like to pick on my friend," he says. "To many Chinese, Wuhan is a city characterized by its customariness." He peeks into the rearview mirror and sees the puzzle expression on Elise's face. "I am not being facetious. I am just saying that Wuhan has a lifestyle and daily parlance representing the common people, which to many people implies a lack of elegance in speech and manner advocated and admired generally by the Chinese."

"That once was true," Bai adds, but due to technological advances in recent decades, the city is breaking away from this common approach in the way they live, but thankfully they hang on to the style and manner in which the Wuhan dialect is spoken and the local customs, such as eating out for breakfast and snacking late at night."

"So," this distinction is more about the common way of life and the everyday language, both of which I find fascinating."

"Ah, you've won another over to your side," Tao teases.

"Wuhan has a dialect and parlance full of slang, with a unique regional flavor. The slang is one of the most renowned characteristics of the vernaculars of the City of Wuhan, not only because it is widely used in daily conversations by people from all levels of society."

Bai smiles as he says to Elise. "What he infers is that from manual workers, officials, doctors, teachers, students, everyone speaks this way."

"Yes, and not only speaks it, is found to be frequently used in literary and artistic works, newspapers and magazines, so much so that the Wuhan dialect may be called a slanguage."

"So, is that so bad?"

"No, not bad at all. It makes Wuhan unique, but China is all about the future."

Tao has a descriptive way of speaking that Elise appreciates immensely. In the lull of the conversation she asks, "Did Bao mention I keep my recorder on all the time."

"That he did, and I would expect you to."

"So, it is all right?"

"Yes, that is fine."

That settled, the conversation turns a corner and Elise listens as Tao speaks. There is no question, Tao is very knowledgeable on the area and begins by explaining that Wudang Mountain is part of a small mountain range in the northwestern part of Hubei, China, just south of Shiyan and that is where we are headed.

We drive a little over a mile and we are there. Once Tao parks the car, the tour begins with him explaining first that the Wudang Mountains stretches for 800 miles and we will have spectacular views if we are willing to hike, because there are a many secluded valleys, peaks, rugged hiking and stair climbing to do.

We follow, listening as Tao keeps a running colloquy going, explaining some and more of what Bai has told her from the other viewpoint of this mountain. "There are approximately 72 peaks, 24 streams, and 11 caves, and ponds." He stops and pointing with his finger, our eyes follow as he explains that this is the main peak called Tianzhu Peak. The other peaks surrounding it and the streams we will find quite interesting as well.

"Bai told me you want to see the less road travel type of tour so that is why I picked this first," Tao says.

"That is right. Thank you, Tao."

Elise feels the change in the temperature as they ascend Wudang Mountain, and she is glad she brought a light jacket with her. But any discomfort is soon forgotten with the splendor of the area.

Tao takes them to see the Five Dragons Temple known as the first site of worship. Even The Gate of Yuan Wu at Wudang Mountains is breathtaking. They visit the Golden Hall, the Ancient Bronze Shrine, Nanyang Palace, and the stonewalled Forbidden City at the peak. From one breathtaking building to the next, Elise stares in admiration.

Elise cannot help herself as she reaches out to touch the wall of the Purple Cloud Temple. Its dramatic appearance on a hill has the trio climbing up several layers of steps to approach, but it is worth it. Once inside they confront several halls and Daoist statues including the Dragon and Tiger Hall, the Purple Sky Hall enshrined with statues of Zhen Wu at different stages of his life, the East Hall, the West Hall, the Parent Hall and the Prince Cliff.

It has been a wonderful tour, long, but full of information that Elise can use in her book. At one point she asked Tao to tell her something that most people do not know about this area and he tells her the story of Zhang Sanfeng.

He starts by saying, "You see, there are really two schools of Kung-Fu in China...There's Shaolin Kung-fu. That was made famous by the Shaolin monks, which most have heard of..." He turns to make sure that Elise does know and sees her nod. "And, then there's Wudang Kung-fu - which originates from the Wudang mountains. Wu-Dang was founded by a legendary man called Zhang Sanfeng."

Tao pauses for emphasis and then begins his tale. "Zhang Sanfeng was a Taoist priest and sage who lived in the mountains. He was a legendary Chinese Taoist who invented T'ai chi ch'üan and was purported to have achieved immortality. According to various accounts, he was born in Shaowu, Nanping, Fujian during the Southern Song dynasty and lived for over 307 years until the mid-Ming dynasty."

"Sorry to interrupt, but what is the Song Dynasty?"

"Yes, well, the Song dynasty was an imperial dynasty of China that began in 960 and lasted until 1279. It was founded by Emperor Taizu of Song following his usurpation of the throne of the Later Zhou, ending the Five Dynasties and Ten Kingdoms period."

"Thanks Tao. Please continue."

Zhang Sanfeng was a man who frankly has a mythical status around parts of China, especially amongst veterans in the World of Chinese martial arts. He was indeed a maestro when it came to internal martial arts and Chi energy, and to what was known as alchemy." Tao pauses and asks, "Have you heard of alchemy?"

Elise concentrates for a while and finally speaks. "I think so. Alchemy is an ancient branch of natural philosophy that is a philosophical and protoscientific tradition that though practiced in Asia, Europe, Africa, China, it originated in China."

Tao nods, impressed. Smiling he adds, "some believers even say Zhang Sanfeng became immortal! And in some ways, you can say he is through the statue of him at the Wudang mountain range."

"Thanks Tao. That was interesting."

"Glad to help, Elise, glad to help."

It was a wonderful way to end the tour for the day. Tao drives them back to the hotel. "My friends, I am going to leave you for a bit. I want to go home and change but I will be back in time to join you for dinner and we can go over my plans for tomorrows tour."

Back in the room, Elise feels shy and nervous as she smiles and says, "I'm just going to change and get ready for dinner."

"Me too," Bai says. She watches as he heads to his side of the living quarters.

When Tao returns, he rings their room and soon they join him. Elise turns and starts walking toward the restaurant, but Tao stops her.

"Oh, no, my sister. They do have excellent food here, but this first meal must be authentic. Hubei cuisine and Sichuan cuisine are typical of Shiyan food, and Wudang food is particularly different. To get the full Shiyan experience we are going to try local snacks on Ancient Street... and, yes, that is the name of the street. There are row upon row of snack bars and restaurant."

And so, they did. With Tao's running commentary and sharing of the food they manage to taste it all. Nothing could please her more as they share a dish of Guandu spiced dried bean curd, a traditional food from Guandu, Zhushan County. Next its Yunxian county Wangyousha made from fine red cowpea served with rice. The cowpea is boiled until its skin comes off. Then they roll up the cowpea pulp before battering it in egg white and yolk powder. Finally, they fry it, cutting it into strips, scattering sugar onto it, and adding some seasonings. Elise found it especially tasty. They finish their food tour with Sanhe soup which Tao says can never be omitted. The soup is made with vermicelli of sweet potato, sliced beef and dumplings stuffed with beef.

At the end of the evening, Tao takes them back to the hotel. "Let's have a drink," Bai says. "Good idea," adds Tao. "I think we should introduce Elise to Chinese beer...what do you say, Elise. Are you game?"

"Bring it on, but you pick it as I must admit, I'm not familiar with Chinese beers."

Tao orders a Harbin Beer for himself and Bai chimes in asking for a Snow beer. He then turns to face Elise and says, "She'll have a Zhujiang Beer."

"It's a pale Lager, Japanese Rice style beer. I think you will like it." She does.

When they finish Tao reminds them, they will be starting out early. Before he has driven off, Elise and Bai are headed toward their room where they say a quick goodnight before going to their bedrooms. Elise falls asleep as soon as she climbs into the bed.

The next day they have a quick bite and then visit what was Yuzhengong Palace where each building is architecturally ornate and some are very colorful, drawing Elise's eye to each detail of their structure. Elise listens and then Tao asks, "Want to know why Zhang Sanfeng's statute sits out here?" Elsie nods.

"In January 2003, the 600-year-old Yuzhengong Palace was burned down accidentally. The fire broke out in the hall, reducing the three rooms that covered 200 square meters to ashes. The gold-plated statue of Zhang Sanfeng, which was usually housed in Yuzhengong, was moved to another building just before the fire, and so escaped destruction in the inferno."

It is like how it must feel to be in an enchanted forest, only this one is enchanted with not only beauty but history and Elise hates to see the end of the day, but she admits she is tired and ready to get off her feet. As they head toward the car, Tao says, "Stop. Look behind us." Bai and Elise stop and turn around. As enchanting as the area is during the day, the night plays a different melody of lights. The three stand there in awe, enjoying the spectacle.

As they stand there, Elise whispers. "Here I am, grandmother. Here I am looking at what you must have enjoyed as a child and remembering how you described your home. I listened, but I thought later it was an exaggeration." Elise smiles and whispers again. "I thought nothing could be so beautiful, but I was wrong. I know it is exactly as you told me."

"Elise, where are you?" It is Bai's voice that she hears.

"Sorry. What did you say?"

"Tao was asking if you would like to do a little souvenir shopping, but I think you've had enough for today."

"Oh, yes, I would. I was just thinking about my grandmother and how she tried to describe the beauty of the area."

"Oh, yes, Bai mentioned you have family from Wuhan, but not from Shiyan, right?"

"Right. They never traveled this far. It is just that the antiquity is something I do not get to see in America."

"I'm glad you are enjoying it, Elise. I am trying to make it informative, but interesting and I think I've done my job." Elise smiles and Tao says, "Okay then, Let's go."

As they make their way into the shopping district, Tao asks, "Do you have something in mind you wish to purchase?"

"Yes, in fact I do. I want to purchase authentic Chinese jewelry. I am thinking a bracelet or a simple necklace for my mother."

"I know just the place. Come with me." They follow Tao expressing their appreciation of his guided tour and he thanks them, expressing that the tour he is giving them is specially tailored to Elise's wishes and it is the first time he has done a tour like this one.

Tao is handsome, smart and has that honest friendliness that she senses in Bao. They walk through throngs of people hurrying in many directions. Soon, Tao stops in front of a store. "This, my dear is the Hubei Zhubao Jewelry Co., Ltd. and it is part of the Jewelry Stores Industry. Here you will get nothing but authentic jewelry. But, first, look at the sky."

"Huh…" I start to say but stop following his instruction.

The sky has changed to a royal blue with a full moon dotting the horizon. "It is magnificent." Tao nods. The three stand there taking it in for several minutes before finally turning their eyes away.

Elise can hardly wait to get inside the store now and once inside, they part ways as Bai goes over to look at some rings and Tao joins him. In minutes of entering the store, the most beautiful woman Elise has ever seen comes forward and smiles. She is quite petite and exquisite with a thick layer of bangs above her perfectly oval shaped face. Her hair is caught up at the sides of her face in jeweled clips that continue in a jeweled band across the top of her head. Her eyes are wide, and her mouth is like those drawn on china dolls. She wears a high neck kimono with a ruffle edge just under her chin. She asks with a slight accent, "Miss, can I help you find what you are looking for?"

Elise cannot help staring. She forces her eyes away from the woman's face and investigates the glass cabinet in front of her as she breathes, glad that the woman speaks English. "Yes, I am looking for something for my mother whose family is from Wuhan."

"Ah, so you are visiting the home of your ancestors?"

"Yes, I am. I am a writer of tour books and I was lucky to get this assignment. I cannot believe I am here. I have always wanted to come and now by providence my company gives me this assignment. I feel so lucky to see this part of my family heritage."

"Well, there is much to see here. Are you exploring alone?"

"Oh, no, I have my guide Bai and he is handling the trips through his contacts. This is the first stop after we toured Wuhan. I am extremely impressed."

"Are you from America."

Elise smiles. "Yes, I am."

The woman leads Elise over to the jewelry counter and Elise watches as her delicate hands move several items on the counter for her to look at. "What is your name," Elise ask. Then embarrassed at being so forward adds, "Oh, that is if you want to tell me. My name is Elise."

"That is okay. My name is Biyu. It means jasper, the precious stone. My father has always been in the jewelry business and he picked my name."

"What a lovely name. It suits you."

Biyu smiles. "Thank you. Here are some jewelry pieces that your mother might like," she says, her hand gracefully waving above the display she has placed on the counter.

With her help it is easy to make a choice and soon she has exactly what she wants. Biyu places the piece in a red velvet box that she puts inside a larger box before putting it in a lovely cloth bag. She thanks Biyu and then leaves to join the men who have been waiting for her. As they step outside, it is Bai this time who says, "Look up Elise."

The sky has changed again. It is like there is a net up in the sky with hazy white dots all over it. And the sky color has changed to a navy blue visible behind the net.

After a bit Tao starts walking and they follow. Soon they are at the car and on their way back to the hotel.

Once there, Tao pulls up in front and gets out. Elise follows suit and goes over to him. She grasps his hands in both of hers. "I have enjoyed the day immensely."

Tao squeezes her hands in return. He looks up so that his vision includes Bai and says, "So, my friends, I will see you in the morning." With that he drives off.

Bao and Elise head for the hotel dining room. After placing their order, Elise is without words as they sit there waiting for their food. She is so happy that Bai chose Tao Chen to be their guide. She has gone on many of these guided tours before, in many places and the guides merely spew the words printed on site placards. But not Bai or Tao. It is obvious how well they know their areas and want to share their knowledge of the actual history and not just what she could read online or in books. So far, between the two of them, it has been the best tour ever. They eat their dinner, enjoying the view from the window and then make their way to the bar for a cocktail. Bai mentions that this is the end of their two-day tour of Shiyan, but Tao has more in store for them. Elise has no doubt he will have them looking at the past and awash them in the memories of the present.

Chapter 10

On waking, the first thought Elise has is today they tour Xiangyang. After a good night's sleep, she is more than ready for the day and when she enters the living room, she looks around for Bai who always greets her but does not see him. To her, this moment is as special as the tours. Disappointed, she turns toward the kitchen in their room and there he is, his radiant smile extending from eye to eye. "Sleep well, Elise?"

"Yes, I did." She can see all his emotions in his smile. It culminates awe, concern, excitement, and tiredness in one beautiful expression. In Elise's eyes, it is the most perfect and beautiful smile she has ever seen. The fact that he is exceptionally handsome helps, too.

They go down to the breakfast lounge for tea and a quick bite before Tao arrives. "Good morning my friends."

Almost in unison Bai and Elise say, "Good morning Tao."

He sits down and pours himself a cup of tea. He wears his feelings on his sleeve and Elise can tell he is pondering a matter. "Tao, is something wrong?"

"No, nothing's wrong. I have just been wondering if I should drive us to Xiangyang or should we take the train for the experience."

"How long is the drive?"

"Hour and a half."

"That settles it. Let us drive. We will see more of the country that way and besides, we will be taking the train again when we return to Wuhan."

Elise can hear Tao's breathe escaping his pursed lips. "That is a load off." Picking up his tea, he leans his body back on the chair.

Tao, more relaxed and Elise excited to be on their way, when Tao finishes his tea, they pick up their belongings and head for the door.

Elise feels the chill when they exit the hotel. She, like Tao and Bai have dressed in layers, and it feels like they will need them all. Once in the car, Bai turns to her and says, "It is a little different here than in Wuhan. It does get cold at night in November, but it is often sunny and pleasant during the day. We are talking 8 degrees Celsius which is 46 degrees Fahrenheit and the average daily high temperature is 17 degrees Celsius or 63 degrees Fahrenheit. "

Tao picks up from there adding, "Around here the hot season lasts for 4 months, from May to September, with an average high of 94 degrees to 76 degrees and our cold season is three months from the end of November to the end of February. The temperature can fluctuate between 29 degrees Fahrenheit to 48 degrees.

Elise is recording all of this. Though she knows that the temperatures match Rochester, she knows that distance can play apart, yet, the reported temperatures, say, on the internet is covering a broad spectrum and not specific places.

During the drive Tao and Bai talk the mingle dialects together, laughing every now and then when Bai falters. Elise pulls out her laptop and begins typing and editing the chronicled information. Every now and then she ask Bai, or Tao for clarification on some points.

Elise does take time to check out the scenery, but since they started out, it has been the same view. As far as the eye can see, small little peaks of orangey yellow among green trees.

Elise looks up when Tao speaks about Xiangyang. He explains that it is a prefecture-level city and at one time was known as Xiangfan. "If you were to see it on a map you would see that it is divided into what looks like three equal land masses as it is divided by the Han River, which runs through its heart and divides the city north-south. What there is of old Xianyang is located south of the Han River and that is where we are going. It contains one of the oldest still-intact city walls in China."

While Tao speaks, Elise puts away her work.

By the time Tao maneuvers the SUV into a parking space all three are anxious to begin the tour of Xiangyang

Their first stop is what is left of the city wall of Ancient Xiangyang City and Tao explains, "This is one of my favorite places to be in Xiangyang. When we get to the top you will see the Han River below and the lights of the modern city of Xiangyang that the wall separates from the old city of Xian."

"What is it made of Tao?"

"Tapered stone with mortar joints. Come on, we're going to access it through the underground tunnel." As they wait for their turn, Tao pays the admission fee and soon they are on their way. Tao gets an electro cart and they take it up to the summit.

The view is breathtaking, much more to attract the eye then the drive there. Then for a break in continuity, Tao takes them on a trip down the Hans River, giving them a different perspective on the area.

Next it is off to see the only city gate left – the north gate "Suo Yue" which means the lock and the key. Tao says, "At one point there were six city gates and four watch towers standing guard of the city."

The walls of the city were covered with golden tiles and colored glazes that made the city wall shine in the sunlight. That along with the architectural details so richly ornate took her breath away." When she says, "I have never seen anything this beautiful," Tao and Bai smile at her admiration and their confidence builds.

They next travel pass the graceful hills and clear waters to visit the place where Zhuge Liang once lived as a hermit and visit Zhuge Cottage, Wuhou Temple built to enshrine Zhuge Liang, Wolong Inchu, and Gonggeng Field.

"Elise, do you know of Zhuge Liang?"

"Yes, he was a key ruler in the kingdom of Shu Han when the Eastern Han Empire fell in 220."

"Correct, but according to historical records, Zhuge Liang invented the land mine, an automatic transport wagon similar to a wheelbarrow, and also the repeating semi-automatic bow called the "Zhuge crossbow.""

That, she did not know.

At the end of the day they dine at the Signature Dish Chinese Restaurant before returning to the hotel. As they part Tao says, "Rest my friends and be refreshed. We have a big day ahead of us in Suizhou.

When they enter their hotel room, they find a bottle of wine has been placed on the table, so Elise gets glasses, Bai opens the bottle and pours a glass for each of them. They toast each other and chat about their lives; but mostly about hers. Then Elise stands and takes the glasses back to the kitchen, rinses them and on her way through the living room says mockingly, ""Rest my friend and be refreshed, Bai laughs, then turns and they go to their separate quarters, over his shoulder he says, "See you in Suizhou."

Chapter 11

In her room, Elise feels the first tinge of anxiety and it does not surprise her. Staying in the hotel suite together at first was not an issue, but now after three nights it feels like they are living together. This will be the third night they sleep in separate beds, but still united in one room, She has no experience being this close to any man and the fact that she is attracted to him makes her heart pound. Elise calms, reminding herself this is a business trip and as such she must maintain a business manner.

She does not get much sleep that night and rises early, expecting to be the first one up, but when she enters the living room Bai is there, his back to her as he stands behind one of the chairs that sits in front of the fireplace. Above him the crystal chandelier dances light over his frame making it hard to turn her gaze away and Bai turns around and catches her staring.

Trying to compose herself she says, "Oh, good morning Bai. Fancy meeting you here."

"Good morning. I woke early so I decided to do some reading." Elise sees he has a book in his hand. Bai turns his wrist and looks at his watch. "Tell you what, let's get coffee downstairs before we have to head out." He pauses, "If that is okay with you."

"Yes, oh, yes, I could use some coffee." They grab what they will need to take with them and leave the room. It is the first time she has felt uncomfortable in Bai's presence. Outwardly nothing has changed, but inside it is another matter. She works on being as nonchalant as possible.

Even though it is early, there are already several people seated in the café, but they manage to find seats near a window. "I like tea, but I really needed some coffee today." Bai says this lightly but there is a tinge of what translates to her to be disrespect for tradition in his voice. She says nothing and they allow silence to fill the space between them.

It is not long before Tao walks in the café. "Well, looks like you two have been up awhile."

I am sure it is my imagination, but I think I hear a tinge of sarcasm in his voice. Does he think... No, I tell myself. It is my imagination.

He sits and chats while he drinks a cup of tea, then stands. "If you are ready, Let us get started." Bai and Elise rise and follow Tao. Tao turns and says, "It is a little far today, so we are taking the train."

He drives them to the train station, explaining that he purchased the tickets last night so they can board right away. When Elise sees the throng, she is glad he had the foresight but had hoped to get a chance to see the inside of the station.

When their train arrives, Tao, Bai, and Elise grab hold of each other and wiggle their way through the doors, then, Tao guides them straight to the dining car. It is a smart move. They find seats and after catching their breath, Tao asks, "Thought you might be hungry. Can I order for you?"

Elise nods. she wants to try a typical Chinese breakfast on a train."

"Yes, please."

Tao orders porridge, pickles, boiled eggs, Chinese breads, and steamed stuffed buns and of course, tea. It smells wonderful and Elise places some of each on her plate and starts eating even before the men have filled their plates.

While they eat, Tao discusses the places he plans on taking them. He will rent a car so they can easily visit more of the sights. Since she has her recorder on, Elise eats and takes in the scenery until they arrive at their stop.

"This is Suizhou," Tao says. He goes on to explain that Suizhou is the birthplace of the legendary Yandi, one of the forefathers of Chinese Nation along with Huangdi. He goes into a lengthy explanation before they arrive at the first point of interest which is to see a set of Bronze Chime-bells excavated from the Tomb of Marquis Yi of the Zeng State.

Then it is on to tour Dahong Mountain where Tao takes them through Hongshan Temple, followed by a view of the Hongshan River and Zhaoquan River.

"We must check out Three-Eye Spring and White Cloud Temple in the north, Kwan-yin Rock in the east, and Xujia Village in the south. And so, they do."

The day wears on and the tour ends at Shennong Cave, followed by a local light meal of a mushroom-based stir fry, lake fish, lotus root, and a fried sesame ball. When they climb on the train to return to Shiyan, they are all spent but happy.

Elise is now nine days into her trip, but more importantly, it is nine days with Bai. What started out to be comfortable, is now becoming dangerous because it is obvious the attraction is on both sides and floating on the surface as they make their way to their suite of rooms. When they part for the evening they shy from touching hands and settle for a smile, but the sexual tension is there, and Elise is not sure how much longer they can avoid acting out their feelings. She uses the evening to concentrate on weaving her recordings into form for her guidebook and when finished, she is tired and able to sleep.

Chapter 12

Wednesday, the eleventh day of November and they are on their way to Jingmen. Tao has advised them to bring snacks and water along with them and they pick up food and drinks from the café in the hotel.

They follow the same pattern as the previous day of taking the train and renting a car to get around and Elise habitually turns on her recorder, the minute they climb in the car so as not to miss anything.

In Jingmen they visit the Ming dynasty Xianling Tomb, the ancient Han dynasty tombs, and Neolithic remains from the Qujialing culture which all of it amazes Elise, but the best is yet to come.

Tao takes them to the Dahongshan Scenic Area, famous for the spectacular Huangxian Cave, which they of course will explore.

But there is much more to see as Tao continues to amaze his guest. "This, my dear is Meiren Valley which means Beautiful Person." Peaceful emerald green water flows over large boulders and in the distance is a small waterfall. "This valley is situated in the Wnfu river Gorge. That is the water you see."

They leave the area and finally are on their way to the Huangxian Cave. Tao pauses at the entrance. "Elise, the name Huangxian means, Yellow Fairy. It is important to know that before we enter." Tao walks in first and then moves aside as he tells the story of the cave. "We are now in the southern part of the Dahong Mountain Range and there is a story to how the cave received its name. We are told that a man named Huang Shigong once rested here." While he talks, Elise takes it all in. On the right side is a great hall with a stone pool, which Tao says was created by a naturally formed dam of calcified rock. The pool, dam, stalactite as well as the three-arched caverns stand in front of her. There are green, pink, yellow, orange and the royal blue of the sky seen through the entrance helping to turn this into a fairy tale place with names like Strong Cave Mouth, Jigong Prays, the Whisper, Panda and Butterfly, Yellow Fairy Promenade, Fairy Path, the First Night, Harmoniously Together, Nezha's Birth, the Golden Shower and a Fairy's Lost Dress, all pointed out by Tao. When it is time to leave, Elise hesitates, wanting to enjoy the beauty a bit longer. But Tao says, there is more to see.

Tao takes them to the Xianling Mausoleum, located to the East of Zhongxiang City, Hubei Province. The mausoleum is surrounded by red walls and is approached by way of long passageway paved with flagstones. On both sides of the passageway are statutes that include, a pair of stone pillars, lions, camels, elephants, unicorns.

Further along the path they see sitting and standing horses and two pairs of statues of generals and arts ministers. Then, at the back are two halls. As they walk, Tao explains. "The Nine Twists River in the tomb area acts as a drainage facility to prevent the water from flowing off Songlin Mountain. All Ming imperial mausoleums have rivers, artificial or natural, for drainage and flood discharge, but the one here is the most outstanding as it conforms to fengshui principles." The expression on Elise's face has Tao explaining further. "The Mausoleum sits toward the east, with mountains at its back and facing water. The coffin chamber rests against the left peak of Songlin Mountain, and mountain ranges flank both sides of the mausoleum all of which conforms to fengshui.

Elise's head is spinning with all that they have seen, and she is happy to hear Bai say, "This has been a lot to take in."

"I know my friend, but that is China. When it comes to ancient sites and nature made attractions, there is much to see. But that is what I wanted to show you today. We will head back to the car and go home."

Soon they are on the road again and Elise feels the fullness of the day forcing her body to relax, but she manages to stay alert as they park the car and as previously agreed to they eat dinner on the train.

Back in Shiyan, they climb into Tao's SUV and head toward the hotel. Elise checks her recorder and then leans back to rest her eyes. The voices from the front of the SUV seem far away as she drifts off.

It is the sound of Bao's voice, now close to her ear, whispering, "It is time to wake, Elise."

That sensation of not knowing where she is or how she got there takes over and her head jerks forward. Her eyes scan the inside of the SUV and soon she realizes where she is. "Sorry. I must have drifted off."

"Yes, you did. Come on. We are here." While Bai helps her out, Tao says, "I will take off." But Bai replies,

"No Tao, this is our last night. Come in, and let's have a proper meal and toast the success of our tour."

Tao turns around to view Elise. "Yes, Tao, besides, I have already had a good rest."

That evening, Tao joins them in the restaurant. They eat a heavy meal and then drink several glasses of wine as they toast each other for whatever pops in their heads. Their laughter fills the restaurant, and, on several occasions, they try to quiet themselves as they can see they are disturbing other diners.

Finally, Tao prepares to leave. "Good night. Get a good night's sleep my friends." With that he drives off.

Elise and Bai go straight up to their suite. "Wow, I do not know about you, but I am exhausted."

"Me too. I think I had a little too much wine with my dinner."

Bai smiles and heads to his room. Elise turns and goes to hers where she prepares for bed, but instead of laying down, she decides to work on her travel guide. Taking her laptop, she sits waiting for it to open and thinks about the fact that this is it. She imagines Bai is sleeping by now and here she sits, her mind mulling over the reality that this will be their last night in this suite of rooms. Tomorrow they will check out and it will be separate rooms in Enshi and then back to Wuhan. She sighs. Elise sits up straight and tilts her head. She hears it again. A light tap on her door.

"Come in," she says, using her hands to smooth her hair.

Bail opens the door and hesitantly stands at the threshold. "I cannot sleep." Not knowing what else to say he adds, "Want to have a drink together?"

Elise pauses thinking about it but knowing what she will say. "Yes, give me a minute and I'll be right there."

In her heart she knows this is dangerous but cannot control her head or body. She tells herself that it will be all right. They are grownups and can handle it. She slips on her robe and slippers then walks as confidently as she can into the shared space.

Bai is standing by the gas fireplace. He has on white cotton lounging pajamas and looks comfortable as his face lights up in a wide grin. "I bought this bottle of Grace Vineyard Chairman's Reserve Bordeaux Blend wine and wanted to share it with you."

"That is a mouth full," she laughs as she takes one of the glasses that Bai has the stems wrapped in his fingers. Her hand cannot avoid touching his and she fights desperately to control her expression as she gracefully moves her hand back.

"I know it is not proper, but I want you to know how special this tour has been and I want you to really enjoy it, so I am going to tell you it costs seventy dollars in American money."

Elise's glass falls from her hand and her heart skips a beat. "Did you say seventy dollars?"

"Yes." There is laughter in his voice as he bends down to retrieve her glass and sits it on the table. He leaves and returns with another one from the small kitchenette in the room.

This time he places both glasses on the table and Elise watches the beautiful bright red wine as it splashes down the sides of the glass.

Bai picks the glasses up and walks over to her, before handing her a glass he smiles. "Maybe you should sit."

She can hear the humor in his voice, but that is exactly what she does as she walks over to the sofa and takes a seat. When he leans over and hands her the glass, he places it firmly in her hand before sitting down next to her.

The tour guide surfaces as he verbalizes, "Here is what I know. This wine has an expressive nose of red and black fruits with a subtle oak dimension. There is a dense, fairly tannic taste…" He sees her puzzled expression and responds. "That term refers to the use of oak and other bark in tanning animal hides into leather." He continues. "The final note is a fruity with spice aromas."

Elise giggles at what he is obviously doing. He tries to relieve the tension by spouting off this in-depth wine description. She goes with it.

"Ah, a wine connoisseur?"

"No, a man trying to impress."

She tilts her head to the side so that she can see his face and their eyes meet. She can feel her face getting warm, so she lowers her eyes to sip the wine. It is good. Exceptionally good.

"Well, Bai, I am impressed. This is incredibly good. I like it. But you shouldn't have. That is a lot to spend on wine, at least in my country it is."

"Yes, I know. It is a lot to spend on wine here too, but I wanted to give you something special and I know you like wine, so I just thought…"

"Enough said. Tell me, have you been to the places we have gone before?"

Bai sips his wine, his brow furrows as he thinks about the question. He answers. "Well, I have visited some of the places, but not all of them." He looks directly at Elise. "I can say that I have not experienced the train as much as I have these last few days and that is a treat indeed."

"Yes, I am glad we have had opportunities to take the train. We do not have trains like these in America."

The casual conversation continues while Elise and Bai finish their glass of wine. Elise begins to feel very mellow. "What is the alcohol content?

Bai picks up the bottle. "It says 12.5 - 13.5%."

"I can believe that." She no longer cares what happens as she holds out her glass. He has spent a lot on this wine, and she intends to see that they drink it.

Between the two they finish off three glasses of wine, their voices softening after each glass until the bottle is completely empty. Now Elise wonders if she can stand as she leans forward and carefully places her glass on the table. Bai does the same.

"So, Elise, I…" he starts and before she can react, he pulls her into his arms and kisses her.

Elise can feel goosebumps on her arms as she freezes, unable to push him away. Instead she melts into his embrace. They both know it is useless to fight it and they do not.

She no longer needs to worry if she can stand. Bai lifts her up from the sofa and carries her into his bedroom, kicking the door shut as if someone is there to see them. It is dark, warm and smells like him, making her body go limp with desire.

Elise does not remember how they undressed, only that his naked body was against hers and their lips never parted. When he enters her, a shiver goes all the way down her body to her toes. She has never felt such ecstasy before. She did not want it to stop.

Their bodies glisten in sweat and their hearts racing frantically as they move as one in their passion for each other. And when they climax it is together. It was as if they are the only two people on this planet.

When they pull apart, Bai holds her close, whispering in her ear and planting small soft kisses along her cheeks until they find her lips again. He kisses her deeply and her body reacts. He enters her body again and they move in unison. Elise, unable to hold it in, screams out in the height of her passion and she hears Bai moaning in her ear.

They make love once more and finally, totally exhausted they part. With a final kiss, Bai slides over to lay his head on his pillow and Elise stares up at the ceiling. Slowly her breathing evens and she falls into a deep dreamless sleep.

Light shining through the window wakes Elise and she has that feeling of not knowing where she is until she turns to see Bai looking at her.

He whispers, "Elise, we overslept."

"What," she asks, her head in a fog.

"We are late. Tao is probably waiting for us."

"Oh my god, oh my god…"

Elise starts to get up, but Bai pulls her over to his side of the bed. "I lov…" he starts, then changes quickly. "I really like you Elise." He kisses her gently and then lets her go.

Elise gets up, heads toward the door, turns and says, "I really like you too." Then she is off to her room where she puts toothpaste on her toothbrush and leans into the shower to turn it on. When the water is comfortable, she climbs in, turning round and round and sudsing her body before rinsing off and drying off. When she leaves the bathroom, she hurries to the dresser and pulls out clean clothes. She breaks her record as she finally emerges in the front room, all dressed and ready for the day.

Bai is minutes behind her. On the way down in the elevator, he gently runs his fingers along the side of her cheek, sending needles of pleasure through her body that linger after he lowers his hand. When they step out of the elevator, they both adjust their faces before heading across the lobby.

Tao is indeed waiting, and Bai has a ready excuse. "Sorry we are late, but we drank some of that wine I purchased the other day."

"Oh, do you mean that bottle of Grace Vineyard Chairman's Reserve Bordeaux Blend wine?"

"Yes, that is the one."

"Did you save me a sip?"

Embarrassed, Bai says, "So sorry, in fact we drank the whole bottle." With that they were on our way.

Chapter 13

That day they travel to Xiaogan. On the drive Tao begins his commentary. "Xiaogan is located in north-central Hubei province, at the south bank of the Hanjiang River and neighboring Henan province on the north." I had looked at the map and know that it borders Wuhan to the east, Suizhou to the north and Jingmen to the west. Tao is weaving his way toward Wuhan in a direct path through the areas of interest.

We all have packed jackets knowing we can expect cool weather.

My interest is drawn to the front seat where Tao is telling a tale of Xiaogan. "Xiagan was the hometown of Dong Yong, whose legend gave birth to the name of Xiaogan."

"Excuse me, Tao, who is Dong Yong," Elise asks, her recorder going.

"Ah, so glad you asked." He looks at Bai and then tells the tale.

"This is a great Chinese Love story of forbidden love. It is the story of a mortal, Dong Yong, and the Seventh Fairy. Tao clears his throat and says, "So here goes."

"Once there lived a very poor father and his son. They worked day and night in the fields to earn enough money to pay their rent and to buy food. One year a drought destroyed the land, and the father died, leaving no inheritance for the son."

"Dong Yong loved his father and wanted to give him a proper funeral, but he had no money. Not knowing what else to do, he sold himself into slavery to pay for his father's funeral and began working day and night to pay off his debt."

"One day, as he rested under a tree, a beautiful maiden approached him and asked why he was working so hard with so little rest. Dong Yong told the girl why, then burst into tears."

"The maiden said her mother had died when she was young and her father had remarried, and now her new stepmother wanted to marry her off to someone. She then burst into tears as well. Then Dong Yong, came up with a solution – he suggested they get married, and maybe they could heal their wounds together. From that moment on, the sorrow that loomed in their hearts drifted away, and they asked the spirits of the earth to marry them then and there."

"After their marriage they both worked for the landlord who told them they had to weave ten items of cloth each night, and they agreed."

"One night Dong Yong was weaving cloth but was sure he couldn't finish in time. But his wife was calm and assured him everything would be fine and ordered him to go to sleep. Dong Yong did not know that his lovely wife was not at all a poor maiden but the Seventh Daughter of The Jade Emperor of the heavens. Deep at night when her husband was asleep, she weaved ten pieces of beautiful cloth with her fairy magic."

"Dong Yong was speechless when he awoke to find ten perfect pieces of fabric! It was then that Dong Yong learned that his beautiful wife was actually a fairy, and that they were going to have a baby. He could not possibly have been any happier."

Tao pauses for effect and then tells the ending. "But all good things must come to an end. When the fairy's father, The Jade Emperor, found out about his daughter's secret husband and her life on earth, he sent messengers to warn her that if she did not come back home to heaven that same afternoon, he would smash Dong Yong into a million pieces."

"The Seventh Fairy had no choice but to tell her husband farewell but assured him that the next year she would come back to the exact same spot and give him his newborn son. So, as the legend goes, Dong Yong keeps returning to this spot, hoping to see his wife and son."

Elise waits, but Tao is done. "No, it can't end like that," cried Elise.

"Sorry Elise, but there is no happy ending in most of the legends."

Elise leans back feeling cheated.

"The legend of Dong Yong has been spreading for over two thousand years and its extremely popular in the rural areas of China. There are things named after Dong Yong, for instance, there is Dongjia Village and elsewhere there is a stele emblazoned with "Dong Yong's Native Place". There is also "Consensual marriage cloth" in Xiaohuai Village in Wanrong County, Shanxi Province. There are even ceremonies that worship such dutiful sons during temple fairs in places like Wuzhi County, Henan Province."

Wanting to change the subject, Elise asks, "Tao, what is the population here."

"Oh, I think it is around 4 million people in an area of 8910 square kilometers," then remembering, says, 3440 square miles.

"Thanks Tao."

"You know, this is a popular city to visit since it is only 20 miles from Wuhan Tianhe International Airport and 37 miles from downtown Wuhan, only an hour's drive."

That day they tour Xiaogan starting at Shuangfeng Mountain at Dabie Mountain's southern slope. The weather is perfect, and the mountains are thickly covered with plant life. Elise records that there is a vast sea of clouds, but the mountain peaks can be viewed above them. Tao takes them to the Baiyun Ancient Village and Qinglong Cave. Elise really enjoys Qinglong cave that has three big cave chambers and four smaller ones. They only have the time and energy to enter two of the largest chambers before moving on.

Setting a different pace, Tao introduces them to the water resources. He explains that minerals are abundant both on the earth surface and underground in Xiaogan area. "Salt, phosphorus and paste are called the Three Treasures of Xiaogan so Xiaogan has long been called Capital of Paste, Sea of Salt, and Mountain of Phosphorus."

When it is time to eat, Tao asks if he can order for them. They both agree. He orders the Four Seasons Soup Bag. Elise peers at Bai, but he only smiles and when the waitress leaves, Tao says. "The soup bag has a thin skin, soup, stuffing, and I think you will like it. I ordered a variety. Shrimp, mushroom, crab yellow soup bag and chicken broth soup bag."

While they wait for their meal, Tao explains that paper cutting is one of the major arts of the region. Elise listens, thinking origami, but Tao surprises her as he shares the legend of paper with them. "The legend states that the Women of Xiaogan city, had the custom of singing Qing Qi songs on the fifteenth day of the first lunar month. At that time, they seek advice from the Seventh Fairy to teach them how to see festive lanterns and how to cut peonies with an ingenious heart. They ask the fairy how to embroider phoenix with deft hands and for this advice they promise to slaughter white pigs and sheep to receive them every year. This reveals the women's desire to seek inspiration."

"So, the legend continues with it becoming the fashion to present the paper-cuttings of Chinese verses to friends and relatives. The people seeking the paper-cuttings would cite a line and the creative paper-cutting artists would cut them with scissors on forms of paper."

"I love that legend, Tao."

Their food arrived and Elise starts to pick up one of the soup bags. "Oh, stop, Elise, there is a proper way to eat these."

Not quite understanding, Elise pauses. "Experienced diners can eat by gently biting the skin of the soup bag, slowly absorbing the soup inside, and then eating the dough and meat stuffing of the soup bag. Only in this way can you genuinely appreciate the unique taste of Xiaolong Tangbao."

Elise tries it and is glad he stopped her from squirting soup all over her companions. After they finish, Tao takes them to the Tangchi Hot Spring. Elise is enthralled by the beautiful surroundings dotted by countless luxurious green trees. They walk by what Tao explains are some of the 88 kinds of bathhouses and pools. As they continue along the path, he explains there are six zones of springs: Japanese-style, dynamical, celebrities, cultural, lovers and Japanese-style wooden houses. Then he asks, "Did you bring your suits?"

"Yes, we did." Thank goodness we had packed all our belongings since we had to check out of the hotel. We go back to the rental car and get our suits and soon we are heading back to the springs.

"Okay, your choice, Which one shall we try?"

In the same breath Elise and Bai say, "Dynamical hot springs." They look at each other and laugh.

They spend the next 20 minutes recommended in the hot springs and then, resignedly get out and dress, the feeling of total relaxation lingering as they get ready to stop for the day.

Chapter 14

As pre-arranged, Tao drives them to Huanggang which takes a little under two hours. All three stay in separate hotel rooms. The hotel is at the foot of Guifeng Mountain proving an irresistible view. Early the next morning they meet for breakfast and then begin their tour from the hotel to the wooden house on the top of the mountain. To get there, the hotel is the starting point. They take the elevator to the sixth floor to walk down a long wooden corridor. As they come to the end of the corridor, they see the wooden house in front of them.

The house sits in a green forest with insects and birds everywhere as they walk along the path further to visit the hot spring pool next to the wooden house.

A breeze blows away the water vapor as they stand in admiration. Next, they visit Yi'ai Lake in the city of Huanggang. Then it is on to visit Yiaihu Park and check out Dongpo Chibi Ancient City. The three pause to picnic at Guifeng Mountain before going to see HuangGang AoKang Shange Ye Bu Xing Jie. They end the day at Chen Tanqiu Memorial before going back to the hotel. In the lobby, Tao announces, "Well, my friends, this is where we part ways."

Being together has been so interesting that Elise has forgotten that Tao would not continue with them. She steps forward and hugs him. "Thank you for a wonderful tour Tao. I can tell you put a lot into making it to my liking and I appreciate it."

When she steps back, Elise sees a slight blush covering Tao's face, but it quickly disappears.

Bai moves forward and hugs Tao, telling him to have a safe trip back to Shiyan and thanks him for his help in showing them the areas. Elise moves aside to give them a little privacy as they talk a bit longer before parting and going to their rooms to gather their things.

Elise and Bai go to the train station. They are now on their way back to Wuhan where they will start their tour of Ezhou. Ezhou is less than two hours from Wuhan so Bai is familiar with the area. At the train station they pick up Bai's SUV and head for the hotel.

Chapter 15

Wednesday, November 18; two days before she will be returning home to Rochester. It does not seem possible she has been here so long. When they arrive at the hotel. Bai asks if she would like to have dinner before turning in. "No, I think I need a good night's sleep."

Bai has a worried expression on his face. "Are you feeling all right, Elise."

"Oh, yes, it is just exhaustion. That and the fact I haven't called my mother in a few days has me feeling down. I wanted to call her each day, but my schedule and probably hers too would not allow it. Besides, I am not used to putting so much into a day and my body is rebellion. I will be fine."

"Well, that is normal when you consider how much we have traveled and toured every day during your stay."

Elise looks at him thoughtfully, "Yes, but it is not like me. I feel fatigued lately after sleeping all night, like I am coming down with a cold. This morning I had a headache. I never get headaches."

Bai is concerned and asks if she wants to cancel the tour of Ezhou.

Quickly Elise replies, "No, oh no. I have been looking forward to this tour. My great grandmother told me many times how she loved going to Ezhou. I will be fine." And she really thought she would be. He kisses her goodnight and she does not linger but goes straight up to her room.

Though the other hotels were nice, they could not compare to the beauty and comfort at Wuhan's Wanda Reign Hotel. Elise waste no time going into the bathroom and turning on the water in the big soaker tub. Sitting on the edge of the tub, she swishes the water a few times to help the bubbles form and then starts taking off her clothes, telling herself this is what she needs to get back to her old peppy self.

While waiting for the tub to fill, she goes over to the sink. The heat from the tub fogs the mirror so Elise takes a washcloth and wipes it clear so she can see her reflection. It is not good. The face that stares back shows exactly how she feels. Her skin has an ashen coloring and as she pushes on her cheeks, she could swear her face is swollen. And those eyes…they are not her eyes at all, with those droopy eyelids and screaming tiredness. "You look awful," she says to the mirror. Trying not to get herself worked up over nothing, she washes her face and puts on her night creams, adding an extra dab of eye cream. That done, she climbs into the tub.

The water is quite warm, but that is the way she wants it as she slowly lowers her body beneath the layers of bubbles. When she sits on the bottom of the tub, she leans her head back and feels her body relaxing. She closes her eyes and gives in to the peaceful sensation.

Elise breathes in the wonderful lavender scent of the bath oil and finds herself drifting into sleep. It is the chill of the water that finally wakes her, and she climbs out, her skin showing the effects of being in the water for a long time.

When she checks her cell, she sees she has been in the tub for almost two hours. She dries herself off and pads across the floor, turning off the lights as she makes her way to the bed. No sooner does her head make contact with the pillow, she falls into a deep sleep.

On Thursday morning, the 19th of November Elise feels much better as she gets dress and goes down to meet up with Bai. She is excited to be going to Ezhou. She has enjoyed the other town tours, but Ezhou is kind of special to her and she cannot wait to see it in person.

Her excitement must show on her face as Bai greets saying, "You look refreshed."

"Thanks. I feel refreshed."

"So, my plan is to head right out and we will have something to eat in Ezhou. How does that sound."

"Perfect."

They start out driving in a comfortable silence, but it has nothing to do with their personal experience and more due to Bai trying to determine what to say about where they are headed.

"So, Elise, Lotus Mountain is just the English name. The mountain is called Lianhua. We will be just across the river from Huanggang when we get there. The first thing we will see is the nine dragon statues at the entrance. The rest you will see for yourself because we are here."

In a little over an hour, we are pulling into a parking space and ready to take in the sites of Ezhou. Elise climbs out of the SUV and looks around. "It is so peaceful here," she says.

"That it is." Bai pauses and adds, "Okay, if you are ready, Let's get started."

Their first stop is to see the Yuanming Pagoda. famed for being the first pagoda in the south of the Yangtze River area. Bai finds a brochure and hands it to Elise. She starts reading aloud. "The Yuanming Pagoda measures 262 feet in height. This white pagoda exhibits golden upturned eaves."

Elise pauses looking up at the structure as nostalgic memories of a grainy, tattered, silvery, photo fills her mind... She takes her hand and wipes it across her eyes and Bai hears a choking sound coming from her throat. "What is it Elise," Bai says reaching out and holding both her shoulders. "Bai, my grandmother had a picture of this in her box of treasures from her childhood. It still looks the same."

Bai sees that Elise is tearing, so he gives her a moment to collect herself. A second glance and he sees she is smiling so he says, "Onward we go."

"So, here we are at Lianhua Forest of Steles. This is the largest cultural forest of steles in the world."

"Bai, what are Steles?"

"Oh, sorry, Steles are stone or wooden slabs, generally taller than they are wide. They were erected in the ancient world as monuments."

They next visit Liuhe Garden that lies in the north slope of Lotus Mountain. They pause at the entrance to take in the Jiulong Altar that can be seen at the entrance. Bai clarifies that "Jiulong" means nine dragons and so Elise sees that the Altar is composed of nine dragons coiling with each other, among which the biggest two lift a lotus ball.

As a little girl when she had seen this picture of the alter and her grandmother must have explained it to her, but all she can remember is something about nine sons so she asks Bai about it.

"Yes, there's the story of the nine dragons being the Chinese mythological sons of the Dragon King. There are many variations in the different descriptions of the nine sons, including in basic facts like their names, but all versions state that there are nine." He pauses and goes over to the side of the wall and pulls out a pamphlet. He studies it, then turns. "This is great, Elise. It explains everything. Just wish they had two of these," he adds.

Elise takes the pamphlet and reads it out loud.

"According to traditional Chinese culture, the dragon has nine sons. Unfortunately, the nine sons of the dragon do not look like the dragon. Instead, they have their own unique appearances. Some are beautiful, some cute, and others are ugly. Their names are: Bixi, Chiwen/Chiwei, Pulao, Bi'an, Taotie, Yazi, Suanni and Jiaotu." Elise pauses, looking up to make sure she is pronouncing the names correctly and Bai nods.

She continues. "Bixi looks like a turtle, fond of carrying heavy loads. He carries a stele all year round. His image can be found in temples and ancestral halls. Chiwen/Chiwei looks like a lizard without a tail. He likes gazing around in precarious areas. He swallows fire and sprays waves to cause rainfalls. His image is found on corners and ridges of a hall and on roofs. Pulao looks like a small dragon and likes to roar. It is said that Pulao lives by the sea and fears whales. Whenever he is attacked by a whale, he keeps roaring. Thus, people put his image on bells and make the wooden striker in the shape of a whale, so they get the loudest possible bell sound. Bi'an looks like a tiger and is powerful. It is said he is interested in prisons and judicial cases. Therefore, people engrave his image on the doors of prisons. The tiger is a brave and fierce animal and the image of Bi'an, is used to enhance the majesty of prisons and to intimidate criminals."

Elise pauses and again looks up at the altar before reading on. "Taotie looks like a wolf and loves to eat. He is seen as greedy, so this imaginary evil beast represents people who indulge in eating and those avaricious of wealth. These people are referred to as "people of taotie". The head of Taotie is often engraved on ritual vessels like bells and tripods as a decorative motif. Baxia looks like a fish but is not a fish and loves water. He is often engraved on top of stone bridge railings. He is the guardian of the ancient bridges. Yazi looks like a jackal, and stares at things with angry eyes. He is fond of bloody killings. His image is often engraved on knife handles and sword sheaths. Suanni was originally the alias of the lion, so he looks like a lion. He likes smoke and fire and often reposes. The lion was introduced into China with Buddhism. Sakyamuni was nicknamed "Fearless Lion", so his image can be found on Buddha altars and incense burners. Jiaotu is like a mussel or a snail with a tightly closed shell. His image is often engraved on doors. Putting Jiaotu's image on doors may serve as a wish for closing the door as tightly as possible for safety."

When she finishes, she looks one more time at the altar and then at Bai. She takes several pictures of the altar and then of the pamphlet before casually handing it to Bai. "Now we both have one."

"How sweet. Thanks Elise, now I know more about the altar. Until now I told tourist only that the altar is carved with dragons because the dragon represents the Chinese totem, symbolizing Chinese spirit."

Bai moves them about so that they can take it all in, especially the population of deer, monkeys, tortoises, golden carp, and beavers.

Bai can see that Elise is tiring though she does not admit it. "Let's stop and go home Elise. We can save something to see for tomorrow.

Relief floods her face as she nods her head. Soon they head back to the hotel where they have a bite to eat and then part ways. Bai informs her they can start later in the morning if she would like to sleep in, but Elise says no.

Bai leaves, wishing he could be with her, but knowing she needs her rest.

On Friday when Bai returns to the hotel, Elise is already in the café having a cup of tea and a slice of toast. He sneaks a look at her and sees she is looking more like herself and as he joins her, he gives her the rundown of what he has planned.

They drive back to Ezhou and this time they begin with the Ezhou Museum, where they are handed a tour book and site to mark of the items they plan to see. After an hour, they leave the museum and head for the bank of the Yangtze River. They stand at the Ehuang Bridge that connects Ezhou to Huanggang. Bai informs Elise that the bridge construction was started in 1999 and it was completed in 2002. He adds that it is 3,245 m (10,646 ft) long and has a main span of 480 m (1,570 ft). This places it among the longest cable-stayed bridges in the world.

Then it is on to the Xiao river to see the Xiao Dong Men of Ezhou City. That needed explaining so Bai filled Elise in. "Back in 617, several military officers at Baling commandership wanted to rise against Sui rule and wanted to support Dong Jingzhen as leader, but Dong pointed out that he was of a humble lineage and would not be respected by others. He suggested that they choose Xiao Xian who was of imperial heritage and would receive the peoples' support. They therefore sent messengers to Luochuan to report this to Xiao, who then gathered several thousand men. So, in winter 617, Xiao built a tall altar and burned a wooden fire. He declared himself the Prince of Liang and changed the name to show independence from Sui China Society. So that is what you see before you and that is where the name came from."

Just outside of Xiao Dong Men of Ezhou City they go to visit a huge rock that sits in the great river. The rock they say looks like a golden dragon and is named Longpan Rock and considered to embody prosperity of the country.

Elise tilts her head, scrutinizing the rock from different angles, but cannot see it resembling a dragon. Wanting so much to see it as a dragon, she walks from side to side and takes steps forward and backward before giving up. She says nothing, just smiles at Bai as if she does.

It is close to dinner time when they reach the shore of Liangzi Lake. Nestled tranquilly it resembles a blue stone inlaid upon the surrounding land. Bai tells her that Liangzi Lake is famous for the unpolluted water and its beautiful landscape, and at that moment a gentle wind blowing in from the mountains not far away ripples this azure lake in the sunlight as Elise takes in the many islets featured around the lake. The water is crystal clear, and Bai informs her that this lake has a large breeding population of Wuchang Fish, which are legendary. "We will be having them for dinner this evening, Elise."

She could stay here forever; Elise thinks as Bai leads her away. He says, "Due to its pleasant environment, this islet is also called Changshou (Longevity) Islet and there is much we need to see before we eat."

"Wait Bai, I read somewhere that Hubei Province is known as the province of a thousand lakes."

"Yes, that is right."

"I know we cannot see them all, but do you have any literature you can give me."

"Yes, I do. Just remind me, okay?"

Elise nods and they continue on their way. He takes Elise to see Kuixing Tower, Liangzi Gate, Siguan Hall, Xianren (Immortal) Cave and a professional Golf Club. "I have a surprise for you, Elise."

"What is it."

"That.," he points at the end of the pier where there is a yacht anchored. They climb on board and the captain says, "Good evening Mr. Zhao", with just a hint of an accent.

"Good evening Senkaku. Me and my friend, Miss McKenna want to tour the inlet and get good views of the area."

Elise starts to say something, having an odd feeling that this is not normal. The feeling puzzles her, but she lets it go when they are out on the lake taking in all its splendor. This time it is the captain who describes the area and Elise finds his voice very soothing. "Liangzi Lake is a winding lake here in the southeast Hubei province. If you look out there you will see the middle reaches of Yangtze River." As they slowly tour around the area, he stops at Kuixing Tower.

"This, Miss is Kuixing Tower, a historic tower built in 1377. As you can see, the tower stands on a hill overlooking the city and is named for the god, Kuixing who is said to live in the constellation of Ursa Major and who governs literature and writing.

They continue the tour until they arrive back at the edge of the islet where Bai and Elise are let off.

"Thank you, Mr. Senkaku. That was wonderful."

He bows and says, "You are welcome. Mr. Zhao, sir, shall I take her home?"

"Yes. Thank you."

Elise has been only half listening as she strolls on the islet, taking in the beauty around her. She does not hear Bai until he is right beside her, saying "…and this is where your dinner comes in."

"What?"

"The crystal-clear water also has a large breeding population of Wuchang Fish, which are renowned, and we will be having this fresh fish for dinner."

By the time they sit down for dinner on Liangzi Lake Resort Hotel, it is among lots of late diners.

"Elise, which do you prefer, steamed Wuchang fish or spicy fried Wuchang fish."

Elise peeks up at him, "Do not know. Tell me which is best."

"Well, the meat is delicate and has plenty of fat." He pauses. "I like it steamed. It brings out the best flavor."

"Steamed it is."

When the waiter comes to the table, Bai introduces himself and Elise thought to herself, one more Chinese custom, since she has heard him do this before. Even the fact that their food arrives at the table quickly is more pleasing then questionable as she tastes the best fish, she believes she has ever eaten before. The freshwater fish has been steamed together with mushrooms, bamboo shoots and chicken soup. Elise is sure she made the right choice of having it steamed.

After dinner Elise and Bai do some shopping before driving back to Wuhan and that is when it hits her—they have spent their last day together.

The thought smacks her in the face. Tonight, Friday the 20th of November 2019 is going to be their last night together. By morning she will be on her way back to Rochester, New York, and all of this will have been the realization of a dream come true with little unexpected pleasures.

She knows that she has fallen hard for Bai and the fact that they have resisted being together after that first night, only makes her want him more.

She should not have allowed it to happen in the first place. He lives in China and she in New York…what was she thinking. That is, it, she meditates, she was not thinking.

It is not like she is alone with her feelings. Bai has approached the subject many times during the final days they have spent together. But at least she has managed to not repeat that night again and it has been extremely hard. She has never felt so close to any man before Bai.

Elise tries reasoning with herself. Maybe it is the romance of the trip that has her feeling so enchanted with him. She ponders the idea for only a minute. The only way she has managed to be strong is to face the fact they live in two different worlds and they have a physical attraction is all. Once she is gone, her feelings will be gone too.

At least she has done the right thing by keeping her distance. China's attitudes towards sex remain, by Western standards, prudish. Advertising with a sexual commendation is tame compared to that in the U.S. There is strict censorship guidelines, promulgated by the state, and supported by the public at large. But the laws have bent a little, as true, premarital sex is acceptable, but not just sleeping around. Elise tells herself that what they are experiencing is animal lust.

It is no use. Her mind is riddled with cogitating how this could work because deep down she believes that her feelings have grown beyond just liking Bai, and she does not want to think of him not being in her life. But long-distance relationships are the most difficult. She is never met anyone who said, "It is great, you should try it."

It is actually a common occurrence in her profession so she does not lack knowledge of the situation and those who have confined in her have said that a long-distance relationship ends with that agonizing feeling of loneliness even though there are many options of visual communication. It is just not the same.

Elise works herself into a frenzy and pays the price. Her head aches and she has a coughing fit before finally accepting the inevitable. The whole matter is out of her hands.

"We are here." Elise does not hear Bai the first time.

"Elise, we are home." That brings her down to earth as she thinks, 'I wish'.

She manages a smile as she undoes her seat belt. Bai is already out of the SUV and walking around to open her door, stopping Jeffries in his tracks.

"What do you say about taking a walk to downtown Wuhan. Sort of like saying goodbye."

A smile plants itself on Bai's face. "Yes, lets." Bai looks at Jeffries who nods at him before taking his keys.

They stroll together, side by side, passing the Huanan Seafood Market and Elise pauses to ask, "Bai, why do they call them wet markets?"

"Well, I believe it is to differentiate them from markets selling dry packaged goods like noodles." He reflects for a moment. "But it could also be because the stallholders' tend to hose down their produce to keep it cool or the ice to keep the seafood fresh."

Elise nods with an accepting expression and they continue down the sidewalk that they share with a crowd of other people. As if reading her mind Bai says that people are always seen walking down the streets. It is like a pastime shared to not only make purchases, but to chat with friends and neighbors.

They make their way to the Han Café and decide to have dinner there. As usual when Bai asks if she would like him to order for her, she says, "Yes." He seems to know what pleases her and she is glad because she has not a clue. Even when she reads the menu which usually has the English words as well, she does not know.

She finds it relaxing to sit here with Bai and listen to him talk about the area and coincidences he has had seeing people he would never expect to see in the area. He shares funny stories with her and when they have finished their meal, Bai has a serious look on his face.

"Elise, I know you must be tired, but can I come back. We can sit in your room where it is quiet and have a toast to your safe trip back."

What can she say but, "Yes, of course, I'd like that." They stop at Om Asian Market and liquor store where he buys a bottle of wine, plus chocolate. "What is the chocolate for?"

Bai smiles, "It is one of my downfalls. I love their chocolate. He holds the bar out so she can see it is locally made." Elise remembers an article her mother shared with her "The Early Stages of Falling in Love," in Psychology Today that said when people are attracted to each other, their bodies release adrenaline and phenylethylamine, which is a key chemical in chocolate. She suppresses a laugh.

They finally arrive at the hotel and Bai gives her a kiss on the cheek that sends shivers through her body. "Listen Elise, I will be back later. Elise is puzzled at first, but it dawns on her it is best they do not go up together. Quietly she says. "See you later."

Up in her room, Elise spends a moment at the window to take in the view, to help inspire her creative juices then scooches to the center of the bed, reaches over for her laptop and while it starts up, adjusts the pillows and leans against the headboard. She takes a deep breath and by the time the laptop is ready, she is ready to begin.

Her mind paints a picture of the places they have been along with minute details experienced along the way. Soon she is reliving her experiences, letting the words flow from her fingers, putting in character and expression until she feels she has captured it all. When she stops, she is happy with what she has written. Later she will trim it for the travel guide version.

Elise closes the laptop and is mentally exhausted. Her head is pounding, and her heart is racing so she takes some deep breaths and tries to relax.

It works. She climbs off the bed and goes into the bathroom to enjoy her last luxurious soak in this amazing tub. When she forces herself to get out, she dries herself off and spritzes her body with a lavender spray she found on the counter in her bathroom. Padding across the floor, she goes into the bedroom area and in the top drawer of the dresser, rummages until she finds the nicest nightie she owns. She slips into it as she walks back into the bathroom. Not wanting to be seductive, she puts on the big fluffy robe supplied by the hotel and tightens it around her waist. Then she brushes her hair till it gleams and falls back into its natural curly state.

She feels like a new person, as she closes the drapes and turns off all but one light near the sofa, ignoring what her heart is leading her to do. She makes a final trip into the kitchenette to get two wine glasses, and the bottle of wine that Bai bought earlier for just this occasion. When he knocks on the door, she is ready.

The minute the door closes behind him, Bai takes Elise's hand and pulls her close for a deep longing kiss. She does not try to fool herself any longer as she feels a jittery sensation in her belly. When he releases her, she wipes her sweaty palms against the sides of her robe waiting for the flutter of electricity to stop coursing through her body. When she chances a look at Bai, she can tell he feels this way, too.

There is no way this evening is going to be about a glass of wine and two friends parting.

Trying to keep focused she is unaware of the activity behind her as Bai removes his jacket, shirt, tie, and undershirt tossing them into a pile around his ankles. He loosens his belt and pushes his jeans down his toned muscular legs, then carefully balances as he slips his feet out of his loafers and at the same time steps out of his jeans.

Elise leans over the table and starts to pick up the bottle of wine, when she feels Bai's arms wrap around her waist. Gently he turns her around to face him. His head is cocked to the left and a serious smile plays on his lips. Elise senses, more than feels his hands releasing her waist and begin to untie the robe which dramatically slides off her shoulders. He then gathers the material of her night gown and slowly starts lifting it up over her head, with Elise raising her arms to help him. Theatrically he tosses it, and the gown catches on a bed post.

Elise turns to face him and cannot control her breathing or her desire to get close to his tanned taunt body with every muscle under his skin dancing with each movement he makes. At that moment, her head empties of all feelings and thoughts except those associated with this beautiful man in front of her. Her body aches, but not with pain.

Bai pulls her into his arms then slowly, carefully he lifts her up and carries her to the bed.

Something deep, mysterious, and wonderful happens when he lays her gently on the bed and leans over to plant the most passionate kiss on her lips. It sets off fireworks and a pleasant loss of balance overtakes her as she tries to move over top of him. Gently he pushes her back against the pillow.

Bai starts slowly and takes direction from her body. He speeds up and she shifts her hips to force him deeper inside her. Bai stares down at Elise and sees a tear well up at the corner of her eye.

He understands and begins their journey, slowing until she grabs his shoulders to pull him close again. It is like their own little dance and when the climax comes, it takes their breath away.

It does not end there. Several minutes pass and they are again as one, fulfilling a deep need to be as close as they can get.

Finally, sated, Bai collapses on his back, breathing heavily. Elise lays, her legs splayed out, staring up at the ceiling, trying to control her breathing.

Several seconds pass and Bai props himself up on one elbow, stroking her abdomen as they remain silent for a while longer. Bai stares so deeply into her eyes it is like he is trying to create a mental picture he can review later.

Even her jaws are exhausted as she tries to smile, the corners of her mouth refusing to obey. Bai lowers his head and kisses her deeply.

That is how they spent their last night. Elise burns the moment in her brain of how his body felt inside hers and how deep her emotions are for this man. She remembers it all up until his last kiss and then, nothing. She cannot remember anything more.

Chapter 16

Most missing people return quickly, but around one percent do not. Sonya had heard this so many times. But she was the mother of this missing person and needed to find her. She has considered that Elise was not really missing, just extending her time in Wuhan. That, she pauses contemplating, is most likely the case. Elise is a grown woman living on her own and has overseen her life for some time.

Again, Sonya halts briefly. Only, why not call. Why not tell her mother what she is doing. She must realize not knowing is traumatizing her. Before she can grasp what she is doing, Sonya's cell is in her hand.

"9-1-1, what is your emergency."

Sonya coughed to clear her throat then calmly said, "My daughter is missing in Wuhan, China."

For a minute, the line is silent, and Sonya is worried they hung up. "This is not a joke. This is for real."

The 9-1-1 responder cleared his throat and asked the proper questions about her, the caller. Then he asked for a description of Elise. He asked her name, date of birth, height, weight, hair color, eye color, skin color. Sonya responded calmly. On the last question, she had to think how to reply and finally added. "She is of mixed race. I am white…. ah….part Chinese and her father is black." Sonya said, "Wait. I guess her skin color is a tan color." Again, feeling like an idiot she manages to say, "Does that sound right?"

"Yes, madam, that sounds like a good description. The police are on their way. If you have a recent picture, they will want to see it."

The police come. All the time notes are being taken though she has the feeling they thought she was jumping the gun. After all, Elise was on assignment in Wuhan, China and most likely not just roaming around on her own. From what her mother had shared about her daughter's heritage, she probably had decided to remain longer. Officer Wendell, though, prided himself in knowing mothers and this one was not the type to whistle blow unless she had good reason to. He took her case seriously and told her.

"Ms. McKenna, do not worry, we will take it from here."

"So, what can I do."

"You can take it easy. Stop worrying yourself sick. That is my job now," he gave her a smile of reassurance and Sonya believed him.

As Sonya stared out the pane glass window of her home that sat up on the hilly part of her street so she could look down and view more than just the area around her, this view that used to make her feel good, now just made her feel alone. Her daughter was missing and her husband, Matthew, was on a major book tour. She had toyed with the idea of telling him Elise was missing, but hesitated. What if Elise was just staying longer. What if she lost her phone and was having a hard time getting another. But all the what ifs were fading so Sonya made the call.

"Matthew, I do not want you to worry, but Elise is missing."

"What do you mean, missing. Where is she?"

"She was on assignment in China, you know, doing a travel guide, but when she was due back to the states, she did not return."

There is a long silence on the other end of the phone before Matthew asks, "How long. I mean, when was she due back?"

Sonya knew her husband and there was something he was hesitant to tell her. She could hear it in his voice. "What is wrong Matthew? Have you heard from Elise?"

There is another pause.

On the other end of the connection Matthew was remembering, remembering something he had overheard on the plane going from Rochester to Washington. Someone was whispering about an Officials' meeting being called between 20 private companies. Being a writer, he was a listener and knew when people speak in a whisper he should listen closely because something important may be going down. So, he eavesdropped and learned that some private companies were summoned to an emergency meeting. They were to meet in Seoul, Korea. These individuals being sent were experts in the medical field. At the time he had thought there might be something secretive going on, but the rest of the talk did not raise any alarms, so he forgot about it. Even now he could not fathom why he was remembering this.

Suddenly frown lines appear on Matthews forehead. In that conversation he now recollected two words that now flashed across his brain…Wuhan! Coronavirus!

Cautiously, Matthew asks, "Sonya, was Elise in Wuhan, China when she went missing?"

"Yes. I told you that."

"I know," he said distractedly, "I also know that she could have been on her way back." Matthew vacillated before continuing. "Listen, dear. I think there is transportation problems going on. Please, do not worry and I will see what I can find out."

"What kind of transportation problems…Matthew, do not hold out on me."

"I am not. I just have to check some sources."

Sonya relaxed. "Thank you darling. Please let me know as soon as you learn something… anything. It is hard for me and for the authorities to do much when we are talking about a missing person in China."

"Now Sonya, we do not know that she is missing. But yes, I will, and you should remember that, when you talk to the police and cut them some slack."

"Honey, you know me," Sonya replied. Yes, he knew her and patience when it came to Elise was not a virtue. He also could tell she was panicking.

"I love you Sonya bear."

"I love you back."

The call ended and Matthew let out his breath, unaware he was holding it in until that moment. Matthew leaned back and allowed his apprehensive opinions to surface. He was about to do what he did best. Research.

Chapter 17

The worse part of Sonya's day became the time when she was alone at home. The one haven that had always bought her calm and peace, was now flashing visions of her daughter that she could not erase. At home, Sonya cannot help but worry. She worries about the police taking her seriously and really following up and she stresses about what more she should be doing. No call? That was reason alone to panic!

Life had been so simple for her and her family in Rochester. They as a family had a wonderful life. They had more than enough money to meet their needs and had given Elise what she needed both mentally and physically throughout her childhood. They enjoyed lots of recreational pleasures: good food, good wine, skiing, scuba diving, lounging by the pool and vacations, which to Sonya, helped Elise relate to other cultures and countries. Elise had grown into a good person, someone who is courageous, honest, trustworthy, kind and she had learned her lessons well. She was self-supportive and well-liked by her peers so for all accounts, she had nothing to worry about. But she did.

She even worried about Matthew. When he hit the New York Times, USA Today, and Wall Street Journal best sellers list once, they were ecstatic. When he appeared on the lists again, they were euphoric, but by the third time, they knew he had his feet cemented in his career and from that moment on, his time was not his own. Of course, he loved it and she was glad for him, watching as he adjusted to the pressure to do all kinds of things that have nothing to do with writing, just to keep his name out there.

She did understand wanting to be a success because she had wanted it too. As for her profession, Sonya recalls what William Osler said, 'Medicine is a science of uncertainty and an art of probability'. There is no such thing as a typical day. Her bread and butter is seeing patients, and each appointment is essentially a meeting with a client. She checks the details of the case, tries to get a sense of what is going on, and then figure out the medicines–often trying to do this within a half hour. When someone comes in with a complaint, you think of a bunch of things it could be and then ask questions to try and narrow it down and separate it from similar problems. Then you choose your tests and hope that you can pin down the source of the problem to something. Next you figure out if the problem is fixable.

There is nothing typical about her day which generally begins performing rounds at the hospital. After two or three hours of rounds, she goes to her private office to begin patient appointments and then there are forms to sign, prescriptions to write and other necessary paperwork to put into the system. Most of the times, she ends her day around 6:30 or 7:00 p.m., but like everything else, it varies.

To Sonya, she sees their choices of careers, though different, being the same in that it takes up a lot of time and they enjoy what they are doing. It has never caused a problem in their marriage because their marriage has always been based on love and wanting the best for each other.

She loved her home and her neighbors, but most of all she loved her daughter. Sonya lets out a big sigh and looks at the clock. "Oh my god. I need to get ready for work."

That day at the hospital she could not help worrying about Elise. Her mind kept going to the dark places and she would see her daughter lying dead in one of those dark dank caves she kept raving about during her calls.

It was hard not knowing but she had to calm down. She could not do her job in a panic state. Besides, she would feel so silly if it were nothing more than her daughter wanting to spend more time in Wuhan. It had always been her dream to go there and she probably decided that once her work was done, she would do a little exploring on her own. Yes, Sonya decided, that was likely what Elise was doing, taking a mini vacation.

But deep down she knew, something was terribly wrong, and it was terrifying her. She was distraught and angry with Elise for not thinking what not hearing from her would do to those who loved her.

Sonya was a mother at home and a doctor at work, but sometimes the lines faded. Her profession was built on saving lives and to do that she had to look at the whole picture and find what was at the base of the problem or illness. Each patient saw her as a healer who minimized their pain, helped them recover from a disease faster or taught them how to live with a disabling injury. She saw it as her job to help her patients enjoy life, even if they could not be cured.

As a mother she wore many hats teaching Elise how to manage her finances to buying groceries and making sure the bills were paid on time. But she was the one that Elise came to when she needed her skinned knees kissed. She was there taking her temperature and giving her a bowl of chicken soup when she was ill. Yes, her "doctoring" skills, make a huge difference in the life of her child and to other families and that made it challenging to keep them separate.

As Sonya gets ready for work, she tells herself that Elise is a grown woman, capable of taking care of herself. By the time she gets in her car she has come up with several logical reasons that Elise has not called her, and they all seem valid. When she enters the hospital, her mind comfortably switches gears. She is on duty in emergency today. Working in emergency requires astute assessment skills, flexibility, and the ability to function in a high stress department. She must have her head into it, and she does. Sonya successfully sets the matter of her daughter aside as she meets her first patient of the day.

"Good morning, Sir, my name is Dr. McKenna."

"Hi Doc. I am Thomas Pritcherd." While he talks, Sonya is digesting the information in the file.

"What brings you here today, Mr. Pritcherd."

He starts at the beginning. "Several years ago, when I was riding my bike, I felt a sharp pain in my chest."

Sonya checks his chart and sees he is in his early forties. She observes him. He seems trim and fit.

"Well, anyway, I have felt a discomfort in my chest for several days, but this time it was more severe: it hurt each time I took a breath. So, I took it slowly and got myself back home. I sat and waited for the pain to pass. But when it did,

I realized it had taken a long time, so I decided to come into emergency.

Sonya listened intently as Mr. Pritcherd describes his symptoms. She observes him diligently working to identify the cause of his symptoms. He is not sweating so she assumes he is not having cardiac distress.

"So where are you feeling this pain?"

"In the center of my chest, first and then it spreads into my arms, neck, and back."

She checks the chart and sees he has never smoked or been overweight. He has no family history of heart attack, stroke, or diabetes.

"Have you experienced any stress at work or home?"

"No more than usual. I'm married and have two children." he says grinning. "I love my family and I love my job."

Sonya checks his blood pressure, which is normal, and his pulse, checks out to be sixty and regular. She listens to his lungs and heart but detected no abnormalities. She next presses on the spot between his ribs and breastbone, and there is no reaction of pain. Further checking found that there was no swelling or tenderness in his calves or thighs.

She writes her findings down and wanting to be thorough, she orders an electrocardiogram, a chest X-ray, and blood tests to measure Pritcherd's cardiac enzymes.

"Tell you what Mr. Pritcherd. I think we should keep you overnight. We should have the results of your test by noon, but I want to keep an eye on you. How does that sound?"

"Fine. Thanks Doc."

"You are welcome."

Sonya leaves the cubicle, walking slowly down the hall as she writes the test order. She stops and gives instructions at the nurses' station before going to check on the next patient. At noon she makes a b-line to her office to try Elise's cell. The cell goes to voicemail just as it should when she does not answer. Yes, Sonya says on a positive note. She is probably on the plane now or maybe in the airport bathroom and missed the call. That is what she hopes. The other reason would be her battery was dead but, in her heart, she knows Elise never let her battery die.

Sonya stares out the window of her office forcing her mind away from her daughter. She needs to focus all her attention on her patients now, even if she cannot shake the feeling Elise needs her. She meditates, forgetting all about lunch until finally she feels calm enough to do her job.

Back on the floor she is focused, doing her job of making her patients comfortable. But unlike most days, Sonya does not hang around the hospital beyond the time she is off duty. Instead she goes to her office and hangs up her duster. Sonya gets her purse from under her desk and switches into her outdoor shoes before walking determinedly down the hall to the elevator.

Several people join her there and she makes sure she can get on the first elevator that arrives. She does not smile or speak as she gets into the elevator and makes a strategic move to the left front side so that she can be one of the first ones off.

When the elevator stops at the lobby, Sonya sidles over to stand in front of the doors and quickly steps out. Her heels, along with those of others make a loud hollow sound on the tiled lobby floor as she rushes toward the hospital exit.

The night air is chilly, and she shivers involuntarily, as she makes her way to her car. Once inside, she turns the car on and sits behind the wheel, trying to relax her mind. When she is ready, Sonya pulls out of her parking space and heads toward home. She makes one stop at the grocery store to pick up something for dinner and a few necessities.

Not living far from the hospital, Sonya soon is pulling into her driveway. She climbs out and walks around to the passenger side to gather the bag of groceries before going up the stairs to her front door. She hears the phone ringing while standing on the porch trying to balance the bag of groceries as she tries to put the key in the lock. Her hand is shaking badly. Finally, the lock clicks open and she leans against the door. Her bag of groceries spill out on the floor, but she does not try to retrieve them as she hurries to the landline. She makes it just seconds before the answering service picks up.

Breathlessly she says, "Hello, this is Sonya."

"It is Matthew.

"Oh, hello, honey."

"Hello wife. You sound out of breath. What are you up to?"

"Oh, I was just getting in from work and heard the phone ringing when I was at the door." Sonya places the phone between her ear and shoulder as she moves across the floor, picking up the groceries and walking back and forth to put them on the kitchen island. "Is everything okay."

"Yes, I am fine. I was worried about you is all. How did your day go?"

"Great, except for the fact I cannot reach Elise. Her cell goes straight to voicemail."

"I know. I have tried several times and got the same result."

"Should I worry… tell me I should not worry."

"Do not worry. If you want, I will come home."

At first Sonya starts to say yes, come home, but she knows this is an important tour and he should finish it. Besides, she would be at the hospital most of the time anyway. So, she tells him she will be fine.

And she is, after having a light dinner of salad and a grilled chicken breast with lots of lemon juice on both. After eating she takes a long luxurious bath and puts on her pajamas.

Not sleepy yet, she goes into the family room and turns on the television. The Big Bang is on. It always makes her laugh, so she stays on the channel and during the commercial pours herself a glass of wine. That is the last thing she remembers until the alarm goes off.

Sonya is shocked awake, and it takes a moment to realize she has slept on the couch all night, though she cannot remember laying down at all. She feels re-energized though and ready to face the day. She goes upstairs and gets ready for work then returns to enter the kitchen where she drinks a glass of water and downs a glass of orange juice. As she leaves, she grabs an apple from the basket on the counter and heads out the door.

Driving to the hospital she notices the change in the weather. It was getting colder each day. Soon there would be snow on the ground which meant snow to shovel to get out of her driveway, but by then, Matthew would be back home, and he could shovel for her. Sonya laughs.

When she arrives at the hospital she is in great spirit. She eases into her parking area and checks her face in the rear-view mirror before bundling up and entering the hospital.

She had just sat down at her office desk when Dr. Evans knocked on the frame of her open door.

"Yes, Doctor, can I help you."

"Got some news for you."

"Come in and share."

"Very interesting case, that man you saw yesterday. I understand his test came back and he had an acute myocardial infraction."

"What?"

"Do not get upset. If I had seen this guy, I would not have gone as far as you did in ordering all those tests."

"I should be upset. That error could have cost him his life. Clearly, I missed it."

"Do not beat yourself up over this. It happens."

"Not to me. Mr. Pritcherd had a heart attack, and you want to know why I missed it. It was not because of any egregious behavior, or negligence. I missed it because I allowed my personal life to cross over into my hospital life. My head was elsewhere, doctor and that is not allowed."

"Okay, you are right Sonya. What can I say." There was a silly smile on his face. "Don't you ever let that happen again, young lady." Then, he turned and went out the door, but not before she saw the exaggerated way, he lifted his head and stepped forward, almost snapping his heels together. She had to smile. And that is how her day started and then turned around.

From there it was all downhill.

Chapter 18

At the Renmin Hospital of Wuhan University, Dr. Haung checks his watch. It is already 6:55 a.m., no time for coffee as he makes his way down the hall to find Dr. Wang who is finishing the night rotation and waiting to brief him on the overnight happenings. When they meet up, Dr. Wang starts by saying, "Let us get some coffee in the lounge." Dr. Haung nods and the transfer of information begins with brief details of new patients, including any outstanding issues.

This evening there have been 25 new patients. A high amount, but nothing to be worried about. By the time they sit with coffee in front of them, Dr. Wang shows him morning labs, radiographic studies, and overnight events. The transfer of information takes some time and when they finish, Dr. Haung realizes it is eight o'clock and time for him to head to the floor to see patients. He has a 10:30 a.m. meeting so he must get a move on. He thanks Dr. Wang and heads to the floor.

With so many years of practice, his day, to him, goes smoothly. He eats lunch on the run to answer a page from a nurse who says the intravenous team is unable to get intravenous access on a patient and they need a central line. Dr. Huang takes care of the matter and throughout the remainder of the day, young doctors page with questions and pharmacists request clarification of medical orders while he works on completing rounds and his documentation. When he next checks his watch, it is seven o'clock in the evening. He heads to his office to finalize paperwork, make calls, and tie up loose ends.

"Dr. Huang?" He looks up.

"Yes, Dr. Wang."

"I need your opinion on something."

"What is it."

Dr. Huang knows Dr. Wang is not a sensationalist and if he is bringing something to his attention, it must be important.

"Take a seat Dr. Wang." Dr. Wang takes a deep breath, a habit Dr. Haung knows is his way of controlling herself before sharing a finding.

"I know you noticed we are up on cases and you probably have noticed the problem, in some cases, being respiratory. I think there is something going on. In a three-week period, dozens of people have come to this hospital with what we have diagnosed as viral pneumonia." Dr. Wang pauses as she pulls out a folder. "Anyway, today this patient caught my eye. She complained of having trouble breathing." Dr. Wang hands a file across the desk and Dr. Haung takes it.

While he checks the file, Dr. Wang continues. "At first, she said, she thought that she had a bad head cold, so she had drunk orange juice and tea, and took a few aspirin. But her symptoms got worse. She took her temperature and found she had a fever of 37.8 degrees Celsius, so she checked herself in. By the time I saw her she was breathing rapidly— at almost twice the normal rate. I listened to her lungs but there did not seem to be any rhonchi but sent her to x-ray anyway. I ordered a chest X-ray, and her lungs did not have the white streaks typical of viral pneumonia, and her white-blood-cell count was not elevated." Dr. Wang hesitates. "I guess what I am saying is that we are seeing a lot of pneumonia cases; way above what should be expected, and... and I do not think it is pneumonia."

It was hard for Dr. Wang to present a scenario with no identified diagnoses except an assumption. Dr. Haung understood. He looked over the information in the folder and reviewed his findings for the day.

"I see," Dr. Haung pronounced as he pulled his tablet toward him and started reviewing information for the past three weeks. When he finally looked up, he stared at Dr. Wang.

"I think you are on to something. I agree, something is off kilter and I will investigate it. Thank you, Dr. Wang."

She was sure that Dr. Haung could hear her nervously exhale as she thanked him, shook his hand, and walked confidently out of his office.

Dr. Haung spends the next hour going over what he sees as unusual inpatient analyses. Could there be a problem or has there been misdiagnoses? It was highly possible since each doctor generally was responsible for 17 to 25 patients and it was easy to take similar symptoms and translate them to the same diagnoses.

Even if there was something going on, RHWU was equipped to handle it. The hospital consists of 76 clinical departments and offers 4000 hospital-beds for inpatients. To help with diagnoses they had top-level medical instruments. They were well staffed, medically advanced and had reached international standards of care for out and in-patients.

Dr. Haung stood and went over to the window as his mind continued to go over the symptoms. A frown creases his forehead as he takes out his notepad. He finds what he is looking for. The annual amounts of patients treated in this hospital were 2.23 million for outpatients and 120,000 for inpatients. There were 60,000 surgical operations annually completed in RHWU. He flipped through pages of data and stops when he learns that the East campus has 2,300 hospital-beds for the patients.

Dr. Haung checks one more thing and learns there are 5100 employees at the campus that includes 580 medical care personnel.

The frown disappears. If there is indeed a rush of patients, they were equipped to handle it. He puts his notepad in his briefcase and makes sure the lights are out before he closes and locks the door. In his mind no matter what happened, they were ready.

He is in the car, just having pulled out of the parking lot when his phone rings. He presses the phone icon on the dash to answer it.

"Yes, hon, I am almost home. I will be there in a few…"

"No, that is not why I called. That, I expected. I want you to stop by the drugstore and pick up some aspirin."

"Are you not feeling well."

"Okay, doctor, settle down. I have a headache and we do not seem to have any aspirin in the house."

"Any other symptoms."

"None. Just hurry home. I will have dinner on the table when you get here."

When Dr. Haung enters the house, he smells the aroma of General Tso's Chicken, his favorite dish. He sits his purchase on the entry way bench and hurriedly takes off his coat and steps out of his shoes before entering the kitchen.

His wife's back is to him, so she does not know he is there. He watches as she turns her head to the side, away from the stove and coughs. It is a dry sort of cough. He cannot stop his medical mind from processing. That is the symptom of a viral pneumonia. If it were a bacterial pneumonia it would be a phlegmy cough and he would treat her with an antibiotic therapy, while viral pneumonia will usually get better on its own. Taking it down a notch he admits she might just be coming down with a cold. He walks over to her and hugs her around the waist, leaning his head against her cheek. It is hot.

Gently he turns her around to face him. Her face is flush, but that might be because she has been standing over a hot stove…

"Hon, it is already."

"I see it is." He says as he can see she is not herself.

His wife knows his worried voice and tells him to settle down. "I am fine. I probably caught a cold, is all."

He nods, giving her a smile as they carry the food into the dining room and sit down to eat.

Dr. Haung watches his wife, Lihua, as she pushes her food around her plate. Every now and then she raises her hand and begins kneading her forehead and he pushes his chair back to get up from the table.

"Hon, where are you going? You have not finished your dinner."

"No, I have not, but I left the bag with the aspirin in the hall and I think you could use them."

Lihua agrees and he goes to retrieve them. When he returns, he shakes out two and puts them in her hand and while she takes them with water, he touches her forehead.

He tries to hide his concern as he goes to get his medical bag and first checks her temperature. She has a fever and its registering over 37 degrees Celsius. Now he is worried, but again he tries to hide it. "Listen dear, I think you need to go upstairs and climb in the bed. Lu will handle cleaning the kitchen. You should have let her fix dinner, knowing you were sick."

"But I am not sick."

"Okay but humor me and get some rest. I will be up later to check on you."

That evening, playing it safe, Dr. Haung works out a worst scenario plan of action and emails Dr. Wang that they will need extra time in the morning to go over his reports. "There is something else I want to run by you too," he adds. He then informs her he plans on being at the hospital by six in the morning. Continuing with the worst-case scenario idea, he outlines an email and sends it to other hospitals in the area to see if they are experiencing the same thing.

Chapter 19

Early the next morning Dr. Huang arrived at Renmin Hospital to meet up with Dr. Wang. He had spent most of the evening reviewing hospital admissions and diagnoses reports hoping to find a key to what was the cause of so many becoming ill with the same symptoms. He explained that he came across seven cases of a virus that he thought looked like SARS and figured that if they got ahead of the game, the virus could be stopped before it took on epidemic proportions.

He had Dr. Wang's attention as he went on to explain that in the earlier cases he found that the virus caused severe acute respiratory infection after symptoms that usually started with a fever, followed by a dry cough.

Dr. Wang sat there absorbing what Dr. Huang was saying and agreeing wholeheartedly.

"So, what now?"

"Well, I think we should warn the staff to suit up."

"You mean, wear protective clothing like we wear with patients with infectious deceases."

"Yes. Better cautions now than later."

"What do you want me to do?"

"Well, you have seen all the files so if you can put any new cases on top, it will save me time going through them all."

"I can do that."

The meeting ended and Dr. Huang immediately sent out an initiative to the staff, keeping it low key though it did not feel low key at all. He called home to check on Lihua, who, trying to be brave, said that she felt better. "Not good, but better."

He could hear the panic in her voice as they spoke and after he hung up, he began planning to have her admitted. Throughout the day he felt confident in his decision and noticed that not all, but a lot of the staff were heeding his warning and wearing protective coverage.

For the next few days, he did his rounds and following protocol had another doctor assigned to Lihua, who kept him informed on her condition and each evening, with his notepad he sat at her bedside.

On the fourth day after he had alerted the staff and contacted the hospital administrators, he was summoned to the Public Security Bureau.

From the minute he entered the room, he knew something was wrong and when they presented him with a letter to read, he knew this was not going to be in support of his initiative. In the letter they handed him to sign he was admitting to making false comments that had severely disturbed the social order. He had no choice, of course. He had to sign it.

But he did not let it silence him. Later when speaking to another colleague he learned that he was not the only one on the hot seat. There were seven others who police said were being investigated for spreading rumors.

From that point on he noticed that the medical staff was leery of taking more than the usual necessary precautions, afraid they would be reprimanded next, so they wore only their usual medical attire. Each evening when he went to sit with his wife, he found she was doing much better and that gave him hope. Maybe this was not a serious matter after all.

Late on December 31, 2019, the WHO China Country Office was informed of cases of pneumonia of unknown origin detected in Wuhan City, Hubei Province of China.

On December 31 in the United States, millions gathered in Times Square in New York City looking forward to a great new year and Sonya McKenna sat in her Rochester home worried about her daughter.

It had been a sad Christmas for them. Sonya spent most of her time at the hospital, only leaving to go home and get some rest, after talking with Matthew who she knew was holding something back from her. In the McKenna household, Christmas never came.

Since talking to his wife, Matthew had heard rumors and had been busy in Europe between his book tour, trying to find out what was happening in Wuhan. He had made several calls to get more details and finally hit the jackpot with a fellow author who lived in Wuhan, China. After making contact he explained his reason for the call.

"Matt, there is something happening here. From what I have heard, in December there were patients tricking into the ER with high fevers and coughs that seemed to be pneumonia."

"Pneumonia?"

"Yes. The doctors were really puzzled by it because medicine did not help. The rumor was it was a virus and they needed to be aware. The leak came as a warning from a Dr. Huang who logged into a group chat to express his concern. In any case, whatever he said the Public Security Bureau found out and made him eat his words."

"What is this bureau?"

"Oh, here there is an entire system of online surveillance, in which they can monitor what is happening, and I think, in this case they picked up on certain words and figured out what the group chat was discussing."

"So why would it interest them."

"Do not know for sure. All I know is the local authorities issued a formal directive ordering other doctors not to discuss the matter.

Across the nation, Americans crowded into New York City Times Square ringing in the new year. What no one knew was that it was going to be memorable, but not in the way they hoped as a highly infections virus was moving toward them.

In Wuhan, Dr. Huang was refreshing his knowledge on the different types and symptoms of coronaviruses. He considered the 2003 severe acute respiratory syndrome (SARS) outbreak. Labeled SARS-CoV, it was a viral respiratory illness that was recognized as a global threat in March 2003. After first appearing in Southern China in November 2002 it was thought to be an animal virus from a yet unidentified animal but most leaned toward bats being the host. But what was positively known is that SARS began with a high fever with temperatures greater than 38.0°C, or 100.4°F.

The fever is sometimes associated with chills or other symptoms, including headache, general feeling of discomfort, and body aches. Some patients also experience mild respiratory symptoms and diarrhea is seen in approximately 10 percent to 20 percent of patients. Later, the patient can develop a dry, nonproductive cough that can progress to a point where the oxygen levels in the blood are low. In 10 percent to 20 percent of cases, patients require mechanical ventilation, and most patients develop pneumonia.

Dr. Haung stops reading and resting his elbows on the desk, he puts his head in his hands. The more he reads, the more worried he is becoming. But, if he is going to break the law, he had to have all the ammunition to do it. He reads on.

Being an airborne virus, it is easily spread through droplets of saliva in a similar way as colds and influenza spread. But unlike colds or influenza, SARS has severe impact on humans.

Dr. Haung reaches over for another pamphlet and flips pages until he finds what he is looking for.

During November 2002 through July 2003, a total of 8,098 people worldwide became sick with severe acute respiratory syndrome that was accompanied by either pneumonia or respiratory distress syndrome, according to the World Health Organization (WHO). Of these, 774 died. By late July 2003, no new cases were being reported, and WHO declared the global outbreak to be over. The CDC recommends that patients with SARS receive the same treatment that would be used for a patient with any serious community-acquired atypical pneumonia. If transmission of SARS-CoV recurs, there are some common-sense precautions that you can take that apply to many infectious diseases. The most important is frequent hand washing with soap and water or use of an alcohol-based hand rub. You should also avoid touching your eyes, nose, and mouth with unclean hands and encourage people around you to cover their nose and mouth with a tissue when coughing or sneezing.

Dr. Haung sighs as he leans back, his eyes blurry and his mind searching for his next step.

Despite the silencing of dissention, there were many Chinese scientists working to map the genome of the virus and the novel coronavirus was very quickly sequenced and found to be 80% related to the SARS coronavirus.

From that point through January 3, 2020, a total of 44 cases of patients with pneumonia of unknown etiology were reported to WHO by the national authorities in China, but not identifying the causal agent. The missing detail was how it was spreading, but given the speed of the subsequent spread, it should have been apparent to all that there must have been human-to-human transmission.

Dr. Huang prepared a list of symptoms for the staff to look out for and for every patient that appeared with any of the symptoms to make note of it on their charts. Fever or chills, cough, shortness of breath or difficulty breathing, fatigue, muscle or body aches, headache, any reported new loss of taste or smell, sore throat, congestion or runny nose, nausea or vomiting, and diarrhea. He knew this was an extensive list, but he was not sure which symptoms were more important than the other.

This seemed a ridiculous list of symptoms and he was glad he could present it electronically and not face to face since he could imagine the thoughts going through the heads of his colleagues. This would cover everything including the common cold but checking with those who came into the ER and questioning about those at home, might help identify how bad this might be. Of course, those who were experiencing trouble breathing, persistent pain or pressure in the chest or an onset of confusion would be easy to diagnose as having something beyond the common cold.

From what he had read on patient charts there were patients complaining of some or all these symptoms and what he planned to do was isolation. For each one of these patients, put them in isolation as they were contagious. How contagious was yet to be known.

At first Dr. Huang thought he was tired from spreading himself out so thinly, but on January 10 he woke up coughing, the next day he had a fever and two days later he was no longer a doctor attending to his patients. He was a patient himself. But Dr. Huang had started something.

Not well-versed on Coronaviruses, Matthew was at that moment conducting his own research. With his experience in seeking background for his books, he was good at research and he found enough information to make him nervous.

Chapter 20

It was beginning. Sonya was in the kitchen busying herself while she listened and every now and then glanced the television screen. Then the anchor caught her attention after coverage of a video of a tourist hit on a Brazilian beach, followed by a Texan struck dead while out running. Those reports barely penetrated her mind. What did was hearing the mention of Wuhan, China.

Sonya stopped what she was doing. It was like a lightning bolt struck her body as it stiffened and the hair on her arms stood straight up. She moved closer to the television and with her elbows on the counter, she leaned in as if being controlled by the voice as the anchor said, "When we return, we will..."

The reporter now had Sonya's undivided attention as she sat down in the kitchen chair waiting for the news to continue. By the time the face of the anchor filled the screen, Sonya was in a state of distress, rubbing her hands along the crook of her arms.

"Scientists worried about China's lack of transparency about a month-old outbreak of pneumonia in the city of Wuhan breathed a sigh of relief today, after a consortium of researchers published a draft genome of the newly discovered coronavirus suspected of causing the outbreak. According to the Chinese state-sponsored Xinhua News, the Wuhan Seafood Market has been traced as the source and on Wednesday, January 1, the market was closed for cleaning and disinfection. The causal agent has not yet been identified or confirmed and the World Health Organization has requested further information from the Chinese authorities to assess the risk."

Sonya lifted her head up. "Oh my God," she said out loud. "That is the market I suggested Elise check out." She stood up repeating, "Oh, God, Oh, God." She quickly flipped the station hoping to hear more, but there was the in-sync commercials happening. Sonya looked at the kitchen clock and repeated, "Oh, God, I am going to be late. She turned off the television and hurried upstairs to get ready for work.

On her drive to the hospital, she kept telling herself to calm down. Just because Elise may have visited the market, did not mean anything. When she pulled into her parking space, she grabbed her belongings and hurried inside.

Between patients she managed some time with Dr. Warren, the head of the department who shared with her that on January 2, there were 41 patients in the hospital in Wuhan who were confirmed to have contacted a novel coronavirus and 27 had direct exposure to a Huanan Seafood Wholesale Market. Beyond that Dr. Warren said that WHO in China has three concerned levels and they are all working together in response to the outbreak.

Each day during the staff meeting, more information was shared. They were advised to bring any cases of what seemed to be pneumonia to Dr. Warren's attention immediately as this is how this virus appeared and by the third of January the World Health Organization said that a newly emerging member of the family of viruses that caused the deadly outbreaks of severe acute respiratory syndrome (SARS) and Middle East respiratory syndrome (MERS) could be the cause of the present outbreak.

At the end of the day, Sonya rushed home to call Matthew. She wanted to let him know what she had heard, which was basically what everyone was hearing on the news and able to read online so Matthew was not surprised.

After that Matthew took over the conversation, letting Sonya know that Elise was still missing, and no one seemed to know where she was. He said he had called Elise's office and they told him they had not heard from her either. When she did not show up at work on Monday, November 25, they had made some calls to the travel agents office and had been informed she had gotten off on time. When Matthew asked, her company shared the airline itinerary with him and then because she obviously had not arrived in Rochester, he asked them to double check. When they called him back, they told him that Elise had indeed checked out of the hotel early on Sunday, November 23rd and had taken an Uber to the airport.

"So, what happened to her," Sonya asked her husband.

"I called Uber in China. They traced the driver who said he had indeed dropped her off at the airport. So then following the trail I called the airport in Wuhan and after waiting for some time on hold I finally reached a person and asked could they check on Elise's flight from Wuhan with the final destination being Rochester, New York and I supplied them with the itinerary for her travel."

"What happened then?"

"Well, I was getting agitated and even more so when I was put back on hold listening to a Chinese woman singing a song that I thought I'd heard before but was not able to identify. But it did what it was supposed to do, relax me. By the time the airline person came back on the line I was quite mellow. It was reported that they showed an Elise McKenna had checked in at the airport on Sunday, November 23 in plenty of time for her flight, but they do not show her as boarding the plane."

"What?"

"So, wait. I made a call to the travel agency that Elise was being sponsored by in Wuhan and learned that her escort was a man named Bai Zhao. In trying to reach Bai Zhao, at his office in Wuhan, I was unsuccessful. The office manager asked for a number where she could have Bai call when he came by the office and I gave them my cell number."

"It was a day later when I received a call from the office manager in Wuhan who told me that Bai had been hospitalized."

"I was frustrated. I asked her why she had not told me this when I called the first time and the woman said that the tour guides were usually out of the office for extended times and had no need to check in. So, she did not know until she tried to reach him."

"So now what, Matthew? What do we do now?"

"Hon, you know I have got this. I think we should contact the hospital and see if we can learn anything more about Bai and find out if Elise is hospitalized too."

"Yes, that is a good idea. I can probably get further with that than you and I speak the language, a little broken, but better than you can."

"You are right. I think you will be able to get more information than I can."

Sonya was nodding her head, then, finally said, "I will call and as soon as I have any information, I will get back to you." As an afterthought she adds, "I love you Matthew."

"Me too."

At the next staff meeting at the hospital, the discussion was the coronavirus and Dr. Warren stressed, "Viruses do not know borders, so going forward we must be

174

more vigilant. We need to ask our patients if they have been out of the country, considering how rapidly global travel can spread a viral respiratory disease." He then passed out new intake forms and asked them to look them over. After a few minutes he asked if there were any questions.

Sonya asked. "So, what have you heard from China?"

"So far what they have shared is that on January 21, there was a total of 314 confirmed cases reported for novel coronavirus globally and of that total 309 cases were reported from China, two from Thailand, one from Japan and one from the Republic of Korea. And of the total cases, 51 patients are severely ill, and 12 patients are in critical condition."

The questions kept coming.

"How many patients have died?"

Dr Warren stated, "Six deaths have been reported from Wuhan."

"How is it spreading?"

"Considering that to date, sixteen health care workers have been infected I would say that it is passing human to human but that has not been confirmed."

Halting the discussion, Dr. Warren said, "People, the genetic analysis of early cases suggests a single line of coronavirus imported from China began circulating in the United States between Jan. 18 and Feb. 9, followed by several importations from Europe. We need to be proactive if we want to get in front of it."

At the end of the meeting, Sonya approached Dr. Warren.

"Doctor, my daughter went to Wuhan back in November and was to be there for 20 days. She was expected to leave Wuhan on November 22nd and be in to work here on Monday, November 25th. Not only did she not return to work, I nor my husband have been able to reach her."

"What have you found out so far?"

"That she did arrive at the airport in time for her return flight, but never boarded the plane. So, what I am hoping is that you could check with the hospital in Wuhan and see if they have my daughter there or, anything else you can discover."

"Do not worry doctor. I will gladly check on this for you."

"Thanks, Dr. Warren."

"You are welcome Dr. McKenna. And Dr. McKenna?"

"Yes."

"Do not worry. I am sure she is all right." He said it, but he was not so sure it was true.

Chapter 21

Reports were coming in from all over the world. South Korea announced the first possible case of the virus coming from China. The patient had spent time in Wuhan, China, but had not visited the Huanan Seafood Market where the virus had been linked.

By January 15, the first known travel-related case of 2019 novel coronavirus entered the United States in Washington. The patient had been in Wuhan and returned to seek care at a medical facility in the state of Washington, where she was treated for the illness. Based on the patient's travel history and symptoms, healthcare professionals suspected this new coronavirus and testing proved it to be true. Then on January 16, Japan joined the ranks with its first case. Again, the patient could not be linked to the Huanan Seafood Wholesale Market, but possibly had close contact with an affected person in Wuhan.

What added to the stress was that with the report of 17 new cases in China, Wuhan City government held an annual banquet to celebrate the Chinese New Year with forty thousand families in attendance. It was unfortunate that the virus outbreak came ahead of the lunar new year holidays in late January when many of China's 1.4 billion people would be travelling to their hometowns or abroad.

At this stage of the game, only the medical profession was taking it seriously. This was the year 2020 and the fact that something as miniscule as a virus could change the world, well no one believed it, not for a minute.

So, it was no surprise when it was learned, a private international sales company meeting of 109 attendees that included 94 from overseas was held from January 20th to the 22nd at the Grand Hyatt Hotel in Singapore. Upon returning home five attendees became deathly sick and were taken to the emergency room. They were diagnosed with the coronavirus. One was from Malaysia, two from South Korea and two from Singapore.

Now report of cases of the coronavirus were confirmed in Macau and Hong Kong, Guangdong, and Shanghai. In China alone, the cases totaled 571 people with 17 deaths.

No one could deny the new data showed indications of the current rapid spread of the disease and an increase in the rate of transmission. On January 23, 2020 at 10:00 a.m. officials in China announced a quarantine of the greater Wuhan, China area. No traffic would be allowed in or out of the city, all planes were grounded, and trains were at a standstill. Wuhan was ground zero for the outbreak. It was eerie for a city that 11 million people called home, but it got people around the world to begin to take notice.

But was it too late?

Just one day later as the coronavirus continued to spread more cases were reported in Japan, South Korea, the United States, Singapore, Thailand, and Hong Kong. Soon, Nepal confirmed its first case, being a student who returned from Wuhan. France reported its first three cases. It was fast becoming a worldwide pandemic with Australia confirming its first four cases, Malaysia reporting its first three cases and Canada confirmed its first case in Toronto.

The World Health Organization had remained in close contact with Chinese as well as Japanese, Korean and Thai authorities since the reporting of these cases. It was no doubt something had to be done.

The three countries shared information with WHO under the International Health Regulations which, first adopted by the World Health Assembly in 1969 and last revised in 2005, are a legally binding instrument of international law that aims for international collaboration to prevent, protect against, control, and provide a public health response to the international spread of disease in ways that are commensurate with and restricted to public health risks and that avoid unnecessary interference with international traffic and trade. The IHR is the only international legal treaty with the responsibility of empowering the World Health Organization (WHO) to act as the main global surveillance system. Back on the 2nd of January, the incident management system was activated across the country offices, regional offices, and headquarters

On January 27, in Germany, the first specific, global case of coronavirus being transmitted by a person with no symptoms was reported. The originally infected individual was from Shanghai.

In the US, there were surging increase of warnings from its intelligence agencies toward the end of January and into early February. The chief of staff began convening regular meetings. In early briefings, however, officials said the President was dismissive because he did not believe that the virus had spread widely throughout the United States.

The outbreak was declared a Public Health Emergency of International Concern on January 30, 2020 and the world as we knew it was about to change.

Chapter 22

Wuhan has been under lockdown since Thursday, January 23, to contain the virus. It is scary to see the streets empty in a city of eleven million people. But, with transportation shut down and shops and businesses closed, there is nowhere to go and nothing to do.

When Meili, wakes on Tuesday morning she feels ill, but knows she cannot take the day off. There is a big reception due at the Wanda Reign planned that day and overseeing the staff she just had to be there. So, she dragged herself out of the bed and managed to gain a little more energy after showering. Soon she was on her way to work. By Thursday of that week she was worse and knew she could not make it into work. But the first thing she heard was that the city was closed, and people are being advised to stay at home.

What did this mean, she wondered as she forced herself to sit up in bed. Does she have what she needs already. She is sick. She needs to get some medicine. Not knowing what else to do she opens her laptop and reads through the comments posted. There is something about patients cannot be hospitalized as there is no more room for the sick.

"That is just crazy talk," she says but not totally believing her words. What she needs to do is call her mother. She will know what to do.

Meili searches the covers for her cell and finds it. She calls her mother who answers immediately.

"Meili, what is wrong?"

"What is happening mother."

Her mother tells her that there is a virus spreading and everything is closed for our own safety.

"But mother, I am sick and need to get some medicine."

"What do you mean you are sick."

"I think I have the flu, or a bad cold."

Meili cannot see her mother who is looking up at the ceiling and slowly letting out air through her pursed lips. She knows the situation with the hospitals, so she says, "Meili, stay in bed. I will go out and get you some food and medicine."

"Thank you, mother."

Meili leans back on her pillow and waits.

Qi is worried about her daughter as she hurriedly gets dressed. She turns on the television and sees how empty the streets are, but there are some people out and about. She sees they are wearing masks. She makes a list of what she will need and adds two masks to that list. In the meantime, she takes a scarf and puts it around her neck. She pulls it up over her mouth and nose as she leaves her home.

Normally it would be difficult to get through the crowded streets at this hour, but it is practically abandoned as she drives to store after store until finally, she finds a drug store open.

Inside the shelves are still stocked and she hurriedly picks up rice and noodles, broth, and a variety of seafood and meats. Most of everything else she has in large supply, but she gathers up a few vegetables thinking, just in case.

Over at the medicines she reads the labels, her mind churning over flu symptoms and what her daughter might need. She checks out and heads over to her daughter's apartment.

It is so eerie. She sees no one on bikes and only a few people on the streets as she puts the groceries in her car. She parks right in front of her daughter's building and spends a minute separating the groceries, planning on taking some of it back home with her. Soon she is knocking on her daughter's apartment door.

Inside the apartment Meili is sleeping. She thinks she hears something but is not sure. It comes repeatedly, and she realizes someone is at her door. It must be her mother.

Slowly she gets her feet on the floor beside the bed and with her legs leaning against the mattress, she manages to stand and put on her robe before making her way to the door, dizzy and disoriented.

"Yes, is that you mother."

"Yes. Open the door Meili."

Meili tilts her head as if she needs to watch her hands so that they can turn the knob and open the door. When the door opens, it takes just one quick look for Qi to see that her daughter is extremely ill.

She says nothing as she helps Meili back to the bed. She goes into the bathroom and gets a washcloth and wets it with cold water. This she places on her daughter's forehead before going into the front room to gather the groceries and take them to the kitchen where she puts away the perishables. Then locating the medicines, she has picked up, decides on what to give her daughter. Taking some pills and a glass of water she enters the bedroom only to find that Meili is sound asleep. She decides not to wake her.

Back in the kitchen Qi calls her husband and fills him in on the situation. She tells him she does not think she should leave Meili and will stay at the apartment. He agrees and asks if she needs anything. Qi tells him no, she can wear Meili's clothes since they are the same size and from what she has heard and seen on the news, it is best he stays put. She tells him she will keep him informed. They say their goodbyes.

Qi remembers she has food in the car and grabbing Meili's keys off the hook by the door, she goes out to get the rest of the groceries.

Qi stays with her daughter feeding her, helping her to the bathroom and giving her the medicine, but she sees Meili is not getting any better.

Outside the world is quiet, and the silence is horrifying. She hears only the occasional noise in the corridor outside the apartment door.

Qi has been listening to the news and knows that this is bad. No one knows how long the city will be on lockdown and there is nothing coming in or going out meaning that supplies will eventually be exhausted. She talks to her husband and he informs her he is fine. He has enough food and his company is shut down, so he has no place he needs to be. He could come and stay with her at Meili's and give her a break.

She has not wanted to think it, let alone say it, but now she must. "No Zhang Wei. Please, stay where you are. I think Meili has this coronavirus they are talking about."

"Qi…are you sure?"

"Pretty sure. I will give it one more day, but if she does not get better, I am going to take her to the hospital."

"But they say they cannot take any more patients. They have no room."

"They have to take her. She is…"

"It is bad?"

"Yes."

"Call me and let me know how it goes."

One of Qi's goal is not to fall sick, so she wears her mask and exercises as she watches the news. The announcer says that this lockdown might last until May. This scares her and Qi works out harder, not knowing what she should do. She goes out while Meili sleeps, wearing both masks to keep safe. The pharmacy and the convenience store are closed. Noodles are all sold out in the supermarkets, but there is some rice. She wonders if she should buy celery, garlic shoots and eggs. It cannot hurt, so she does.

After returning home, she strips at the door and puts everything into the washer before going into the bathroom to take a shower, thinking that going out makes her feel that she is still connected to the world, but she might be bringing this deadly virus back on her clothes and body. Being a kind, concern person, Qi finds it difficult to imagine how elderly citizens living alone and people with disabilities will get through this.

She cannot get Meili to eat anything that evening and she knows in the morning she will have to take her to the hospital. She is too ill for them to turn her away. Over dinner, she video calls several friends and there is no escaping talk of the virus. Some people are in towns near Wuhan, some chose not to go home because of the disease, some still insist on gathering despite the outbreak.

A friend coughs during the call and someone jokingly tells her to hang up!

They chat, filling each other in for at least an hour which tells Qi they are feeling anxious in isolation too. When they are gone, she feels helpless, angry, and sad and for the first time, entertain the thought that Meili could die.

Their life is turned upside down and it is a challenge to accept.

The next morning Qi gets Meili ready and practically carries her out of the apartment and into the car. A couple wearing masks pass her but do not offer to help. Panic has driven a wedge between people.

When they are finally on their way, Qi goes directly to the emergency department of the Wuhan hospital and pulls up to a group of what appears to be sentries. She lowers her window and tells them that her daughter is extremely ill and that she thinks her daughter has the coronavirus.

"Wait here."

There is a scurry of activity as someone exits, dressed in protective clothing and has not only a mask but a shield over their face. When they ask Qi to lower the passenger window, she does it. The hands that come into the car are encased in plastic gloves as they move over Meili, checking her pulse, testing to see if she has a fever and try to get her to talk. They do not need to tell her. It is as she assumed, Meili is gravely sick.

A stretcher appears and Meili is taken out of the car. Qi starts to get out, but her door is held shut. All she can do is watch as Meili disappears inside. Qi starts up the car, but is told, "No."

She follows the commands. She is taken out of the car and walked behind the hospital where there is a tent erected. Once inside, Qi finds herself in a sheltered hall like area and is told to strip. Qi knows she has no choice, so does as she is told.

The water is surprisingly warm as she is instructed to wash herself with the soap they supply. Then, when she is done, they shooed her ahead and Qi enters another enclosure where there is a cotton dress like item, woven shoes, and a mask.

"What is this?"

"You have to remain here."

"For how long?"

"Fourteen... or more, days."

"But my daughter…" Her words fall on deaf ears.

When Qi steps out of the second enclosure, she realizes she is not alone. Inside the massive tent there are at least 30 people that she can see. They are all dressed similar and moving around, looking confused. Qi sees there are tables and chairs in this main area and off to the sides there are enclosures. Qi is led to one of these and told this will be her room. Women on the left and the men on the right.

"Any questions?"

Qi has many of them but does not say anything but two things. "I need my cell and I need to know about my daughter."

To the first she is handed a bag that contains plastic bags with her personal possessions and told that after they have been sterilized, she will get her clothing back. As for her daughter, they ask her name and tell Qi that they give a daily report to everyone who is here.

What can I do but thank them and accept my fate.

There are televisions everywhere and she hears the announcer say that some people have sealed up the doors of others who they decided to self-quarantined themselves. Hearing that Qi shivers. That could have happened to Meili.

Qi, glad to have something to do, joins the other quarantined individuals in the gathering area. Immediately when she enters, someone yells out, "Stop right there."

"What," Qi says.

"You cannot be in here without the head gear, booties and disposable gown." The speaker pauses. "Did not you read the directive in your assigned room?"

One of the others in the group could tell she was near tears. "He means we need to protect each other if we ever want to get out of here. We have all been exposed and this is for our protection."

The information was softly given, and Qi was able to give a grateful smile before returning to her room and getting into the proper attire. She then joined the group that sat in chairs spaced apart and unmovable from their location.

Qi turned her attention to the screen. "Wuhan health officials reports that the pneumonia-like illness appears to be viral and that the patients are in isolation. No obvious human-to-human transmission has been observed, and no healthcare worker infections have been reported."

The man who had interrogated her earlier, got up and switched the channel. No one complained and it is obvious that the same news is being reported again, but in a different format.

"So far, the cause of the outbreak is still under investigation. News of the outbreak triggered rumors of possible severe acute respiratory syndrome (SARS). A SARS expert from Hong Kong University, told Radio Television Hong Kong, a public broadcasting service, that it is too early to say the outbreak is a SARS event." He added that the emergence of atypical pneumonia cases requires identifying the responsible pathogen and ruling out SARS or other types of coronaviruses."

The outbreak was declared a Public Health Emergency of International Concern on January 30 and by the 11th of February 2020, WHO announced a name for the new coronavirus disease. No longer would it be called novel coronavirus, but instead it would be known by the name, COVID-19, meaning the coronavirus of 2019.

Chapter 23

It continues to get worse. After hearing on the news that the number of cases of Covid-19 has spiked in Europe, Matthew fears that if he does not make a move now to return home, he might not be able to. Only his focus until now was on the book tour and on Wuhan and not Europe so, as he opens his laptop to check airline schedules, a popup caught his eye. He clicked on it and read. **Disaster at Milan**

Bergamo is a city in the alpine Lombardy region of northern Italy, northeast of Milan with a total population of just over 1.1 million. On February 19, the soccer team of Atalanta took to the field in its match against Sassuolo. This was the team's first game in more than three months as Series A. Atalanta won that first-leg match 4-1, and won the return leg 4-3 to reach the quarterfinals of the Champions League in its first ever season in the competition.

Roughly 40,000 fans made the 35-mile journey from Bergamo to Milan for the Valencia game that followed. Kids were taken out of school, with parents' mischievous notes to teachers explaining that their offspring needed to participate in a "cultural-historical" moment making international headlines. Just to play in such a game, for a club of Atalanta's means, was already a cause for celebration.

On March 10, the day of Atalanta's return game against Valencia, the number of confirmed coronavirus cases in the province rose to 1,472. Across Lombardy, the region containing Bergamo and Milan, there had already been 468 deaths.

Less than a week after the game, the first cases were reported in the province of Bergamo and the greatest achievement in Atalanta's history was swiftly marred.

Hours after Atalanta departed, Italy's lockdown was expanded to cover the whole country. By the time they arrived home, the government was drafting tighter restrictions, obliging most businesses, besides food stores and pharmacies, to shut down.

Matthew scanned through the article, his anxiety mounting. He was interested in the article because it was all people were talking about, but now it struck fear in his heart. He immediately placed a call to his agent, Randolph Peters.

"Hello."

"Hi Randy. Have you been watching the news?"

There is silence on the line. "Ah, yes."

"This is serious. I need to get home."

"I take it you are talking about just the game."

"No, of course not. I am talking about the lockdown. I know you had to know about it."

Randy had a worried look on his face now as he said, "Look Matt, so we miss a few author readings. We just stay put and schedule them later."

Trying to remain calm, Matthew filled Randy in on Elise being missing and needing to get to Wuhan. There is silence on the line, but Matthew gave Randy time to absorb what he told him.

"If anything, Matt, you should aim for home. Going to Wuhan is a bad idea. A really bad idea."

"I know, Randy."

Again, silence and finally, "Okay, listen. I know you are right, but at least consider going home, not Wuhan and in the meantime, I will handle rescheduling the tour."

"Thanks Randy."

Bergamo, Italy had become the epicenter of Italy's outbreak. Ten people from the hospital in Bergamo went to see the game and ten of them were infected. Word came down that the head of the hospital was quarantined at home after catching the virus, along with two main outbreaks in Spain near Madrid and Valencia, the home of the opponent team. Just like in China and Iran, Italy was slow to react.

It was apparent that the people of Italy continued with their social life and the fact of their hospitals not being overwhelmed by patients seemed to support their lackadaisical attitude. Even hearing that flights were being cancelled in China did not faze them. Italy decided to take the US attitude and wait it out and so they lost valuable time.

No sooner had Matthew disconnected his call to Randy, his cell rang. It was a friend in Europe.

"Listen Matthew, I think we need to cancel our dinner."

"What's up?"

"Well, my daughter is ill. She has not been herself the last few days, but she woke up this morning saying she ached all over and the pain was like being stabbed all over with a knife. At first, we figured it was because she did not want to go to school. Later today she was running a high fever and could not keep anything down, so we took her to emergency. She has this coronavirus."

"I see. I am so sorry to hear that."

"Yes, well, there is nothing we can do, but I thought I should make you aware, since me and my wife are now under quarantine."

"Thanks, my friend, I understand. Take care of yourself and your family. I will be in touch."

Matthew sat wondering what the best alternative was now. He called Sonya to tell her he was going to catch the next flight home and then went online and turned on the television.

As far back as the end of January there were cases of pneumonia being reported in Wuhan. Those cases of pneumonia were now said to be the coronavirus. There were a total of 581 confirmed cases showing up in China, Thailand, Japan, Hong Kong Special Administrative Region, Taipei Municipality, China, Macau Special Administrative Region, United States of America, and the Republic of Korea. It was spreading across the world rapidly.

When he had talked with Sonya last, she had mentioned that the growing outbreak was said to be due to an ongoing exposure at the Huanan Seafood Market in Wuhan. She had totally stressed out on that because she had encouraged Elise to make sure she visited that market during her trip.

Now, knowing the situation, Matthew began checking the two airports in Italy, for flights. He was told there were no flights available, so he tried impressing upon them it was an emergency. He had to find his daughter. They expressed concern, but still he was told all flights were cancelled going in and out of the city. It was not their decision alone as there was a lockdown on the whole of Italy in an emergency attempt to contain the coronavirus outbreak in the country.

Matthew did not give up. He checked other city airports in Italy and received the same message. Matthew decided to hold off, hoping the situation would change, before he called Sonya. He spent the next hour just listening and reading the news.

The World Health Organization (WHO) declared COVID-19 a pandemic, on March 11 pointing to the over

118,000 cases of the coronavirus illness in over 110 countries and territories around the world and the sustained risk of further global spread.

"This is not just a public health crisis, it is a crisis that will touch every sector," said Dr. Abaynesh Wodajo, WHO director-general. "So, every sector and every individual must be involved in the fight."

Making sure he understood, Matthew looked up epidemic and read, 'refers to an uptick in the spread of a disease within a specific community'. He next checked out pandemic 'A global spread of a new disease. The term is most often applied to new influenza strains, and the CDC says it is used when viruses are able to infect people easily and spread from person to person in an efficient and sustained way in multiple regions.' Nothing he reads was encouraging. This was not going to go away anytime soon.

How had he missed this! It was like he had been asleep and woke up to find a changed world. There were reports of a nearly deserted Piazza di Spagna in central Rome on Thursday, as Italy shut all stores except for pharmacies and food shops in a desperate bid to halt the spread of a coronavirus.

He watched in surprise and horror as the television broadcast images of hundreds of people storming Milan's central train station, desperate to catch a train out of the city after rumors circulated of the coming of a quarantine being issued.

Matthew raised his arms above his head. He walked around the room trying to not panic. As it stood now, this was fast becoming the reality not just here but everywhere.

Finally, he calmed himself down so that he could make the call.

"Sonya?"

"You do not need to tell me. I know. There is no way in hell you can get home."

"I am so sorry. I should have made arrangements earlier, but after talking with you about Elise…"

"It was me too. I told you not to come."

They were silent both wondering what to do or say next.

"I will keep in touch and keep trying to see what I can find out about Elise. She is resourceful and we can go crazy thinking the worse, so we need to remember she is capable of handling herself."

"You are right Matt."

Reluctantly they ended the call, with neither one able to think positive in a world that had suddenly gone haywire.

Chapter 24

The first two cases of the new coronavirus in Italy hit near the end of January and the beginning of February 2020. From that point the total number of cases in Italy increased steadily. People went about their daily lives oblivious to the threat that soon would cause them harm. It was no more at the outset than the threat of rain has on life, but it would soon blossom to the harm caused by the release of an atomic bomb.

When he first arrived in Italy, at the end of February 2019, the people continued to go about their busy lives, which in Rome includes long hours at cafes that were open late at night. Stores operated full-time and nightlife in youth bar districts went on full blast. The city's multitude of museums were open with visitors waiting in line for their first time seeing the exhibits. But it was unrecognizable now. Rome was quiet.

The buses of tourists that usually clog the city's main arteries around ancient landmarks are long gone. Cafes hosted dwindling numbers, but kids still spilled into malls and fun parts of town. A few days later they dropped the next bombshell. Conte ordered nearly all retail businesses, museums, and other places where crowds might gather to close. The only exceptions were pharmacies and food stores.

Tired of staring at four walls, Matt went for walks each day and from one to the next everything was changing. The streets were even emptier. He went to a pharmacy and customers were ordered to maintain "secure distance."

As big a change as it was, it did get worse. Streets were haunted with silence. Stores had closed signs out during normal business hours. Businesses were not open for business anymore. The depth of the effect of this virus kept getting worse. When Matthew happened upon a cathedral that used to have a sign saying, 'Enter as Friends, Leave as Family', the magnitude of the unseen enemy registered. The sign now in front of the cathedral read, 'No masses are being held until further notice'. Even the doors to St. Peter's Basilica were closed.

It was a different, unrecognizable Italy. When he opened his window in the evening he is met with silence. Nightlife has been extinguished. And the daytime joys of morning coffee and friends strolling the streets linked arm in arm is at an end.

Watching the news, it was evident it is the same everywhere. Day after day one more norm was taken away.

Japan postpones the 2020 Summer Olympics, which were originally slated to be held in Tokyo starting July 24, until summer 2021. Countries had already announced that given the public health risk of the COVID-19 pandemic, they would not be sending their athletes to the Games.

The cancellation of school attendance is followed by the cancellation and suspension of all kinds of sports events.

Matthew is watching when one anchor says, "The International Olympic Committee (IOC) President Thomas Bach is facing the media in Lausanne, after a two-day executive board meeting. Tokyo 2020 organizers have agreed to scale back the torch relay in response to coronavirus, with the lighting of the flame due to take place in Greece next week."

That is all he can cope with as he flips off the television.

Chapter 25

Like most medical professionals, Sonya is more than aware of the seriousness of the situation as patient after patient is admitted to the hospital. The first coronavirus infection in western and central New York was confirmed late Wednesday night, March 11 in Rochester. The patient who tested positive for the virus was in isolation at home and recovering nicely but the test results triggered an aggressive attempt to identify the man's associates, some of whom have already been placed in quarantine. Health investigators continue to locate people who might have been exposed in hopes of short-circuiting the local spread of COVID-19, the disease caused by the novel coronavirus. Some would think this was overkill, but Sonya knows they are facing a serious medical event. She prays each night that Elise is okay, because with the travel bans there is no way Matthew can get to her.

Before life turned upside down, she would go to the hospital with a smile on her face, ready to face the patients; giving them the time and compassion they deserve. But now, when she enters, the hallways are barely walkable with patients ill enough to be here, but the rooms are needed for those patients who need to be quarantined. It seems hopeless no matter how long or how hard she works each day her patients are not getting the best of her.

There is no need to shower at home as she must immediately shower once she enters the hospital. Then she must put on her nursing outfit that she leaves on the premises and over that, the huge white jumpsuits that covers her from head to the tops of her booties over her shoes. Finally, she puts on a white elastic headpiece, a mask, and a face shield. She looks like something from outer space.

She is exhausted when she finally takes herself home, grabs a bite to eat there as there is nowhere open to order food or arrange for a delivery. It prays upon her so that she cannot fall asleep right away and ends up torturing herself, listening to the news as the announcers cover one devastating report after the other.

"More than 3,600 passengers are quarantined on a cruise ship off the coast of Yokohama, Japan, while passengers and crew undergo health screenings. The number of confirmed cases of coronavirus on board the ship is more than 700, making it one of the largest outbreaks outside of China."

"Kirkland, Washington Medics transport a person on a stretcher into an ambulance at the Life Care Center of Kirkland, a long-term care facility linked to several confirmed coronavirus cases."

"The first COVID-19 death is reported in Washington state, after a man with no travel history to China dies on Feb. 28 at Evergreen Health Medical Center in Kirkland, Washington."

"Two earlier deaths at a nearby nursing home are the first COVID-19 deaths to occur in the United States and in Santa Clara, California, the first dead from COVID-19 was reported."

It is not until March 13, 2020 The U.S. President declares a national emergency and the news just gets more tragic with the coronavirus present in all 50 states.

The CDC warns against holding or attending gatherings larger than 50 people, including conferences, festivals, parades, concerts, sporting events and weddings for eight weeks, recommending that individuals cancel or postpone those events to avoid spreading the virus or introducing it into new communities.

With tears of frustration flowing uncontrolled, Sonya falls asleep with the television still on.

The order is out to shelter in place as COVID-19 continues its march across the world. When Italy's death toll tops 4,000, it becomes the first country to report more deaths than China, despite its much smaller population. Spain followed, going over the count of deaths in China.

In the United States, the symbol of the effect that COVID-19 has is exposed by the usually busy New York City Grand Central Station being uninhabited as the announcer states that New York City is being declared the US outbreak epicenter

New York City reports more than 15,000 people testing positive for COVID-19. The United States now has more confirmed coronavirus cases than any other country in the world, with cases topping 82,000 and deaths topping 1,000.

The virus knows no bounds when at the end of March, the United Kingdom Prime Minister Boris Johnson registered a high fever and a persistent cough. He tests positive for COVID-19, but as a leader announced he will continue to lead the government via video conferences.

Chapter 26

By the beginning of April 2020 the global cases of COVID-19 hit 1 million, but given testing shortages, undiagnosed cases and suspicions about governments obscuring the scope of their respective outbreaks, the actual number of people falling ill is believed to be much higher.

The coronavirus causing people to stay at home is bad news for populaces but good news for much of the world's wildlife. With people staying at home and travelling less, animals have been spotted in unusual places and air pollution has dropped in some areas.

In the Welsh countryside, goats were out and about as lockdown measures cleared the streets of humans and traffic. A wild puma was seen prowling the streets in Chile and a coyote stalked the San Francisco Golden Gate Bridge.

With less human interference and light pollution, sea turtles across the world are daring to lay their eggs on beaches they once avoided.

We are beginning to see wildlife that stay hidden from view and we are seeing clear skies with the reduction of pollution. Smog has lifted in New Delhi, one of the most polluted cities on Earth. Nitrogen dioxide pollution in north-east America is down 30 per cent and Rome's air pollution levels are down more than half compared to a year ago.

The air along the U.S. Interstate 95 corridor from Boston to Washington is the cleanest it is been since 2005, after a severe decline in vehicle traffic. Air pollution over China too has shown improvement since December. What we are envisioning is the rare absence of human activity grants us a special glimpse of what the world might be like without us in it.

That is the somewhat good picture, but so much of the bad overshadows it. It is apparent that several months of sheltering in place has affected life as we know it. We are forced to depend on a supply chain that is local rather than global as countries hoard what they produce. We shop, work, and play online. Retailers with physical stores are struggling to compete with online shopping. As the last online laggards adjust to online commerce, they will likely not go back. So, in-store shopping and commercial real estate will take a long-term hit.

Many workers are put on furlough. Even students are attending online classes and finishing their school year at home. Those with connectivity and technology jobs and skills are working remotely unaffected during the shelter in place order.

All people and all industries are under the coronavirus affect.

Danger of becoming affected is everywhere and people lose the ability to trust what they have taken for granted. Cruises, air travel, or travel by train is no longer the first choice mainly because it is now unavailable, but later caution will hold people back from these modes of travel.

Talking face to face with a neighbor, or friend is kept at a social distance and with a mask. Even letting a repair man in the house is scary enough to try and handle it first before making that service call.

Being what has been deemed necessary workers, Sonya has not faced furloughs or downsizing. Instead it has become impossible to keep ahead of the patients being assigned to her and to the other doctors. No one has a spare moment between COVID-19 patients and those who are suffering from other severe illnesses.

When Sonya goes to work during that first week in April, she senses something is different. At first, she cannot put her finger on it and has no time to give it much thought. That is until she decides to check on one of her COVID-19 patients.

"What are you doing, doctor?"

Sonya unnerves Dr. Henderson. Hearing her voice quickens his pulse as he searches for words.

"Dr. McKenna, ah…how are you doing."

"I am doing fine. That is my patient, Dr. Henderson," she says, stepping forward and nodding her head in the direction of the door."

Dr. Henderson takes a moment to collect himself and then responds, "Not anymore. The patient has gotten worse and I am taking over his care."

Stunned into silence, Sonya stares stupidly at the doctor. She can take care of a terminally ill patient and he knows it.

"What is going on," she asks.

"Nothing is going on doctor. We are dealing with this coronavirus and are shorthanded. I have been assigned to take over on cases where the patient is getting worse."

It sounded sensible to have one doctor recording changes on the patients who appeared terminal so that the data of their recovery or demise is a roadmap prepared by one person. Sonya must admit that Dr. Henderson is very capable of being that one doctor.

"Oh, I understand. I did not get the message." She turns and heads down the hall, ignoring that twinge that threatens to force her to question him further. Instead she goes to check on her other patients.

There were so many. It was a wonder that the right patient got the right drug, therapy, or meal. Having someone assigned to the more seriously ill patients, Sonya found gave the other doctors more time to deal with the ones that were recovering.

Each day Sonya spent going from patient to patient and each evening she spent talking with Matthew who was not going to get transportation home any time soon, and of course, they continued to see if they could find out more about their daughter.

Matthew had managed to contact a fellow author who lived just outside of Wuhan and he had learned that Elise's tour guide, Bai Zhao had come down with the coronavirus. Matthew's friend was facing a stay at home order from the government and unable to check on Bai.

Sonya told Matthew she had contacted the hospitals, of which she found two through the internet, and was told they did not have a patient by the name of Elise McKenna, at least that they could trace. She left her contact information with the staff and they said they would get in touch with her if they were able to locate Elise. She had also talked with the hotel personnel and they assured her that Elise had checked out and they had not seen her since.

"So, Matthew, what else can we do? If it were not for this coronavirus, I would catch a plane to Wuhan myself and look for her. I just feel so lost."

"I know. I feel the same. Here we are facing a crisis and we are all three in different countries."

The call always ended with an uplifting thought as they tried to cheer each other up. One evening call, Matthew said, "Hey Sonya, I have got a joke for you."

"Do tell, my love."

"I was up late last night. I was doing some work, and I got so upset with my computer that I flung my keyboard across the table. some keys popped off, and I learned a valuable lesson: Do Not Lose CTRL!"

It took a moment, but Sonya got it and started laughing. "Thanks. I needed that." From then on, Matthew brushed up on jokes to tell her.

When Sonya arrived at the hospital the following day, she was greeted by her friend, Dr. Tina Williams.

"Hey, Sonya, do you have a moment?"

"Yes," Sonya said absentmindedly as she stared around the hallway. "What?"

"Yes, indeed, what! I cannot believe what I am seeing Sonya. Not only have patients with the coronavirus been removed, but they seem to have disappeared."

Dr. Williams walked with Sonya, stopping to peek into hospital rooms and seeing only a few of the many coronavirus patients.

"What did they think," Dr. Williams said to her friend, "That we would not notice."

"Have you talked to anyone about this?"

"Yes, I did. I was told that we should be happy to see our situation lessening, but…"

Sonya interrupted her. "Look, it is Dr. Henderson." She grabbed a stunned Tina by the arm and dragged her into the well in the hallway where the fire extinguisher resided so that they could see Dr. Henderson, but he would not see them. They watched as Dr. Henderson went down to the end of the hall, turned to check to see if anyone was watching and when he saw no one, he opened the emergency door and disappeared.

Sonya held Tina back a moment longer until she was sure he was gone and then they stepped out into the hallway. "What was that about Sonya?"

"I am not sure, but I think it has something to do with the decrease in our coronavirus cases."

"What do you mean?"

"Well, I do not think that is officially an exit off the floor to any other patient floors. If I remember correctly, that is the staircase that we were told to refrain from using at any time as it was for maintenance only. We usually take the stairs over by the elevator to go from floor to floor if we do not want to wait for an elevator."

"You are right, but, maybe because of our current situation, it is open so that it is allowed to be used."

"Let's find out."

Tina was not sure what Sonya was about to do until she followed her to Dr. Warren's office. "He'll know what is going on."

At the door, Sonya knocked lightly, waited a second and then opened the door. Tina followed her in.

Dr. Warren was sitting behind his desk staring down at his hands as if he were not sure how to make them work.

"Dr. Warren. Can we have a moment of your time."

Dr. Warren looked up, a dazed expression on his face. "Yes, of course. What can I help you with?"

Sonya asked him about the missing patients on the floor and the strange way that Dr. Henderson was acting. "So, Dr. Warren, what is going on?"

Dr. Warren did not answer right away and when he did, he seemed to sidestep the issue.

"Yes, of course. I understand. Sorry to bother you."

Sonya grabbed Tina's arm and walked toward the door. As soon as they were back in the hallway, Tina pulled against Sonya and said, "I know that tone you used with Dr. Warren. You are not letting it go, but I am telling you to, please let it go.'

"Okay, okay. I will."

"No, Sonya I need you to say it. Say, I will let it go."

"Yes, Tina, you are right. I will let it go."

But Sonya could not just let it go. It might not be obvious to Tina, but something very odd was going on and she had to get to the bottom of it because she felt it had something to do with the welfare of the patients.

Even at Tina's insistence to forget about it since those in authority were aware of the matter and seemed fine with the situation, Sonya could not. What she could do, though, is investigate on her own.

Chapter 27

For the next few days, Sonya continuously had patients taken out of her care and placed in Dr. Henderson's hands. Tina was finding the same happening with her patients, but she was fine with it. Her plate was too full to worry about the patients who were taken out of her control. It was not that Tina cared less; Tina was just being more realistic. If she wanted to take care of her patients, she needed to have time to do it.

Sonya was convinced whatever was happening surreptitiously was happening unlawfully. There was no legitimate reason for seriously ill patients in a hospital to suddenly disappear. If they had died, the doctor in charge of their care as well as the family would be notified. At one point she started to ask Dr. Evans if he had noticed anything strange happening on their floor, but when they were in the doctor's lounge, she saw him standing off in a corner, talking with Dr. Henderson. She decided not to mention it.

Was she just being paranoid? These were doctors and doctors cared for patients. They like herself lived by the Hippocratic Oath written by Hippocrates and still held sacred by physicians: to treat the ill to the best of one's ability, to preserve a patient's privacy, to teach the secrets of medicine to the next generation and so on, and so on. Maybe whatever was happening would have a logical explanation, but not knowing what it was, bothered her.

So, Sonya took the next logical step. At noon she went to her office and looked up the charts for her missing patients.

No matter what was going on with a patient Rule #1 was to note it on the patient's chart. In this hospital they aimed to complete charts immediately after treatment when details are still fresh. The doctors as well as any nursing staff had time limits for when documentation is due: within 24 hours for admitting notes, 48 hours for surgical procedures and 15 days after discharge for completing the record.

In the midst of pulling up the first patients chart she paused. Fifteen days after discharge for completing the record. Sonya leaned back in her chair. "No way," she said to herself. "No way these patients were discharged." Her fingers fumbled trying to open the first patient folder. She knew each of her patients well enough to know they were too ill to be discharged.

She read the chart thoroughly, looking for anything abnormal. She saw nothing. Again, she sat back, and tapping a pencil against her lips she mumbled. "Not even a death recorded. If the patient had died, there would be a record of the date and time of the patient's death along with the name of the health care provider who pronounced the death.

She was just about to check another file when her screen went blank. At first, she thought she must have hit something, but her hands had been away from the keyboard.

Sonya stood up and went to her office door. She peeked out but saw no one. She went back to her desk, gave a futile effort to get the file back, knowing all the time that was not going to happen. Her screen was back at the list of patients. She clicked on another of her patients and as soon as she clicked, the name disappeared from the list. She started to try another but saw the time. She had to get back on the floor.

Her mind was working in overtime. She knew the morgue was full. She knew that the bodies of coronavirus patients were being put in refrigerated trucks behind the hospital. Both were unusual circumstances, so this might be too.

Nothing she thought or said would change the fact she had to find out for herself. She just couldn't let it go until she knew for sure what was happening. Something was just not right.

Sonya hurried down the hospital corridor with now far fewer patient beds. She should be glad that the quarantine was working, and the coronavirus patients were getting better, easing up the space in the hospital. But she was not. It took her about three seconds to decide what to do.

Cautiously, making sure no one was watching, she hurried down the hall and to the door to the back staircase, praying it was still unlocked. She turned the knob and heard the latch mechanism release from the strike plate. She turned to face the hallway and seeing no one, opened the door and slipped through.

The stairs were made of metal with an embossed surface like beaten silver on the steps and she was glad for the flat surface of her medical shoes. As her eyes adjusted, she noticed the walls of the stairwell were made of cinder block and looking up she could see the bare bulb hanging above each landing.

When she reached the fourth floor the bulb was out. The relative darkness forced Sonya to slow down and proceed with caution, advancing her foot to find the first stair of the next flight.

Sonya leaned out over the metal banister and could see down into the subbasement. Sonya felt slightly ill at ease but despite the disquieting sensations she continued slowly, deliberately, being careful of each footstep because if she should fall, she would die, and no one would find her. This was not the stairwell taken to any of the floors.

Keeping her mind off the danger of what she was doing, she turned her mind to the real problem. Dr. Henderson had said he was to take care of the patient and she had learned that this situation was happening to a lot of the other doctors; even though they, nor the nurses were saying anything. More than once she saw puzzled expressions on the faces of nurses and doctors as she passed them in the hall, only until now, it had not registered. She had assumed they were expressions of concern.

Sure, they were dealing with an uncommon situation, but there still was a set protocol in place. Sonya stopped. Like turning a page of a book, her mind going backwards. She remembered something that one of the nurses had said just a day or two ago. The nurse was new to the staff, but she was doing a good job. The nurse was in one of the isolation rooms talking to someone, that Sonya could not see. The conversation was muffled but she was sure she heard the nurse say that the anesthesiologist was giving succinylcholine. "Oh my god!" the words popped out of her mouth, echoing in the hollow stairwell. These patients were already having trouble breathing.

Snapping out of her reverie, she continued until finally she was in the subbasement area. Once her foot stepped down, lights in the ceiling turned on giving her a fright. She had never been down this far in the hospital. This was where the guts of the building lived and as far as anyone knew, that was it. Two floors above this was the morgue and that was a floor she tended to avoid. This was the subbasement a story below the basement and she had not known it existed until now. Sonya is surprised by how clean and well-lit the area is. Sonya paused and put her face gear back on in case there were any fumes she should not be breathing.

She stepped forward and continued down the corridor. When she thought she reached the end, she stopped. It took her a moment to register that she was not alone anymore. She turned to see a woman dressed in white from head to toe. Sonya, being in her infectious care gear was unrecognizable.

Sonya remained silent. The woman asked, "Can I help you?"

Sonya paused, quickly going through her mind trying to come up with an acceptable answer. There was none. She could counter and ask this nurse what she was doing here, but that would not buy her anything. But luck was on her side.

"Ah, you must be the replacement." The woman in white pronounced.

Not sure what that meant, Sonya tried for a look of annoyance on her face and then turned to face her captive. "Yes, I am the replacement."

"Sorry doctor. It is just that it takes them a while to send a replacement on short notice."

Cautiously Sonya asked, "So why did the doctor leave without giving notice?"

"I am sure you will be able to answer that yourself once you see what we are dealing with."

Smartly, Sonya stopped the interrogation and let the nurse do all the talking. "That is fine. I do not get many coming down here, so my manners are not the best."

Sonya stared at the nurse. She was not wearing any of the standard infectious disease uniform, so Sonya assumed she was on her way in to work. She had a sense about her that said, 'I am the boss'. Her short, straight white hair with the uneven thin bangs emphasized the eyes that were open only enough to let Sonya know they were checking her out. As Sonya looks intently, she sees two vertical wrinkles, either side of the nurse's mouth that was thin lipped and curving downward. She was wearing a pale purple scarf around her neck, a light gray long sleeve sweater that seemed to have a cranberry long sleeve shirt under it. She had glasses on a strap dangling over her scarf as the only jewelry visible.

Sonya immediately knew this was not the type of person who answered a lot of questions.

"As you undoubtedly know, this is a care unit for chronic patients. Most of the patients are in some level of coma. We use this area to free up beds in the ICU."

The woman paused and turned. "By the way, my name is Lottie Bond, but most call me just, Nurse. I have been down here since the start of the virus, learning the routine so I do not expect you to catch on right away. I must caution you that we have developed a very new technique of caring for these patients and that is why it is secretive. No family or even other hospital staff are allowed down here. And most doctors relinquish the care of their patients when they are moved here."

Nurse Bond pauses, giving Sonya a moment before she says, "So, if you are ready, let's get to it."

Lottie walked slightly ahead of Sonya and stood in front of what appeared to be a mirror. She placed her hand on a silver box attached to the side of the mirror and it opened, gliding off to the right soundlessly.

"Hurry up Doctor... ah, what is your name."

This time she was quick on her feet as she scurried through the doorway and said, "Dr. Weston."

Lottie followed hastily, explaining as she slipped through. "It is usually only one at a time so when two go, we have to scurry fast. Once you are settled, we will make your print for the door."

Lottie paused and looked at Sonya. "Now, we do not sit on ceremony here. We go about doing our job and waste not a second as there are only a few of us on the staff. Understood?"

Sonya started to say, listen lady, I outrank you and will not be talked to like this, but something about her expression kept her mouth closed and she nodded instead.

"Okay, follow me." Lottie walked forward. It was like being in a room of mirrors as they were everywhere. So tiny, she almost missed it was a little silver pendant like fixture and Lottie whispered something. The entrance glided open. Over her shoulder, Lottie said, "Quickly." Sonya did as she was told.

She had barely stepped through when the entrance seemed to disappear as it glided into its place.

Sonya looked around her and saw her reflection everywhere looking back. She followed Lottie who was walking nimbly down what seemed to be at least a fifty-foot-long hall made of mirrors. As they advanced, Sonya glanced up and noticed, the ceiling was also mirrored.

Sonya wanted to ask what was with all the mirrors but decided to hold her tongue. She figured that even if she asked, she would not get an answer. This was all secret. They passed through one more hidden door with no hardware, apparently automatically activated.

When they reached the far end of the corridor, and Lottie opened the door, Sonya entered a familiar looking room. It was open and exceedingly long. It reminded her of the intensive care unit upstairs. There were the usual assortment of gadgets, EKG, and other medical equipment. Sonya barely had time to look around before Lottie was on the move again heading toward the far wall that was like all the walls in this place. Lottie opened it and this time did not rush her through, but the minute her feet were planted across the threshold, the door automatically slid close.

Once inside this new space, the first thing Sonya was aware of is the light, there was something strange about it and she lowered her head. Next, she felt the warmth and the humidity weighing heavily on her and she wished she could shed her coverings. As she was trying to adjust, she finally started to raise her head, but stopped in utter astonishment.

There were what appeared to be thousands of patients in the room and all of them were completely suspended in midair starting at about a foot from the floor. All of them were naked. Looking closely, Susan could see the wires piercing multiple points on the patient's long bones. The wires were connected to complicated metal frames and pulled taut. The patient's heads were supported by other wires from the ceiling which were attached to screw eyes in the patient's skulls. Susan had an impression of grotesque, horizontal sleeping marionettes.

"As you can see, the patients are all suspended by wires under tension."

"It is rather gruesome," Sonya said. She inquired, "What is that strange lighting."

"Oh, yes, we should put on glasses if we stay in here much longer. "Nurse Bond pulled out two pair of goggles.

"There is a low-level flux of ultraviolet light in here. It has been found useful in controlling bacteria as well as helping to maintain the integrity of the skin."

"The temperature in here is maintained at 94-point five Fahrenheit plus or minus five hundredths of a degree. The humidity is held at 82 percent with a one percent variance. That tends to reduce patient heat loss and hence reduce the patients' caloric needs. The humidity has reduced the respiratory infection problem which you know is critical for coma patients."

Sonya was spellbound. She gingerly moved closer to one of the suspended patients. A profusion of wires perforated various long bones. She looked up at the ceiling and saw that it was a maze of tracks for the trolleys.

"And there are no nurses."

"I am a nurse Sonya and there are two others on duty, plus one doctor. That is all that is needed"

"Well, so, we will head back and discuss your role in this project."

As they made their way down the halls of mirrors, Sonya was deep in thought. She had noticed something very strange about the patients and wondered if it had anything to do with the lights or the humidity. They were all blue.

"So?"

Sonya had only been half listening. "Sorry, what did you say?"

"We need to go to the office and get you processed. By the way, when do you start?"

"Ah, soon, soon. I have a few things to clear up. Can I come back and fill out the forms?"

She held her breath, waiting for Lottie's answer.

"Sure, Dr. Weston, no problem, but make it soon and call first. I will need to get out the paperwork for you to sign."

Sonya stopped at the exit door, turned, and put out her gloved hand. Thank you, Nurse. See you soon. With that, Lottie opened the door and Sonya walked out.

In the hallway she stopped to breathe. "What was that?" she whispered to herself. "Just what was that?"

As she hurried back up the stairwell Sonya understood the patients being naked. That allowed them to eliminate any contamination on clothing or blankets. The blue tinge to the skin of the hanging patients was a whole other issue to think about.

She knew there was a condition called methemoglobinemia that could be the cause, but that was an inherited condition and that many patients with the genetic mutation was an impossibility. So, she wondered, what else could it be. A low level of oxygen in the blood can cause the skin to appear bluish but that would require treatment and it did not seem to bother Nurse Lottie.

Chapter 28

"We have been called together for this virtual meeting to address an important issue. When diplomats met to form the United Nations in 1945, one of the things they discussed was setting up a global health organization. And that is when WHO came into existence as the essential leader to improve global health outcomes. Today WHO is perceived as the most effective organization at influencing policy for improving people's health at the global level."

"This COVID-19 pandemic is out of control and we as the heads of WHO offices in countries, territories and areas across the world must take action while there is still hope of controlling this virus." Director-General, Dr.Wodajo continued saying, "I have come up with a solution that needs to be presented to each Regional Director, but to eliminate bias and misunderstanding, I have asked the assistance of certain individuals to present the facts that lead to the solution we are about to present."

"Before reaching this conclusion I have monitored the health situation, trends, progress and performance of health systems around the world and reviewed the health data from household surveys, civil registration systems of vital events, and institution-based sources."

"I ask that you keep an open mind as the details will support our theory of what we must do to survive this pandemic. Just as it is done at our general meetings, this meeting is being translated directly to each of you in your own language. So, let's get started."

The view of the faces of those in attendance can see that they are anxious to get underway feeling quite certain that during the months of dealing with COVID-19, there cannot be any new way of approaching this pandemic, but they are willing to listen.

As for Dr. Wodajo, on one side he is glad they are doing a virtual meeting as he feels as though the group is more focused. Yet, on the other hand he worries that without hearing what needs to be said, some of the members will click out of the meeting. All he can hope is that the majority remains. There is no more stalling as he begins.

"The first speaker is Dr. Nathaniel Reed, an expert on the 1918 great flu epidemic. Dr. Reed…"

"Good morning. I will get right to the point." Dr. Reed is comfortable with virtual meetings as he has attended many of them during his life, maybe not with such dignitaries as those pictured in front of him now, all at the same time, but no matter. He clears his throat and begins.

"In 1918, the great flu epidemic took the world by surprise as it ravaged even the young and healthy. An estimated forty million people died as the epidemic stormed through the world. It would become the worse pandemic in recent history. This flu was given the designation "H1N1" for its unique traits. The "H" stood for hemagglutinin and the "N" for neuraminidases which are proteins found on the outer shell or envelope of the virus. As best could be discovered, this flu was a virus with genes of avian origin. Although there is not universal consensus regarding where the virus originated. What is known is, it spread worldwide during 1918 and 1919."

"In the United States, it was first identified in military personnel during the spring of 1918 and it is estimated that about 500 million people; or one-third of the world's population became infected with this virus. The number of deaths was estimated to be at least 50 million worldwide with about 675,000 occurring in the United States."

"At this 102 year anniversary of the 1918 pandemic of the H1N1 flu pandemic, which is sometimes referred to as the "Spanish flu," we still shutter at the high death rate it caused among healthy adults from ages 15 to 34 years. This pandemic lowered the average life expectancy in the United States by more than 12 years and until now, there has been no comparable death rate observed during any of the known flu seasons or pandemics that have occurred either prior to or following."

"Like a thief in the night, the 1918 virus arrived on a chilly autumn day in September of 1918. The illness spread to remote parts of the world practically decimating some Eskimo villages from the face of the earth. It was recorded that nearly twenty percent of Western Samoans perished. But what stood out was that the virus attacked the young adults who generally are spared the ravages of infectious diseases. Children were orphaned, families destroyed. Attempts to gather personal data was hard as those who lived through it said it was so horrible that they would not even talk about it."

"At the outset it was theorized that the virus was created by Germany and planted in Boston Harbor. One day you are fine, strong, and invulnerable. You might be busy at work in your office. Or maybe you were providing necessities for the war when it struck. You wake up one morning and find you have a headache. By the end of the day you announce you are not feeling well and need to go home. Your eyes start to burn, and you cannot stop shivering. You grab spare blankets and put them on the bed, but no number of blankets can keep you warm. You fall into a restless sleep, interrupted by nightmares brought on by delirium as your fever climbs. And when you drift out of sleep, into a semi-consciousness, your muscles ache, and your head throbs so you know that you are moving steadily toward death. It may take a few days or only take a few hours, but there is nothing that can stop the disease's progress. You die a horrible death. That was how it was described by non-medical victims of this virus who lived to share the memory."

Taking a sip of water gave him a chance to survey the faces. Dr. Reed knew he had their full attention.

"There were no requirements in those days to report cases of influenza, but it became a practice in the United States after, the second wave of the 1918 flu. Reports on the flu's reaches were reflected mostly from such places as prisons, the military, and some industries, which simply recorded absentees. There was no systematic attempt to track an epidemic."

Dr. Reed looked through his notes to come up with some examples to support the sources of information. When he found what he was looking for he began again.

"It moved quickly, like a thief in the night. In the U.S. the Ford Motor Company had more than 1,000 workers call in sick with the flu in March. In San Quentin prison, 500 of 1,900 prisoners became ill in April and May. On March 4, the flu came to a training camp for 20,000 recruits in Kansas. That month and the next, it also arrived at more than a dozen other Army camps."

"It spread just as quick. In April 1918, the flu epidemic appeared in France, the next month, it was in England, where King George V contacted the flu."

Dr. Reed put emphasis on King George V getting the flu before going on."

"The epidemic crested in England in June; at the same time, it cropped up in China and Japan. Asia, named it the three-day fever or, wrestler's fever."

"Germany labeled it the Flanders fever as it thwart battle plans there. The flu added to the troops misery of fighting hungry, cold and wet, weakening the men, and lowering their morale."

"Yet although much of the world fell ill that spring, there remained large areas that were untouched. Most of Africa and almost all of South America and Canada had no flu epidemic. And then in the summer of 1918 the flu seemed to vanish without a trace. But a few months later it was back with a vengeance. The second wave of the 1918 pandemic still was highly contagious. But this time it was a killer. By August it reached the populations of the Indian subcontinent, Southeast Asia, Japan, China, a large part of the Caribbean, and parts of Central and South America."

"Although about 20 percent of its victims had a mild case and recovered without incident, others almost immediately became deathly ill, unable to get enough oxygen because their lungs had filled with fluid. They died in days, or even hours, delirious with a high fever, gasping for breath, and finally lapsing into unconsciousness. In others, the illness began as an ordinary flu, with chills, fever, and muscle aches, but no untoward symptoms. By the fourth or fifth day of the illness, however, bacteria would swarm into their injured lungs and they would develop pneumonia that would either kill them or lead to a long period of convalescence."

"The second wave of the flu arrived in the United States in Boston, appearing among a group of sailors who docked at the Commonwealth Pier in August. The sailors were simply in transit, part of the vast movement of troops in a war that transformed daily life. And then some of those sailors in Boston got sick. On August 28, eight men got the flu. The next day, 58 were sick. By day four, the sick toll reached 81. A week later, it was 119, and that same day the first civilian was admitted to Boston City Hospital sick with the flu. Deaths soon followed. On September 8, three people died from the flu in Boston. That same day, the flu appeared in Fort Devens, Massachusetts, thirty miles west of Boston. Overnight, Fort Devens became a scene out of hell."

"The disease crept into Philadelphia. Philadelphia was among the hardest hit of all-American cities. And it was almost completely unprepared. Yet as the flu spread, the city did take a few precautions. On September 18, its health officials began a public campaign against coughing, spitting, and sneezing. Three days later, the city made influenza a reportable disease, which meant that records had to be kept of numbers of cases. On that same day, September 21, however, scientists reported good news-it seemed that the battle against influenza was won."

Dr. Reed paused to let the momentum sink in before starting again.

"But by October 1, the city was under siege. In one day, 635 cases of the flu were reported to public health officials. That, however, was an underestimate. Doctors had become so overwhelmed caring for the sick that most cases went unreported and the true numbers will never be known. On October 3, the city closed all schools, churches, theaters, pool halls, and other places of amusement in a frantic attempt to slow the spread of the disease. In the week that ended on October 5, as many as 2,600 were reported to have died in Philadelphia of the flu or its complications. The next week, the flu death reports reached more than 4,500. Hundreds of thousands were ill. Sick people arrived at hospitals in limousines, horse carts, and pushcarts. Within a month after the flu arrived in Philadelphia, nearly 11,000 people died from the disease."

Dr. Reed glanced around at the faces on this screen, hoping to get a read on them before presenting the rest of his talk. Everyone was still there, and everyone had expressions of interest.

"Undertakers were overwhelmed. In some cases, the dead were left in their homes for days. At the city morgue, bodies were piled three and four deep in the corridors and in almost every room covered only with dirty and often bloodstained sheets. Most were not embalmed and without ice. Some were mortifying and emitting a nauseating stench. The doors of the building were left open, probably for circulation of air."

"By the first week of October, the flu had spread to every part of the globe except for a few remote islands and Australia. Few public officials anticipated the disaster and almost no members of the public did. The outbreak, in fact, was preceded by soothing words from medical authorities not touting the severity of the situation. No one from any walk of life or in any location around the world was safe from the virus and it was taking out the much needed health workers who tried to save lives to those with the knowledge to combat the illness as well."

"Public health departments gave out gauze masks for people to wear in public. In Tucson, Arizona, the board of health issued a ruling that no person shall appear in any street, park, or place where any business is transacted, or in any other public place within the city of Tucson, without wearing a mask consisting of at least four thicknesses of butter cloth or at least seven thicknesses of ordinary gauze, covering both the nose and the mouth. In Albuquerque, New Mexico, the schools were closed, and movie theaters darkened "

"Trying to identify it, the plague of 1918 is deemed influenza, even though it is like no influenza ever seen before. Some likened it to a biblical prophecy coming true. But though influenza never makes the list of deadly plagues it indeed is in that category. It was not just that the epidemic struck during wartime, when the nation was distracted by the horrors of battle. It was also that the epidemic came before scientists had any idea of how to isolate an influenza virus and no one understood what viruses were, since DNA and RNA, the genetic material of viruses and the clues to their destructiveness, had not yet been discovered."

"So, the 1918 flu pandemic swept the globe in months, and ended when the war did, disappearing as mysteriously as it appeared. And when it was over, humanity had been struck by a disease that killed more people in a few months' time than any other illness in the history of the world."

Dr. Reed pauses to let the enormity of the situation sink in. He takes a sip of water, frowns, and starts again.

From the inception of WHO we made important decisions to combat influenza virus pandemics starting with the Asian Flu from 1956-1958 that resulted in a death toll of 2 million. We traced its origin to China in 1956 and in its two-year spree, the Asian Flu traveled from the Chinese province of Guizhou to Singapore, Hong Kong, and the United States. Estimates for the death toll of the Asian Flu vary depending on the source, but the World Health Organization places the final tally at approximately 2 million deaths."

Then in 1968 another flu pandemic arrived and was named the Hong Kong flu, responsible for one million deaths. We traced its source to the H3N2 strain of the Influenza A-virus a genetic offshoot of the H2N2 subtype. From the first reported case on July 13, 1968 in Hong Kong, it took only 17 days before outbreaks of the virus were reported in Singapore and Vietnam, and within three months had spread to The Philippines, India, Australia, Europe, and the United States. While the 1968 pandemic had a comparatively low mortality rate of .5% it still resulted in the deaths of more than a million people. Estimates for the death toll of the Hong Kong Flu recorded by the World Health

Organization places the final tally at approximately one million deaths, including approximately 500,000 residents of Hong Kong."

Dr. Reed breathe a sigh of relief at reaching the end of his talk. "Thank you for your kind attention to my windy report."

Dr. Wodajo gave it a moment and then thanked Dr. Reed. "I think we should all take a slight break now and then return to hear our next speaker.

Sounds could be heard of chairs moving, and voices chatting between members with personnel in their remote locations. When all had returned, the meeting was again called to order.

Chapter 29

"Next we will hear from Dr. Aresenio Petuka on the 2009 H1N1 pandemic in the same manner as Dr. Reed to help each of you see the obvious -- that we are facing a real enemy and if history is correct, we need to approach this with vigor and knowledge. Dr. Petuka."

"Thank you, Director General."

"Influenza pandemic H1N1 of 2009, also known by the name swine flu, was the first major influenza outbreak in the 21st century. It was noted for its rapid global spread, facilitated by an unusually high degree of viral contagion as modern-day travel increased passenger travel."

"At the time obtaining accurate global data was obstructed by underreporting and difficulty in obtaining samples from affected individuals, especially in developing countries. This played a part in the accuracy of the final figures of 622,482 cases and 18,500 deaths confirmed by laboratory analysis. Indeed, later analyses based on statistical models considering countries with limited influenza-surveillance data indicated that the actual total number of deaths from the outbreak ranged between 284,000 to 575,000."

"The H1N1 virus symptoms varied from diarrhea, chills, and vomiting, and in rare cases respiratory failure. It passed from human to human primarily through inhalation of infectious particles or contact with an infected individual or contaminated surface."

"The modes of transmission increased the potential for global spread with at least 22 percent of the people who came into contact with an infected individual coming down with the virus."

"The virus first appeared in February 2009 in a small town called La Gloria in Veracruz, Mexico. A young boy, who later became known as patient zero, was discovered to be infected with a previously unknown strain of influenza virus. Although the boy represented the first known case, researchers who continue to investigate the virus suspect that it emerged sometime in 2008. The following month the virus materialized in Mexico City. The virus was exposed as a strain of swine influenza and was then referred to as the swine flu."

"By the end of April more than 2,000 cases of the swine flu had been reported in Mexico. This new H1N1 virus emerged in the United States in Texas, New York, California, and several other states. Two days later, CDC laboratory testing revealed the first two cases of this virus as an 8-year-old living in California about 130 miles away from the first patient who was tested as part of an influenza surveillance project. The individuals had no known connection to each other and the strain differed in some ways."

"Testing showed that these two viruses were resistant to the two antiviral drugs Amantadine, used to treat the symptoms of Parkinson's disease; and Rimantadine, used to prevent and treat infections caused by influenza A virus. But the two viruses were susceptible to the neuraminidase inhibitors Oseltamivir and Zanamivir that work by stopping the spread of the flu virus in the body and shorten the time that flu symptoms such as a stuffy or runny nose, sore throat, cough, muscle or joint aches, tiredness, headache, fever, and chills last. CDC began an immediate investigation into the situation in coordination with state and local animal and human health officials in California."

Dr. Petuka paused, taking a sip of water as he surveyed the video faces. As had been predicted by the Director General, he had all the members undivided attention. He had thought this kind of reporting was not necessary, but the recounts opened his eyes to the gravity of the situation. Dr. Petuka continued.

"On April 25, 2009, the Director General declared the outbreak a public health emergency of international concern. Within days of the announcement, the H1N1 virus reached Spain, having been carried to that country by individuals traveling by airplane from Mexico. Confirmed cases of H1N1 infection also occurred in Germany, Austria, the United Kingdom, Israel, and New Zealand. Several provinces in Canada, including Nova Scotia, Alberta, Ontario, and British Columbia, also were affected. Although most persons who fell ill recovered, there were deaths in Mexico and the United States. In addition, many more cases of the disease were suspected in other countries, including Australia, Chile, Colombia, and France."

"Although it was not clear whether all the cases in these other countries were caused by the H1N1 virus, several of the already confirmed cases in multiple countries demonstrated evidence of human-to-human transmission. This evidence 4 days later prompted the Director to declare a pandemic alert for the H1N1 outbreak. A level 5 pandemic alert indicated that WHO believed a swine flu pandemic was imminent and called for accelerated distribution of drugs to treatment facilities and rapid implementation of measures to control viral spread."

Dr. Petuka paused again to take a drink of something stronger than water. He leaned back in his seat, taking the upper half of his face out of the camera and then slowly his full face reappeared.

"By late April 2009, Mexico had become the epicenter of the H1N1 strain and things got crazy because of the label of swine flu. It was called swine flu because in the beginning, the people who caught it had direct contact with pigs. This of course led to people afraid to eat pork, but it all changed when a new virus emerged that spread among people who had not been near pigs. So, from that point on it was officially renamed Influenza A (H1N1) or called 2009 H1N1."

"As early as May 1, 2009, CDC test kits began shipping to domestic and international public health laboratories. From May 1 through September 1, 2009, more than 1,000 kits were shipped to 120 domestic and 250 international laboratories in 140 countries."

"By June 2009, more than 70 countries had reported cases of 2009, H1N1 infection, and community level outbreaks were ongoing in various parts of the world. By June 19, all 50 states in the United States, the District of Columbia, Puerto Rico, and the U.S. Virgin Islands had reported cases of the virus infection. The United States continued to report the largest number of H1N1 cases of any country worldwide, although most people who became ill recovered without requiring medical treatment."

"It became obvious by late June when more than 30 summer camps in the U.S. reported outbreaks of 2009, H1N1 influenza illness and the estimated number rose to at least 1 million cases of influenza that group gatherings needed to be eliminated."

"As the outbreak spread, the CDC began receiving reports of school closures and implementation of community-level social distancing measures meant to slow the spread of the disease. School administrators and public health officials were following their pandemic plans and doing everything they could to slow the spread of illness. Measures included staying home when ill unless to seek medical care, avoiding large gatherings, telecommuting, and implementing school closures. When the second wave of illnesses struck schools had reopened. St. Louis Children's Hospital set up two tents and a waiting room in its parking garage after a 30% surge in emergency visits for flu and asthma."

"By early June 2009 more than 25,000 cases and nearly 140 deaths from H1N1 flu had been reported worldwide, the majority of deaths having occurred in Mexico and the greatest number of cases—more than 13,000—having appeared in the United States."

"After mid-July, disease activity in most countries decreased, but by the last two weeks of August 2009, H1N1 influenza activity again began to increase in the United States. In September 2009, the Food and Drug Administration announced its approval of four influenza vaccines to protect against the virus and were able to place their first orders for the vaccine."

Preparing to go into his summation, Dr. Petuka paused and the members waited. He was silent, sitting as still as a statue, no part of his body showing any movement, then suddenly he began talking again.

"A human-to-human spread swine influenza virus had been rarely documented and had not been known to result in widespread community outbreaks among people. CDC remained in close contact with the international health community as the outbreak unfolded and on April 18, 2009, under the International Health Regulations the United States International Health Regulations Program reported the 2009 H1N1 influenza cases to the World Health Organization (WHO). The cases also were reported to the Pan American Health Organization (PAHO), Canada and Mexico, as part of the Security and Prosperity Partnership of North America."

"That summer, in preparation for an increase in H1N1 activity, the U.S. Department of Health and Human Services had secured resources for the production of 120 million doses of vaccine, expecting that the full stock would be available by mid-October. However, only about 11 million doses had been delivered by that time, and delays in vaccine production left a large percentage of the population susceptible to infection."

"The CDC estimated that from April 2009 through mid-April 2010 between 8,870 and 18,300 deaths, between 43 million and 89 million cases, and between 195,000 and 403,000 H1N1-related hospitalizations had occurred in the United States. In India, 44,987 cases, with 83 deaths and by August 2010, worldwide more than 214 countries and overseas territories or communities reported laboratory confirmed cases of pandemic influenza H1N1 2009, including over 18,449 deaths. In Argentina, Chile, New Zealand, and Australia, overall influenza activity remained low. In Asia, the most active areas of pandemic influenza virus transmission were in parts of India, and to a much lesser extent, in parts of Nepal and Bhutan."

Dr. Petuka then went silent.

Dr. Wodajo, unsure that Dr. Petuka had completed his report, waited for a sign. The space of silent time stretched beyond five minutes when Dr. Wodajo could wait no longer and taking the initiative said, "We thank you Dr. Petuka for your report, which I assume has ended."

Dr. Petuka nodded.

"Let us break for lunch and when we return, Dr. Neil Warren will talk to us about the COVID-19 virus. Let us say that we will reconvene at 2:00 p.m. Eastern Standard Time. Please shut down your connection and I will send a fresh link for each of you to rejoin at that time."

One by one the screens went blank and then disappeared entirely as the connections were dropped. When the final screen was gone, Dr. Wodajo shut down his connection.

Dr. Wodajo stood and stretched his body. He then tried to suppress a yawn as he turned to face his staff member whom he had chosen to be part of the initial meeting. He seemed to need reassurance of the outcome thus far and with a rise of his eyebrows his staff gave him that.

"Sir, you are doing the right thing and from the reports given they cannot expect to be safe from this new coronavirus."

Dr. Wodajo nodded.

"Plus, with the average age of this group, most can expect to not recover."

"Yes. You need not worry sir. They will be willing to proceed."

Dr. Wodajo thanked his adviser and then they sat down to eat lunch together. Done buffet style, there were cold cuts, cheeses, lettuce, tomatoes and onions and a variety of breads. Dr. Wodajo felt surprisingly relaxed as he prepared his sandwich and even made a joke about the drink bar that included fruit juices, water, tea, and coffee. "So, where's the real drinks," he said jokingly. They knew as well as he that he had to be totally present during this meeting.

The hour passed quickly and soon it was time to resume the meeting. Dr. Wodajo took his seat and the links were sent out for the members to rejoin. He watched as each member activated their reconnection to the session.

Chapter 30

"Welcome back. I can see everyone is in attendance so we will begin. Dr. Neil Warren, our expert on COVID-19 will take us through what we have all been experiencing this year. Dr. Warren…"

"Thank you Dr. Wodajo." Dr. Warren cleared his throat and not wasting a second, started right in.

"The most important difference between the two pandemics of the 21st century, H1N1 illnesses responded well to anti-viral drugs already used to treat the flu. People in close contact with someone who caught H1N1 were commonly given the drugs as a precaution, limiting its spread. But there is no approved treatment for COVID-19. The incubation period for H1N1 flu was about one day to one week, meaning people learned more quickly that they might be infected, and therefore contagious. It is thought that COVID-19 symptoms may appear up to two weeks after a possible exposure."

"So, my friends, how did we get here? The novel coronavirus outbreak, which began in Wuhan, China, in December, has expanded to touch nearly every corner of the world. Hundreds of thousands of people have been sickened and thousands of others have died. We had to declare the virus a global health emergency. We had to rate COVID-19's global risk of spread and impact as at the most serious designation the organization gives."

"There are many who close their ears and eyes to the seriousness of this situation, but that needs to stop. I want to start at the beginning."

"On December 31, 2019, we were aware of a mysterious pneumonia, sickening dozens in Wuhan, China, and that many of those patients had visited a live animal market in Wuhan. At that time, the authorities said there was no evidence of the virus spreading from person to person."

"On January 11, 2020, China reported its first novel coronavirus death as a 61-year-old man who had visited the live animal market in Wuhan. By January 21st, the first case was confirmed in the United States as a man in his 30s from Washington state, who traveled to Wuhan. Japan, South Korea and Thailand also reported their first cases one day prior."

"By January 23, China imposes strict lockdown in Wuhan, China, and residents begin wearing protective mask and can be seen walking down deserted streets in a city with a population of 11.08 million. And, Wuhan, China became known as the epicenter of the outbreak, suspending flights and trains and shutting down subways, buses and ferries to stem the spread of the virus."

"By January 30, for the sixth time in history, the World Health Organization declares a "public health emergency of international concern and the world takes on a new face."

"On February 5, buses arrive near the cruise ship Diamond Princess that carried 3,600 passengers. The ship is quarantined off the coast of Yokohama, Japan, while passengers and crew undergo health screenings. The number of confirmed cases on board the ship would eventually swell to more than 700, making it one of the largest outbreaks outside of China."

"On February 11, the novel coronavirus was renamed COVID-19. "Co" for coronavirus, "Vi" for virus and "D" for disease. They purposely avoided naming COVID-19 after a geographical location, animal or group of people, so as not to brand people or places."

"March 2, 2020, we began our daily briefings on the new coronavirus dubbed COVID-19, at the WHO headquarters, in Geneva and by March 3, 2020 the: CDC lifted restrictions for virus testing from only those who had traveled to an outbreak area, or had close contact with people diagnosed with COVID-19, or with severe symptoms."

"People began hoarding hand sanitizer, paper products as shipments of goods were hampered by the virus and grocery store shelves began to show the results. No one could count on getting all the items that they usually expected to find in stores."

"It wasn't until March 13, President The U.S. President finally admits there is a crisis going on in America and declares a national emergency."

Though Dr. Warren says this as not confrontational, the expression on President The U.S. President's face shows his distaste. Dr. Warren continues.

"On the heels of that announcement, the CDC warns against holding or attending gatherings larger than 50 people, including conferences, festivals, parades, concerts, sporting events and weddings. The warning extends for eight weeks to avoid introducing COVID-19 into new communities, but by March 17, the coronavirus is present in all 50 states. Northern California issues a 'shelter in place' meaning residents are required to remain at home unless they are leaving the house for an essential reason or are exercising outdoors."

"While this was happening in the US, on March 18, China reported no new local infections for the first time since the outbreak began. It is hopeful that it could be that China's outbreak is ending and a second wave of infection can be eliminated even if they lift their government's strict lockdown measures. This gives hope, but it is quickly dashed."

"By March 26, the United States leads the world in COVID-19 cases with 82,000 and 1000 deaths they outnumber any other country in the world. With businesses closed all around the US, they are facing financial effects and on March 27, The U.S. President signs $2 trillion stimulus bill guaranteeing loans to small businesses and creates a lending system for distressed companies. It also provides financial aid to hospitals on the frontlines of the crisis."

"New York City reports that more than 15,000 people tested positive for COVID-19 and that would account for roughly half of the infections in the country. New York City has just over 8 million people with the total population of New York State being in the range of 19 ½ million. That designated New York City as the epicenter of the COVID-19 virus.

"With the increase in cases in the United States, it is Italy that reports on March 19, its death toll surpasses China's as it tops 4,000 despite its much smaller population of just over 60 million. The following week, with a population of around 47 million COVID-19 deaths in Spain would similarly eclipse deaths in China."

"In India measures are taken to enforce the lockdown. One incident reported that three men were forced to perform sit ups while holding their ear lobes, as a punishment for stepping out without a valid reason during a lockdown in Ahmedabad, India after the country issued on March 24, a 21-day complete lockdown. This is a country with 1.3 billion citizens, making the need for social distancing even more advantageous to halting the spread of the virus."

"In London, the Prime Minister of the United Kingdom gave daily COVID-19 press briefing at Downing Street starting on March 22, 2020. On March 27, the prime minister tests positive for COVID-19 after having a high fever and persistent cough. He announced he would continue to lead the government via video conferences."

Dr. Warren pauses to let this sink in before adding, "He has been effective in ruling electronically."

"April 2, 2020 the global cases of COVID-19 hit one million cases around the world. Given testing shortages, undiagnosed cases and the possibility of obscure government reporting of outbreaks, the actual number of people effected is believed to be much higher."

"Attempts to trace the infections has revealed additional information. For instance, the United States found that the coronavirus reached them in February 2020 instead of April and that it did not come through China, but Europe. Facts are still being gathered, but what remains constant is everywhere in the world, the virus has swept and taken away the basic staples of our way of life."

Dr. Warren again pauses for emphasis as he brings his talk to a close.

"Countries are prematurely lifting lockdowns and closures even though there are reports of a second, and possibly a third wave. We tend to lean toward information mainly coming out of the United States as it is the country that feels it is the most impenetrable, yet we know that is not true. But consider now the numbers across the globe. There have been a million and a half cases of COVID-19 reported with over five hundred deaths and six million recoverees of those human cases that we know."

"Thank you for your attention."

Dr. Wodajo gave the group time to settle after hearing Dr. Warren's report and then began his presentation of what they must do now.

"What I am about to say to you will only strengthen our cases for what we are going to propose and that is until now and not broadly announced, this virus has gone beyond the human element. It has now been found in the common household pets like our dogs and our cats, birds, and amphibians. Soon, even as we find a way to contain it in humans, we will be faced with another level of decision."

"The question is are you ready for this? Do you know what to do? We are a group of brilliant individuals but being under the pressure of running a country, playing the politic games and forced to travel around the globe for face to face encounters, we are the most frangibility of all the population and our 'jobs' force us to make major decisions on what needs to be done. Decisions that if we are honest would be best made from those highly acclaimed in the medical profession."

Dr. Wodajo stood, his face no longer present on the screen. Slowly he sat back down. Took a sip of water and reached the point of the discussion they have all been waiting for.

"Our hospitals, our medical staff, and sadly, our morgues are all overtaxed and with no hospital beds or medical professions to take a special interest in a person because of their status, is not going to happen. So, to speak on this situation, listen to the famous Dr. Sun Simiao. Dr. Simiao if you please."

Chapter 31

"Thank you, Director-General."

"The development of a vaccine is not going to happen any time soon."

The tenseness of every muscle in his face is apparent as he continues.

"So, what happens in making the right vaccine? Live attenuated and inactivated vaccines are easy to make. They are the 'classic vaccines' that we know from the measles and the flu. You isolate a little bit of virus, weaken, or 'inactivate' it, and then inject it into a human being in a portion that is small enough to trigger a reaction from your body. Production capacity for such vaccines has existed since the 1950s. If such a vaccine would work, you can go to market relatively quickly."

"We also have experience with recombinant protein vaccines used, for the human papillomavirus that causes cervical cancer, or for the hepatitis B vaccine. The latter vaccine exists since the 1980s. This type of vaccine does not use the virus itself, but the proteins on the outside of it."

"In the case of the coronavirus, these vaccines would use the 'spikes of the crown' of the virus which the virus uses to attach itself to our cells. If you inject a vaccine that will make us produce antibodies to block the protein from attaching itself, then, the virus might not be able to enter our cells."

"It is not certain whether human antibodies, elicited against those proteins, will protect you from the virus. For the novel coronavirus, there are good signs it could work since it did for SARS and MERS, in some animal models. Still, if this technique works, it might take a little longer to set up the production and administration, but it is certainly possible since it is already in use for papilloma and hepatitis B."

"Finally, if one of the above three principles does not work, there are also the DNA, RNA or Vectored vaccines. The principle for all of them is that you take a piece of the genetic coding of the virus, and inject it into the human body, where it is taken up by your cells and they produce the 'spike protein' of the virus, against which your immune system will make the antibodies.

The technique is new and complicated, and it is part of the 'third generation' of vaccines. Clearly, this technique could work, but we have less experience with it, especially to produce and use it at scale. It would, therefore, take more time."

"A commission, such as the National Institutes of Health in the US, or the Coalition for Epidemics Preparedness Innovation in Switzerland, would have to decide whether the various vaccine candidates have to do testing with animals for safety. If the technique is deemed safe, it will go quickly. If not, you will need to do a toxicity tests with animals and such tests can take at least six months in a traditional program."

Dr. Simiao seems to be looking at each face in the various screens, giving the sense that they are all included, and it is important for him to see their individual reactions. He then continues.

"After this phase, the real race to a vaccine starts, with clinical tests on humans. It starts with Phase I, with a few dozen patients. It is a safety phase. This Phase I takes probably at least two months, because you first need to inject the vaccine to a small number of patients and wait a week or longer to get results. Then you do the same with another few people, and with a higher dose, and you wait and continue the process until you get to a target dose."

"Then comes Phase II, with hundreds of patients, to prove the vaccine candidate creates anti-bodies and creates immunity response. This phase uses healthy people who are not necessarily faced with the virus, and it will also take a few months. You need a 3-4-week interval in between each to see how the body reacts. So, for this phase again you need at least two--up to three months."

The doctor can see from the expressions that the members are counting the time spent on testing. This pleases him.

"Then comes Phase III, where you do a real test for effectiveness, and protective immunity. This is the 'make or break' phase to determine whether we have an initial 'winner'. But the phase will take even longer, as you will need to include a lot of people in your trial and you need to follow them over time to know if there is a difference in infection between the groups. Right now, the problem is that many areas have either strict lockdown measures in or they have very few infections anymore. That is until the second wave comes."

"Either way, this phase will last six months, or longer, and for the front-runners, will likely start in the fall of 2020."

"Once we have a winner the vaccine then goes to manufacturing, distribution and administration. How long this phase lasts, depends on the category that comes through. You can look at a few to many months. A good example is the influenza virus. That is being made every year in a couple of months."

Dr. Simiao looks as overwhelmed as the information he has shared. He swings his arms out from his side as he slowly rises until his face and arms are no longer visible. There is a long period of silence as the members lean forward in their viewing screens trying to see Dr. Simiao. Finally, he sits back down.

"So, my colleagues, in the end, SARS-CoV2 vaccines will not be realistically available for another 12-18 months. And even then, we must be lucky through every phase of the process. Until then, we better get ready for a summer like no other."

"Thank you Dr. Simiao. We will take a half hour to think over what you have shared and then reconvene for the final presentation."

When the group return it is obvious, they are exhausted both physically and mentally, which is the exact state the leader had hoped for, since this mental fatigue would serve two purposes. It would take more of an effort on their part to focus and in so doing, make it easier to convince them that what he is proposing is the best alternative.

Chapter 32

"Welcome back my friends. I know you are tired and ready to call it a day, but believe me, you must be adequately informed to make an intelligent decision on what we are suggesting. So, Dr. Sun Simiao if you will continue."

"Let me begin by saying that pandemics are large-scale outbreaks of infectious disease that can greatly decrease morbidity and mortality over a wide geographic area and cause significant economic, social, and political disruption. What we can predict at this point is that the world's food will be limited and all resources taken up and that the only alternative is to create a drug that would put people asleep until the pandemic is over and they have the cure."

It is easy to read the expressions on the faces of the members. They are shocked, but they are listening. It is exactly the reaction they had hoped. There are separate conversations going on. Then, one member after another talk over each other, trying to be heard by the group.

For the first time in a long time, Dr. Wodajo raises the gavel, lowering it quickly on the top of his mahogany desk. "Please my friends, order...order."

After a moment or two, the silence returns as each member leans closer to their monitor as if sure they heard wrong or are afraid they did not.

"So, we are suggesting that each of you be sedated."

The rumpus starts up again.

"Here me out...please."

Dr, Wodajo decides to take over and deliver the final blow. His voice is loud, ringing above the murmurs and direct confrontations from those faces on the screens. He speaks confidently and assuredly.

"I know what you are thinking, and it is only half the reality. We are talking about sedating each of you…"

The uproar starts again and Dr. Wodajo lowers the gravel once more. When he has their attention, he continues.

"All of you, along with your heads of state, will be taken to a location, that must remain secret and safe. You will be sedated so that each of you will be unaware of where you are and upon your arrival will be monitored by a medical professional you trust to care for you personally and one who will not disclose any details. You will also have another individual who you have total confidence in that will be your direct contact to your country while you are sedated. This person will 'run the country' with the information you relay to them. These two individuals will be the only ones you will be in contact with. Then when it is deemed safe, each of you will be returned to your countries."

"Is not this being a little dramatic? Why not have us sequestered in our personal residence in our countries."

"Yes, it may seem dramatic, but it is the only way we can assure that you will live through this second wave that is about to hit and if it is like the 1918 second wave, you will not want to be around for it. Plus, it would be very costly to keep each of you in a facility separated and in need of many things that we will provide equally to each of you."

"Then as has already begun, there is always someone who takes advantage of a crisis and might blame one, or both of you for what is happening and threaten your life. We do not want to take that chance. The country is already struggling with the coronavirus and the results it has on our economy. We need you, Health Representatives, and you, Heads of State to be safe."

The message is clear, noticeably clear, and now made sense of why they were asked to include their Heads of State at the meeting. Dr. Wodajo gave each of them time to consult and slowly witnessed nods from the members that he hoped meant they were on board. The first question was no surprise.

"So, what is the assurance that the medical assistant or the advisor we choose will not bring the disease to us," asked the U.S. President.

"I am glad you asked. What we will do is have each of them put through a full checkup, cleaned on the premises and redressed before they can enter the area."

"So, how will we know that the country is being run according to our instructions?" asked Europe's W.H.O. member.

"Because you will have a private data connection securely connecting you to your country with high data speeds. It is a private network data transport service which does not traverse the public Internet and is inherently secure with no data encryption needed."

Another member asks, "So, we, nor anyone else beyond this point will know where we are, or physically see us. Wouldn't that cause suspicion?"

"Think about it. Recent research supports the idea that visual communication can be more powerful than verbal communication, suggesting in many instances that people learn and retain information that is presented to them visually much better than that which is only provided verbally. So, you will be visually and verbally available and for all intents and purposes your country will assume you are doing and being where you always are."

"And where is that?"

"In your homes, on a jet, visiting other dignitaries…all in the name of running your country. The only impossible piece is you will have no face-to-face contact with anyone."

"Yes, so there it all falls apart."

"No, not necessarily. In the interest of keeping you safe, your country will not want you to be doing any face-to-face confrontations. They will understand you are practicing what you preach. Social distancing, remember, is the name of the game."

"So, answer me this. What if a revolt starts? What then?"

"Well, we've thought of that and it won't make a difference. You will be handling it like you always do…send out the troops and give them instructions after talking with your internal staffs. You will always have your thumb on the country. Just like always. And a revolution can only be initiated by you or another country. You are all here and on equal grounds, making it easy to solve the problem before it festers."

The members again are talking to their constituents. The Director-General was right. Everything he said is true and whether they wanted to admit it, they were the talking marionette, handing out orders, but only participating through others. The times where they would make an appearance and not show, would not matter because they were under the cover of the pandemic.

"So, how soon?"

Dr. Wodajo, pauses rubbing his hands together.

"Now."

"What?" Dr. Wodajo is again glad they are all separated from one another as voices raise and insults are slung, blaming each other for the predicament they are in now. China takes the blunt of the accusations with the United States close on their heels.

Not letting the disruption continue, Dr. Wodajo shouts, "Now each of you already know the people you trust in this situation and can relay their names. You can prepare a statement for your country informing them that you will be in dispose to prevent being infected and that the advisor you choose will be responsible for running the country in your physical absence. In this statement you will inform your people that the advisor will be in close contact with you daily for instructions on any issues either ongoing or presented in the future."

"So how long are we talking?"

The director general clears his throat and says, "We are talking at least one year!"

Then came the question most anticipated. "You do not think I am going to go away and leave my family? That is the craziest thing I ever heard of." He could not determine who spoke, but the concern was repeatedly echoed by other members of the group, some getting up and moving out of camera range.

The director-general understood their frustration and in the back of their minds they knew they had to leave their family behind. As they mulled the matter over, they realized that if the whole family disappeared, it would cause a sensation especially for such an extended amount of time.

When all the leaders were seated in front of the camera, the director-general could tell, they were accepting that though undesirable they could see no alternative to the decision handed down. There would be no more resistance.

"Listen everyone, we are running out of time. You must make a decision."

As Dr. Wodajo waits, he tries to convince himself that he will get positive responses from all 194 member states. He must.

"We will be safe? We have your word?"

"Yes, to you, and a big Yes to the safety of your family and country. Now, on a different note, we have assigned younger medical workers to treat coronavirus patients to avoid endangering more seasoned employees. To be honest, if older doctors get infected, their immune system is much weaker, but their knowledge is what will eventually lead to a cure and the end of the pandemic."

"As for you, you will be in the hands of your countries medical advisors who are the most knowledgeable on your care, and medical research. Your doctor will be with you at all times making sure you remain in the best of health throughout this pandemic."

Dr. Wodajo paused and glanced across the screens before adding, "Tell me, who among us could not go for a nice long rest."

That eases the tension, and he hears a few chuckles. These are leaders of countries who are used to not letting the country or even their family know where they are every minute of each day. It is for their own safety and their families. So that would not be a problem if they continue to provide the guidance the country needs and are able to relate to current as well as past issues. It could work. No, it would work.

"So, are all of you in agreement. It would not be fair or ethical otherwise."

"Director-general, you said 'the members. What about Liechtenstein, Cook Islands and Niue, they are not members."

This was an easy one. "Well, as you know Liechtenstein is one of the world's two doubly landlocked countries, the other being Uzbekistan. The Cook Island is a group of 15 islands scattered over a vast area. The largest island is Rarotonga, but again, the country is landlocked. And Niue is a small island nation in the South Pacific Ocean. Each of these are separate from our countries and have not been found to have the virus at all and to make sure that continues to be the case, each of our countries is blocking them from travel to or from the islands. They are the easiest areas to be totally isolated without force if each of your countries do not allow contact or travel. Does that answer your question?"

There are several nods and verbal positive expressions.

Dr. Wodajo gives them a chance to talk further with their medical advisors.

"So, it must be all or none. To eliminate any confusion, you have two signs in front of you. One is 'Yes' and the other, 'No". You will hold the sign up so that every member can see it. To have you respond verbally will be difficult."

Dr. Wodajo holds his breath, waiting. He sees the signs being raised, one after the other. Finally, all 194 members have their signs held up in front of them and Dr. Wodajo scans the monitors, silently counting. His shoulders drop down and his head raises. Out of the camera view, his fingers tap the desk. The anticipation, the tension has made him speechless as he tries to mouth the words that each of the members already knows. Finally, he pulls himself together. "It is unanimous. Thank you for believing in us. Thank you for giving us this time to explain such a difficult matter."

"So now, what happens?"

"Yes, your medical advisor has papers for you to sign. You will then read the prepared statement to your country, explaining that you will be indispose, but running the country and that whoever you have appointed to act in your stead will be announced. That person will be informed by your medical advisor and share only the information we have given him in a prepared statement."

"Once you have signed the papers, you will be flown immediately to an undisclosed location and because no one is aware of what is going on, no one will be trying to find out where you are going."

That ended the meeting. Dr. Wodajo watched as each screen went blank and then he turned to his assistant. "So, that went well?"

They laughed finally allowing themselves to relax. The worse was over. Now it was out of their hands and the responsibility of the staff in Virginia where their new quarters would be.

Chapter 33

Doctors, researchers, and scientists around the world spend days in labs searching for new cures and treatments that could counter the effects of COVID-19 and so far, it alludes them. They work in a constant state of tension hammering away years of their lives into research and knowing that while they search the patients whose life, they fight for continue to suffer and even die. It is the same old story of the hunt for the right drugs to save life and the resulting failure after failure before they succeed. No one wants COVID-19 to continue its onslaught and end with months of work flaming out along with the people.

But this is what they do even knowing that the chance of that miracle of success will meet with so many promising ideas turned into dead ends and even when there is hope, getting the drug approved by the Food and Drug Administration takes a long time and could be too late to do any good.

Day after day their minds focus on the oxymoron combination of accuracy and speed. Even when medical science moves as fast as it can it is still an agonizingly slow process.

They split up in teams of expertise to deal with the specific issues of the body versus COVID-19. They depend on the technological advances in biomedical sciences as their hope that the process will not lead to failure.

Taking it cautiously was the beginning course, but as time passed, lives were loss and COVID-19 was quickly becoming the winner, they took a more aggressive method.

At the hospitals when the first few patients took a serious turn for the worse, they worked diligently trying to keep them alive with the drugs and equipment they had at their disposal. From country to country the word was passed on that nothing was working. When the few became many, desperation set in and the word went out to find something that would work before the whole world population disappeared from the face of the earth. It seemed dramatic at first, but then time proved that this was a high probability. So, the search for a cure or even a treatment began with every possible theory for development being the focus.

Therefore, when the good news came, no one second guessed it. Researchers are constantly coming up with advances in medicine and no one worried that this vaccine was not touted as a cure, but a treatment. They understood not all medical treatments end with the patient no longer having the condition. There have been many, like hepatitis B where the person will always have the condition, but medical treatments can help to manage the disease.

It is a fact that it is possible that a disease that can be treated but not cured today may be cured in the future, giving them more time to find the right medicine or scientific development to end the recurrence of such a thing as COVID-19.

Sometimes it comes down to want to save lives and will do whatever it takes to achieve that goal.

Only COVID-19 seemed to reduce the trend. Every possible drug alone or in combination had been tried with little success in combating the effects of COVID-19 until they came up with this drug cocktail of basically Methemoglobin and Methamphetamine. It seemed to work.

From a group of scientists working on the effects this disease has on the human body came a brilliant deduction. Methemoglobin normally exists in small amounts in the blood. However, when methemoglobin levels increase, the blood is less efficient in circulating oxygen. The resulting lack of oxygen throughout the body can cause symptoms such as pale or blue-colored skin. To counteract the negative effect, they added Methylene blue injection, used to treat methemoglobinemia. It works by converting methemoglobin to a more efficient type of hemoglobin to better carry oxygen throughout the body. The Methylene blue oral works as a mild antiseptic to kill bacteria. Then they needed an antibiotic medication to treat the infection.

At the same time this research was going on, another group worked on the effects of COVID-19 on the human brain, the most complex organ in the body. The brain regulates your body's basic functions and to find something that could control and regulate this process could fight COVID-19. They looked at adding Methamphetamine. It being a highly addictive stimulant that speeds up central nervous system function to produce effects of increased energy and heart rate could work to save these patients, short term, which was the plan since long-term meth use can cause memory loss, paranoia, hallucinations, and decreased thinking and motor skills. Repeated meth use can also lead to aggressive or violent behavior. So, to counteract this in cases where extended use might be needed an antipsychotic was added.

The final drug cocktail of Methemoglobin, Methamphetamine, and an Antipsychotic medication was named Methchotic.

Chapter 34

When the decision was first made all the arrangements for secrecy had been put in place. The chosen new representative for each country has now been briefed and all the details that were inaugurated were signed. The worse of it was over. There is no doubt the hardest for all concern is not knowing where they will be quarantined and for how long. But the not knowing assures there will not be a leak.

For Dr. Wodajo and his immediate staff, there is still much to coordinate and not wasting a moment, they initiate the orders. Unbeknown to most, Russia's fifth-generation stealth helicopter is a reality. The Central Aero-Hydrodynamic Institute has several operable prototypes available for their use in transporting the members and heads of state. The helicopters are radar invisible, have an extended flying range, are equipped with an intellectual arms control system, and can reach a speed of up to 370 mph.

As an extra precaution, each of the 194-member country leaders along with their heads of state is transported to the World Health Organization site in Geneva, Switzerland. At that point, the group is sedated, and the untraceable helicopters begin the transportation to their final destination.

The idea of how to protect the world leaders first emanated when the United Nations discussed the fact that the heads of states were most vulnerable. The head of state being primarily a representative, they serve to symbolize the unity and integrity of the state at home and abroad and that requires travel about their country and others.

It was not an overnight decision on how to protect these world leaders during the pandemic. Many suggestions were made but the only one that made sense was one that knowingly exactified the position of each of them. That concluded in quarantine in a secret, secure location.

At that point, the search began to look for the state-of-the-art in innovative technology sites. At the time, the United States' efforts to develop such facilities have been modest and consist primarily of small underground laboratories. The same held true for most of the countries, but at least some had larger underground facilities on the scale of major laboratories. As a result, they gathered a force that would assess areas around the world and bring their findings for the one that would be logical as an underground science and engineering laboratory.

The ideal location would be several city blocks with complex layouts and multiple stories. Since it would be in use for an undetermined amount of time, it had to be energy-efficient and provide a comfortable, tranquil, weather-resistant dwelling.

The ventilation must be carefully planned and have a direct source of outside air and vent combustion gases directly to the outside as well as avoid indoor pollutants such as formaldehyde from foam insulation, plywood, and some fabrics. An energy recovery ventilator, which exchanges heat in the outgoing exhaust air with incoming fresh air, must be installed to minimize heat loss while ensuring good indoor air quality. Finally, with the count of the 194 members and the heads of state, along with advisors and staff the facility would need to be able to support an underworld population of 5,000.

Following the instructions, they came up with several alternatives.

The choice was the South Shore Operations Center in Virginia. It was for years used as the retreat of government and Presidents and as such was perfect in size, location and equipment. It was large enough to house all of congress and was equipped with a television studio, hospital and living quarters for all members of Congress in the event of a nuclear war. That meant that the full staff and world leaders would have adequate space and luxury room accommodations. Here they could ride out whatever natural or manufactured events may come their way. What was more important, very few people were aware of the location.

This site was 112,544-square-foot, built 720 feet into the hillside. The facility was maintained in a constant state of readiness by a small group of government employee workers. It had four entrances: three to The South Shore Operations Center grounds and one to the main building. There is a 25-ton blast door that opens with only 50 lbs. of pressure, Decontamination chambers, 1000 massive units for living quarters, power plant with purification equipment and three 25,000-gallon water storage, along with three 14,000-gallon diesel fuel storage tanks.

There is a fully equipped communications area that includes television production area and audio recording booths. There is a clinic with 100 hospital beds, medical and dental operating rooms, laboratory, pharmacy, fully equipped intensive care unit, cafeteria, and meeting rooms. The location had been decommissioned in 1992 after its existence had been exposed and soon it was forgotten. There was work on the facility that needed to be done to bring the electronics and other equipment back to state-of-the-art for 2020. That and a little window dressing would have it up and running in a short period of time.

For months, the work that hired builders undertook at the South Shore Operations Center fueled speculation, but in time the memories dimmed, and the rumors died as the facility under extreme secrecy was brought back to life.

Situated in a lush and remote valley in the Allegheny Mountains five hours' drive southwest of Washington, made the South Shore Operations Center one of the nation's premier facility. The above ground spread over 6,500 manicured acres, with golf courses, skeet shooting, spas and a stream stocked with rainbow trout. Back when the above ground resort was built no one would guess that the place had a bunker. The South Shore Operations Center is the only significant private employer in the County, and its workers - - many of whom are second- and third-generation employees -- do not have to be reminded of the secrecy of the facility. Few have direct knowledge of the installation, but no one will talk openly about it.

They used top-secret clearance individuals to coordinate the set-up arrangements and the members of WHO made a unanimous decision on Fritz Bugas to head the operation.

Fritz Bugas a short man with a salt-and-pepper beard, sporting a dark hairpiece and thick glasses became the main man. Bugas was a career officer in the Army Signal Corps with a top-secret security clearance. At one time he had served as a secret service agent for the President. By law, the Secret Service protects the president and his family, the vice president and her family, the president-elect and his family and the vice president-elect and their family.

One other thing that made him ideal was his honesty and nonpartisan attitude. Whoever he was asked to protect, he would be more than willing to do whatever it took to do the job. More importantly he would be able to staff with little supervision.

After 34 years and a short stint in the private sector, he still wanted to serve his country. As the former Army Signal Corps chief information officer, leading the U.S. Secret Service's IT management made him a perfect fit.

During his briefing he said that IT and cybersecurity are integral to keeping our nation's leaders safe. Once on board, Fritz Bugas took some time to assess the current situation and talked to key stakeholders to fill the position requirements. He knew the importance of knowing the people around him whether on site or off. He had proven this by meeting the responsibility of protecting former presidents and their spouse, but if the spouse remarried, they lost their Secret Service detail, but were always under surveillance.

Fritz Bugas would serve as the Director for the facility. In his office on his desk, behind his nameplate, is a small American flag with gold braid and behind the desk on his bookshelf is an eclectic collection of books. From the moment he entered the room to be interviewed for the position, he was seen as the most obvious choice.

Bugas's assistant, John Nemcik, worked as an Air Force radio operator and had a top-secret clearance and Bugas trusted him.

Across the hall from Bugas's office is his secretary, Gladys Childers. The office contains a networked HP high capacity computer, a bank of HP Officejet and LaserJet printers and in a corner, a high-speed shredder. Gladys had top-secret clearance and was one of the best at her job.

For the most part the equipment and furnishings were transported to the site at night so as not to draw unnecessary attention, but there is always someone watching and because of the history of the South Shore Operations Center it was to be expected. But they had quick responses on the ready

First, WHO dispatched two men who had not been briefed on the project to mingle with the locals, posing as hunters, to learn just how much was known and what was being said.

Most of the residents thought it was owned and run by the mafia in the day. Others referred to it as an elite country club that they could not afford to join. In the end there was little known. Not surprising those who thought the place was a front for maybe a bomb shelter, believed the South Shore Operations Center current staff statement, "There is no bomb shelter, no government facility. I can tell you what I know to be the truth." And that was the end of it.

The director general went over the paperwork on the facility with his advisor and they prepared a report for the different acting leaders in each country to be viewed once they had arrived. The report did not reveal the location.

When the facility was complete the director-general and several others went on a tour. They check out the exhibit halls that have been updated according to their instructions. Even though he knows they are below ground it is hard to believe. The exhibit hall measures 89 by 186 feet beneath a ceiling nearly 20 feet high and lined with 18 massive support columns. Through a vehicular entrance, they can drive truckloads of equipment and displays into the facility over a floor finished with a beautiful terrazzo tile designed to support unlimited weight.

Both the vehicular entrance and a second, pedestrian entrance can be sealed off by blast doors on very short notice.

At the rear of the Exhibit Hall are two smaller auditoriums the larger of these seats roughly 470. Navy blue leather covered chairs with armrests that raise up to become desks are locked into rows. A navy-blue patterned carpet leads to the stage. The smaller of the auditoriums has a seating capacity of approaching 130.

Not far from the auditoriums is a large white door with four metal bolts: two lock into the floor and two into the ceiling. It leads to a corridor, perhaps 20 yards long, that ends at a locked door where a sign with red letters against a white background caution: "Danger: High Voltage Keep Out." Overhead are a large emergency lighting system, vents and what appear to be sensors. Few people have been beyond this door, which can be opened only with a special key card.

When the director general first entered the facility, he was amazed by what he saw. Along the left side of the wide corridor leading further into the hillside was an infirmary complete with an operating table, then the individual doors leading to many suites of rooms that contained beds, bathrooms and all sorts of medical and electronic equipment.

Beyond these rooms was a television studio from which the leaders would be able to address what was left of the nation. Still further into the compound was a radio and communications room, then a room with phone booths that had been specially soundproofed and fitted with cryptographic machines. To the right of the corridor as one entered the door was a dining room where several place settings had been neatly laid out. The walls of the dining room featured false windows complete with wooden frames and country scenes painted on them. The idea, apparently, was that the illusion of being above ground might counter the sense of entombment that could come from a prolonged stay in the facility.

There was also a kitchen and storage area. In the very rear of the compound was a power room, with two diesel generators, standing two stories high, ready to supply all electrical needs. In the same room was a device identified as a "pathological waste incinerator" (translation: an oven for cremations). Once the blast doors were sealed, no one could enter or leave until the crisis had passed. Burial or other disposal of bodies would be impossible, the former official was told. The details and the existence of this area would be kept secret for logical reasons.

Beyond the installation, a vehicular tunnel led through the hill and out to the rear of the South Shore Operations Center property, invisible from the road, but convenient to both Route 60 and a railroad line. Supplies for the facility came in through this tunnel, usually at night.

Chapter 35

At first it was determined that it would not be necessary to have the leaders sedated, but the problems identified if they were not, outnumbered them being awake. This way they can operate without influence from other countries. It was the only way this could work.

In their current state, it was easy to transfer them to the unmarked black helicopters. Of course, US law enforcement agencies, and FBI are known to use black helicopters for surveillance and transportation, so if the helicopters were spotted, they would only draw slight interest.

It would have been easier if it could be done with one, but there were slightly over a total of 582 people being transported. Then there was the space needed for the medically equipped gurneys. That is why military helicopters were used. Their size and ability to be modified or converted to perform other missions such as the current case in point allowed for a safe transport of this valuable cargo.

They needed 3 helicopters to transport their sensitive cargo. Three would not cause too much of a stir, but they planned on spacing out the helicopters, allowing one to take off every 4 hours.

They had a total of 4,990 miles to cover and that increased their chances of drawing attention as they flew from Switzerland to the United States. A plane would make it in 9 hours, but the problem would be in finding a place to land a large plane. The idea of transporting from a plane to a helicopter once in the United States was considered, but that again would draw attention. No, the best way was to use the helicopters. Using the stealth helicopters equipped with air refueling capability was a wise choice. At the top speed of 370 mph it would take them a little over 13 hours to complete the flight pattern.

So, in loading the helicopters they kept the country groupings in mind of Africa, Americas, South-East Asia, Europe, Eastern Mediterranean, and Western Pacific.

The first helicopter lifted off at 12 pm, UTC+2 time in Switzerland. The second helicopter followed at 4 pm, UTC+2 and the last took off at 8 p.m. UTC+2 time. It all progressed as planned and by the following day, all three helicopters had landed, and all passengers were less for wear.

Personnel met each helicopter and as instructed, began the process of taking the passengers to their prescribed rooms underground. Once placed in the rooms, the dignitaries were made comfortable in their beds and their vitals checked. The support staff members were placed in the remaining two rooms of the members quarters where they were checked and once found to be in fine health, left to rest until the sedative wore off.

It was clearly understood that all staff now in place would remain for the duration. No one could leave for any reason and no calls, accept those sanction could come in or go out from the facility. All but the necessary personnel had any ideal who the occupants were and that was how it must remain.

It was time to admit success and Dr. Wodajo and Dr. Simiao breathe easier. The transport had gone smoothly, and all the amenities had been met. Now it was a matter of getting through each day without thinking about the length of time they were in quarantine because that was out of their control and in the hands of the COVID-19 virus.

Chapter 36

As Sonya tried to understand what she had witnessed in the subbasement of the hospital, she knew she had to be careful. She did not know who she could trust at this stage of the game.

Scared and frustrated, she tried to find another way back to her floor. Using her pen light, she flashed around thinking there must be a way back upstairs besides the one she had taken.

As she explored, she remembered. "The freight elevator," she whispered. Now, she stood, trying to get her bearings and once she did, headed just slightly from where she stood. Using her pen light, she walked up to the wall at the far end of the basement. Slowly she moved the pen light around the area, then moving a step at a time, she continued until finally she found what she was looking for.

It did not faze her that the lights on the buttons were not lit until she pressed the one that should open the door and take her upstairs.

She heard nothing. She put her ear to the door. Still nothing. She pressed the button again. Nothing. The elevator was not coming down.

Tears welled in Sonya's eyes and she fought to hold them back as she turned around and started back toward the stairs.

She was almost there when she heard something. She paused, turning out her penlight as she moved back against the wall.

She could see someone coming out the door to the staircase, but she was not close enough to make out who it was. She remained still, watching as the figure moved determinedly toward the mirrored entrance as if knowing it was there. She was too far away to see, but she thought the person had opened the entrance unassisted. She was not sure of it, but it appeared so.

As soon as the figure disappeared inside the mirrored enclosure, she rushed to the door, checked behind her, and then slipped through. She stood there in the stairwell darkness listening for any sound that someone was approaching and hearing none, she hurried up the stairs as fast as she could. When she reached the top landing, she was out of breath. She took a couple deep breaths, listened to hear if anyone was near, then slowly opened the door, little by little until she was sure it was safe. She slipped onto the floor as if nothing had happened.

Back on the floor, she tried to look inconspicuous as she peeked into offices checking to see who was missing from the floor. With a sigh she continued to her office where she quickly changed into fresh protection gear and then went to the COVID-19 isolation area to visit her remaining patients. No one else seemed to be missing as she made her way from one bed to another, checking pulse and taking temperatures. When she had finished each one, she entered comments on her notepad that she would finalize later.

As she was on her way to take a shower, she passed a doctor in the hall who seemed to stare questioningly at her. Was it her imagination, or did he know where she had been. She turned slightly so that she could see him, but he was already heading down the hall, paying her no mind. She was just being paranoid. With a shrug Sonya went in to take a shower and change into her regular medical coverings to visit patients that were in the special care unit where few patients remained.

At the start of the initial wave of the Covid-19 pandemic, like most of the hospitals worldwide they had diverted inpatient critical care to outpatient clinics so they could meet the surge in demand. So, there was a dramatic decline in non-COVID-related health emergencies, which lessened the number of patients in this wing demanding her attention. It was a bad time for anyone to get sick.

All the time she spent with patients she was anxiously churning in her mind who she could turn to for help. Should she go to the authorities? No, she decided. Who would believe her and not knowing how high up the authority on this zone rose, she might find herself in more hot water than she could handle.

Now, along with the worry of finding her daughter was added this new mystery.

By the end of the day she felt paranoia set in. It felt like everyone was watching her. She was afraid to do any research on her computer in the office for fear they were keeping an eye on her computer activity. Each time she stepped out of a patient's room; she was sure someone was watching her.

When her shift ended, she hurried to the doctor's lounge, showered, and changed out of her hospital clothes and into her street clothes. She rushed to her office to pick up her personal belongings and put on her mask and sunglasses before even entering the elevator.

When the elevator arrived, she stepped in and pressed the lobby button. It seemed like forever as she waited for the door to slide closed and once it did, she tried to calm herself. The elevator made several stops as people got on and off until finally, she was in the lobby.

Sonya stepped out and jumped when the guard said, "Have a good evening Dr. McKenna." She was glad her face was hidden behind the mask. "You too," she managed before exiting the hospital.

In the parking garage she felt disoriented, unable to find her car as she rushed down aisle after aisle until remembering where she had parked. Just when she had her finger over the panic button, she saw her car.

It was not until she climbed inside and locked the door did, she allow herself to relax. She started the engine and backed out of her parking space weaving through the parking garage and constantly looking out of the rearview mirror wondering each time a car appeared, were they after her.

By now she was sure the word would be sent to those in power that someone named Dr. Weston had been at the facility saying she was the new doctor assigned to the area. Yes, they would be checking to find out who this Dr. Weston was, but would they be able to identify her. For once she was thankful for the full isolation gear that everyone had to wear, making them all look alike. She was quite sure they could not immediately identify her, but she was sure they eventually would.

Chapter 37

Life was so different now. It used to be easy to shut down and put on her family hat, but now, the devastation caused by the coronavirus was everywhere. There were very few cars on the road with her as she made her way to her destination and when she arrived at the restaurant, she could tell by the parking area, no one was here. A shopping center, empty of cars was so far from the norm, it scared her.

Not in any rush, Sonya parked her car away from the building so that she could get a little exercise. She knew the rest of her evening would be sedentary and this walk in the fresh air would do her good.

Inside the restaurant it is quiet. No one sits dining and there is no one at the takeout counter. She had often stopped here for Chinese food and there were always people dining or waiting for their takeout order. But not now. Who wants to dine out if they always must wear a face covering, except when eating?

It is bad enough to have to lower the mask to take a drink of water and then put it back in place. Try enjoying doing that repeatedly as you attempt to consume a meal. As for takeout she knew people thought they might catch COVID-19 if they did, even though there is no evidence to suggest that handling food or consuming food is associated with COVID-19.

When they said this to her, Sonya would calm her patients by saying, "Coronaviruses, like the one that causes COVID-19, spreads mostly person-to-person." And the patient would come back with, "How do you know someone did not cough, sneeze, or talk with another person while they prepared the food." Sonya had a comeback for that as well. "Because even if they did, they were wearing masks."

She felt for the owner and his family. They must be facing a financial crisis since they had been closed for so long and now, that they were open again, people were afraid to go out to eat. Procuring the dinners was her way of offering a helping hand. She had enough food at home to make a meal, but they needed every customer they could get.

The minute Sonya put down the menu, the man behind the counter hurried up to her. "Can I help you, Miss."

"Yes, thank you." Sonya gave him her order and while she waited, the owner came out to chat with her. He told her that the family was doing fine, but getting bored with staying in. "First, they complain about having to get up so early to go to school, now they complain that they cannot go. Children." Sonya smiled and nodded.

So, how are you doing, Ty."

"We are fine doctor, just fine."

"Good to hear."

When her food was brought to the counter, Sonya watched the owner, Ty as he dropped soy sauce and ginger packets into the bag. He reached into a bowl and pulled out a fortune cookie and added it to the contents saying, "Hope it brings you luck."

When Ty reached for napkins and chopsticks, Sonya reached out to stop him.

"I have them at home so you can save them for the next customer."

She could see it in his eyes that he appreciated her consideration and with that they said their goodbyes.

Sonya left the restaurant and when she was outside the entrance, she pressed the button to unlock her car. She walked across the parking area enjoying the aroma of the Chinese food that made her realize how hungry she was. She was right by the door of her car when she paused. She turned slightly and out of the corner of her eye saw nothing, but she felt someone was watching her.

Her mind frantically tried to decide what she should do. She had her purse and her keys in her hand. She could use them to protect herself if she had to.

Quickly Sonya turned, hoping to catch whoever it was off balance, but all she managed to do was watch her purse slide down her arm and over the key she held in her hand.

She saw no one. Sonya looked all around the empty parking area and saw no one anywhere near her. She let out a shaky laugh as she turned back around and climbed into the car, swiftly closing the door before placing the food on the passenger seat feeling silly, but still being cautious at the same time. She quickly started the car, then checking around her, pulled out of the parking area and on to the street. Her breathing slowed as she headed toward home.

By the time she pulled into her driveway, she was feeling less paranoid, but still had her key ready to put in the front door lock even before she stepped out of the car. It was not until she was inside her house, did she feel safe.

With the door closed and locked, Sonya went straight for the kitchen to put her food into a bowl and pour herself a glass of iced tea. She did not like eating out of the containers, just like she did not drink her wine out of a paper cup. It was more than just the taste, but the taste and the presentation that made it interesting.

As soon as she had her food on the table, she went to her office and retrieved her laptop. She carried it into the kitchen and placed it next to her food.

While she waited for the laptop to boot, she ate greedily, stopping now and then to wipe the juice that dripped down her chin. She had not realized just how hungry she was until her food was gone and her laptop stood waiting for her to initiate the password. She had forgotten all about everything except filling her stomach.

Now she entered her password and then leaned back comfortably sipping her tea, her mind filled with the mystery that had been bothering her all day. There was so much wrong with what she had seen, and did not understand, but first she wanted to search on the condition of the patients.

She did a google search on the condition, methemoglobinemia and it is just like she thought. The condition was inherited, and it was rare. Just like in the James Cameron's "Avatar," the forest loving Na'vi have stunning blue skin and these patients were the same. She searches further and reads that there actually is a family living in Appalachia that had the condition, methemoglobinemia and family members had blue skin.

Even so, she now knew that was not what caused the blueness of the skin on all these patients.

She continued her search, aware that many conditions can cause your skin to have a bluish tint. In instances of small areas of the skin there were bruises and varicose veins, but this was not limited to a small area.

She started reading an article on poor circulation and inadequate oxygen levels in your blood stream. They can both lead to a bluish tint of the skin. Sonya stretched her body. This seems reasonable, but she continues her search.

"Ah," she said as she began reading aloud. "Cyanosis is the bluish or purplish discoloration of the skin or mucous membranes due to the tissues near the skin surface having low oxygen saturation. Most cyanosis occurs because of a lack of oxygen in the blood and is associated with cold temperatures, heart failure, lung diseases, and smothering."

She continued to read knowing, only hoping otherwise that there was more to it, but she knew, the blue discoloration is seen most readily in the beds of the fingernails and toenails, and on the lips and tongue.

Sonya rested her back against the chair, then sat forward again. What she wanted to do was call her husband and tell him what she had seen, but she knew he had a lot on his plate trying to find Elise. She did not want to change his focus and have him worrying about her, so she continued her search.

She read that some people get blue skin through another route: silver poisoning, known as argyria. Argyria occurs when people are exposed to silver dust, and the most common symptom is skin that turns bluish gray.

Could that be it. Did they try a cure on these patients that had silver in it? Colloidal silver can kill certain germs by binding to and destroying proteins and is used for infections, hay fever, skin conditions, and many other conditions, but there is no good scientific evidence to support any of its uses.

She found another site in her search that reported that despite some claims, there is no good evidence to support using colloidal silver for COVID-19. In fact, it can be unsafe.

She was not getting anywhere as she tried to keep her mind from going where it wanted to go. These patients were blue, and they were alive, only maybe in a coma. She paused trying to take it all in. They were in a medically induced coma for some reason.

Now she is on her feet and walking around the kitchen as she gets out a glass and finds an open bottle of wine in the refrigerator. She practically fills her wine glass and sips away, trying to get her mind to stop seeking explanations that did not exist. She finishes the first glass and pours a second. But her mind keeps churning as she says aloud. "So, they are alive and being kept in a coma." She thinks on that, leaning her head back and forward again before saying, "So Nurse Lottie said that they were strung up to save space." Sonya pauses in thought and takes several large sips of her wine. "That could be true, but the way they were suspended would be painful, if..." Just the idea of what entered her mind was frightening.

"My god, could they be alive, but not fully alive...living dead?"

Sonya leaned against the counter to steady herself. "No, that cannot be. I am being stupid."

Yet, the more she thought about it, the more she tried to reason through it she came back to the fact that these bodies...people were not being suspended in that manner to save space, but the quick thinking of someone who needed to protect us from them. She could give the need to save space some consideration, but the method used would then be considered torture.

Her brain hurt trying to figure it out. "Give up and get some sleep, Sonya," she said to herself. "Just give it up and forget it."

Sonya went back to the table and sat down, but she could not stop her thoughts. She was a doctor, and this was a medical situation that a doctor could not easily forget. Plus, she had a feeling that Nurse Lottie would soon wonder where her replacement doctor was and then get suspicious and check on who sent her Dr. Warren and she needed to know what she was dealing with before that happened. Sonya had to hope they could not figure it all out too soon.

So, Sonya forced herself to cover every detail she remembered from that visit. The low-level flux of ultraviolet light could control bacteria, but it was not doing much where the skin was concerned. The skin on those patients looked like it was deteriorating.

"Okay, so what does that mean," she asked herself. It means that the tissue is dying because, maybe, the patients are dying or dead.

She did not like where all this was going and wanted to stop. She got up and poured herself another glass of wine giving herself time to adjust before going on. After a few sips she was back at it.

She focused on the temperature settings. Nurse Lottie had said it is maintained at 94-point five Fahrenheit plus or minus five hundredths of a degree. And the humidity is held at 82 percent with a one percent variance.

Sonya thought she understood the reasoning behind that. It was true those settings would reduce patient heat loss leading to a reduction in their caloric needs.

Her satisfaction with that lasted for one cool minute. Why did they need to reduce their caloric needs? Usually patients are encouraged to eat or absorb calories through feeding tubes. Why did they not want to nourish these patients?

As for the humidity settings, there was nothing odd about that at all.

She filled her bowl with the last of the Chinese food and started eating even though it was now cold. She chewed slowly as the information swirled through her head. Absently she reached for her wineglass and is surprised to find it is empty again, so she got up and taking her empty bowl and glass went over to the sink. She washed out the bowl and then placed it in the dishwasher, then went to the island and started to fill her wine glass. "Oh, what the hell," she said as she picked up the bottle along with her glass and carried them both over to the table.

While she filled her glass, she allowed her mind to continue to test what she had seen. Why were they suspended like that? No matter how much they needed to conserve space, there had to be a better alternative. No matter how desperate for space, they would never go to this extent. There was a profusion of wires perforating through their bones. "God, that is inhumane on any level."

Then she remembered something that had almost slipped her mind. She had moved closer to one of the suspended patients. The patient's eyes had opened, and spittle had dribbled from her lips. Sonya could have sworn she heard a growl, or maybe it was a groan before Nurse Lottie had pulled her back.

"Not so close," Nurse Lottie had said, and Sonya could hear the fear in her voice. Nurse Lottie sounded scared but because she was shocked by all she was seeing; Sonya had not questioned her. Now she wish she had.

What she did know for sure was that Nurse Lottie was terrified of these patients and knew they were not in a 'real' coma. Yes, Nurse Lottie knew.

Chapter 38

At the South Shore Operations Center facility in Bluemont, Virginia things are running smoothly. The leaders are comfortable and being well cared for both physically and mentally and the first test of the transfer of orders from the leader to their advisor went smoothly without a hiccup.

Even though they had tested this method for several months before it had to be put in place, there were doubts that it could fail. But everyone felt relieved as each member was able to translate their directives to their advisor and from them to the acting head of state. And, as they had assumed, outside of their headquarters in their countries, no one questioned not seeing them at all. Even if they had, they had thought through that as well and prepared tapes of the leaders addressing the country. It worked because the leaders wore a mask, and no one would know they were listening to recorded responses and not hearing the words from their mouths.

On that end, everything was going as planned. On the other hand it was those who were quarantined with them, sought privileges like making a call home to talk to family or friends and at the least, asking for permission to go up to ground level and just go for a walk over the grounds. Unfortunately, this could not be allowed and eventually they stopped asking as they went about their jobs.

Food was flown in nightly or bought in by rail to the facility and quickly transported into the building. At least once a month medical supplies arrived for not only the members, but also in case anyone sustain an injury. Having so many medical professionals on staff gave an ease of comfort knowing that the staff was in the hands of the best in the country if they were to become hurt or ill.

Since the facility was several levels below ground, they could use lights without fear of drawing attention to what appeared to be a deserted building. To most in the area, they were accustomed to seeing the secured building being manned to protect whatever was inside. Most had not noticed that the amount of security had increased, nor did they care.

There was games for entertainment as well as a gym to let off some steam. There were even televisions in the main area as well as the staff rooms so that they were aware of what was going on around the world. That was important, especially since they were not allowed to have any personal electronics like computers or cell phones.

As for the director-general and the main leaders in this facility, they were busy. At first the attention was given to making sure the leaders of the country, their advisors and doctors were comfortable and felt confident in keeping their countries running smoothly. They too had access to televisions and when needed could go to a secured, locked facility to surf the internet for details and make calls from specially designed 'burn' phones that were constantly replaced. On each of these visits they were joined by one of the security staff who stood alert, listening for code words or details that were forbidden. If that were to happen, they were equipped with a hypodermic needle that had serum to render them immediately unconscious. Again, if they had anyone viewing them, the mask would cover the fact they were sedated.

It was a new world for all of them and they were adjusting.

But not all the news was relayed to the staff or the public and that was good. Only the higher ups were being briefed on the 'special' effects that a trial cocktail of drugs had on some patients or of the resulting sequestering of these patients who were assumed dead by their loved ones.

This had caused a major scare, but quick action was taken to scour the testing centers of all vaccines, files, and test subjects, whether appearing to have ill effects or not. These test subjects had been successfully corralled in a special facility, secured and under constant surveillance. Yet they had not figured out how to reverse the effects, so they were kept restrained. Of course, the specifics on the quarters for these patients was not shared beyond a need to know basis so those at the facility were only aware it had been successfully handled and any change on that level would be relayed.

Yet on the forefront they were cautiously optimistic about a COVID-19 vaccine that may be ready by the end of the year or as early as the beginning of next year. This was the top priority, and all hands were on deck working on a vaccine to end the pandemic.

Chapter 39

By now everyone is aware that the coronavirus infection happens when the germ enters the body's airways through the nose, mouth, or eyes. From the entry points it passes through the body, lodging in the cells lining the lung and from there, quickly starts making millions of copies of itself, inserting its own genes into cell's genetic structure and from there wreaks havoc on the lungs.

Knowing this the scientists retreated to taking another look at remdesivir, an anti-viral drug designed to target the system the virus uses to replicate itself. Remdesivir could prevent the virus from making new copies of itself or infecting other cells. Whether this works in people to reduce symptoms of COVID-19 or shorten the length of the disease is not known but it is worth a try.

There never is time on the scientists' side as they need to search for cures and advance clinical science and patient care while combating the pandemic. All around the world all kinds of studies are moving ahead at breakneck speed to find the next best treatment or vaccine for COVID-19.

The scientists can now incorporate machine learning to identify hundreds of new potential drugs that could help treat COVID-19. This type of computational strategy linked to artificial intelligence uses an algorithm that can knock off years of human exploration. The development of any potential drug begins with years of scientific study to determine the biochemistry behind a medical problem for which pharmaceutical intervention is possible. The results are then used in determining what compounds will interact with the virus in some fashion. At this initial stage of drug development, it does not matter what effect the compounds have on the targets. It simply is the desire to find anything that binds to the virus in any fashion.

From the release of reports across the world new ideas are presented including hydroxychloroquine, known for 50 years to have nonspecific anti-viral properties. But it is still remdesivir that remains the preferred choice.

The anti-malarial drugs chloroquine, like hydroxychloroquine is considered as potential treatments for COVID-19.

But since the testing results review are anecdotal in their use for COVID-19, they have not received approval from the FDA. They need testing data driven for FDA approval and it was not forthcoming.

So, the test trials begin. A number of medical centers around the world are involved in global trials and in the end, the infectious disease doctors have enrolled 30 participants in two trials — one for severe and the other for moderately ill patients — who were receiving the drugs intravenously.

The world-wide spread of the new coronavirus is throwing into disarray studies critical to the development of promising new medicines. There just is not enough time. Plus, the pandemic is causing delays in starting clinical drug trials and temporarily halting others as patients enrolled in some studies have stopped showing up for new ones. That is the case when thinking out of the box the combination of Methemoglobin, Methamphetamine and an added Antipsychotic medication was developed and named Methchotic

When bringing this forward as a possible cure, to the FDA the lab technician said, "We arranged everything in a week and are ready to roll." This was record time. But the pressure was on.

The drug is tested before going to the FDA and they state these tests prove the drug is safe and effective for its intended use and the drug's health benefits outweigh its risks.

But before a drug can be tested in people, the drug company or sponsor must perform laboratory and animal tests to discover how the drug works and whether it is likely to be safe and work well in humans. Then and only then can a series of tests in people begin to determine whether the drug is safe when used to treat a disease and whether it provides a real health benefit.

During normal times, a phase 3 clinical trial — the final step in the process of drug approval — typically takes months of planning, after years of research, before it is underway. But these are not normal times. With a fast-moving pandemic bearing down and no approved treatments available, researchers are, like everyone else, desperate for answers, and they have ramped up their efforts to find solutions.

Pressing their point further for sidestepping the process was that fewer test candidates were being found quoting that two studies in China, were halted due to lack of patients. "We urgently need a safe and effective treatment for COVID-19."

The scientist knew that a randomized, placebo-controlled trial is the gold standard for experimental treatment, but they had to act fast.

Methchotic looks particularly good in the lab. In cell cultures, it is also been more active in fighting the coronavirus than other drugs. That is why it is promising.

They are anxious to see what the clinical trials would show. So, the clinical trial flouted just about every norm in the book: American patients were flown into the Caribbean island of St. Kitts for experimental injections. Local authorities did not give permission. Nor did the Food and Drug Administration. Nor did a safety panel. And unreported was the use of a local clinical lab in the United States.

Chapter 40

That is how they were put in this predicament. Scientist not working on a new vaccine to cure COVID-19 were trying to find a reversal for the Methchotic vaccine. Not only did they perform the clinical trials outside the

United States with American citizens willing to participate, the majority of test subjects reached an all-time high when they learned they would be flown to the Caribbean island of St. Kitts for an all-expense paid trip.

Desperate measures called for desperate action and at the rapid spread of COVID-19 before the testing was completed, Methchotic was given to these patients who were assuredly dying if something was not done.

That is how there was now a group of contractors sworn to secrecy building the basement facility in a hospital in Washington DC. Because of the number of patients given Methchotic was kept secret, the number of actual deaths from COVID-19 was again misreported, though the patients were not actually dead. That and because of the need to house so many patients, someone came up with the suspension method.

Thank God they had done limited testing at one site only or else the situation would have been far worse. As it was, they now had 100 test subjects fall ill and quickly flown back to Washington and placed at a secure testing site, away from the public and away from other patients. If they had not moved quickly who knows what would have happened. Well, they were about to find out.

As if things were not bad enough, all hell broke loose. Sara Brown, the head nurse on the COVID-19 testing was the first to alert Dr. Griffin Warren that something was wrong.

Today is the second anniversary of Griffin's wife's death. He was already in a funk when the call came in from Sara Brown, thinking about the last words he had shared with his wife. Because she was just recovering from her chemo treatment, they made plans to spend a quiet evening at home. For some reason that night he was not sympathetic when his wife, Martha, instead of preparing for their small celebration came into the family room to show him another study about a possible experimental cancer treatment that she found online. He snapped.

"Can't we just have one night off from cancer?" he yelled.

Martha had been taken aback. Her posture straightened and her neck stretched up. She stood there, the paper dangling from her hand and tears gathering in her eyes. When she was finally able to respond she replied, "I don't get a night off from cancer!"

Now instead of fond memories of their wonderful life together, he remembered that one black spot in their marriage. Doctors are not superhumans or saints. So, what happened to Martha made him feel helpless, sad, mixed with fear, and rage. He was a doctor, a healer and when the person he loved most needed him, he had let her down.

He heard a tune playing and he mouthed the words,

All alone am I ever since your goodbye
All alone with just a beat of my heart
People all around but I do not hear a sound
Just the lonely beating of my heart

It was an old song by Brenda Lee, his wife's favorite. Now it was the song that fit his mood.

The tune came again, and this time it snapped Griffin back to the present as he reached for his private cell.

"Hello," he cleared his throat. "Hello, this is Dr. Griffin."

Chapter 41

Sara Brown had held off calling. She had insisted she could handle this job and she did not want to admit that she and her staff needed assistance. Veronica Peters, the lead tech, told her she had no choice. They needed help.

"Sara, we need someone to tell us what to do. We cannot handle this," Veronica demonstrated with outspread arms."

Sara knew she was right. The test subjects were getting sicker by the day and getting supplies to the Caribbean was taking more time now that the Covid-19 was spreading rapidly throughout the world. That, she was sure had not been anticipated any more than the condition of the test subjects, who were now more like patients than test subjects.

Dr. Warren had been understanding and the arrangements were made. The fact that she was not fired raised her spirits. Instead of just shutting down the project, they opened one up in Washington with all of them set up in the new test facility.

Sara had wondered about that. Why did they not immediately hospitalize the test subjects? If they were to continue testing, they needed new test subjects and the new facility barely held the ones they had. But she finally stopped thinking about it and did her job which was no longer heading a testing facility but trying to take care of these patients.

It was less than a week later that Sara made the frantic call from the secure test site in Washington.

"Something is happening here. The test subjects are out of control. We did not know what to do…what should we do?" It was Sara.

"Can you safely put them into restraints."

"Not by ourselves. There are 10 of them and only 10 of us," added Veronica.

"So, what have you done?"

"We locked them in the testing room. That is all we could think to do."

"Good, that was good thinking. We are on our way. Do you have any sedatives on the premises?"

"No!"

"Okay, we will bring some with us. Just wait for us."

With that they hang up. Sara had seen a lot in her days of service in hospitals and test sites, but nothing like this. It was her job to keep everyone safe, so she said, "Step back and remain calm."

Veronica had to know what was happening in that room and she moved closer to the door.

"Veronica, don't."

Veronica turned around. "Don't worry Sara, I am not going to open the door."

Veronica stood on her tippy toes and stared through the wired glass window. Inside the test subjects are behaving in a disorganized, confused, and some in a violent way.

It was alarming, no doubt to see such easy going, friendly people, now walking aimlessly around, while others bang their heads against the wall.

"Are they messing with the drugs or equipment, Veronica?"

"No, but that is the least of your problems."

"What?"

"What…" She paused, "What you have here is a room full of blue zombies. They do not seem to know anything, like what to do with themselves."

Veronica examined the faces of the group behind her, observing their expressions change from worry to absolute fear. She had to lessen her drama, or they would go stark raving mad. "I do not think we need to worry. I do not think they know how to open the door and they are not trying. It is disturbing, really creepy, but we are safe."

That little piece of news ameliorated the situation. Afraid to move, the 10 staff members sank down to the floor and waited for help to arrive.

They did not have to wait long before military men arrived with special clothing for them to put on before they opened the door.

"Here is what we will do." The leader said as he walked, handing them syringes. Each of you now have syringes with a high dose of sedative. You will walk behind us and our medical staff, along with each of you, will give as many shots to as many patients as you can. We must work quickly as we do not know how violent they might be. Are you ready?"

"Yes."

Leading the group, the soldiers opened the door and began grouping the patients against the walls of the room. Just as quickly everyone sprang into action dosing the patients until the site was under control.

Everything was moving at breakneck speed with no time to think. Then as quickly as the patients were sedated, the lead soldier put out a call and in minutes the sound of helicopters could be heard. The staff of ten were first sent out to a helicopter while the soldiers placed the patients on stretchers. Sara and Veronica held hands and peered out the helicopter windows watching as the test subjects were briskly disappearing into the other two helicopters.

This time they all were taken to the hospital, a short ride away. The helicopters landed on the roof and as soon as they were down, Sara started to open the door, but did not have the strength. Before she could say a word, the door was opened and she, along with the rest of the staff climbed out. Sara stepped forward but was pushed back. "Wait."

They stood watching as, like ninjas all dressed in black the soldiers moved the patients from the helicopters and disappeared down a hatch. When the last patient was moved, the commander turned to the 10 and said, "Follow me."

They felt safe as they made their way into the bowels of the hospital, taking a flight of steps that were obviously not the regular steps leading to the different medical floors. When they stopped, the staff of 10 could easily tell they were in the basement, but in front of them was an elaborate structure of mirrored walls and doors. The commander made another call and soon the door opened, and they faced a nurse who said, "Hello. I am Nurse Lottie Bond. Welcome to your new home."

The first wave of COVID-19 ripped through the world at rapid speed from the Winter of 2019 to the Summer of 2020 when shields began to be lowered…way to soon.

Chapter 42

It was beginning to effect all walks of life and it became even more apparent when Japan postponed the 2020 Summer Olympics that originally were slated to be held in Tokyo starting July 24, until summer 2021 but countries including Canada and Australia had already announced that given the public health risk of the COVID-19 pandemic, they would not be sending their athletes to the Games.

Use to observing, the population around the world did celebrate Christmas, Hanukkah, New Years, Chinese New Year, Ramadan, and Eid al-Fitr. The celebrations continued to Easter, Valentine's Day, Mardi Gras, Basanth, St. Lucia Day, Kwanzaa and Diwali, all cause for merriments. They even managed a few parades, and festivals and so the inevitable happened.

A second surge of the coronavirus arrived before fall of 2020 with much of the blame falling on the shoulders of the population. So many, tired of the restrictions, refused to entertain social distancing and the wearing of masks. It will take weeks for the number of COVID-19 cases to change after this major behavior shift.

Not known at the time, the global pandemic was expected to last for two years. No one wanted to hear that. No one wanted to hear of a second wave either, but that became apparent when a significant number of deaths were packed into three especially cruel months in the fall of 2020. This highly fatal second wave was responsible for most of the deaths attributed to the pandemic.

The reason was blatant. Before the second wave it looked like we were in for a long haul under lockdown measures, but then, suddenly, the picture changed.

Restrictions were being lifted in Greece, Germany, Spain, and elsewhere. The United Kingdom, which has seen some of the highest numbers of infections and deaths from COVID-19 in Europe, is thinking about reopening too.

Earlier that year, India extended its lockdown for another two weeks concerned that if nations ease restrictions too soon, the world would find itself in a second wave of infections. They would be proved right.

It began slowly. The German government and health authorities agreed to partially reopen schools for those sitting for major exams or moving from primary to secondary schools in the autumn. The schools set about redesigning classrooms and segmenting concrete playgrounds into safe zones, to ensure they met physical distancing and hygiene guidelines which included wearing masks.

Zoos and museums were also reopening with new physical distancing rules, ensuring that people remain apart from each other. And on their heels, playgrounds opened.

The federal government has left it to the states and municipalities to track developments, and lockdown again if they saw 50 new cases of coronavirus per 100,000 people in any given week.

None of this disturbed Matthew McKenna. He had enough to deal with. For the first time he felt blessed to have a GSM compatible cell phone. So, use to being on the road and calling home, he never more appreciated this fact then right now.

While much of the world goes in one direction, the U.S. tended to do the opposite by balking international technology trends and standards like the metric system and Matthew did not mind it. So, at first when Sonya had pushed him to get a Smart Phone he had balked, "Come on honey, they cost too much. All I need is a phone that will let me call home."

"Yes, and that will be all you can do."

So, for a little over a year he continued with his flip phone and he only used it to call Elise or Sonya, and sometimes a friend or two. It only began to become difficult when his books started to hit the Best Sellers Lists and he had an agent who was good. No, not good...fantastic.

Randolph Peters knew everyone in almost every country and as such had Matthew traveling all over the world for readings, interviews, and book signings. And that was when he stood in front of his wife, his hands in a prayer position as he lowered himself to his knees saying, "You were right. I should have listened to you all along. I need a smart phone."

Sonya could not stop laughing which was what had made him fall in love with her in the first place. That spellbinding, peals of laughter that seemingly burst from deep within her soul and yes, the fact she not only loved him unconditionally, she trusted him explicitly. No one could have a better wife.

When they stopped laughing, Matthew asked Sonya, "Now, what do I do?"

"You have to go directly to the top or you will be on overload when you finish."

"What do you mean, babe...it's a phone, just smarter."

"You would think so, but when I got mine...she continued talking and he heard things like correct hardware GSM or CDMA standards and multi-ban to operate on the correct frequencies.

Matthew rose from the desk and went into the kitchen to pour them each a glass of Sauterne wine. It was Sonya's favorite.

While Matthew is busy with the wine, Sonya pulled out a pamphlet she had been given when she purchased her smart phone. She only used it to give herself a brief update as she had just looked at it when she heard Elise was going to Japan.

That paused her for a moment, "Elise," she whispered. She allowed herself a moment and then quickly went over the details again, though she knew most of them by heart.

When he returned to the office, Sonya was walking toward him on her way to the family room. He met her, sat down the glasses, and hugged her tightly before putting his hand under her chin and bringing her lips up to meet his. "You are amazing, and I love you."

"I know, my dear. I know."

"Matthew, we are buying your phone outright so that you will not have to worry about having it unlocked. And I chose a service where you can get a SIM card to join networks in Asia since you have only a few stops there for the time being. If you tend to travel more than that, we can always change the service."

"I am not sure about using SIM cards..."

"Wait. I can change it if you want, but international roaming can get awfully expensive since you will pay each time that someone calls you or vice versa.

Matthew nodded in agreement. "So, explain this, CDMA vs. GSM."

"Most of the world uses the Global System for Mobile Communications standard, better known as GSM.

The exceptions are the U.S., South Korea, and Japan, which use Code Division Multiple Access known as the CDMA standard. But having a phone that works on the correct standard is only half of the equation because the American CDMA cell phones operate on the 850 MHz and 1900 MHz frequency bands, while South Korean and Japanese phones use the 2100 MHz band. Your cell phone will have to be tri-band or quad-band to work abroad which was the choice I made for you."

As always, when Sonya shared wisdom, Matthew's whole body responded. That night they left the wine sitting in the family room. They did not take the time to drink it, or for that matter to go upstairs. Instead, they worked their way across the family room to close the drapes before they dropped down to the rug. The last words Sonya spoke was, "I thought you would never make your move."

All this plays in his mind as he sits with the phone at his ear trying to find a passageway from Italy to China. He starts calling the airlines, starting with Alitalia, then China Southern Airlines and six others before giving up. Every airline he called was limiting passengers on their flights and as luck would have it, he was unable to obtain a seat. By plane it would take almost 10 hours to make the 4,700-mile trip, but that was not happening, so he started checking out taking a train.

Online he learns that to travel to China by train it was best to book online for proper link of connections that would run from Milan, to Venice, onto to Vienna and then Austria. From there the train would head to Warsaw in Poland, then Moscow in Russia and on to Beijing China before finally arriving in Wuhan, China. There were several alternatives including night train connections and either high-speed train or standard trains.

It looked promising so Matthew began to reserve a seat. He had barely started before he ran into a stumbling block. Travel is restricted within and to China due to Coronavirus (COVID-19).

It was impossible. Matthew put his elbows on the desk and leaned his head into his hands with frustration. He sat like that for some time before he lifted his head and rubbed his hands along his cheek.

"There has to be a way!"

Matthew stood and walked around the hotel room trying to think. When he stopped, he picked up his cell and placed a call to a friend at the United States embassy.

"Ryan, this is Matthew McKenna. I need your help."

Ryan is silent.

"Ryan, it's me, Matthew."

"I know, I know. Just trying to get use to that American way of greeting an old friend."

"Hello, Ryan, how are you?"

"That's better. I am fine. Obviously, you are not."

"Sorry. It's just that I have a problem." Matthew pauses. "I hope you can help me."

"Where are you?"

"I am here, here in Italy on a book tour?"

"How's Sonya and Elise?"

"They are fine…. I mean Sonya is, but I do not know about Elise. Elise is why I am calling. I need to get to Wuhan, China."

"What!"

"I know, believe me I know, but Elise was there on assignment and we have not been able to reach her or find out anything about her. Her cell went dead, and she was last seen checking out of her hotel and taking an Uber to the airport."

"Matthew, Italy is under a travel restriction and so is China. I am sure you have checked the airlines?"

"Yes, and trains, but with no luck. Do you think there is anything you can do?"

There was a long uncomfortable pause on the other end of the call and Matthew held his breath. He had first met Ryan at the University and not only did they take different classes but were not part of the same social group until one night, Ryan was down in the dumps. His latest girlfriend and dumped him and he was falling apart. Matthew happened to walk by him as he sat leaning against a tree in an obscure part of the campus.

At first Matthew, like most young men of the times, did not want to get involved, but he could not help himself. He stopped and sat by Ryan, not saying a word. Finally, Ryan turned with a quizzical look on his face and asked, "What is your problem?"

Matthew gave him a serious expression and replied, "Thought you had found something and wanted to come see."

That broke the ice and the two started laughing. And from that point they were friends. But that was years ago. Since then when Matthew came to Italy, they would arrange to meet up when they could. Now as he holds the phone to his ear, he hopes that friendship is enough to get him the help he needs. Finally, Ryan says, "Let me try and I will get back to you. Stay put."

"Thanks Ryan. I will wait for your call."

Matthew tries to relax. He calls down for room service and orders a sandwich and a beer. When it arrives, he tips the person and closes the door. He does not sit the food or the drink down, but instead stands balancing his food as he manages to pull the sandwich out of the bag and then moving the beer against the palm of his other hand, he uses his fingers to unwrap the sandwich. He takes two bites of the sandwich. It is good.

Matthew, still holding on to the sandwich frees his fingers by moving the sandwich just so that the side of his thumb and palm support it. He then opens the beer. He takes a big gulp. This act of normalcy settles his nerves as he moves across the hotel room over to the window.

His mind wanders as he stares out the window of the St. Regis hotel in Castro Peretorio. He has stayed here many times before and each stay has been perfect in this lavish hotel occupying a belle epoque palace. Matthew turned and looked around at the plush, antique-filled room. He remembers the first time he stepped into the marble bathroom with frescoed walls. It felt like he was showering outside in a fancy garden. It was like he had gone back in time, but of course there were all the modern amenities to disprove that. Just staying in this hotel he experienced the sensation he had made it in his profession when his editor booked him here, but now it was even more elaborate as the company upgraded him to full 24-hour butler services and a Jacuzzi on a small patio.

It's like being in a fairy tale he once read to his daughter, then to add a little upscale normalcy to the atmosphere there is a fireplace in the separate living area and over the dining table is a Murano glass chandelier.

Matthew smiles as he remembers moving around the suite with his phone so that Sonya could enjoy it with him. She was the one who filled him in on the furnishings and he can remember her saying, "You are being treated like royalty, but you better not go matching that life up against ours. Ours is the best." He had laughed and she joined in because they both knew how they felt about each other and their life together.

This he can still enjoy, but COVID-19 has cheated him out of the rest. He no longer can enjoy the art-filled Mediterranean restaurant, the spa, or the bar, instead he is served in his room.

It is torturous waiting. He turns on the television and tries to find something to distract him. He comes across 'The Ghost Writer'. This is a movie he has meant to watch but had not found the time. He sits back with the last of his beer, his eyes glued to the television and his mind slowly finding space to enjoy the movie.

His cell rings. Matthew has been so distracted he almost forgot he was waiting for a call. When he picks up his cell, he sees that two hours have passed since he called Ryan.

"Hello."

"Hi Matt. This is Ryan."

"Yes, Ryan. Any good news to report."

Ryan hesitates and Matthew knows before he says, "No, nothing. Ran into roadblocks at every turn."

"I understand. Thanks for trying."

Matt is about to disconnect when he hears Ryan. "Wait, Matt. There is another way."

"What do you mean."

"It sounds crazy, but, well, hear me out...You can drive."

"Drive, are you crazy."

"No. It is the only way. Just listen. The driving distance between here and Wuhan China is 8,662 km. It takes approximately 5 days to drive there which if you break it up with rest stops is possible. Not ideal, but not impossible."

Matthew, getting over his initial shock knows he is right. Secretly he had hoped that they had a private jet or helicopter to use to get him there, but even they would be under the same limitations as he was finding himself. "Are you sure that is the only way."

"I am sure. What I can do is give you a route that will be safe for you and get you reservations at the best hotels and motels along the way."

"That would be helpful."

"Okay now, I know you already have a VISA. The drive from Italy to China can be fascinating and I admit a challenging endeavor, but it is possible. Because you will have to go through many different countries, while crossing the continent you will realistically need to acquire assistance and I can give you that. I have planned such a journey before and know the preparation can be complicated. I will set up your stop points and help with the necessary paperwork, which we should get started on right away."

"I have a VISA already."

"Yes, I know, but you are going to need a lot more. Got your note pad?"

"Just a minute." Matthew put his cell down and hurried over to the desk set up by the window. There he sees his notepad and he takes it with him back to the sofa. He turns off the television while picking up his cell. When seated he says, "Okay, I am ready.

"Okay. You will need a passport, valid for at least 6 months, Chinese tourist VISA, Vehicle registration certificate, Vehicle inspection report (TÜV, MOT, DEKRA, Contrôle Technique, ITV etc.)"

"What?"

"Do not worry, I will take care of it."

"Vehicle photos, ID photo of you so you can get a temporary Chinese driver's license. Though not needed in China, you will need a national driving license as well."

"Wow!"

"Wow is right, but don't stress, we can do this. You need to come to the Embassy as quickly as you can so that we can get started on the paperwork."

"Ah, well, I can be there in 30 minutes."

"Ask for me when you get here. While I am waiting, I will get an itinerary together for you. See you soon." With that Ryan disconnected the call.

Ryan got busy. The ideal route may depend on where in Italy you start from and where you are planning to travel to in China. However, a basic route, which should offer both efficiency and practicality, will take him through Austria and the Czech Republic, then through Poland and Belarus, before arriving in Russia. From there, he will travel through Kazakhstan and have the option of either passing through Mongolia, taking him into China via Inner Mongolia, or travelling through Kyrgyzstan, bringing him into China via the Xinjiang region. Ryan knew some people opt for other routes, but they may lengthen the journey and complicate matters further. Matthew was in a hurry and did not need to deal with any complications.

Ryan painstakingly documented the trip which he would have to offer alternatives since he was not sure what Matthew might run into. So, he began. On the first leg of the trip Matthew could enter China from Kyrgyzstan going from That route would take him through Italy, Slovenia, Hungary, Ukraine, Russia, Kazakhstan or Uzbekistan, Kyrgyzstan, Turkut Port or Irkstan Port, China.

Tapping his lip with a pencil, Ryan studied the routes and noted his connections to contact before mapping out the next. He could enter China from Mongolia which meant he would go from Italy, Austria, Czech, Poland, Belarus, Russia, Mongolia, Bulgan Gol or Zamiin, Uud, China. Again, he checked out his connections in each location.

He went on to the next route being China from Kyrgyzstan going through Italy, Slovenia, Croatia, Serbia, Bulgaria, Turkey, Iran, Turkmenistan, Uzbekistan, Kyrgyzstan, China or he could route him to China from Pakistan, taking him from Italy, Slovenia, Croatia, Serbia, Bulgaria, Turkey, Iran. The last one he dismissed it was best that he stay away from the Iran-Pakistan border.

Ryan sat back looking it all over. Just the names of the places along the route was enough to tire him out. This would be a long journey to map, so he took a breath and began again.

Most of the European leg of the journey should be fairly simple, as Matthew would not need separate visas to cross borders into countries like Austria, the Czech Republic and Poland. Similarly, Kazakhstan can usually be accessed without a visa if you are not staying for more than 30 days. However, he would need visas for countries like Russia and Mongolia, and his fingerprints taken.

Chapter 43

From September through November of 2020, the death rate from COVID-19 skyrocketed. In the United States alone, 195,000 Americans died from COVID-19 in just the month of October. And unlike a normal seasonal flu, which mostly claims victims among the very young and very old, the second wave of COVID-19 exhibited what is called a "W curve"—high numbers of deaths among the young and old, but also a huge spike in the middle composed of otherwise healthy 25- to 35-year-olds in the prime of their life.

The medical society was exasperated. Not only was it shocking that healthy young men and women were dying by the millions worldwide, but it was also how they were dying. Struck with blistering fevers, nasal hemorrhaging and pneumonia, patients were drowning in their own fluid-filled lungs.

The COVID-19 outbreak triggers a dangerous immune overreaction in healthy individuals leading to severe inflammation and the fatal buildup of fluid in the lungs.

The deadliest week in 2020 was from October 11 through the 17th, the same time New York City's numbers of cases and deaths were cresting during the second wave of the pandemic. The highest count of deaths reported is 5290 deaths throughout the United States alone and this leads to talks of a national health insurance plan in Congress.

All over the world, schools, churches, theaters, and public institutions in every community are closed. But the truth is that the there is no way to put a nationwide closing order into effect, as this is a matter which is up to the individual communities. In some states, the State Board of

Health has this power, but in many others, it is a matter of municipal regulation.

It is stressed that the disease is spread by breathing germ-laden matter sprayed into the air by the infected person in coughing, or even in ordinary breathing. Everyone is cautioned to wear a mask over mouth and nose along with keeping socially distant from each other. But not everyone follows the mandates.

Lack of quarantines allowed the flu to spread and grow and at least partially to blame are public health officials unwilling to impose a second quarantine. In Britain, for example, a government official knowing full well that a strict civilian lockdown was the best way to fight the spread of the highly contagious disease decided against it. The same held true in the United States were things were returning to normal and they did not want to risk crippling the workforce again by keeping workers' home.

The relentless needs of the workforce to keep the world on a path to normal where the food and other supplies were at levels before the pandemic hit became most important. Yes, this is the justification for incurring the risk of spreading the infection.

What is worse there is a severe nursing and doctor shortage as thousands come down with COVID-19. To try and remedy the situation, medical students are enlisted to fill in on the front lines at least until the worst of the pandemic has passed.

But chief reason that COVID-19 claimed so many lives in 2020 is that science simply cannot develop a vaccine for the virus. What is graver the virus mutated resulting in a more infectious strain that is particularly severe and the resulting second wave of the epidemic dwarf the current outbreak.

Quarantine fatigue was behind Philadelphia's decision not to cancel its Liberty Loan parade in late September resulted in 1,000 deaths in the span of 10 days. Other cities like Denver lifted restrictions that November on Armistice Day only to experience a deadlier spike.

Pretty much all, cities in most countries, reported on huge crowds immediately congregating downtown in stores, cafes, theaters, and bowling alleys; starting on the very day social distancing orders were lifted.

It was harder to enforce such control in certain countries, taking away the rights of the citizens because of the vastly different economic landscape. So many more people, retail, restaurants, movie theaters and other small businesses were everywhere. All of which depended on the manufacturing sector to keep them afloat.

By December 2020, the deadly second wave of COVID-19 had finally passed, but the pandemic was far from over. But it at least became clear that governments realized they had to delicately balance the needs of the economy and social life with suppressing the spread of the virus.

At this point the focus turned to preventing a third wave. Researchers sought answers by studying the effect social distancing had on limiting the spread of the virus. That research was used to inform the public and aid in their cooperation with banning public gatherings.

In fact, worldwide orders making masks mandatory and shutting nonessential businesses is widespread in 2020 and heading into 2021. To support the mandate, fines are imposed on business owners and workers as well as the public who are found not wearing a mask or practicing social distancing in public places.

Chapter 44

Ryan has supplied Matthew with two routes, suggesting which he should follow first, and if he ran into any problems, to switch to the second choice he had been given for each leg of the trip. It made Matthew comfortable to know he had an alternative.

The first leg of the trip was from Italy to Slovenia and Matthew would cover 772 kms. Ryan informed him it would take 10 hours and 43 minutes as the route curved around the Adriatic Sea but there would be no border controls between Italy and Slovenia so no unnecessary stopping. Matthew made good time. The route swung to the west to Tuscany then headed north through a town called Emilio-Romugna. From there he continued north and slightly east to Veneto, skirting by several small towns until he reached Slovenia.

It was easy to keep to the speed limit since most of the way it was 130 kilometers per hour. That and the fact that the road signs were white-on-green which he was familiar with as this was the same in Italy.

As prearranged, Matthew checked in at the Antiq Hotel, near the Ljubljana Castle and offering him a view of one of Slovenia's most kayaked rivers, the Soča. The brochure in his room said that it flows for eighty-six miles, passing through Italy before emptying into the Adriatic Sea. He found the room comfortable and the view of garden courtyard added to the appeal. Since he would not be staying long, he need not unpack nor was there time to explore.

More importantly, he needed to get as much sleep as he could so he could start out fresh in the morning.

He ordered room service and ate alone in his room, getting up now and then to gaze out the window and doing some yoga to relax his body before turning in for the night.

The next morning, bright and early he checked out of the hotel. There was a café in the hotel set up with prepared breakfast items, wrapped and ready to go. Matthew grabbed a bagel and egg sandwich and poured a cup of coffee into a paper cup. He seized a banana and a muffin for later then made his way out the door to his car.

The route from Slovenia to Croatia was 277 km and would take him just shy of 4 hours to cover to the border between Slovenia and Croatia. He would be crossing the border on the southeastern side of the Schengen Area, which was a passport-free zone shared by members states of the European Union.

Once over the border, Matthew continued to Serbia. Ryan had him driving the 463 km along a great route and he made it in 6 1/2 hours. Because Slovenia and Croatia are members of EU there was no border to cross even though Croatia is not incorporated within the Schengen border treaty.

As much as he wanted to push it, he could tell by the feel of his body, it was best to call it a day and according to the itinerary, this was where Ryan had set up a hotel for him.

From the parking area, Matthew could tell that The Damianii Luxury Boutique Hotel & Spa in Omis was high end. It is a quaint hotel, by the Adriatic sea, just steps from Duce Beach and a 4-minute drive from Cetina Gorge.

Matthew is beginning to see the picture. Ryan has made sure he can enjoy the moment by going the distance on putting him up in great hotels and so far, ones that offer him a view. With the pandemic there is not much to do except stay in his room.

Here again the room is nicely furnished with a jacuzzi on the terrace and a spa like bathroom. As soon as he had settled into his room, Matthew could not resist a walk on the beach before sitting down to an outdoor seafood dinner. Later in his room, he called down for a beer. He was about to take a shower when there is a knock on the door. Not expecting anyone, Matthew is cautious and puts his eye to the peephole before opening the door.

"Hello," he says.

"Your beer, sir."

"Just a minute." Matthew grabs his wallet and unlocks the door.

"Thank you."

He relieved the waiter of the beer and handed him a tip. "Thank you."

The man bowed before turning and heading down the hall. Matthew closed the door.

Instead of a shower, Matthew changed into his trunks and taking his beer with him, climbed into the jacuzzi. Once settled he gazed out over the Adriatic Sea. Everything around him seemed to melt away as the sea seems to take him over. The water is the deepest blue he has ever seen. He sits there, his body relaxing and his mind focusing only on the sea until his beer is gone and the sky darkens.

Regrettably, he climbs out of the jacuzzi and heads to the bathroom to prepare for bed. He rinses out his trunks and hangs them on the towel rack to dry before leaving the bathroom.

Settled in, he places a call to Sonya. The call goes to voice mail, so he leaves her a message. "It is me, lover. I am on the shore of the Adriatic Sea in Croatia and besides missing you, I am in heaven. I will call again, but for now, I am turning in for the night. Love you."

Matthew wiggled around making the bed form to his body and in minutes he fell into a deep sleep.

Used to the one nighters, Matthew appreciates the fact there is no packing and unpacking to be done, except for his toiletries, and in this instance, his trunks.

So, when the alarm on his cell goes off, in a matter of minutes, he is awake, dressed and on his way to the café to fix a cup of coffee. This is day three of his journey and already he feels a coolness in the air as he makes his way to the car to begin the 10-hour drive ahead of him to the next stop.

The trip to Bulgaria will cover 482 km and clock in at around 6 ½ hours. Ryan has sent him travelling through Serbia, rather than Romania as the roads are better going via the Trakia motorway designated A1 and going through Sofia and Plovdiv.

Checking the GPS, Matthew observes he is making good time. Ryan had advised, he fill the tank in Bulgaria since Turkey had the highest gasoline prices and Matthew does this before continuing through Bulgaria and heading to Turkey.

Ryan has him completing a 416 km trip on E80 that should take another five hours before stopping for the day in Istanbul. At that point he will be almost halfway to Turkey.

The High-Speed Toll System put in place on E80 means he cannot pay highway or bridge tolls with cash or credit card. It must be paid in advance. Thank goodness for Ryan or he would not have known that or had the proper funds to cover the tolls.

Matthew spends the night at the Swissotel The Bosphorus, Istanbul a five-star luxury hotel right in the center of Istanbul on the European banks of the Bosphorus. Matthew cannot help thinking that under normal conditions, this would be a great place to vacation as driving up to the hotel he noticed a lot of world-class shopping places and night clubs. Only none of this is available now as he reaches the hotel and checks in.

"Sir, if I leave my soiled clothes outside my door, can they be cleaned and returned before I leave in the morning?"

"No problem, Mr. McKenna. We can probably have them back to you this evening if you like."

Matthew sighs, "That would be wonderful."

He has been trying to record the experience of this trip which he might consider for a book. So far nothing but routes, hotels and views are all he has to offer but he faithfully continues to journalize.

When he finishes, he tries to reach Elise, but there is no answer. He next tries to reach Sonya. Again, no one answers. She must be busy at the hospital, he assumes. Otherwise she would have returned one of his calls by now. He does not worry, instead he studies the itinerary for the following day before calling it a night.

It is sheer exhaustion that allows him to sleep so soundly. He is used to being on the road during the early release of his books, but with his mind a jumble with thoughts of his missing daughter, he should not be able to sleep. Only he does and each morning when he wakes refreshed, he knows it has been a dreamless night.

The first thing he does is go to the door of his room and open it. As promised, there is a bag waiting for him. Matthew closes the door and carries the bag over to the bed where he opens it, smiling. "It is only at hotels they iron underwear, " he says as he removes the freshly laundered clothes and adds all but one set of jeans, a collared shirt, socks, and underwear to his suitcase, along with the laundry bag that can come in handy.

With his clothes laid out, he goes into the bathroom to get ready. It takes him little time to shower, brush his teeth, and comb his hair, placing each of his toiletries into his travel bag. He takes one last look around to make sure he has everything, then, does the same in the bedroom. Assured he has not missed anything; Matthew anxiously heads for the door.

In the lobby, Matthew fixes a cup of coffee to go. Matthew, a people person, misses being able to say hello to a stranger, or smile as someone passes by, but that does not happen. The stay in orders across the nation has turned the world into a ghost town along with taking away all the pleasures of life. To get his mind off this trail of thought he reflects instead on this being day four of his journey which means he is almost to his destination.

With that thought in mind, he heads to the car and puts his belongings inside before climbing behind the wheel. He is on his way to Turkey and following Ryan's notes, he gets on E80 and begins the endless Fast Transit System (HGS) ride. He is well prepared, having the HGS transponder on his vehicle and all tolls paid in advance.

And there are lots of toll booths on the motorway, as he goes through Serbia, Belgrade to Nis which is around 100km from the Bulgarian border. Today he is going to be on the road for at least 10 hours and once he reaches Turkey,

Ryan has included vignettes in his travel package. These he will need for Austria and Hungry.

The roads are excellent and well surfaced, but Ryan had caution him that in both Serbia and even more so in Bulgaria to be VERY careful about observing speed limits as it is a huge obsession in both locations. He warned him that the police hide in the most amazing places and in Bulgaria are in almost every village.

It was a great stretch with amazing scenery from Nis to the border crossing where Matthew drives through tunnels and at the bottom of one is a spectacular gorge with a river. He reaches Turkey in a little over the time estimated by Ryan as he was indeed careful to stick to the speed limits and may have slowed a bit to take in the view.

That day ends in the same manner as all the ones before.

Day five Matthew faces the longest stretch of his trip. Turkey to Iran would take 26 hours to cover the 2,300 km and he will be traveling via Route 2. The route has tolls and crosses a country border putting him into a different time zone. His aim is to get halfway, and Ryan has warned him of the dangers on this leg of the trip.

Matthew covers the first 901 kms in 8 hours, bringing him to the Iraq border. He continues for the same amount of time to reach Kirkuk.

As forewarned by Ryan, Iraqi Kurdistan is by far the safest region in Iraq, but there is still high risk of terrorist activity in certain areas. The contested city of Kirkuk is not safe for travel, and neither are the disputed areas outside Iraqi Kurdistan's official borders. So, Ryan has cautioned him to lay low.

Matthew does, making sure he does everything right. He is booked at the Kirkuk Plaza Hotel and follows the instructions to the letter, so he does not make any miss turns. Once he checks in at the Kirkuk he stays in his room, ordering room service and watching a little television before writing in his journal. After that, he turned in for the night.

He wakes earlier than usual, but that is fine with Matthew as he prepares for day six. Matthew uses discretion as he finalizes his stay and soon is on the road again. By now he knows his friend's itinerary by heart, that, along with using his GPS make it easy to find his way. This route he must follow to the letter.

Ryan had said rather than coming from mid-Iran at Van's Kapıköy Border Gate he wanted him coming in from northwest Iran at Ağrı Province's Gurbulak Border Gate which brings him in close by Doğubeyazıt and the ethereal IshakPaşa Palace. From there he would follow a well maintained busy direct highway route taking him through Erzurum, Erzincan, and Sivas. He had 1500 km to go to get to Iran and he had to make it without any problems so he drove vigilantly and when he tired, he stopped at a rest stop to stretch his legs. He was going to make it. Ryan had him pushing it, but it was for the best and after a little over 13 hours of driving on Route 80, Matthew arrives in Sivas, Iran.

Days blend one into the other with no deviance from the normal pattern. Since he has not been able to reach Sonya nor Elise, he does not try to reach them that evening, knowing if it continued that he could not reach either of them he would start worrying even more so, so on day seven he is up and about driving from Iran to Turkeminstan, crossing the Iran-Turkmenistan border which takes him around 8 hours. He is still feeling competent as he continues to Uzbekistan, which is another 504 km.

Matthew sees a pull off ahead and takes it so he can text Ryan.

"I am not going to stay at the hotel in Turkeminstan. Please cancel the reservation. Nothing wrong, feeling good, going through to Uzbekistan."

At first, he is feeling great as he starts on his way but after a few hours he begins to feel fatigue, but he pushes on, thankful the roads are in good condition. He drives with the window down allowing the air to keep him alert. All goes well and he crosses from Turkmenistan to Uzbekistan at the Farab-Alat border crossing.

In Uzbekistan he drives to the Hilton Tashkent City and checks in, wanting to just go up and get some sleep, but instead he orders dinner and when it arrives, he is surprised at how hungry he is. He eats greedily and downs two bottles of water with the meal. He has ordered a slice of pie for dessert and finishes that off before leaning back feeling completely satiated.

Day eight, his body screams for a day of rest, but Matthew takes a hot shower instead. He realizes that Ryan's scheduled stops had been well thought out and he should have followed it and stayed at the hotel in Turkeminstan. One of Ryan's 'must have' was a thermos that he could fill with coffee. Until now, a quick cup has done him fine, but he now knows he needs it.

Matthew feels a little selfish as he fills the thermos using up almost all the coffee set out for the customers of the hotel, but at least no one is around to see him do it. He grabs two wrapped bagels made up with ham, cheese and egg and a muffin before heading to his car.

He begins the 19-hour trip via A373. He drives the distance between Uzbekistan through Navoi, Khujand and must stop to stretch and move around. But he does not give up as he climbs back behind the wheel making it through Andijan and into Krygyzstan covering 1266 km in one stretch and polishing off the coffee and the two bagels. He drags himself into the hotel and once in the room, he falls on the bed, fully clothe. He does not wake until morning.

It is now day nine and Matthew is physically and mentally exhausted. He starts out much later than he intended and begins the drive from Krygyzstan to China; a distance of 2,613 km. According to Ryan it should take him 17 hours. Ryan has stressed the need for him to take rest stops and Matthew does.

He thinks back to the day Sonya had purchased his smart phone and must laugh. She had been right and was right again when two years later he was traveling excessively to not only Europe, but Asia as well. Sonya had said, "I am changing your smart phone to not have to use the SIM card anymore. It can be hard to get to places selling the SIM cards, or for that matter to always find someone who speaks English." As usual, she was right.

This leg of the trip calls for strategic time. Matthew needs to purchase a Torugart Pass to use the China-Kyrgyzstan-Uzbekistan International Highway. Since Beijing time is two hours ahead of Kyrgyzstan, he must plan well so that he can get through the Kyrgyz formalities and at the gates well before 11.30 a.m. in Kyrgyzstan, which is 13.30 a.m. in Beijing time. This is important if he is to get to the first major checkpoint and avoid waiting through the lunch break.

Ryan had suggested, he have snacks, water, and weather-appropriate clothing because if he did end up stuck outside the gates, he would have to wait on a barren, rocky hillside with no cover until the Chinese side opens again.

Matthew had water, but outside of the left-over muffin from a few days ago, that is the limit of his snacks. As it turns out, it does not matter as he makes it in time and is able to cross the border without any delay.

From there he passes through a lot of checkpoints before he finally sees the sign announcing his arrival in Beijing. Matthew is now in Mainland China. He sighs with relief. Now to make it to Wuhan.

Matthew was tense from his drive and admittedly needed to sleep. That is what he would do after seeing if there had been any word from his daughter. So, after checking into the W Marriott Hotel in Beijing Central, Matthew makes a call to Ryan.

"Hello."

"Hi Ryan."

"Matthew, is everything all right?"

"Yes, thanks to you, this trip has been long, but a breeze. I cannot thank you enough."

"You are welcome, my friend."

Matthew hesitates. The US Embassy in Beijing serves as the bilateral mission between China and the United States and its mission is to advance the interests of the United States, and to serve and protect U.S. citizens in China. If anyone could locate his daughter, it would be the embassy. "Ryan, I need to ask another favor."

"Go ahead."

"Can you contact the Embassy in Beijing and see if they can locate my daughter?"

"Sure Matthew. I will just need some information from you."

Matthew gave Ryan the details he needed and after hanging up, he felt confident the embassy would find her or at least have some information to share.

Matthew had not anticipated that it would take some time so when he did not get a call back that evening, he had to force himself to sleep. Then, not hearing anything the next morning, he felt panicky and anxiously texted Ryan.

"Have you heard anything. Leaving Beijing and on my way to Wuhan now."

From Beijing to Wuhan Matthew headed south to begin the 1172 km drive via route G412. It should take him 12 hours to reach his destination.

He drives through Baoding and onto Zhengzhou, his eyes constantly looking at his cell to see if he missed a text or a call from Ryan. He starts wondering if maybe there is not any reception on the highway, but he knows better.

Matthew does not stop to rest or take on any nourishment. Instead he keeps wondering what he will find at the end of his journey. Was Elise okay, or did something awful happen to her. Where was his daughter.

His mind has been so occupied he is surprised when he realizes he is here. Using his GPS, he drives up to the Wanda Reign Wuhan Hotel in Hubei, Wuhan, in the Wuchang District. The same hotel where his daughter had stayed during her visit to the country.

Chapter 45

As confused as Sonya had been on seeing THAT room of suspended bodies, so were the testing site employees who had to call in help when the test subjects got violent. Now, though as Sara sat with her nine employees, she did not feel like a leader. She had freaked out.

It was not like her. She had seen a lot of outlandish happenings at the test site and before that at the hospital where she worked. But this, was beyond anything she had ever perceived. They had turned smart, capable people into blooming idiots and to add to that, they were blue. Not barely blue, but totally blue.

"I am going to lose my job," Sara whined softly. She was good at her job, but she was about to lose it now. So then what, she wondered, would she have to go back to the hospital and be a nurse again. She had always thought she loved nursing and at first, she did. But then she did not. At first, she anxiously went to work each day caring for patients, communicating with doctors, administering medicine, and checking vital signs. Sara could not put her finger on what had changed, only that she knew she had to leave the hospital nursing job and think of something else.

First, she worked at a hospice thinking what she needed was a place where the patients depended on her and she could give them comfort. But, no, that was not what she wanted. So, from there she left and worked at a care facility and it was okay, but there was little aspiration in that job either. The people were old, and some were sick and there was nothing she could do to give them hope.

Then she found what she was looking for. She had gone to lunch with her roommate, Tempest and she had lamented her need for a change.

Tempest, listening to Sara, was giving thought to Sara's dilemma. She was and had always been that way; a person who had to find the right answer to help a friend out and she had no better friend then Sara. So now, as she listened to her once again searching for something more rewarding, it finally came to her. She waited until Sara finished her sorrowful rendition.

"Listen, Sara, do not fret. I have it! You need something in the medical field, but not too medical and you want to use your nursing skills, but not too professionally medical. What might be your cup of tea is working at a research center or at a clinical trial facility."

Sara had only been half listening, but then she lifted her head. Tempest was pleased with her reaction. From a frown Sara's mouth slowly worked its way to smile at Tempest. "You are a genius, Tempest. That is exactly what I need to do."

From that minute, Sara had gone on several interviews and with her experience and credentials was confidently seeking just the right job. When questioned about her change in fields, she had a ready answer. "I want to experience working in several fields using my nursing skills."

That led to the next question of could they depend on her to remain on the job. To that Sara would smile sweetly and say, "Yes. The work is less demanding, but the rewards are many." That got them every time.

It turned out that this job had met her needs. Her joy in coming to work each day was noticed by her peers and before long she was the head nurse, running her own facility.

Every clinical trial was designed to answer certain research questions and each clinical trial mapped out what study procedures would be done, by whom, and why. On staff there was a doctor, herself and one other nurse and several other health care professionals. Everything had been tested and reviewed so that when the trial on actual subjects came, which was her level of involvement, it was a matter of following protocol. She made a difference and in most cases the ending was 'happily ever after".

She loved it and now she was about to lose it. Something had to have gone wrong. She had authorized the wrong dosage, or maybe in the physical checking of the candidates she had overlooked something; a virus or infection that led to this reaction.

Sara knows that is impossible. The reaction on one test subject was logical, but all one hundred. That was insane.

Chapter 46

At some point during the fall of 2020, Andrew Matthews grew tired of throwing up constantly. At first it was fine but vomiting three days a week at an inpatient clinical-trial site was not worth it. He decided to be a clinical guinea pig when a friend mentioned he could get paid $2,500 just to get maybe a few shots and let them test his urine and such. It sounded too good to be true, but he decided to check it out.

He had been working a hodgepodge of part-time restaurant and factory jobs and Andrew was intrigued by the promise of an easier way to make money. He enrolled as a guinea pig in a four-week study testing a drug that might be the cure for the coronavirus.

From the moment he met the doctors and nurses, he had total confidence in them. For the first time in a long time, someone showed care and concern for him and did their job with devotion to detail. First, he was given a complete physical exam and blood analysis. Then they gave him a two-hour briefing about the trial – how long it would take, what would happen and who would be carrying out which part of the study with him. He felt perfectly safe and appreciated. Also, as with all clinical studies, he was told he had the right to withdraw for any reason, at any time.

The unasked question on his lips was, "Do I still get the money." Besides, he was sure he would go the length.

As it turned out, it was severe. Many of the participants became violently ill and he vomited while having his blood drawn. The clinic staff told participants to use a bucket rather than the toilet if they felt like vomiting, so that they could look through the vomit to see how much of the pill had been digested before it came back up. Now if that was not dedication, what was.

After the first round, Andrew began sneaking into the bathroom after each dose and forcing himself to throw up the pill, to stave off the side effects, but the staff caught on and told him he would have to leave the clinical test if he did not want to participate. He told them, no, he wanted to participate and would not do it again.

He did not, he suffered through the vomiting and eventually it stopped for him and all the others. At least that is what he heard since after the testing began, they would come and go individually. But several times he ran into one or another at a bar he frequented or just in passing on the street. It was not like they were out in the country somewhere amongst farm animals only. From what he

314

figured, there was somewhere around one hundred participants in the case study.

The visits were staggered and each of them had been taken to separate rooms so, there was little contact between them. When they arrived, they would be only waiting a matter of seconds before they were whisked away.

Matthew did not understand why. He wanted to ask if they felt different like he did. Heck, he could barely operate his brain anymore. But he never got the chance until now.

It was like he was sleep walking. He just left the examining room and walked down the hall. He was not the only one either. Doors opened and others walked in front and behind him. Only they were not walking to the exit. They were walking to the large laboratory on the floor.

He tried to think, but no thoughts came to him. He tried to speak, but his mouth would not work. All he could do was walk and he did not do that well either. His legs were stiff, and his body swayed with each step as he advanced to wherever he was going.

Chapter 47

Sara Brown was scared; they were all scared. It had to do with the test subjects....no, creatures who were still under their care. Something was wrong and whatever it was, they were responsible since they oversaw the testing facility. Whatever had turned these perfectly normal people into...what. She could not finish the thought.

The day had begun as normal as most days. The subjects involved in the test study arrived at the proper time slot and were taken to one of the rooms. The nurse, following the directions on the chart, administered a pill to certain subjects while others were given a cocktail. Every night when Sara sat with the charts, she reviewed all details making sure everything was in order. It always was.

Only this time, instead of leaving the building, one subject after the other, left the testing room and seemed to be on their way out, but they had not left. No, they all eventually ended up in the lab.

There had been signs. Several of the staff, during the recent staff meetings had mention changes in the behavior of their patients. Sara had listened to their comments and made note of them, but she was not too worried.

Her plan was to check in during several patient checkups but there was always more paperwork and less time to make physical contact with the test subjects. Besides, she had a great staff, and they knew their job. Now, though it was something. Confused and unable to make sense of what was happening, Sara had to call for help. There was no way she and her staff could handle this…What, what should she call it…an outbreak.

Sara's mind was racing back remembering the day that her staff member, Veronica had said she was noticing physical and mental changes in her test subjects but could not explain it.

"Dr. Brown, they are turning blue."

Sara had jumped up out of her chair. "They are dying. You are telling me that our test subjects are dying?"

"No, no, that is not what I meant." Veronica paused before blurting out. I think they are…you know…like zombies!"

Sara just stared at Veronica. She was confident and dependable, but now she was acting like she had no medical training whatsoever.

"Listen, sit down and explain what is happening."

"I wish I could, but I think you need to come with me, and quickly. You need to see for yourself."

Sara did just that. She put on her lab coat and while walking down the hall she pulled on her plastic gloves. "Which test room?"

"Any one of them," Veronica replied. "Anyone will do."

Sara stopped, keeping her face from showing the irritation she felt. She walked over to the test room door next to her, removed the patient folder from the plastic pocket affixed to the door and turned the door handle.

"Careful, Dr. Brown."

This was becoming ridiculous. Slowly she turned the doorknob and pushed the door open enough so that she could look inside.

The room looked fine. Nothing was out of order nor was there any signs of chaos. Sara pushed the door the rest of the way open and stepped in, not noticing that Veronica remained in the hallway.

Sara opened the folder. The name of the test subject was Andrew Matthews. She looked up and walked in a little further and said, "Good morning, Andrew. How are you feeling today?" When there was no reply, she looked up.

At first, she did not see him as her eyes moved around the small room. He was not on the examination table, which is where she had expected to see him, but then she heard movement off to her right.

Sara turned her body in that direction and stared at the wall, allowing her gaze to move slowly across the area, only looking up, instead of down. When she lowered her eyes, she could not believe what she was seeing. Sitting off in the corner of the wall was what must be Andrew, only it bared little resemblance to his picture clipped to his folder.

There was barely enough skin covering his limbs that were totally blue, and from the way his gown hung, there was barely anybody under it. His hair was askew as if he was trying out some new punk hairdo.

Andrew did not see her at first as he sat there wondering what was happening to him. He could barely understand or question anything. All he could do was sit there, until he heard something. He looked up and saw someone looking at him and his body took control. He slid up the wall until he was in a standing position.

Sara was frozen to the spot, unable to make a move, watching him until she heard Veronica, "Sara, get out of there…. quick."

That shook her out of her stupor and without thinking she backed out of the room, closing the door behind her.

"What was that? I mean, what happened?"

"We do not know."

"We?"

"The staff. All the test subjects are like that."

"I do not understand…are they violent?"

"Not all of them, yet. We locked three of them in the lab at the end of the hallway."

Sara was trying to take it all in, but she did not know what she was dealing with. What she did know from what Veronica was saying they had to act quickly.

"Okay, we need to get…" she started to say, but then looked up and saw the rest of the staff standing in the hallway as if waiting for her to make it right.

"Okay, everybody, we will open the test room doors close to the lab first and together get the patients to move toward the lab."

Sara hurried down the hall to join those closest to the large laboratory doors. Her thought was if there were only three in the lab now, they had seventeen more to go. Keeping it moving her staff followed her directions. She carefully opened the test room door, stepped in, and moved slowly until she was at the far side of the room, then gradually moved behind the test subject. As she had hoped, this forced the patient to stumble forward until reaching the door, then as prearranged, the staff moved behind her. Together they guided the subject to the lab. Once there she opened the door and with a gentle push, got him inside with the others.

They continued doing this in the same pattern until the only patient left was the one, she had first seen, Andrew Matthews. She recalled that he was the first who had a reaction to the medicine at the outset. While the others had a problem in the beginning, it seemed to lessen as their bodies adjusted. But not Andrew.

So far it was going as planned as one by one they managed to get the patient into the lab without coincidence. But something told her it would be different with Andrew.

Sara was aware that Andrew was Veronica's test subject so he would know her best so, this time instead of entering the room alone she asked Veronica to come in with her and do exactly as she did.

Listen everyone, no matter what happens, "You need to be ready and do as we have been doing. No matter what. We can do this."

"Sara, maybe we should get something for protection. You know, just in case."

"What?"

She was right, Veronica knew Andrew. She watched as Veronica reached in her pocket and pulled out a syringe. Surprised, but remaining calm Sara asked, "What is in that?"

"A mild sedative. We gave it to all the others earlier when they started changing, but we were unable to get to Andrew. Besides, we wanted you to see him fully alert…well, as alert as he can be so that you did not think we were doing anything crazy."

Sara was dumbfounded. They had taken it upon themselves to sedate the test subjects without her permission. She made a mental note to reprimand them later. But for now, she would follow Veronica's lead.

"Okay. So, we will see where he is in the room and I will administer the sedative while you keep his attention on you." Sara nodded and they entered the room together.

At first it seemed to be working. Andrew was calm and leaning against the wall. Veronica moved in a little closer and when she did, Andrew looked up and stared at her while Sara moved out of his range of site until she was almost next to him. And that is when it stopped working as planned.

Andrew was confused and defensive, wondering what was happening. His arm swung out, catching Veronica in the face, and forcing her back against the far wall, causing her to lose her grip on the syringe. Sara's mind quickly registered, what was happening. Andrew was strong. Stronger than he looked.

A little dazed, Veronica tried getting up on her feet and saw Sara as she quickly rushed across the room, avoiding Andrew, and grabbing the syringe. Andrew swung his arm out again and caught Sara across the cheek, but she was prepared and held her ground. Before he knew what was happening, Sara pushed the syringe into his arm and quickly back stepped.

It was done. Sara let out her breath as she went over to help Veronica up on her feet and they stayed where they were, watching as the sedative began to take effect. The weird thing was that it did not put them to sleep. It only made them docile.

"Come on Sara, we have to get him into the lab before it wears off. I have a feeling the sedative will not last long." While she was talking, Veronica had already moved across the floor and over to the far side of Andrew. Sara only needed to be told once as she rushed up behind Andrew.

Sara directed Andrew's body while Veronica supported him with one hand on his shoulder and the other at his waist. The three in unison made their way to the door. Once there Veronica released her hand from his waist and opened the door.

Worried expressions greeted them as Sara said, "Quick. Help us get him down the hall."

No one hesitated as they lined up behind and beside Sara. The procession moved as swiftly as they dared toward the lab, trying not to focus on the bruises on Veronica and

Sara. When they arrived at the lab, they could see activity through the window in the door.

"Come on, someone open the door," Sara said. As soon as the door was open, Sara pushed Andrew forward and through the door. Veronica closed it quickly.

At that moment they all felt relieved while Sara, peeking through the window counted the bodies inside. When she was sure all 10 test subjects were now inside, she stood watching, trying to decide the next move.

It was decided for her. As the sedative wore off, the test subjects became more animated, moving about the room stiffly. Veronica moved up beside Sara and practically whispering said, "They cannot get out...can they?"

"What makes you think they cannot get out. We do not have a lock on this door so they can if they want to."

"No, they cannot." It was Stephanie, one of the other trained nurses on the staff. "When I finished checking my test subject, I noted several oddities, so I went to check out Theo's. The EKG showed that only the brain stem and small regions around their brain was active. Their sensoric, problem-solving and, as you can see, their coordination centers were completely disabled and inactive. That means they are incapable of figuring out how to open a door."

Sara turned to face Stephanie. "Stephanie, really. You watch to many scary movies. That cannot be or I would have seen it in the report.

"You will when you see today's reports. It only started happening today."

"Whatever. But I do not want to chance anything so humor me now and find something to hold this door."

At that moment, they heard a crash and looking into the room she saw the test subjects just swinging their arms out blindly and knocking each other out of their way. The strength they seemed to possess forced the other test subject to collide with the far wall just as Sara had. They did not seem to have any purpose as they moved around and not one of them seemed interested in the door.

The violent motion continued within and Sara observed that some of the patients were bleeding. That is when she made the call. They needed help and a direction. They could not just leave them in the lab.

At her interview for the position she had been given emergency numbers to contact in case anything went wrong. Knowing that was a formality, she did not ask what could go wrong, though now she wish she had, even if there would be no answer forthcoming.

"Okay, everybody, stay alert. I am going to my office to get a phone number and I will be right back."

Sara rushed down the hall to her office and went to the corkboard, looking for the emergency contact list that she knew she had put there. Finally, she saw it, took the pin out and with it and her cell in hand, started dialing as she made her way back to the lab.

After only a brief explanation of what was happening, the emergency recruits said, "We are on our way." In what seemed like merely seconds, she heard the helicopters on the roof and lights from the emergency vehicles flashed across the back windows of the center. Sara went out to meet them and as they made their way into the facility, she explained what was happening.

"Where are they now?"

"We herded them into the lab and have been watching the area as there are not any locks."

Sergeant Barnes tried not to appear shock as he asked if everyone was all right. She told him the staff was fine, but the test patients were showing agitation. "It is not like they know what they are doing. It is like they are trying to conserve their space and in doing so, they are knocking each other around. Sergeant, let me tell you they are strong, too."

"Okay, that is all we need from you. Is this all the staff?" Sergeant Barnes saw that there were only 9 people in the hallway with Sara.

"Yes, that is all of us."

"So, all of you, listen up. There is a helicopter on the roof. You need to go up the back stairs and aboard the helicopter. Me and my men will handle things from here."

"Are you sure. You might need us."

Trying to keep the irritation out of his voice he managed to say, "Yes, I am sure."

More men appear and Sara feels confident they will be able to take care of the situation. She figures they probably will be taken to be questioned on what had happened to the test subjects and then they would all go home; probably with no job to return to, but at least they were all safe.

That is what she thought would happen, but it was not that way. Sara and her staff were transported to the hospital by helicopter. Once they arrived on the roof, they were all put into one elevator with two security men. The elevator went down and down, and Sara noticed that there were no more floors listed, yet they continued to descend. When the elevator finally stopped, one guard stepped out and issued all of them to follow him. The other guard brought up the rear.

What was happening. Were they under arrest? It was at that moment that Sara began to worry, really worry, but she tried not to show it.

They were marched down a hall until they reached a mirrored enclosure that filled up a large portion of the area. The security guard took out his phone and in minutes, the door opened. Sara started to move forward, but the guard stopped her.

Soon a woman appeared in the doorway. "Hello, my name is Nurse Lottie Bond. You can call me Nurse Bond. Come in."

The security guards herded them in and followed behind them. As soon as everyone was inside, the entrance door closed, and Sara went from worry to being terrified. This was not according to any procedures she had read or been told.

"Where are we? How long will we be here? I for one want to go home and forget this day ever happened."

"Well my dear," Lottie leaned in to read her name tag. "Nurse Brown, you and your colleagues will be here as long as we feel necessary."

"Did we do something wrong? This does not make sense; we did not make this happen. We followed all the rules and protocols and cannot figure what we did to cause this."

"Oh, no dear. You did not cause this, and you did not do anything wrong. It is just that…well, for safety sake we need to isolate all of you for a while. You can understand that, can't you."

"Ah, we are being quarantined."

Lottie nodded. It was okay for them to think that and not the real reason. There was no way they could allow them out in the public with what they had seen. To keep it hush-hush they could not leave or make contact beyond these rooms.

The security guard stepped forward. "Okay, if you will all get in a line for me." They did. "Now, we need to pat you down."

"Why, what do you want."

"This is a medical facility and there are patients down here, so we need to keep them safe. We need to make sure you do not have any medication or any electronics that might interfere with the machines."

That made sense. "People help them out. Pull out what you have on you for them."

"Thanks. We will still need to pat you down."

"We understand," Sara said.

She really did not but she wanted to be as cooperative as possible so that they would be able to get home. She figured they would be examined, tested for the virus or any other infections and maybe be held for a few days at the most. The sooner the quarantine started the faster they were out of here.

Once they were processed, they were taken to a mirrored area where there was two mirrored doors: one labeled men and the other women. Sara went in first and the others followed her lead. It was like a high school laboratory, but only cleaner and smelt better.

Veronica, chatty as ever turned to Sara and said. "What do you make of all the mirrors?"

Sara thought for a moment then answered as best she could since the other staff women were waiting for her reply.

"Well, we all know about halls of mirrors at carnivals. There the basic concept is to be a maze-like puzzle, you might say. It can be confusing yet challenging to find your way to the other side."

"Is that what you think this is?"

"I do not know, but since we are not or have not seen any mirrors of different curves, in the glass to show confusing reflections of us, "she started jokingly, "I think it is a way to brighten up the area. We are in a basement, after all."

Several of her staff nodded. Sara smiled considering her remarks had settle them down, though it was not a true answer. Sara wanted to know why the mirrored walls too, but she kept that to herself.

Veronica reached her hand out and grabbed Stephanie's hand and Stephanie gave her hand a squeeze. It was not that they believed Sara, just that they chose to. Any other explanation was too terrifying.

The police who brought them here, turned them over to another group of uniformed men who led them down the mirrored hallway that was surprisingly long. As they advanced, it was not just Veronica and Stephanie holding hands, it was each of them finding a hand to hold. When the men stopped, they pushed open a door and moved aside. "Go in, ladies."

Sara turned and tried to pull off a look of confidence before turning around and entering the room.

She looked at the long table with several chairs and the brightly upholstered seats set off to the sides of the room. She continued surveying the premises until her eyes met those of the men on her staff.

Sara wanted to say something reassuring, but instead tried to appear confident as the women moved over to the end of the conference room where the men had taken seats.

They sat in a huddle at the long table, waiting, for what they had not a clue. No one spoke and Sara knew they were trying to make sense of all this. How long they sat like that, no one could say, but it felt like an eternity.

Worried and afraid, Sara wished it were over. That whatever they intended to do to them, they would just get on with it. She was about to say something when Nurse Bond entered the room. She was not alone.

They watched as Nurse Bond moved to the front and began speaking.

"Ladies and Gentlemen, I know you are wondering what is happening right now, but we need you to listen to what we have to say. This gentleman with me is from the World Health Organization. I am sure you know, W.H.O. is a United Nations agency so you can trust what he is about to say to you."

Nurse Bond stepped back, and the man stepped forward. "Hello, my name is Dr. Helmut Menz. During your stay here you will meet Dr. B.J. Vickery, Dr. Andre Ling, and Dr. Genevieve Krauss. They are also from W.H.O. To help put you at ease now, I will answer any questions you have, but first have something to share with you."

"What you have witnessed in your test facility has happened at another test facility in the Caribbean." Sara looked up, knowing that was the site set up at around the same time as hers. "No one knows why or what to do to stop it. So, we had to get a strategic plan quickly in order before the public was made aware."

"People are dealing with the threat of the coronavirus and if this, ah, misstep were to be found out, there would be panic. That panic might cause people to refuse a vaccine when we finally have one. So, you can understand why we have taken such drastic measures. We are hoping that putting all of our heads together, we can make this, ah, isolation work in our favor and not only find a cure for the coronavirus, but understand what went wrong and how to prevent it happening again."

Sara interrupted. "But what about us? When can we go home?"

Dr. Menz was sure he had been perfectly clear. He wanted to talk first and then they could ask questions later. He hated being interrupted, so to assure he was back in control, he went off script and did not try to hide his irritation.

"Something I am sure none of you are aware of, is that each of you was chosen for the test facility because you did not have anyone waiting for you or wondering where you are. You are dedicated individuals who focused on your careers and any socializing you did, you did it with each other. That made you perfect for this task and now that it has gone awry, it makes it easier on us to not have to put out a story to cover the whereabouts of each of you."

It did not seem to trouble him in the least as shock appeared on their faces. Nurse Bond could not believe the cruelty in his words, though she knew each declaration was true.

Dr. Menz continued, "Now that I have your undivided attention, I want you to just think, you might find yourself on the leading edge of science when a cure is found."

Sara Brown could not believe it. It could not be happening. "In other words, we are prisoners here."

"Now, Nurse Brown, do not look at it like that. You are not prisoners."

"So, we can go home, if we want to."

"Well, no, at least not right away."

"When." The word was spoken in unison by Sara and her staff.

Dr. Menz knew he needed to soften the blow of his words, so he gave it a try. "Listen. You are not prisoners; you are welcome guest and will be treated as such. We have set up nice quarters for each of you and we have a chef to do the cooking and a staff to clean up after you."

He paused and could see interest on their faces. "You are all known for your active minds and we will utilize them. You will not be just sitting around twiddling your thumbs. After today and you have rested, you will meet the other groups and we will begin our work. Each group has an assigned task and location so that we will not be stepping on top of each other. Some areas will require clearance and if you need to enter, that clearance will be given, but do not try to wander around beyond the areas that are marked, 'common area' unless instructed."

There was a titter of conversations in low whispers until Nurse Bond said, "I have folders with information for you to review," As she spoke she walked over and placed one in front of each of them. "Some of the information needs to be signed by you. You can take it with you and when you are done, let one of us know."

"How do we get in touch with you?"

"Excellent question. Your rooms have microphones in them. All you need to do is say, "I am done, or if you need a clarification, state it."

"So, if there is not anything else, you should get ready for dinner. You can even discuss the information in the folder amongst yourselves. After dinner, you can go to the television lounge, or even the recreation area where you will find everything you might need to keep in shape or just relax. The officers will take you around so that you get a feel for the place and where things are located. That is all for now."

Those five words rang with authority. There was a rustling of chairs as each of them stood with folders in hand to follow the officers out the door. Since their watches and cells had been confiscated, and there were no windows to see out, they had no idea what time it was. "What time do you have?" Sara hesitantly asked the officer leading them to the dining room.

"It is after six."

Alarmed, Sara asked, "after six in the evening?"

"Yes."

It had been just before noon when all of this happened. She could not believe it was that late, but why would he lie.

It was like being in a hall of mirrors as they saw their reflections everywhere. Even when they looked up, the ceiling reflected their image back to them. It was so weird and unsettling. There were reflections of her everywhere she looked with walls and even the ceiling mirrored.

Sara decided that this man was not from the police. He, she decided was some type of security for the place. As she followed the guard, Veronica moved up closer to her and whispered. "Once on the sitcom the Guiding Light, Rita Bauer was pursued through a hall of mirrors by Roger Thorpe. Just saying…"

"Shh," Sara responded.

The guard stopped in front of a lady who they had not seen before. "This is Mrs. Eduardo. She heads the cleaning staff. They had not noticed Nurse Bond was in the room until she spoke. "Mrs. Eduardo will take you on a tour of the facility and show you your rooms."

"Hello everybody." Mrs. Eduardo had a welcoming smile. She wore her black hair pulled back into a ponytail at the nape of her neck and she appeared to be in her late thirties, early forties. She was dressed in a black uniform with white V-neck collar and short black sleeves with white cuffs. Her features were even and quite pleasing as she smiled, exposing her white teeth.

The tour began. It was hard to determine the length of hallway with all the mirrors around them, or if there were any rooms off the areas that they passed. Finally, they arrived at a full wall, again mirrored, in front of them. She felt Veronica tap her on the shoulder but decided to ignore her.

Like magic the mirrored wall opened and from the double mirror door entryway, they entered what appeared to be the main living areas.

Over her shoulder, her words dripping with pride, Mrs. Eduardo said, "This is where you will be living. Follow me. We have a lot to see."

They were on the move again with Mrs. Eduardo giving a running commentary. "This is the study, the wall and ceiling color may be dark, but the tall mirrored windows on two sides of the room make this space feel bright and sunny. I think the art with thin black frames on this wall adds bold color and personality to this space with a good dose of drama and glamour."

Mrs. Eduardo gave them a minute to take it all in then was on the move again. "We are now in the dining room and as you can see there is bold art and botanical-patterned drapes to balance out the seriousness of the paneled walls. I personally love this room with its elaborate chandelier and velvet seating. Again, in here we have a lot of color. Look up at the ceiling." All eyes looked up. "That color is called artichoke. Don't you think it adds a punch of color and personality to the space."

Sara was thinking, it beats seeing your reflection staring down at you.

Her captive audience nodded. By now two things were obvious to Sara. Each room was designed to heighten the background and give them flair that removed the sterilization of the hall, plus the dark features and lots of lights made it believable that these mirrored windows could be just windows. And the added effect of someone they had thought was only a house cleaner, turned out to be a great tour guide and even had an eye for style was clever.

It did not go unnoticed by Sara, that to be this familiar with the area, Mrs. Eduardo has been here for some time.

"Please, follow me. We are on our way to the kitchen."

The kitchen had off-white cabinets and ivory-gray floors combined with charcoal walls, countertops, and decorative accents to create a chic and inviting cooking and eating space. A large island covered in a charcoal-hued quartz countertop is the central hub providing plenty of prep space, and seating for six. Floor-to-ceiling mirrored windows in the breakfast nook give the impression of flooding the kitchen with lots of natural light and warm ambiance. A doorway between the breakfast nook and kitchen connects to a hallway that leads to the laundry room, powder room, mudroom, and garage.

They were next taken into the great room which was an open space in the center of the area. There was a faux-steel facade on the fireplace transforming it into a sleek focal point. Four side chairs in cream with round bolster pillows were seated on either side of the fireplace. There was layers of cream, gray and deep wood tones in the great room playing off the color scheme and hues found in the adjacent kitchen and giving the quarters a cohesive, easy ambiance.

Someone had taken pains in putting this prison together so that the façade did not betray it as such.

"Next, my friends we are going to the gym. You will like it."

They did. The gym had a large black-and-white-striped indoor/outdoor rug for cushioning underfoot, ten digital weight systems, ten treadmills, and other assortments of equipment, plus a movie screen set up with a virtual personal trainer.

As they stepped out, they followed Mrs. Eduardo up a beautiful curving staircase to what she announces will take them to the second floor. Sara was quite sure, like herself, they were all in awe and doubly so as they ascended the steps. From the minute they had seen them, Veronica had poked Sara with an elbow and pointed a finger at them. "That must be fake, right?" Now they were about to see they were not.

The landing in between the first and second floors is outfitted with a set of benches under two large mirrored windows. In the evening when the stairwell is not lit with natural light, a vintage-inspired chandelier with leaded-glass reflectors illuminates each step. Mrs. Eduardo explains this as she leads the entourage the rest of the way up the stairs and opened the first door on a beautiful bedroom suite filled with plush bedding, a large upholstered headboard, glamorous metallic details and, of course, the latest technology including a custom smart mattress. A Hollywood regency-style globe light add a glamorous touch to the bedroom. The bright white walls of the master bathroom stand out against the charcoal-brown walls in the bedroom, creating a dynamic contrast. There is traditional recessed-panel cabinets with modern black pulls, a splash of yellow in the floral Roman shades and a hint of feminine style to balance the room's handsome, spa-like aesthetic. The luxurious standalone bathtub with its unique asymmetric design has Sara visualizing leaning back and enjoying a relaxing soak.

"One of the two bathroom lighted mirrors is Wi-Fi-enabled and voice-activated so you can use your voice to adjust the mirror's lighting or get the latest news and weather, play music or even hear a joke to start the day right."

Sara could not help thinking, this was most likely the extent of their electronic entertainment with the outside world.

They checked out the shower's six wall sprays, one traditional showerhead, a hand-held spray, and a rain head. Inside the water closet, an intelligent, toilet offers custom personal cleansing options, a heated seat and water-saving technology all within a sleek, modern design that does not take up much space.

The master closet had tons of functional storage, lots of lights to give it an open and spacious feel. There was enough carpeted floor space to do a few morning stretches or a little yoga and even one of those high-tech mirrors that doubles as a personalized workout portal.

Mrs. Eduardo turns to face the group. "There are twenty-five bedrooms on this floor. Each equipped with the same high-end furnishings, only different décor that we hope appeals to at least one of you. You can pick your own rooms out of the group of bedrooms.

"What now, Mrs. Eduardo."

"Now, you will follow me to the dining room where I am sure the evening meal has been set. After dining, you are free to go to your rooms or any other area within this space." The group does not miss the stress put on those last words. "In the morning, Nurse Bond will contact you and your day will begin."

Dinner was served to them and being famished, all they wanted to do was eat. While Sara ate, her mind was going a mile a minute. This was their prison; beautiful and well equipped, but a prison.

Chapter 48

Sonya knows the area in the lower levels of the hospital is being kept secret. She knows this because she has discreetly asked about patients she knew were no longer on the floor and then listen to what their caretaker had to say. It was always the same. The nurse in charge of the patient would basically reply, "I do not know where Mr. Smith is. He was gone the next day and when I asked where my patient was, I was told he had to be moved to another location that was better equipped to deal with him."

After hearing the same thing repeatedly, Sonya was sure that though they might not accept the reason verbatim, they were too busy to do anything about it.

Sonya tried to carry it a little further by asking if they had noticed anything medically weird happening with their patient. She would see their heads pull back on their neck as if they did not understand the question and then they would generally say, "All of this is weird, Sonya."

Sonya knew that what she was hoping was just one person thought something was going on at the hospital and she would have an ally. But she now knew she was on her own. She wanted to call Matthew, to hear his soothing voice and his thoughts on what she should do. But she did not want him to start worrying about her and be pulled two ways. No, she wanted him to concentrate on trying to find their daughter.

So, Sonya spent the next two days designing a plan to get into that room again. She waited wondering if anyone had figured out it had been her who went there and pretended to be the new hire. For all they knew, it was the expected doctor who went there and after seeing what would be involved, backed out. At least that is what Sonya wanted to believe because to consider anything else scared her.

If that happened, what would they have done to that person. They could not let her or him just leave and not say a word, could they?

No, she would not allow herself to get upset with wild thoughts. Most likely that new hire did show up and took the job and now they knew that the person who had showed up earlier and who was aware of this facility needed to be found. They would be trying to find her, so she needed to be careful. Luckily, she had not touched anything while she was in the facility and was totally masked with a visor and all the paraphernalia they were required to wear on the infectious wing of the hospital. There is no way they could identify her unless she did something stupid.

So, Sonya talked herself out of doing anything. She reviewed what she knew and that was their patients who were dying were moved off the floor and being placed in an underground facility where they were hung by chains and pulleys from the ceiling. The reason they were suspended she was told had to do with space savings.

None of that was illegal if they were receiving medical attention and were in a medical facility, there was no wrong doings.

The next day at work she is feeling more like her old self as she studies medical records of a new patient. She familiarizes herself with the latest lab tests and other diagnostic results. After that record introduction, with a genuine smile Sonya introduces herself to the patient, trying to establish a personal connection with them through brief, informal conversation to put them at ease before she examines them, explaining what she is doing in a calm voice.

She does this even though she is not sure the patient hears or sees her.

Once the physical examination is completed, the patient is still only slightly aware of the situation so, Sonya sits on the metal chair next to the bed so that she is at eye level with her patient.

She can now take the time to read the details beyond the previous testing. She sees her patients name is Coretta Stevenson and she was rushed by ambulance to the hospital, and has been three days in the ICU, before being moved to the coronavirus-only ward. The patient is female and first complained of having a constant headache. Later she had a fever, dry cough, and occasional shortness of breath that she thought was due to overexerting herself.

She had become tired all the time and her muscles ached even when she was not active. By the third day, scared and unsure of what was happening, her husband had taken her to the hospital. She was diagnosed as having pneumonia.

By day five her symptoms worsened. By day eight she had shortness of breath, pneumonia and acute respiratory distress syndrome with abdominal pain and appetite loss. And now, twenty-seven days later, she was barely holding on.

Sonya gave her hand a squeeze and said, "You are in good hands. Try and rest now."

When Sonya returned to her office, she wonders again about the patients in the basement facility. She wonders if they were at the point of Coretta Stevenson when they disappeared. She decides to check out the online records.

She logs into her account and begins checking charts of patients on the floor. She opened a word document to enter notes. She is so engrossed in what she is doing, she does not hear Dr. Warren enter. It is when she hears her office door shut that she looks up. Startled at first, she does not know what to say, but she recovers quickly. "Hi, Dr. Warren. Can I help you?"

Dr. Warren walks over to her desk and takes a seat in front of her. His look tells her everything. He knows.

Chapter 49

It seemed ages ago when reports surfaced out of China that a cluster of pneumonia cases in the central city of Wuhan may be due to a new type of coronavirus. The World Health Organization responded at the time they were still assessing the extent of the outbreak and at first found no reports beyond Wuhan, but then the situation changed drastically. Life as we lived it is no more and front-line workers are facing a frightening new normal.

Across the world people have been asked to maintain social distancing, or 6 feet, at all times and the majority have been asked not to leave their homes except for essential needs, such as medical care, groceries or exercise.

Politicians across the spectrum had been forced to respond as the novel coronavirus pushed the 2020 presidential primaries into uncharted territory. Alaska, Connecticut, Delaware, Georgia, Hawaii, Indiana, Kentucky, Louisiana, Maryland, New York, Ohio, Pennsylvania, Rhode Island, West Virginia, and Wyoming, as well as Puerto Rico postponed their primaries and others followed. Presidential debates were virtual and voting was offered earlier.

It was to be a busy election year for Africa with presidential, parliamentary, and municipal elections in at least 20 countries. It would begin with the Comoros in January and end with presidential and parliamentary elections in Ghana in December 2020. As more African countries started announcing their first cases of COVID-19 each country played it by ear. By June, some countries had already chosen postponement for some form of scheduled election. This includes parliamentary and regional state council polls in Ethiopia and legislative elections in Chad.

In the end at least 71 countries and territories across the globe have decided to postpone national and subnational elections due to COVID-19 and at least 60 countries and territories have decided to hold national or subnational elections despite concerns related to COVID-19.

People are stocking up on hygiene products food and medicine and it causes a worldwide shortage everywhere. And frustration is at a high level as stay-at-home orders, along with public gatherings of any kind are being banned. That means festivals have been postponed and restaurants and bars have shut their doors, only allowing for pick-up or delivery.

One of the few places where crowds do form is at the grocery store, where customers often queue outside as stores have enacted new policies limiting the amount of people inside.

The International Monetary Fund announces that the world should be prepared for the worst. COVID-19 has disrupted our social and economic order at lightning speed and on a scale that we have not seen in living memory. Meanwhile, unemployment reaches staggering numbers.

Following the lead of other countries, the U.S. State Department issued a Level 4 advisory, aka a Do Not Travel advisory, for all international travel.

Stockpiling and price gouging becomes the norm and people head to grocery stores in droves, as daily news coverage shows photos of empty aisles and lines out the door and people wearing face masks is mandatory at most public places. With day-to-day life at a standstill, anxieties around the disease and the future heightened.

The world has changed. Schools are closed and no one knows if or when they will open again. All major events have been canceled around the world. No Olympics, no sport events, etc. Food is even at a premium and for now gas prices are at a low along with the stock market plummeting.

Hospitals are filled and alternative measures have been taken for the sick. Even visiting loved ones at nursing homes is curtailed.

This was now the reality of life and it spread across the world. Even checking into the hotel was different. He had to have his temperature taken and COVID-19 swab administered. Since he did not have a temperature or show signs of illness, he was able to stay at the hotel.

Matthew was thinking about all this as he wakes in the Wanda Reign Wuhan Hotel in Hubei, Wuhan.

He had slept well but his journey and its purpose had not allowed for restful sleep. For him it would be a busy day, so he wasted no time getting ready.

He had to be prepared for anything so he checked his pockets to make sure he had all his credentials with him and then checked his brief case to make sure he had his lists of the places he needed to go and the people he needed to see. He looked at his Fitbit and noted the time. It was too early to call on anyone, so he decided to go down for breakfast.

Masked, he entered the elevator, no more surprised by the lack of hotel guest. He had run into this throughout his trip. No one was staying in hotels or visiting foreign countries with the pandemic roadblocks in place.

It was a beautiful hotel and quite pricey. During normal circumstances he could tell there would be all types of amenities offered. He wondered how his daughter had been able to swing these accommodations.

Used to being stared at, Matthew had a keen ability to ignore eyes upon him. It came with the territory. At first it had been exciting to be recognized, but it started getting old when he found it disrupted is everyday life. He would be approached in the supermarket and asked for an autograph when all he wanted to do was shop and go home.

Here, he figured he could be invisible, except for being a tall black man in China. He managed to make it almost through the lobby when he hears his name called. He pauses, works on his smile, and then turns to face the speaker.

"Yes, can I help you."

"Yes, you can. You are Matthew McKenna, right."

"Yes, I am. May I ask your name."

"My name is Vincent Peone."

"Should I know you."

"No, but I saw your daughter, Elise McKenna."

Matthew could feel his heart pushing blood rapidly through his body as he tried his best to remain calm. The man who had spoken was his age or maybe older. He had a scraggly beard, a thick mustache and one eye seemed off, but he could not figure out if it was a fake eye or just the way he did not open it all the way. His size was imposing too and if he had to guess, he presumed him to be at least six-three or more. Heavy set and looking like a boxer, he carefully chose his words. "Yes, I am Matthew McKenna. How do you know my daughter?"

"Mr. McKenna, I was sent here to keep an eye on your daughter, and I did, but my job stopped once she made it to the airport and checked in on her flight home."

Matthew was speechless, not sure what to say. "Who had you watching my daughter."

Matthew could tell that Mr. Peone hesitated before he finally said, "It was her boss in Rochester. This was her first major assignment and he wanted to make sure she was safe, so he called my agency, and we were asked to keep an eye on her until her flight home."

Matthew began breathing easier and managed a smile as he said, "Well, I thank you, Mr. Peone. Thanks for watching out for her."

"Do not thank me. I should have made sure she boarded the plane, and I did not. I have been trying to find her ever since, but with the lockdowns, it has been impossible. I will continue looking for her, but you, being her father, can probably find out more than I can. In any case, here is my card and if you give me your number, I will call you if I have any luck."

Matthew took the proffered card and gave Mr. Peone his. "That is my cell so you should be able to reach me at any time. And again, thank you."

Matthew continued his way to the restaurant area of the hotel where there were a few seated guests, all wearing masks. Instead of being shown to a seat, he was told to sit anywhere there was not a distancing sign.

Once seated he looked over the menu and the deep-fried dough sticks, served with a steaming bowl of sweet soymilk for dipping sounded good. When the server came to take his order, he added a pot of Oolong tea.

While he waited for his breakfast, he pulled out his agenda. He had the address of the travel agency and the name of the man he needed to talk with. He needed to talk with staff at the hotel in case there is something they forgot to mention. Then he needed to go to the airport and see if there was anything that might give him a lead. He was hopeful someone would remember something.

When his breakfast arrives, he said, "Thank you in Chinese as his wife had taught him."

When the server responded in English, he is glad since he could not carry on a full conversation in Chinese and needs to ask her about Elise. "Miss, can you look at this picture. Do you remember seeing this woman?"

The server hesitates so Matthew pulls out his license showing his name and adds, "It is my daughter, and I am looking for her."

The server relaxed. "Yes, sir, she stayed here."

"Well, she is missing. Did you notice anything...someone following her, just anything to help me?"

"No, I only saw her when she came to the restaurant. She did have a friend who met her here."

Matthew dug into his briefcase and pulled out a picture of Bai Zhao. The server blushed as she looked at the picture. "Yes, that is him...he is so handsome..."

"Thank you," Matthew said, then looking at her nametag added, "Soui thank you for your help."

The server paused. "Sir, you might check with the front desk, the front office manager and the concierge. They may be able to tell you more.

Matthew thanked her again. He quickly ate his breakfast and once he was done, he went directly to the front office manager's desk. Yes, he remembered Elise and could verify that she checked out on time and he had an Uber called to take her to the airport. He directed Matthew to the concierge who was able to add that he had personally helped Elise into the Uber and when Matthew asked what did the

Uber driver look like, he had told him he knew the driver personally and could vouch for him.

"Good, that's good. Can you give me a name and where I can reach the driver," Matthew asks then looking at his name plate adds, "Fritz, I trust your judgment, but he might have more to add."

Matthew waits while the concierge takes out his wallet and finds a piece of paper. He writes the information down for Matthew. He does it slowly and carefully and Matthew knows it is because he is not used to writing in English. "Thank you, Fritz."

Matthew next makes his way to the travel agency and as luck would have it, Bai Zhao is in the office. He begins by introducing himself.

"Good morning Mr. Zhao. We briefly spoke on the phone. My name is Matthew McKenna, and I am looking for my daughter, Elise."

Bai tries not to look shocked. He is surprised to see this handsome black man informing him that he is Elise's father. Not that it mattered, but he just was not prepared for this. Elise had told him her father was a writer, but not that he was black.

"Yes, ah, Mr. McKenna. Your daughter was my client while she was here. When I heard she was missing, like I mentioned to you on the phone, I went to the airport myself. They told me she checked in, but never boarded the plane."

"What do you make of that, Mr. Zhao?"

"Please, call me Bai. I do not know what to make of it. Something may have happened, but I do not know. I suggest we go to the airport together. Not all the employees speak English so I can help you there."

"Thank you, Bai. When can you leave?"

"Right now. I will drive."

The men talked on the way and Bai found himself liking Mr. McKenna. Matthew liked Bai, too. They conversed easily about Elise, and the tour Bai had taken her on. At one point Bai started to share his personal feelings for Elise but thought better of it. Besides, behind masks, it would not be easy to see his reaction. By the time they arrived at the airport they were like two friends catching up with each other.

After the initial greetings, Bai and Matthew had removed their masks so when they arrived at the airport, Bai reminded him to put it back on before getting out of the car.

With masks on, Bai and Matthew went into the airport. They had just stepped inside the door when they were asked to step aside. They did. In a few minutes, their cheek was swabbed, and their temperature taken. A few minutes later they can put their masks back on and enter the airport.

Even though they knew Elise was said to have arrived at the airport, they went to the reservation counter.

"Hello, my name is Matthew McKenna and…"

"THE Matthew McKenna,"

Matthew had been searching in his briefcase for Elise's flight information. He looked up and smiled. "Yes, if you mean the author. That is me."

The flight attendant blushed. "Oh my. I am sorry, but I am a big fan." She took a deep breath then said, "How can I help you Mr. McKenna."

Matthew had the confirmation number for the flight and a copy of the full itinerary. Smiling, he handed it over the counter. "Can you check to see if Elise McKenna checked in and if she made her flight."

"Sure, no problem. Just give me a minute."

Matthew felt Bai tap him on the shoulder. He turned. "So, you are a celebrity. I did not know."

"No, I am an author and there are people who know me from my books."

At that moment, the flight attendant returned with a frown on her face. "I am sorry, Mr. McKenna, but we do have her checking in, but never boarding the plane. I wish I could help."

"No, you have helped. We just need to figure out what happened after she arrived at the airport. Was there any commotion that day, something unusual that happened?"

"I cannot say but let me ask one of the other attendants."

Matthew and Bai observed as she went to speak to her co-workers, telling them the date and time she was interested in. Just when it looked as though no one could help, they heard someone say, "Wait a minute. I remember that day."

Their attendant returned bringing another woman in tow.

"This is Mr. McKenna and the girl I was asking about is his daughter."

"Hi Mr. McKenna."

"Hello. You remember something?"

"Yes, I do. I remember asking someone to cover for me while I went to the restroom. I went in and saw her. This woman was on the floor by the sink and she was bleeding. I immediately called for help. They asked me who she was, but I did not know, and they took her to the hospital."

"Oh my god. Was she alive?"

"Maybe…I do not know. She could have been just unconscious."

"Where did they take her."

"I think it was to the new hospital, Huoshenshan. The other hospital is overloaded with the coronavirus patients. This one was built for them, and, it is where they said they were taking her."

Anxiously, Matthew asks, "Where is the hospital."

Bai spoke up. "I know exactly where it is. Come on I will take you there."

"Thank you miss. You've been a big help." He raised his eyes and gazed around at the faces behind the counter. "Thank you, all of you."

Bai and Matthew walked quickly through the airport and back to Bai's SUV. As he drove, Bai filled Matthew in on the hospital. "Huoshenshan Hospital is an emergency hospital built near the city of Wuhan. It is in the district of

Caidian which is one of the western neighborhoods of Wuhan. When COVID-19 hit they built this one thousand bed facility in two weeks. It has all modern and up-to-date medical technologies and is served by the country's best qualified staff. If she is there, she is well cared for."

"I think I heard about that. They started working on it sometime in January and you say it was totally completed in two weeks?" Matthew thought about it. "Oh, come on. That is impossible."

"It would seem, but they did it. They had over 7000 construction workers working around the clock."

"It is a real hospital. Not some tent for overflow."

Bai laughed. "Yes, Mr. McKenna, it is a real brick and mortar hospital, and it has a thousand beds."

"That is quite big."

"Yes, it is. It covers 60,000 square meters which is equal to 645,000 square feet."

"What about staff... what about equipment."

"Come on Mr. McKenna...No shortage of people in Wuhan," he said it with a light lilt in his voice.

"Please, call me Matt."

Bai looked at his passenger. Just those four words meant a lot to him. Matt accepts him.

"No problem there. Hundreds of doctors and medical personnel were drafted in from China's military to treat patients at the hospital and many of the fourteen hundred medical specialists have worked in the treatment of severe acute respiratory syndrome, or SARS, which the new coronavirus is related to."

At that moment they were pulling up at the facility. It was massive, but Bai seemed to know his way around. He easily found the parking lot nearest the main entrance and in minutes they were walking toward the massive front door.

"Matt, I will do most of the talking for us. I do not think many of them speak English, and if they do, they appreciate being spoken to in Chinese."

"That is fine with me, Bai."

"Okay, Let's put on our masks."

Once inside, Bai paused at the entry way. The guard says, "Gentlemen, please step over here."

Matthew follows Bai and soon they are having their temperatures taken and their cheeks swabbed. They continue to wait while some quickie process is administered to verify they are clean.

"They are checking it now?"

"Oh, yes. I have heard of the procedure. Molecular tests are considered fully accurate when properly performed by a health care professional."

Soon they are released to enter the hospital. Bai walks confidently up to the front desk and speaks to the receptionist. The little Chinese that Matt knew, he was able to decipher enough words to follow the conversation. When the exchange ended, the receptionist picked up the phone and in a few minutes is talking on the line. When she hangs up, she smiles at Bai and says in English, "Your girlfriend is in Room 5270. She is fine. Simply fine. Her doctor is with her now."

"Do we have to wait?"

"No, you are both expected." Without asking, the receptionist gave Bai a sheet of paper that when Matt looked over his shoulder, saw that it was a layout of the hospital and she highlighted the way they needed to go.

"Thank you."

Matthew noticed a change in Bai's voice. It was more than that of someone having been worried or that of someone feeling responsible, feeling relieved. Matthew thought that there was more between his daughter and this man than just comrades.

The receptionist paused, then added, "That is in case you need to return on your own." At that moment, a gentleman dressed in a white hospital coat came to join them. He was taller than the average Chinese with black glistening hair, thick eyebrows, and an enchanting smile. He walked up to Bai and Matt and stuck out his hand. "Hello, Mr. McKenna, I have been expecting you." He let out a laugh."

At first Matt did not catch the joke, but then it came to him. It was a line out of his recent book that turned out to become the title, 'I have Been Expecting You'. "Ah, I see you have read my book."

"Yes, sorry, just had to say it. When they called back to say you were here, I hurried up to walk you two back. It is a ways down so I can give you a quick tour."

"Thank you, but first, how is my daughter."

"When she first arrived, she was in bad shape, but she is fine now."

"Do you know what happened."

"We were not sure at first, but from information from the airport attendant that found her, it seems she slipped on the floor and hit her head against the edge of the sink. The airport attendant was a mess, seeing all that blood, but we explained to her with head wounds there is always a lot of blood. But by the time we got her into the ambulance we knew there was more going on than that. She had a fever."

"At that point it became mass hysteria. We needed to call for help to sanction off the area and keep the airport attendants away from the rest of the public. Thank god it was early or otherwise we would have been dealing with a lot more people. When the ambulance left with your daughter, the other personnel quickly gathered up all those in the area and took them to quarantine. You can imagine the commotion that caused, closing that whole wing of the building. Anywhere else it would have been a big problem, but here in Wuhan there is always someone to fill in, especially at the airport."

Matthew interrupted. "Oh, so that explains why they didn't all know about it. If it had been the same employees, they surely would have known about it if they had to go to quarantine."

"Yes, it was probably all new employees that you saw there, or a later shift. But it worked out and kept everyone safe. I understand that the workers went in and sterilized the area and at the end of fourteen days, most, but not all the personnel were released. There were several with symptoms of COVID-19, so they were taken to the isolation ward here."

"Wow. Wow, my daughter caused all that?"

"You can look at it that way, but yes. That is why she is known so well; almost as well as you are known, Mr. McKenna."

"If she is so well known, why did not someone get in contact with us to let us know she was here. We have been worried about her since she did not return home from her trip here."

"We did, once we found out who she was. You see she had no ID on her when she arrived here. We think that she had checked her luggage and her ID was in her purse, but we could not find it anywhere in the bathroom. Mind you, we did not check for it when we found her, it was only later that we asked the workers to let us know if they found a purse in that vicinity. We never heard back."

"Couldn't Elise tell you?"

"No. She was unconscious when she arrived, and we had to deal with her head wound as well as the coronavirus. Her symptoms escalated fast which might have been caused by the head injury and she eventually was in a coma that lasted several weeks. We gave her the best of care, just like we do with all our patients and she made it through, but it was touch and go. It was only the last couple of days that she was fully awake and able to remember because she was delirious at the beginning and we could not learn anything about her. But now she is okay and is ready to leave the hospital."

"Is she in isolation."

"No, not anymore. She was moved to a regular room and has shown no signs of the virus or ill effects from the head injury. She is as good as new. Except she is missing a patch of hair."

Matt smiled and felt Bai pound his shoulder lightly. Matt looked at the plate on his jacket and saw his name was Wang Xiu Ying. He said, "I do not know how to thank you, Dr. Ying."

Dr. Ying smiled sheepishly. "An autographed book?"

Matt laughed, reached out his hand and grabbed Dr. Ying's. "You've got it."

Chapter 50

The tour began. As the men headed down the hallway with Dr. Ying explaining as they went.

"We made the hallways wide, very wide as you can see so there are no traffic jams with beds, people or traffic.

He paused. "Here, this room is available. Most of the rooms look exactly like this one as you will see when we get to your daughter."

Dr. Ying pushed open the door and they stepped inside.

"The Huoshenshan Hospital, which means Mount Fire God Hospital," he pauses when he sees the look on Matt's face. To ease Matt's worried expression he adds, "It is well built and is safe from ever catching fire. The hospital is an emergency specialty field hospital. I am sure you noticed outside that it is built near Zhiyin Lake and this is the Caidian District, of Wuhan. The hospital is modeled after the Xiaotangshan Hospital built in the suburbs of Beijing. There are a thousand beds which spans over an area of two floors and there are thirty intensive care units, medical equipment rooms, and quarantine wards."

"Each unit is fitted with two beds. Each room is negatively pressurized to prevent airborne microorganisms from spreading out of the hospital. It also has specialized ventilation systems and double-sided cabinets that connect each patient room to hallways, allowing the hospital staff to deliver supplies without the need to enter each patient room. The hospital is linked by a video system to PLA General Hospital in Beijing so doctors can talk with outside experts over a video system and about half of the building is isolation wards."

"Mr. McKenna you might like this. It makes for great writing material." Dr. Ying paused for emphasis. "The hospital received a donation of 'medical robots' from a Chinese company for use in delivering medicines and carrying test samples." He gave his same laugh and Matthew not wanting to offend, joined in.

"This is one of the standard hospital rooms," Dr. Ying continued. As you can see it contains two beds, two storage dressers and the usual bar of plugs and equipment above them. There are good size bathrooms and ambient light and like most hospital rooms, the walls are beige, and the ceiling and baseboards are light tan making it seem light and airy. It is practical and efficiently laid out."

"Now, we are going down another hallway which is away from the area your daughter is in, but it is where she was taken when she arrived. This leads to the Isolation Rooms." They continued down the hall until they came to an area that immediately changed in complexion.

"We are now in the isolation wing." At the entrance was a closet and Dr. Ying opened it to display paper hospital gowns, hats, shoe booties, masks and plastic shields and rubber gloves. "Here gentlemen." The doctor pulled on a temperature gauge and checked them both. "Okay, you are fine. We need to put these on before we go any further."

Once they were dressed, they stepped all the way in and proceeded to the first area on their left. Matthew had expected to see tented beds, so he is unprepared for the actual layout. There was a big metal door with an oblong window to view the inside. The grey metal door handle gives it the appearance of a walk-in freezer unit. Inside the patients are separated by an interior wall with a large oblong window, allowing light to shine into both areas."

Dr. Ying motions them back to the entrance and they remove all the gear that is tossed down a shoot. When they step over the threshold, Dr. Ying starts back down the hall they left and continue to almost the end. He pauses, smiles, and hands Matthew his card, saying, "It has been a pleasure."

Matthew counters back. "Thank you, Dr. Ying. It has been a pleasure indeed and I will send you an autographed copy of my book."

They watch Dr. Ying leave and then open the door to Elise's room.

Chapter 51

Dr. Warren strolls into Sonya's office and walks leisurely over to her desk. He takes a seat in one of the chairs stationed in front and once seated, peers into her face. His expression says it all.

Sonya starts to speak, but Dr. Warren, raises his hand. He places a finger vertically over the lips and she is silenced.

"Dr. McKenna, we know it was you so there is nothing to say. You just need to listen. Do you understand?"

Sonya nodded.

"So, I do not know how you found out about the facility, but you did. My hope is you did not share what you saw with anyone else."

"I did not, sir. "

"Good. That is very good. We do not want to cause a panic with all that is happening. We had your phone tapped so we know you have not talked with your family. We also know that outside of your mother, your family is out of the country so I think it will all work out."

Sonya breathes easier. "Thank you, Dr. Warren. You can count on me."

Sonya starts to get up.

"Sit back down Dr. McKenna.' The sternness in his voice was petrifying. Sonya swiftly plopped back down on her chair. "We are not through here. You need to know what happens next."

She could not breathe, it felt as if someone were choking her. Her heart was racing and all she wanted to do was curl up into a ball and wait for someone to save her. But no one would, no one was there. It seemed as if this was the end of the road for her.

Seeing the effect his words had on her, Dr. Warren tried to calm her. "Nothing bad is going to happen, but you will be unavailable for a while."

Stuttering, Sonya repeated, "A while?" Then feeling a little more in control added, "What are you going to do to me."

"Do not worry Dr. McKenna. What we are going to do is take you down to the facility. You will be staying there until we get everything cleared up."

"What cleared up?"

"A vaccine to cure COVID-19, of course. Hopefully, that will reverse the effects that the patients in that facility are experiencing and all will go back to normal."

Sonya was about to say something when there was a knock at the door. Dr. Warren looked expectantly as he turned his head and said, "Yes." The door opened and a doctor that Sonya had seen once or twice before stepped into the office. He moved forward so that he is looking directly at Dr. Warren who responds, "We are ready. Come, Dr. McKenna."

Sonya knows she does not have a choice. She stands and with Dr. Warren behind her and the other doctor in front, they walk her out of her office and down the hallway to the back staircase. If anyone saw them, they would see two doctors and maybe notice there was someone with them, but she was basically shielded from view.

As they walk her down the stairs, they explain that she will be living in the facility and assisting Nurse Bond with the patients. I and Dr. Henderson check in daily on the patients as well as the residents.

"Um, the residents?"

"Oh, yes, unfortunately there are 10 other medical staff who just recently joined the facility

"What, did they find out about your secret facility."

Dr. Warren had been civil up until then. Where did she get off calling it his secret facility? He decided to tell her exactly how they chance to be here.

"No, they did not sneak around and find it. They were at the test center where we were investigating a new vaccine for the coronavirus that was showing effective outcomes. The results were so promising that we decided to use it on the patients here at the hospital who were beyond our help."

"What happened?"

"Well, the outcome speaks for itself. Since you are now aware it might interest you to know that we had a test center in the Caribbean that we used as well as one here, but neither performed well. As you saw, those that lived turned blue, like the patients you saw and seemed disoriented and could be dangerous, so we sedated them, and they are now in the patient room of the facility. We have them in suspended animation in the hopes we will find a cure and save them."

"Let me guess, the staff from the test center are imprisoned down here."

"Not imprisoned, Dr. McKenna, more like quarantined. They are also being utilized in the care of the patients.

They were at the door of the mirrored room and Dr. Henderson stepped forward. The mirrored doors opened and the three of them entered. They were barely over the threshold before Nurse Bond appeared in the hall. "Welcome to the facility, doctors."

"Thank you, Nurse Bond."

Nurse Bond tilted her head toward Dr. Henderson. And then Dr. Warren. "Ah, and this must be Dr. McKenna."

Sonya was not surprised that Nurse Bond knew her name. She probably had blown the whistle when the new assistant did not show. Nurse Bond was smart, which is why she was the head nurse here. Just her first visit, she could tell that the nurse was not only efficient, but shrewd. Obviously when no one came, she figured it out that the person who did show, was not supposed to be there.

While the two doctors spoke with Nurse Bond, Sonya's mind was going warp speed. Should she turn and run. No, that would not work. They had voice or touch code on the door. She was not getting out of here until they decided to let her go…if ever.

Finishing their discussion, the doctors turned and headed towards the door. She could follow and force her way out... She turned her head. No, Nurse Bond was staring right at her as if she knew what she was thinking.

Nurse Bond smiled, saying, "from now on, please call me Lottie. We will be working together."

Meekly Sonya responded, "Okay."

"Now walk with me, Dr. McKenna. We are going to the staff quarters." Sonya had not gone this deep into the bowels of the facility and now as she walked with Nurse Bond, she is impressed. The mirrors were everywhere and created an optical illusion of a larger space by drawing the eye farther than the existing wall. They were in a basement, a sub-basement but with the mirrors there was the feeling of light in this windowless hall.

As she thought this, Nurse Bond spoke her contemplations aloud. "Clever, huh. The mirrors are a masterpiece. They make the areas feel larger and reflect both natural light; of which there is none, and artificial light to make a room brighter during the day and night."

She gave Sonya an enchanting smile. "You will not be alone. There are ten medical assistants, plus the cook, cleaning staff and security. I am sure they explained why they are here, so I will not waste time with that."

"What about the staff from the Caribbean Test Center?" Sonya asked.

"What? I don't know anything about a Caribbean Test Center."

Sonya said nothing. That could be possible. They probably only told Nurse Bond what she needed to know. So that inferred that the staff from that location were not brought here, or anywhere else. She hated to think what might have happened to them.

Nurse Bond paused and Sonya could see her lips move but could not hear what she was saying. She had not realized that they were at an entrance until the mirrors parted and in front of her was what looked like a living room.

Beyond that she could see a kitchen. It took her a minute to adjust as this area was not all mirrors. It was tastefully decorated. "So, this is where you will be living for now. The others are working but should return shortly. Upstairs are the bedrooms, and I am sure you can figure which ones are still available. If not, you can check with them when they return."

"So, what am I to do."

"That we will cover in the morning meeting. We have a full itinerary in place that covers our jobs, reporting system and time schedules."

"What else can you tell me."

Nurse Bond looks perplexed at first, then grins. "Dinners will be prepared for you, but if you want, you can cook something. This is to be treated like your home. Okay? I will leave you now."

And she did. Sonya watched Lottie depart. When she is alone, she cautiously searches every area of the downstairs, smiling pleasantly when she sees one of the staff and tries to look as though she is just exploring the areas. "Getting my bearings," she says as she continues to search for a phone or any communicating electronic device.

The living quarters are massive as she scurries from area to area until returning to the living room. She stands there and her eyes fall on the staircase. Even as she approaches the stairs, she is fascinated that the facility is two stories. When she first saw the stairs, she thought they were an optical allusion, but they are real.

Sonya has been combing the areas for some time and decides she must hurry before the others return. Frantically she races up the stairs and begins checking and each room…even the bathrooms. She finds nothing. There are no computers or phones anywhere.

There are radios and televisions everywhere, but no way to contact the outside world.

Chapter 52

The third wave of the COVID-19 occurred during the winter and spring of 2021/2022 and after the devastation of the second wave of the coronavirus there was not a soul left who thought it was all a farce and that life would be back to normal in no time. COVID-19 takes over the world for two long years and in its wake left an ungodly number of deaths.

Hope had risen when the number of cases dropped during the summer of 2021 giving false hope to the world. By August of that year the opinion was the virus had run its course. But, in retrospect it was just the calm before the storm when starting in Europe, a mutated strain emerged and in 24 hours killed millions of perfectly healthy young, men and women.

What finally grabbed even the non-believers was the fall of 2021 when in three especially cruel months the death toll rose implausibly. Global deaths from the third wave, while still in the millions, paled in comparison to the apocalyptic losses during the second wave, but it ranked close.

The powers that be sent the message that any man, woman or child who will not wear a mask will be fined.

Every person who attended or arranged large gatherings would be fined. Social distancing and proper hygienic requirements must be adhered to with no exceptions.

With most countries having lifted bans and opened stores, gyms, and recreational facilities, they had to reverse orders and introduce stringent lockdown measures once again.

As dark as the coronavirus crisis had been, the fact is it could get much worse and it did.

Cornelis Wilson was in her garden pulling weeds from between her flowers when she saw a squirrel just at the edge of her garden. "Come to eat my sunflowers some more my friend," she said. "Well you have to wait while I clean the area for you." Cornelis made a face at the squirrel then continued with her weeding. She loved working in the garden and enjoyed the beauty of her garden creations, that is if the bugs, animals, and birds allowed it. She started humming a tune as she worked diligently.

After that first initial confrontation, she forgot about the squirrel until, weeding at the back of the garden, enjoying the shade from the tree above she felt teeth sinking into the flesh at the back of her neck. Cornelis jumped up, surprised, swinging her arms and knocking the squirrel off her. "You bit me?" She reached to the back of her neck and her hand came back with blood on it. "You really bit me." Cornelis rushed back to her house and only when she was inside, did she check to see if the squirrel had followed. The squirrel was nowhere to be seen. She locked the door and then went upstairs. In her bathroom she washed the bite with soap and water and then planting her feet firmly, she reached under her sink and pulled out the alcohol. She soaked the washcloth with it and pressed it against her neck. Luckily, there was no one to hear her scream.

Nothing happened immediately and Cornelis pushed the matter out of her mind, but several days later she started feeling sick. She had been out in the garden in the hot sun when she felt her stomach do a flipflop. She stood up, wiped sweat from her brow and said to herself, "That is what you get for staying in the sun so long, you ninny." Yesterday it had been so sunny, she had worked in direct sunlight most of the day.

Cornelis felt it coming and leaned over quickly so that when she vomited, it did not get on her clothes or her shoes. It did take out one of her beautiful tomatoes though.

After that incident Cornelis stayed inside the next day, drinking lots of water and pampering herself. It seemed to work so she decided to chance gardening on the following day. She warned herself to keep track of the time.

Cornelis sat up, confused and scared wondering why she was laying in her garden. She feels very weak and sick as she sits there, sure she cannot walk so does not. It is dark out she realizes as she looks up at the sky. How long had she been out?

She amuses herself, waiting for her strength to return and then she slowly pushes her body up into a standing position. She lists back and forth at first, then feels confident enough she can make it to the house.

It is a slow progression with her mind going over what could have happened. All she can remember is waking up. By the time she makes it to the house and opens the door, she knows she passed out and it felt as though it was about to happen again. Quickly she made it to her phone and dialed nine-one-one.

Cornelis remained in the hospital for three days and underwent dozens of tests: X-rays, EKGs, MRIs, blood tests, stool tests, urine tests, and more. The doctors officially diagnosed her as having pancreatitis, an inflammation of the pancreas that can have the same gastrointestinal symptoms that she was experiencing.

"So now what?" Cornelis asks.

"You need to stay in the hospital so we can treat your dehydration with fluids and, if you can swallow them, fluids by mouth. We will be giving you pain medicine, and antibiotics and start you on a low-fat diet for the next few days. If everything goes right, you should be back home in no time.

"So, I do not have COVID, then?"

"No. No signs of that."

She did get better and was soon back home. She had been told to drink plenty of liquids and to call if she had any more problems.

At first, she was feeling great, but it did not last long. She kept getting worse. She threw up all the time, often after eating or drinking, and her heartburn would not go away. She called the doctor.

Another battery of test and then… "You tested positive for…" Cornelis interrupted him, "COVID-19'.

"No, Yersinia."

"What is that?"

"It is the bacterium that causes the bubonic plague."

"The bubonic plague...I have the bubonic plague?"

"You are lucky."

"Lucky? How do you figure I am lucky?"

"Other types of Yersinia can kill you within days."

"Ah, I see. So now what?"

"Well, I need to issue a public health warning even though this strain you have is not contagious, and we need to tell them where and how you contacted it."

"I do not know..." she starts, but then she remembers. "Ah, yes, a few weeks back, a squirrel bit me on the back of my neck. I'd forgotten all about it...You do not have to give them my name, do you?"

"No, that will not be necessary."

Her doctor gave her a simple course of antibiotics, which successfully killed off the Yersinia bacteria in her system and soon Cornelis was as good as new.

That was how it started before the reports came pouring in. A tiger attack in a wildlife park in Beijing. Then there was a bear attack called in from Yellowstone National Park. Still this did not raise concern, but a warning to carry bear spray, stay in groups, watch for signs of the animals, and keep away from areas with animal carcasses. Though the doctors had made their report, it was not being connected.

The news told of a woman who had been killed by a great white in the first fatal shark attack on record in the US state of Maine. A nearby homeowner said she saw and heard the horrible incident mentioning that first she heard the woman giggling and laughing and then seconds later, she heard her screaming for help.

Still no connection is made. But there was more. A hippo chased a boat in Africa, but hippos are known to be aggressive, then there was a bull attack on a farm in the Yucan, followed by a swarm of bees attacking the beekeeper. Still no cause for alarm.

The attacks become more aggressive. A herd of elephants stampeded a village in Africa and killed most of the villagers. Coyotes moved in packs down the streets of a North American town, and it takes the whole police force to stop them.

No one was now able to ignore that this was unusual vicious actions of animals of all types continuing to surface. From the smallest to largest of mammals taking over outdoor space, forcing residents all over the world to stay in their homes, People went from house to cars in their garages and when going grocery shopping, found the automatic open doors were turned off and had to be manually pushed to enter and exit the premises.

When the world was headed for its new normal with people back to work, stores opening and again able to go out and enjoy a meal, it all changed. Only this time no one complained about social distancing, wearing masks, and not congregating in large groups. Instead they cherished the seclusion of their homes, hoping that they would not have to go out at all.

As dark as the coronavirus crisis seems, the fact is it could get much worse and it did.

In some ways the Yersinia bacterium aided in the populations willingness to stay in their homes. No more were people mobile or having large parties. There was too much at stake now.

The world scientist were now able to concentrate on finding a cure for COVID-19 instead of defending their position. As for the governments, they were able to spend less time policing the population. There no longer was protesting or a clamoring to get back to life as normal. With the animal scare, everyone was more than willing to isolate.

But then people begin to determine it had to be safe and one by one they began taking chances to reclaim their lifestyle.

With partial seclusion the count keeps growing. In Europe, a Catholic Church nun died, along with six of her young charges. A service was held and from that initial count, at least 250 of the children became ill with COVID-19 as well as twenty of the Sisters.

In Spain a Reverend, wearing his mask and gloves visited a sick church member and along with his infant son was stricken with COVID-19.

Reports circulated that the person who coughs or sneezes discharges a spray more deadly than bullets or poison gas, unless the mouth and nose are covered by a handkerchief or they wear a mask.

Some took the advice seriously, others did not. There were places that refused, for the entirety of the pandemic, to close their businesses. There not being enough personnel to police every inch of the country, another directive came down that various businesses stagger their hours of operation to decrease the density of clients, customers, or students. And as for the danger of infected animals, well, nothing would stand in their way of being social because that is what humans do.

As time marched on, by the spring of 2022, countries such as China, South Korea, New Zealand, the UK and most European countries, have now substantially reduced the infection, while Sweden and Russia reflect an increase in the number of cases.

But three extensive pandemic waves of influenza occurring in succession, with only the briefest of quiescent intervals between them, was unprecedented. With a world population of over 7.8 billion an estimated 1/3 of the world's population or roughly 234 million was infected with COVID-19 and over 75 million deaths were reported worldwide. With those figures, who could feel invulnerable.

It was not until the summer of 2022 that the third wave of the pandemic subsided.

With the research reaching a climax, the vaccine dosage was being prepared and distributed and people drove to areas to be tested for COVID-19. It was all coming under control, along with the end of the animals claiming domains. How that was managed was not shared with the public.

Chapter 53

The first step after making sure that it was safe, was to decide on the patients in the special facility in the basement of the hospital. Because of the secrecy of the area, the meeting was to be held at the home of Dr. Warren.

Dr. Warren spent the morning trying not to think about it until he absolutely had to. He knew Dr. Henderson was spending an uncomfortable evening as well.

Hoping to ease his own mind, Dr. Warren went to the door off the bedroom and stepped out on the upper deck. He looked out over the panoramic view of Lake Ontario and took a deep breath. The sun was just coming up making a shimmery path across the water and immediately he felt the tension lessening. He stood for a moment longer then returned to the bedroom to get dressed.

As expected, Dr. Henderson was the first to arrive and Dr. Warren immediately took him to his office. "Make yourself comfortable. I will be right back."

Dr. Warren and Dr. Henderson oversaw the project. They were the ones to track the patients and those who had been sequestered for their knowledge of the vaccine program or the existence of the facility. They felt they had done the right thing. The key word was, 'they'.

Dr. Griffin Warren had to take a moment to remind himself that he was one of the head doctors at the hospital and was held in esteem and as such his peers would recognize his reasoning in this matter. Feeling more confident, he returned to the office to join Dr. Franklin Henderson, his colleague who was looking over records in preparation for the meeting. Dr. Warren did the same.

Coming to this meeting were the top physicians in their field. Some he had only talked to but never met in person.

He personally knew Dr. Timothy Evans, soon to be a leader in his field. It was Dr. Evans who had found the cause of Dr. McKenna's patients illness had to do with his heart. There had been several puzzling medical cases like that where Dr. Evans took it upon himself to review the files and his determination led to proper medical treatment for the patient.

Remembering he was the host, Dr. Warren excused himself again and went to the kitchen to make sure Hattie, their cook had everything under control. Hattie had been with the family since the day they settled into this estate, going on twenty years ago. He depended on her more these days, since Martha, his adored wife passed following a two-year battle with breast cancer.

When Martha became ill, he had searched for a cure. Even though he knew there was no hope, he could not give up. They chose to keep her fight private, so he had taken her to a cancer center outside New York State and he constantly was at her side, watching as her body deteriorated.

Saying goodbye to her had been one of the hardest things he had done in his life. No amount of witnessing death in his patients could prepare him for the hole in his heart and in his life. If it were not for Hattie, he would not have made it. They had no children, and they were both the only child of their parents. There were cousins somewhere, but for them, they were enough for each other.

This house, way too large for the two of them, was even more so for just him, but it was Martha who had worked with the builders to design the home and Martha had picked out each piece of the furnishings. He could not let it go.

Now, forcing himself to return to what needed to be done, Dr. Warren, took a deep breath, blew a kiss into the air, and started down the hallway. Everything had to be perfect and as such, Dr. Warren had given Hattie directions on the types of food she must prepare. From the smells in the kitchen, fighting against each other, he knew she had done just that.

Himself included there would be four in attendance at the meeting and to make it as comfortable as possible, they would be sitting around the conference table in his office.

Dr. Warren was proud of his office with its dark tan walls that worked well with the oak trim around the oval topped French doors overlooking the lake and the lower oak wainscoting on the walls. The floor was hand scraped wide oak boards with area rugs providing designated sections of the room. From the oval simplistic desk and its high back, black leather chair, to the almost rugged looking coffee table it was apparent a lot of thought and love went into the décor.

There is a fireplace set in the corner of the wall next to the French doors, adding a touch of ambiance and a perfect location for the television, disguised as a mirror on the wall above it. Two sconces surrounding the mirror were part of the control pad he kept at his desk. It turned on the television, lights, and the fireplace. There was another control pad at the conference table with a few additional features on it.

The room at night would be dark, except that there are recessed lighting in the ceiling and in a channel around the edges of the ceiling is hidden a string of lights.

The area of the room where he was seating his guest was at the large oak conference table that looked sleek and inviting, but, just like the right side of his desk that had the only panel below the desk top, this conference table had a secret. There were a total of twelve sitting positions and a hardly recognizable panel cut out at each. This allowed those in attendance to have a flat surface to eat at, and then by a push of a button on the side of the desk, raise a computer that was also attached to a video camera located in the underground facility of the hospital.

Once everyone was gathered in the office, Dr. Warren did an introduction, though most either knew or knew of the other. He gave the men a chance to talk amongst themselves then announced, "Gentlemen, if I can have your attention. I would like you to all take a seat at the conference table. My cook has prepared a few dishes for you, along with several drink choices."

There is a rustle of movement in the room as the attendees make their way over to the conference table. Dr. Henderson lags. "Grif, you were right to have the meeting here. This is a grand home and this office is fit for men of their stature. They will be quite comfortable and that will soften the edges of the conversation we are about to present."

Dr. Warren patted Dr. Henderson's back. "Thank you, Franklin. I hope you are right."

With that they took their seats at the table.

Dr. Warren waited until everyone had finished eating and was enjoying a cup of coffee or tea before he looked over at Franklin. Dr. Henderson nodded.

Slowly, Dr. Warren stood, waited until he had the groups attention and then began. "Gentlemen, we are here to discuss what needs to happen with the facility now that it is again safe, and the coronavirus vaccine has been successful in bringing the world into balance again. There have been no more cases of the virus found in our countries and those who had it have recovered and are no longer contagious. We have made it through these past two years and come out a little wiser on the other side of this pandemic. Now we have to make some hard decisions and the 'facility' is one of them."

Everyone at that table knew of the facility and what it was used for. They had unanimously backed the decision and helped finance the project to build the space. It was their unanimous decision to test this vaccine on the patients who were dying when there was no other solution available to help them. They had also been part of the decision to have the one testing center set up where the vaccine had been simultaneously tested and were aware of the results that led to their addition to the facility.

Several of those present had gone to the facility to examine the patients and look over the area which they found surprisingly fascinating.

"Gentlemen, as you know there are several individuals in the facility whom we need to deal with."

Heads nodded.

"In front of you is a button on the edge of the desk. Please press that now."

Dr. Warren watched as hands were lowered and moved along the side of the desk in front of them until they found the button. Slowly the computer monitors appeared. When they were all up, Griffin pressed a button on his control pad and the screens illuminated. When they came into focus, they were seeing the underground facility. Dr. Warren gave them a minute to view the activity there.

"There you can see, Nurse Brown who has been the head of the facility since its inception."

They watch as she heads down the mirrored hallway and pauses before the hidden mirror doors to open them. She continues until she reaches the last door and when it opens, the décor changes to what looks like the inside of a home. They can see the entrance to a living room, further back, a

375

kitchen. Everything is light, neat, clean, and impossible to believe it is all underground.

Soon she is joined by the rest of the residence. "Now, gentlemen, you can see Sara Brown who headed the test clinic where the vaccine was administered. At that point Dr. Warren pressed a button so that they saw on their screens the actual incident of the test subjects going awry in the clinic and the sedation of them to finally get them into the helicopters and on their way to the facility. That video was followed by Sara Brown and her staff being herded onto another helicopter.

"All of them were taken to the facility and the area you are now seeing," he flipped back to the live video of the facility, "is where they have been residing since then."

"It looks like they have been well taken care of," said Dr. Evans.

"Yes, they have been."

"So, they have been there for almost a year?" This came from Dr. Evans.

"Yes, and before you ask, they have wanted to go home almost every day of their confinement, but of course, we had to sequester them. They understand that, but still they wonder when they will be able to go home."

"Of course, we have not allowed them to have phones or computers, just television so that they can keep up on what is happening beyond the facility," added Dr. Henderson. "And, as you are aware, we had chosen individuals not only with the skill to run the test clinic, but individuals who, if something happened, had few friends and family. In that way they are not being reported as missing by anyone and we have had no backwash since they were sequestered."

Dr. Warren could see from their faces that they approved of how they had handled everything up until this point. He wanted to feel confident the group would agree with him, but because it was not something, he totally approved of himself, it made it hard. But, before he put the final decision in their laps, he had to explain one more thing.

"If you will look at your monitors, gentlemen and on the right side of the room you can see a woman with long black hair." After seeing nods, he added. "That is Dr. Sonya McKenna. She was the head of the COVID-19 unit, but she noticed something was going on when patients were being removed from the floor. She started getting nosy and calling herself Dr. Weston, she managed to get into the facility and took a tour of the front end with our Nurse Lottie Bond."

"Why would Nurse Lottie let a stranger in?"

"Well, she was expecting us to send her help, after, as you know, we had to terminate the previous assistant."

"Yes, I remember that well," said Dr. Evans. "She threatened to go to the papers and tell them about the way the patients were suspended with wires. She thought it inhumane and would not listen to reason. We had no choice in the matter."

Of course, this had been a cover story and not true. Dr. Warren cleared his throat, "You are right. We had no choice."

This next is hard, but he had to go on.

"Right now, we have Nurse Sara Brown and her staff of nine from the test facility, Dr. Sonya McKenna and Nurse Lottie Bond. All the patients, as we had suspected would happen, have died and been removed from the facility so these are the ones we need to focus on."

"We were very discreet about the removal of the patients. We contacted their immediate families and advised them of their deaths and that they were still contagious. Our advice to them was to have them cremated immediately."

"How did that go over?"

"Believe me, we were shocked at how easy they accepted that, but you have to remember we were in that time of the beginning of the third wave of the pandemic when animals as well as the coronavirus was a threat. No one wanted to take a chance."

"So, the real problem here is Dr. McKenna. She was not expected to be involved in anyway and she put herself in the matter on her own. She, unlike the others, was not handpicked and has a family. It is only because her husband and daughter were still in China...Wuhan, when the third wave hit that they were unable to get back to the U.S. Since she is a doctor, they have not been too worried that they cannot reach her, or she has not called them. That, gentlemen, is a part of the 'new normal' we are facing. Anyway, that is where it stands for now."

The members started talking amongst themselves while Dr. Warren pressed the control pad again. Now on their screen was a document.

"Gentlemen, this is a ballot to vote on the step we take from here."

He watched as they looked over the ballot that had everyone in the facility listed and boxes to check on the right. There was also a listing for what to do with the facility and that was followed with two boxes as well.

"I trust each of you will come to the right decision, no matter how hard it is. At the bottom if you wish to add a comment you can. This is anonymous and I, nor anyone else beyond yourself, will know your vote. Please vote now."

Chapter 54

Elise stood staring in the mirror at herself as she brushed her hair, glad to see her face without all the bruising. She was herself again. "Ow." Her hairbrush hit the bruise on her scalp which was not totally healed, alerting her to the fact she was not totally her old self again. Luckily, her curly hair easily hid the bald spot.

Leaning into the mirror closer, she thought she saw more than her face in the mirror. She blinked. Blinked again to clear her head. The images remained. Slowly she turned around, with her head slightly down and tears of hope welling up in her eyes. As she slowly raised her face, Elise placed a hand on her throat as she realized this was not a dream. She was staring into the faces of her father and Bai. "Oh, my god! You found me."

Bai wanted to rush to Elise and capture her in his arms. He wanted to tell her he loved her and that he would never leave her. But he did not. Instead he allowed her father the privilege of holding his daughter first.

Matthew closed the distance between himself and his daughter. His eyes were wet, and furrows appeared on his brow as he whispered, "You are really here, really here." When he stood in front of Elise, he pulled her gently into his arms and Bai could see her body melt into his embrace. There they stood as if they were the only humans on earth.

Bai overhears Matthew whispering to her as he expresses how scared he was at the thought of losing her. He would take his arms from around her, then put one hand under her chin to lift her face so that he could see her and then press her head to his chest again, whispering "I love you Elise," then after hugging her closer he would whisper. "We were so afraid....so afraid."

Through her tears, Elise whimpers, "Oh dad, I cannot believe you are here either. I love you too. I missed you too."

Finally, the two move out of the embrace, but Matthew still holds his daughter's hand as they stand over by the side of the bed with joy written all over their faces.

Then, as if she has forgotten, Elise turns her head quickly and stares into his eyes. "Bai." Is all she says before she rushes into his arms, almost knocking him down.

Bai feels a genuine high when their bodies meet in a tight embrace and their heartbeat synchronizes. When he sees her coming toward him, he has this urge to take in a deep breath because by doing that, he is trying to relax and gather the courage to not have a meltdown at the first word she says to him because at that moment Bai knows it is real. He genuinely loves her and never wants to be separated from her again.

Finally, Matthew realizes they need a moment alone. "I will be right back. I need to call your mother."

Elise turns her head and smiles. "Thank you, dad. I love you." Matthew grins and raises his arm with two fingers up in a salute as he walks out the room.

Matthew needs to call Sonya and let her know he has found their daughter. And this is a good time to do it. It was easy to perceive the two of them need time alone.

The minute Matthew stepped out; words rushed out of Bai's mouth. "Elise. I have been so scared. I did not know you were missing right away as I had COVID-19. I was hospitalized, and barely knew who I was, at first, then when I finally recovered, I was unable to call you. I gave them your name as someone I had been in contact with so that they could alert you. They needed to put you in quarantine so you could not spread the virus further. But they could not find you. I told them that the last time I saw you, you were headed for the airport the next morning. When they told me that you had not gotten on your plane, I was panicked, but unable to look for you."

"Bai, it is not your fault. It is no one's fault. I was sick, too. I knew it, but figured I had a cold. It never dawned on me I had the coronavirus. Between COVID-19 and a head injury, I was told I was in a coma for almost two months."

"So, you had COVID too?"

"Yes. I think I had it before you did and gave it to you. They told me I was found passed out in the bathroom at the airport and had hit my head on the sink. I do not remember any of it and only lately started remembering even who I am."

Bai, grinned.

"What is that look, Bai."

"Sorry, it is probably good you did not remember. Did they happen to tell you the commotion you made at the airport."

"Yes, they did," Elise said as she gently punched his chest."

Matthew dialed his wife's number and listened to it ring, endlessly. He then disconnected the call and tried her work phone. Again, there is no answer. He paused a moment and then tried the home phone, listening as it rings until the service picks it up.

A frown appears on his handsome face as it dawns on him that her cell did not go to voicemail. Was it that her box was full?

Matthew is beside himself with worry. He cannot even leave her a message to let her know he has found Elise and it is not like her to let her voicemail get filled. He stands there until he cannot find any excuse that he can accept and will not allow himself to think something has happen to her. He gives himself a minute to calm then turns and enters Elise's room.

Announcing himself, he says as he opens the door, "Well, are we ready to get out of here."

"Yes, I have my release papers over there, Elise says as she points toward the dresser in the room."

"So, the doctor's say you are all right. Are you all right?"

"Yes dad. They told me what happened to me. I must have been feeling dizzy and a bit disoriented when I went to the bathroom at the airport. I fell, hit my head on the edge of the sink and passed out. From what they could determine, my head striking the edge of the sink produced a severe contusion causing my brain to swell and not get proper oxygenation. That along with me testing positive for the coronavirus it was a matter of what came first. They saved my life, dad."

"Your doctor told me you were in a coma and that you had the coronavirus. We stopped at the airport before coming here and that is where we heard you had been taken to this hospital, and here we are. But, Elise, when talking with the airport they did not find any ID on you. They could not even find your purse. Do you know where your purse is?"

"I am not sure, but I think I left it on a hook in the stall before I went to the sink. I was so sick I was not thinking right at all."

"Well, it is over. We will get your credentials replaced and then we can go home."

Neither Elise nor Matthew saw the wrinkling of Bai's forehead at the mention of going home. He had a chance to tell her he loved her and could not live without her, but he let it pass.

"So, where are your things?"

"I have nothing but the clothes on my back. The rest of my luggage probably is sitting at lost and found at the airport, maybe in New York."

"That is okay. We will get you some things before we leave for home."

As they prepared to leave, Dr. Ying enters and hands each of them a card verifying they had tested negative for the coronavirus.

"Show this when you are stopped, and it will save you some time."

"Thank you, Dr. Ying."

The three put on their masks and prepared to leave.

As they walked out of the hospital, Bai walks a little slower, his mind churning, wondering when and if he would get another chance to be alone with Elise. When they reached his SUV, Elise said she would sit in the back and let her father sit in the passenger seat. Once seatbelts are hooked, Bai starts the car and says, "Where too, Matthew."

"Now that is a good question Bai. We could check into the hotel again…"

"No, I will not have it. I am going to take you to my home."

"We do not want to put you out," Matthew says.

"You will not. I insist."

They drive in silence for several miles outside the downtown area into a residential area with large houses seated on big lots. As they make their way up the steep driveway of one of the residences, shielded by large trees on either side of the driveway, a house comes into view. It takes Elise's breath away when she catches the first glimpse of the white concrete house in front of her.

"Bai, this is your house?"

"Yes, I inherited from my father. He died a few years back."

"What about your mother."

"She died when I was born. It has been just me and my father for a long time, but not long enough. He built this house for her, but she only lived in it a couple years."

"I am sorry."

"No, do not be. It was a long time ago."

By now they had parked the car and were heading up to the oversized front door that looked like it was made of steel. Bai entered a code into the pad next to the door and it opened.

If she had been shocked by the exterior, the interior almost made her faint. It was enormous.

"Bai, how big is this place?"

"It is almost 10,000 sq. ft. up and down."

Matthew suddenly realized his mouth was hanging open as he stepped over the threshold. The house was expansive and open. From the foyer he could see a large dining room table with black upholstered seat chairs on stainless steel legs. They were situated around a long dark wood table that looked capable of seating at least 20 people, easily. The ceiling above the table was like nothing he had ever seen. It was a coffer ceiling with two rectangle glass cutouts around oblong panels. The far wall of the dining room had a floor to ceiling Red Black And White Cherry Blossoms Wall Mural. Across from the dining area was a credenza that ran the length of a dove grey, half circle sectional. Across from the sofa he could see a marble encased fireplace with two beige side chairs.

The ceilings had to be 20 feet in the main area, and on the back side of the living room area, he could see that this was open all the way to the ceiling of the second story. There was a glass railing for a wall situated along that whole side of the room.

Everywhere he looked there was glass French doors and windows reaching from ceiling to floor.

"Come on, I will show you around."

Stunned they followed Bai as he took them through the first floor to just beyond the dining room where there was a kitchen that any chef would love. It had everything in oversized capacity, including a huge island with 10 chairs around it. It was all stainless steel and tile and with the light coming in, the kitchen sparkled. They continued through to an office area and then what looked to be a movie room. There were several recliners and a 100-inch screen.

"It is so light in here Bai," Elise said.

Bai walked over to a panel on the wall and pushed a button. She watched in amazement as blackout screens lowered over the windows. "Please, step inside," Bai said. Matthew and Elise moved forward and once over the threshold, Bai pressed another button and doors lowered from above to seal them in. It was perfect for theater viewing. They waited while Bai opened the room again, then they continued their way to a room that was what they would call a mud room at home. There was laundry facilities, upper and lower cabinets and even a folding table beyond the countertops.

From there they entered a small room that held a coffee maker, beverage fridge, sink and stove top, which seemed strange until she saw the view through the French doors. This room was situated before a cement patio with chairs and umbrellas scattered around before the longest pool she had ever seen.

"I cannot believe this. I have always thought of China as having nice areas, but this is ah, exceptionally nice."

"Thank you. Less international does not mean Wuhan is less modern. The city just had not registered with many people outside China, unlike the first-tier cities of Beijing or Shanghai."

"That is so right. It is hard for Americans to understand that a city as big as Wuhan is not a big deal in China, because 11 million people is not second-tier in the United States. Yet it is bigger than the biggest city they have ever been to."

"What did your father do, Bai."

"He is what you would call an entrepreneur. He leased lands to the United Kingdom, France, Germany,

Russia, and Japan. Wuhan was important as it has always served as a transportation hub. Besides the busy waterways, most of China's major train routes go through the city, as does the fast-developing, high-speed train network. Millions of Wuhan residents commute by bicycle, and the city was the first in China to set aside bike lanes."

While he talked, Bai showed them upstairs to their rooms. Each was elegantly furnished and had their own bathroom and sitting area.

"Listen, why don't we head into town and get Elise some clothes and we can grab something to eat."

"Bai," Elise said, "I agree with getting me some clothes, but I would love to cook us something to eat...that is if you do not mind. I have been living off hospital food and want a home cooked meal."

"Great, but I have a cook. She has a small house just beyond the pool area. I could ring her and have her fix us something."

Elise thought about the kitchen and doubted her capability in doing it justice. "Sure, that sounds wonderful."

Chapter 55

All hell breaks loose once the leaders wake. At first it seems it is going to be fine as they slept for almost two days. Their medical assistants were at their sides making sure they were all right and at the first reporting session it is the consensus they were exhausted more than sedated.

During those two days, the advisors met with Dr. Wodajo to give a report on what they had learned was happening in their country. Each medical assistant reported on the condition of the leaders until it was reported they thought they would be awake enough for their first joint meeting.

After the announcement, Dr. Wodajo declares, "It is important that we handle this right, gentlemen. We will not meet on any affairs or talk of any decisions until all the leaders are able to join us, understood?"

They are all in agreement. Though it had not been part of the plan, Dr. Wodajo and his staff saw an association or maybe a mutual respect developing between the doctors who had only one job, being their one patient to keep an eye on. After the first session all of them gave their reports and went separately to the room of their leaders. There they stayed, taking their meals and, Dr. Wodajo surmised, stared at the four walls.

Only this time when the medical assistant arrived to give their reports, they came together and seemed to be conversing as they made their way to the conference room. When the meeting ended, they grouped together speaking with each other until reaching the room of their leader. That second night they still had their meals sent to their rooms, or to that of their leaders, but they had showed an ability to be friendly with one another. That Dr. Wodajo took as a good sign.

It had been agreed upon that an initial tour of the place would not take place until the leaders woke, but the advisers and medical assistants were told they could explore on their own. No one did.

So, for the first few days of the leaders being sequester, it had been quiet as if they were in a tomb and then one by one the leaders awoke.

Insanity stole into their minds like a deranged thief, adding dangerous ideas, seeding a new personality. New sparks of ideas that once they would have dismissed as bizarre started to grow roots, to make sense of it all, cascading out of control, luring them further and further from the self they once knew, until they remembered and realized. Those who woke alone in their rooms stared at the unfamiliar walls around them and the gown they did not recognize but was covering their body. The panic grew before it settled and once it did, they were the same as they had been before bringing them here. Some, with the help of their advisors or assistant remembered before things got too dramatic.

It was not Dr. Wodajo's job to quiet them so he allowed the advisors and doctors to calm their leaders before he gave his first message over the sound system, opening up all channels so that his voice penetrated every part of the facility.

"My esteem members of the World Health Organization, we are glad you are awake. We have had reports on your condition from medical and your advisors have been in contact with your country, keeping up on all matters of importance. We believe fully that because of the pandemic your public absence has been unquestioned. So now, you will be briefed by your advisors and either share your meals together in our dining hall, or, if you wish, have your meals sent to your rooms. I, myself will be in the dining room if anyone cares to join me."

"I understand you might need a day to return to full awareness so, we will wait until tomorrow to do a full tour of the facility and have our first briefing. Until then, gentlemen, I hope you are comfortable."

Dr. Wodajo understood their anger. It was not that it was toward anyone, but more at themselves for having done what they are never allowed to do…sleep for days! Once they accepted that this was what they needed and that their country faced no ill effects, they would calm down. His only hope was that it would happen before the morrow.

No one came to join Dr. Wodajo in the dining room so feeling foolish seated there alone, he asked to have his meal sent to his room.

If there was ever a time to worry it was now. Soon he would be ordering members of W.H.O. as though they were children. As Director-General of W.H.O. he presides over meetings, but now he was talking about directing the lives of a Queen, Kings, Sultans, Supreme Leaders, Presidents, Emirs, Emperors… Dr. Wodajo could feel his breathing quicken. He was on the verge of a panic attack. He needed to settle down. There was much to do if this was going to work.

As he gained control of his faculties, he reminded himself he had been smart to sequester all the leaders, their advisors, and medical assistants. That was good thinking. It gave each leader the daily support they were used to having and the two individuals that they had always trusted with their lives. He had done that right. Now came the part he could not prepare for.

They had thought of everything, from the designed areas that mimicked those of their homes, to their personal expectations and food…it had all been studied. There were chefs renown for preparing native cuisines, assistance who knew the protocol of each heads of state, and all the entertainment found in their countries laid out in special rooms for their joint or individual use.

Tonight, he would take the transport down the connecting routes to the various areas of this underground city and make sure all was on the ready. He would not sleep tonight, even if he tried. This was too important. He was about to do something that no one had attempted, ever, and that was to make 194 heads of government remain stationary for almost a year.

Of course, he would not be doing this alone. There were the 15 Council Members who agreed to this arrangement, vested in this as much as he. Dr. Wodajo returned to his office and pulled out his folder. There were the five permanent members of the council -- China, France, Russian Federation, the United Kingdom, and the United States, and ten non-permanent members that included Belgium, Dominican Republic, Estonia, Germany, Indonesia, Niger, Saint Vincent and the Grenadines, South Africa, Tunisia, and Vietnam. When they had reviewed the plan, it felt as though they were about to become gods taking on the whole universe. That was the good feeling he had; the rest brought him down to ground zero.

When the members had initially designed this plan, it was determined that these 15 council members would be the governing force in this facility. It was these members who were trained and would be working with him from this point on. If was too much for one person to headline, even for fifteen it seems impossible.

There was a knock on his door. Dr. Wodajo's assistant, not waiting for permission, enters the office.

"Dr. Wodajo, you need to go to your quarters and sleep. You have a lot on your plate tomorrow and if you want to be ready, you need sleep."

"You are right. You are right."

And so, Dr. Wodajo stopped what he was doing and slept.

After the heads of state were awake, that first week held all the signs of failure. There was threats upon threats. Even though they had agreed to accepting this drastic step, the next World War began.

What happened that day was a battle of words but if it had happened under other circumstances, lives would have been taken. There was China who threatened military action against the United States if they were not informed of their location. That fire began a debate that would last for months until it became clear that it was crazy to consider a worldwide conflict over a demand to know their whereabouts. After all they had agreed to that from the outset.

Others fought over being in power. These rulers have delusions of taking over major chunks of the world by military force and think that is what the United States and North Korea are up to. So, as they had managed on the outside of the facility, they now tried to find a way to become the most powerful country in the facility.

Slowly the battles became less violent as the months progressed. There is nowhere to go beyond the areas in the facility and spending time alone becomes their enemy if they do not reconcile their differences. More than the members of W.H.O. could have hoped, they saw the leaders begin to bond together spending personal and professional time together as they set differences aside. They were here to save their lives and in turn, save their countries from challenging not only the coronavirus, but the loss of their leaders.

Except for their daily briefings with their heads of government, the members found themselves co-existing no longer filled with political ventures. It was all going smoothly. The coronavirus was becoming the focus beyond these walls and there was no need to worry about the invasion of their country by anything but the virus.

It seemed that the coronavirus not only kept countries and people at bay for fear of infection, it had done the unforeseen in giving their leaders a chance to realize they were all just people surviving on the same planet.

The change did not happen all at once but seemed to sneak in unseen and unannounced. The heads of states began sharing their ideals and talking amongst themselves.

There is time now to reflect on the current state of the world today and each member could not help but wish it were different. At first the methods of changing the world into their own utopia where there is no conflict and everyone is happy was envisioned differently, but eventually the differences between the members softened until they began to flow in the same direction and getting there in the same way. The talk centered on the need to try and solve the problems we have in this world and not how to take it over.

Each day they would take the time to discuss the visions of a perfect world and the foremost topic was no political parties outside or within a country. They saw these parties created a rupture in countries as well as individuals within a country. They determined that political parties lead to judging others because of their political opinions instead of discussing the problems they face.

That became the topic of many discussions. There was a consensus growing that politics is an extremely sensitive subject and needed close scrutiny. That necessitated they learn how to agree to disagree and respect the opinion of others instead of trying to find fault in their opinions.

During a group discussion, one of the leaders stood and addressed the assembly saying, "We need to be open minded and see the good in people instead of the bad. We need to ignore those who cause harm and sadness and praise those who go out of their way to help others. We need to learn how to simply be nicer to people and only in this way will we be able to unite as one.

There was so much time and energy to diffuse that instead of the leaders becoming bored with the isolation, they seemed to grow stronger both physically and mentally. Of course as had been predicted, there were injuries sustained from trying to impress each other in the gym, or other sports that were initiated in turn by the members themselves and even this open their eyes to see other avenues.

And open their eyes they did, along with their hearts as they begin to think beyond themselves and to the people of their country. It got even better as the months rolled by and the leaders all agreed that people in their countries should not have to wonder where their next meal will come from or wonder where they will end up sleeping each night. At that point, the members knew the world leaders were entering a new phase of understanding. They wanted everyone to have a place to go to that they could call home. A place to sleep at every night and be given a chance to reach their fullest potential. Yes, they had come around to this idea before, but now they expressed the reality that this could only happen if each of them helps the other first and then pass it down the line. Once one person starts the change, it will hopefully cause a domino effect throughout the world.

It was then that Dr. Wodajo presented his talk on the matter. "I am not saying it will ever be easy to alleviate the problems we have. People all over the world are trying to solve these problems but we just must accept the fact that the world will never be perfect. We have to look at the beautiful things the world does offer us and hope that one day, maybe one day, we will be able to see happiness in every face, that the world will be a less stressful space for everyone and that we can all live in peace and harmony on this planet."

In those last days of the pandemic it was obvious that the leaders felt they had too much to lose and were willing to listen. No one asked when they would be released as they began to enjoy being in the facility. It not only had everything they could desire, but it also had given them a chance to understand other heads of countries on a personal level.

They were now seeing each other as just people. People with a lot of responsibility, but still just people and as such they learned about each other and found a way to accept their differences.

It had gone beyond their realm of expectations from the start of this project. The hope was to first protect the country leaders and help them learn how to live amongst themselves peacefully. No one could have foreseen that the outcome would lead to them accepting each other on a whole different plane. And now the day that Dr. Wodajo and his staff had looked forward to is here and instead of rejoicing, they feel a little sad. The pandemic is over, and the leaders can return to their homes and their countries.

On the day before they are to depart there is a big celebration in the huge ballroom. The event had been planned over several months and the outcome was spectacular. It begins with a travel theme as a fun way to connect the countries and provide cohesiveness to the event. To welcome each guest there were directional wooden signpost with arrows pointing from their facility residence to the party. The halls were decorated with Around the World travel of world flags, luggage, maps, globes and posters and when they entered the ballroom it had been transformed with a main bar, an airline ticket counter, a cruise ticket booth with posters of countries in a particular region, such as a Mediterranean, South American or Caribbean to visit. There was also a booth for transportation by train to specific cities and countries across the world.

Throwing an Around the World party in honor of an international holiday and some of the sporting effects they prided themselves in added a fun and distinctive theme for the social gathering. There were lists of international holidays throughout the year as part of the centerpiece at each table and the drinks were delivered with country flag stirrers in them.

There were favors to mark the occasion given to each leader and a skit put on by the staff, as their way of saying goodbye. Each leader came dressed in their fanciest clothes and the celebration went on into the early morning hours with just enough time to pack, be given a light sedative, and meet the helicopters that would depart from the roof the next morning and take them to the W.H.O offices where they would be placed on their personal jets.

As Dr. Abaynesh Wodajo saw them off, he said a prayer.

"All that you do. All that you say. All that you stand for. Let us do it with love. For perfect love, casts out all fear.

And that is what gives us power to move forward, propelled with strength, surrounded in peace, filled with greater unity in our land."

Chapter 56

Just as doctors take a Hippocratic Oath, nurses take a pledge called the Florence Nightingale Pledge. For Lottie Bond, this was what she lived by.

"I solemnly pledge myself before God and in the presence of this assembly, to pass my life in purity and to practice my profession faithfully. I will abstain from whatever is deleterious and mischievous and will not take or knowingly administer any harmful drug. I will do all in my power to maintain and elevate the standard of my profession, and will hold in confidence all personal matters committed to my keeping and all family affairs coming to my knowledge in the practice of my calling. With loyalty will I endeavor to aid the physician in his work and devote myself to the welfare of those committed to my care."

She had said it to herself so many times during her life and had taken the words literally which is why she never married or had any children. Those words, 'to pass my life in purity' and 'I will abstain from whatever is deleterious and mischievous,' flashed across her mind whenever she found herself even thinking about a man.

Her job was her life, but it had not always been that way. When she was young, less than half her sixty-five years now she had wanted a husband and a family. More than once she had fears of insecurity and loneliness that magnified whenever a friend or relative got married -- and she still is not married. As the years progressed, every time she saw a happily married couple, she was given the awful reminder that no man had even come close to asking her to marry him.

Lottie was five feet eleven inches in height, making it hard for her to find a man she did not tower over. Yet, she had all the right equipment from her long shiny blonde hair she wore down to frame her face and her features that seemed comfortable on her visage. She was not a raving beauty, but more than just acceptable in the appearances department. At least that is what her friends told her. She knew that her most outstanding quality was her green eyes and she played upon them. Her figure was shapely, even if she was reed thin and she dressed to show it off. So, she often asked herself, why could not she find Mr. Right.

At her last close friend's wedding she was feeling despondent as she forced a smile in passing. She would never be married. She was doomed to a lonely, unmarried life. She was so engrossed in her pity party she embarrassed herself by spilling her drink on her beautiful new green chiffon dress when he spoke to her.

It was his way. He loved surprising women and then pretending he did not mean to scare them.

"Oh, I am sorry. Look what I have done. I did not mean to alarm you."

Lottie peered up at the most beautiful man she had ever seen. He was easily over six feet in height. He leaned down toward her and a lock of his black hair that seemed to be under control and freshly barbered fell on his forehead.

She felt her head pounding as she stared into his dark brown eyes before allowing her gaze to take in his wide, sensual mouth that was slightly parted in a grin.

"Miss? I am so sorry, Let us go inside and see if we can find something to take care of that spill before it stains your lovely dress."

"Ah," Lottie was having trouble controlling her tongue, but she finally managed to say, "thank you."

He laughed making Lottie feel uncomfortable. This was a joke to him. He tried to humiliate her and now he was enjoying it. She wanted to say something sharp, to give him the impression she could care less, but instead she lowered her eyes. She was about to get up and excuse herself when he added, "It was funny to hear you thank me and all I did was scare you and make you spill your drink. Please, let me help you."

He was charming as well as handsome and Lottie Bond knew what it felt like to fall in love.

"By the way, my name is William Harding Peterson, III."

"My name is Lottie Bond."

"I like that," he said with a studious expression. "Now that has a ring to it."

That was how they met and from that moment her life blossomed in ways she could never dream of. They were brought together by mutual affection and intimacy and spent every day together. Lottie was bathe in happiness. Every moment was filled with romantic tension and finally she heard the words she longed to hear. "I love you Lottie Bond."

"I love you too William. I have loved you since the first time I saw you."

That evening was her first sexual experience with a man. Her mind never let go of one minute of that night.

William at first was so gentle, moving slowly, kissing her first, deeply on the lips while his hands traveled down her body until she found herself leaning in ever closer, wanting more of him.

Her hips had a mind of their own as they pushed against him and he moved his hands down and in one sweep lifted her skirt and wiggled a finger through the elastic of her panties until it reached its target. Lottie's body melted and he picked her up and carried her over to the bed. He laid her down and slowly slid her panties down her legs and over her feet. Then she watched as he lowered his pants, waiting for him to step out of them, but he did not. Instead, before she knew what was happening, he flipped her body over.

Lottie was in shock. She screamed when he penetrated her from behind. William put a hand over her mouth and pushed down on the middle of her back, making her helpless as he rammed into her and all she could do was sob uncontrollably until finally it was over.

Lottie was humiliated as she struggled to turn over, despite the pain. Her mind was as bruised as her body as she remembered her best friend telling her, people who cannot tolerate pain end up living tiny, sad lives. Well, she had tried to step out of her fear of being rejected and look what happened. She was angry as she finally managed to flip over so that she could stare up at him and with tears in her eyes, managed to whimper, "Why did you do that to me. Why."

William was looking at her with contempt and she could not understand why. why you hurt me. Tell me why."

Lottie watched as he pulled up his pants, then left the room without saying a word. She could hear the water running in the bathroom and became more confused.

Finally, William returned, his hair back in order, and his clothes neatly arranged on his body.

He looked over at Lottie with that same expression and before she could ask, he said with disdain, "I am married, and I cannot afford to have some broad get pregnant. Can you understand that."

She found her words then. It had all been a game and she had been the patsy. It had taken him some time to get what he wanted, but she had eventually fallen for his charm. "Get out!" She screamed. "Get out."

"With pleasure."

Those were his last words and the last time she saw him. He was the reason she had given up on finding love or even capable of any relationship with the opposite sex that was not work related. Lottie vowed never to let another man get close enough to touch her and she kept that promise.

From that day on she took her oath literally. She was a nurse who only allowed herself to think about her profession and dedicated her life to caring for others. It was this commitment that they saw in her and why they asked her to head the underground facility. To her it was what she was meant to do. She was in charge, she did not have to interact with others, and she could just concentrate on caring for the patients placed in her care. Her answer was, "Yes."

Of course, she had not known at the time that the patients would be beyond medical help when they came to her, but that was fine. She saw it as her chance to prove her skills. She would nurse them back to health.

And that she tried to do, right up until the time when she was informed by the head doctors that there would be men coming in to do some work in the patient ward and that she was to stay in her quarters until summoned.

Lottie did not ask questions but did as she was told. When they told her to go to her quarters, she had obeyed and when they asked her to join them, she came.

It took all she had to not scream, and she was thankful she was wearing her mask under her helmet. Before her were more than the initial patients she had started with. There were indeed three times that in the room, but that was not what bothered her.

She remembered how she felt that day with William and experienced that same sensation again. That shock of surprise returned as she stared at the patients. They were hanging from the ceiling, three deep in row after row. There was a canvass sling under them, and wires connected to their bodies that kept them in place. Lottie turned to the nearest doctor and before she could speak, he said.

"Nurse Bond. We are in desperate times with this coronavirus and desperate times call for desperate measures. We need space for these patients."

The way he spoke set Lottie aback as she watched dumbfounded him showing and explaining her new role. "This is a control that you will use to lower the patients when you need to check on them, but we have them connected to the monitor in your office so that you will not need to physically take their vitals or even administer any medicine. That will be done by us," he added spreading his arms to include the other doctors who were with him."

Speechless, Lottie nodded her head. She wanted to ask if this suspension mechanism hurt them in any way or how was she and her small staff going to wash and feed them. They answered her questions before she had a chance to express them.

"This unit is basically self-contained now. There are tubes that connect to this control panel and a temperature check as well as all vitals being operated mechanically, and the results are sent to your computer. If there is a problem, the computer will alert you. Your part in this venture is to keep close tabs on the monitors and alert us if there is any change in the vitals. Any questions."

"How do I let you know what is happening?"

"Oh, yes, I forgot to mention that. There will be reports prepared each day by the system. You are to print them out and when we come to check on the patients, have them ready for us to review."

The doctors had left and as promised came regularly to review the reports. Lottie went from head nurse to secretary in one shake.

There came a time when she felt she needed more help. There were so many patients, so many reports to review and prepare. When she presented the request, she was told they would send her someone to interview. Little did she know that they were only telling her what she wanted to hear, and they were not inclined to send her anyone.

Since Lottie had not known this when Sonya McKenna had come, posing as Dr. Weston, she had not thought anything of it. A resident doctor was just what she needed in the facility. It was not until she had not returned that Lottie had announced the visit to the doctors and that was the last, she knew until suddenly Dr. Warren was back, but not on her own volition.

Stranger things were happening, and Lottie was getting suspicious about what her role really was. From the arrival of Dr. Weston who she learned was not her real name, but in fact she was Dr. McKenna everything changed. Next came Nurse Sara Brown who Lottie learned was the head nurse at the testing center for the coronavirus and she was joined by her staff of ten. They had arrived along with another batch of patients which, were 'fitted' into the patient care unit.

She had more than enough help now and as each day progressed, Lottie's eyes were opened. This was not a facility to cure, but instead a facility to test vaccines on those who were already critically ill.

Furious at how she had been played, Lottie contacted the doctors. Dr. Franklin Henderson, along with Dr. Timothy Evans and Dr. Griffin Warren arrived and in no uncertain terms told her to do her job and keep quiet. They did not let her speak her piece, but left her standing there, confused, and upset.

She fumed over the matter and finally decided she had taken enough. She was not going to let one more person step on her and accept the consequences. She would pack her stuff and leave the facility in the hands of the newcomers. Defiantly she did not waste time and without announcing her intentions was ready to depart, only the door would not open. It was not until later that she realized the voice control to the exit no longer worked. She was a prisoner in the facility.

Those on the other side of the door had all the power now and she had no choice but to relent. What could she do but defend the facility to the new occupants who were as discombobulated as she.

So, Lottie continued faithfully in the role of head nurse of the facility making sure that everyone stayed in line and performed the duties she assigned to them.

Chapter 57

Dr Warren had not wanted it to go this far. When he learned of Dr. McKenna sneaking around, he was livid and had no choice but to take her down to the facility before she had a chance to talk to anyone about what she had seen.

His original idea was to find a cure for COVID-19. He was not a medical research doctor, but he knew a lot about medicine and their effects on the body. So, he had set up a laboratory in the basement of his home, working evenings on various formulas, hoping that before the test facility found a vaccine that worked, he would have his own.

But he knew that if he was to get credit for the vaccine, he had to administer it separately from the test facility. That is when he got the idea of setting up the facility in the basement of the hospital. He needed somewhere near the patients for testing and a place where large shipments of medicine would not be questioned. He also needed space; much more than his basement could provide. He thought about it long and hard and finally made the decision. He had the money to finance the venture and now he had the place.

It was easy to get plans drawn and workers assigned to build the unit, which he thought out to the last detail. It would require living quarters for the staff as well as a place to take the patients that he would test the vaccine on. It had to be on the lowest level, below the parking ramp so that it would not be happened upon by accident and he had to have as much technology as possible to support staff as well as the patients.

It was not easy, and it took months to finalize, but he had done it. It was the first time he really appreciated the fact that his wife was rich.

Thinking of his wife always hurt. He had loved her dearly and when she first found that she had cancer, he was sure he could cure her. Finally he had taken her to every cancer clinic and had her seen by the best cancer doctors, but they always left with the words trailing behind them, "We are sorry, Dr. Warren, but we cannot save your wife."

He did not want to accept it and had worked night and day in his lab trying to come up with a way to cure her cancer. He knew that he was being rough on his staff at the hospital, but he did not care about anyone except his wife. He used all his medical knowledge, but she died. It had been a year ago, a year before the COVID-19 hit.

COVID-19 for him, became his focus, helping him to achieve his desire to find a way to save people with a medicine he had developed. So, with the money from the estate, which was substantial, he was able to build the unit secretly in the basement of the hospital, only letting a few doctors he trusted explicitly in on what was happening. He had hired Nurse Lottie Bond because of her reputation and the fact she would not be missed.

At first all was going well, but the turning point came when the patients were metamorphosing. They were blue and unresponsive. That is when he knew he was failing. When the same thing was happening at the test facility, he had immediately transported those patients, along with the staff to the facility. Their testing had been on healthy patients. He had thought his vaccine would work on them where it had failed on those critically ill with COVID-19.

By the time the patients were put in the facility, the others had started dying and been removed. Their family and friends were told they were contagious and so it was easy to have them eliminated and buried without anyone blinking an eye or asking too many questions.

Then he had started on the new patients. There were only a hundred of them, so it was easy to fit them into the facility and there was no need to suspend them. He had already decided that this would be it. Any other critically ill patients would not be brought down to the facility. These would be the last ones.

And so, he continued with his experimental drugs, until just recently, when the last of the test center patients had died. It was now that he needed to decide what to do with the staff.

Chapter 58

Dr. Franklin Henderson was a bully and used to getting his way. When he took over Dr. McKenna's patients, it was not the first time he had made such a move. He did whatever he wanted to satisfy his need to feel superior. That is why he began his career as a trauma surgeon. Just the title made him feel superior.

He had been raised by a father who seemed to have the Midas touch and everything he linked with turned into gold. It was not like that for Franklin. He had to struggle to get even a slight bit of acknowledgement. But there came a time when his past caught up with him and he spiraled into depression and burnout having to face the fact it would take more than a title to become superior.

He recounts how, during his residency, he was "rewarded" for being on call for 24 hours by being allowed to scrub into the operating room for surgeries that made him the envy of the other doctors. Only now, years into his profession he feels like just one of the staff and at every opportunity he takes that step to make himself noticeable. It is a cruel irony that doctors and nurses are drawn to medicine to care for others, yet the majority have been bullied by their colleagues and superiors. That was the reality.

When Dr. Warren had approached him with his idea, he saw it as an opportunity to once again become that doctor that others would admire. He would be able to stand out among his peers and beyond. It was the opportunity he had been waiting for.

When Dr. Timothy Evans was a medical student trying his hand at a variety of specialties, he spent two months on the surgery service. The days were rigorous, starting before 5 a.m., when he was expected at the hospital to do his round on patients who had recently undergone surgery. He would then scrub in to his first operating room case of the day, at 7 a.m. Depending on the complexity of the procedure, Dr. Evans would not emerge from the O.R. for hours. His biologic needs such as going to the bathroom or eating be damned. That would not be the end of it. There was always another case, more rounds, and he typically surfaced from the hospital at dusk, completely exhausted.

As the years progressed, he realized that there would always be this rigorous schedule if he remained one of the herd. That is when he decided to take charge. It happened one day when he scrubbed in on a patient undergoing coronary artery bypass surgery, an intricate procedure in which the heart is actually halted from its inexorable beating while the surgeon attaches new vessels supplying it with blood. He felt such power, especially when he held the patient's heart in his hands. He felt like a god and he wanted to feel like that every day. That is when he decided that the critical ill in the hospital would give him that feeling he craved and because of their conditions, would not take up much of his time.

When Dr. Warren had approached him with his offer he at first wasn't interested until it was explained this would be only a small group of doctors, working with a small group of patients and their work might lead to a Nobel prize. That is all it took for him to say, "Yes. I'm in."

Dr. Griffin Warren placed a call to Dr. Timothy Evans and Dr. Franklin Henderson, inviting them to his house that evening. Nothing needed to be said about the reason for the gathering as they were all aware of the issue confronting them.

That evening after a nice dinner prepared by Dr. Warren's cook, the group retired to his office where he had a stocked bar and invited his guest to make themselves a drink.

They looked relaxed, like friends spending a quiet evening together, but nothing was further from the truth. Each of them was already thinking about the issue they needed to deal with. No one had thought it would get this bad. Their sole purpose had been to move the uncurable COVID-19 patients to the facility that Dr. Warren had built and there, with advanced medical treatment, help them to survive the virus.

They had admired him for using his own money to create the facility in the subbasement of the hospital and provide all sorts of amenities for the staff. They were impressed by the electronics installed so that there was not a need for a huge team. They also applauded him on the use of mirrors to make the facility virtually disappear unless one was looking for it. They even went along with it being best not to let word get out.

The one thing they did not know at the start up was that Dr. Warren was using these patients as guinea pigs too, testing vaccines he was creating himself.

That piece of information was revealed at the proper time because when he told the other doctors what he had been doing, they could see that even the vaccines being created by scientist ended up killing the clients who then became patients at the facility. So even if what Dr. Warren was doing was illegal, others, following the route of legality were seeing the same results. Dr. Warren had been smart to point that out and also the fact that he, at least at first tested on COVID-19 patients who were beyond help.

They now were all in too deep to want the facility to become public.

"Okay, gentlemen, we need to make a decision. There are several subjects left down there and we need to decide what to do with them before we disband the facility."

No one said a word.

"Okay, let me tell you what I think we need to do. First, Let us review. The test center subjects had been relocated to the facility with the worse cases of COVID-19 patients. Those patients have all died and their families were contacted and told they had a reaction to the vaccine being tested and could not be saved. Because of their physical condition, we kept the family and friends at bay stating they were contagious. Some of the families wanted to have a closed casket ceremony and others wanted to have the body cremated. We finally convinced them for the safety of themselves and family they should all be cremated. So that was that."

"What we need to do now is going to be harder, but not impossible. The word must go out that the staff at the testing facility were exposed and succumbed to the coronavirus and as such should be looked at as heroes. We build that up and it becomes the focus while we pay our respects to any family and take care of the expense of having them cremated. This third wave of the coronavirus gives us the authority to make drastic decisions so that we eliminate the spread of the virus."

The doctors nod.

"So, gentlemen, let me make myself perfectly clear. We need to eliminate them."

Silence followed.

"We are in this too deep now and we cannot let it get out or we will find ourselves in jail and stripped of our license. You know that is true."

Both doctors gave the matter some thought, knowing there was no alternative. Finally, Dr. Evans said, "Yes, I agree." He really did and had no qualms about taking care of the situation. He even had an idea.

"I think it will not be easy, but I have a proposal. After several minutes Dr. Evans offers his suggestion.

"Why not use fentanyl. It is a powerful synthetic opiod analgesic and we can easily get enough for our purposes."

Dr. Evans watches his comrades' faces, then continues. "We need something potent enough to act quickly. Fentanyl is 50 to 100 times more potent than morphine."

Dr. Henderson nods in agreement. "That would work, but what about Carfentanil. Carfentanil is one of the most toxic opioids currently known, with studies showing it to be 10,000 times more potent than morphine, 4,000 times more potent than heroin, and..." he turns and peers directly at Dr. Evans... "100 times more potent than fentanyl. In humans, a dose as small as 1 microgram is enough to elicit a response to the drug and about 20 micrograms, which is less than a grain of salt, is enough to be fatal."

"Hmmm, great ideas doctors, they both sound promising, but we need the most potent so I would lean toward using the Carfentanil."

Dr. Warren pauses, then asks, "So, how do we do that?"

There is silence while they think about it. It must be administered at the same time and to make sure they each get a lethal dose; it must be prepared in a way they are individually dosed.

The room fell silent as the doctors searched their brains for how they could accomplish this feat. They have been, in a sense, bedside to patients dying from COVID-19 searching for a way to cure them. Now they were searching for a way to kill their caretakers.

As Dr. Warren watched them, he knew he had chosen the right men for the job. If they had succeeded, they would be able to enjoy the fruit of their labors and now, that it had gone the other way, they would be able to accept what needed to be done.

Now it is his turn. They have come up with excellent suggestions so he needs to give them the proper stage to employ the idea and a method of administering the drug.

"I have got it," said Dr. Warren. "We are going to dismantle the facility and as a final goodbye we meet with all of them in the facility and tell them of our plans and that they should be prepared to leave the following day. Then, we have a bottle of champagne to thank them. We have the Carfentanil premixed in the champagne bottles and have the cook and her helpers pour the champagne and once everyone has been served, including the maintenance staff, cook and her helpers, along with the medical staff as well. we give a little speech and watch as they drink, and we pretend to take a sip. We will have it potent enough so that if we have any nondrinkers a sip is all they will need to overdose."

The doctors peered at one another then slowly one after the other they nodded in agreement. "That can work. That is good. We can dispose of the bodies in the same way as the patients and put out the word that they had a fatal case of the coronavirus." There is a pause as he thinks it through before finally adding, Yes, that will work."

The doctors head down to his well-stocked lab in the basement and search through the shelves. They come up with enough Carfentanil to do the job. No one blinks an eye as they know Dr. Warren had set up the lab in his basement to find a cure for his wife. Having carafentanil handy for her pain was reasonable.

Dr. Henderson does the math outloud. "Let's see," he says, "One 750-ml bottle of Champagne fills five regular Champagne glasses and we want at least to be prepared with 20 glasses?"

Dr. Warren thinks about that and says, "Not quite sure, but to be safe, let's say at least 25 glasses."

Dr. Evans breaks it down. "Ten people: 2 bottles, 20 people: 4 bottles, 25 people: 5 bottles, 30 people: 6 bottles, and so on."

Dr. Warren explains, "Best to over plan then to be short. "We'll go with 30. I know there are the security men as well, but that would not bring the total over 30."

"Okay, doctors, my wine cellar is over there," he says pointing to the left of the lab. "Let's get 30 bottles of Moët or Chandon," he says thoughtfully. "I think it is appropriate in this situation to offer nothing but the best."

They follow the doctor and soon are standing in his wine cellar. Before entering they had expected a dark, cavernous space, peaceful and unassuming, filled with dusty bottles slowly maturing, but that is far from what they see before them. They are in a room with precision humidity, insulation, and temperature controls, with modern LED lighting giving the room a dazzling futuristic feel.

Dr. Warren gives them a minute before leading the way to the section where he has the champagne they are looking for. Then, they each begin filling a box that Dr. Warren supplies until they have all 30 bottles packaged for transport.

"Are we ready, gentlemen?" Dr. Warren asks. "I don't want to allow a temperature change."

"Yes, I'm ready," they say in unison. They each carry a box of 10 bottles as they move back to the entrance. Dr. Warren opens the door, and they hurry forward so that he can close the door quickly.

Once back in the lab, they find long needle syringes and work out the mathematics for the dose needed for each of the bottles of champagne. That figured, they get to work.

The rest of the evening they prepared the bottles of champagne, enough and a little extra to go around. They go over the rest of the details necessary to make sure the job is done as quickly and efficiently as possible. They call it a

414

night in the wee hours of the morning with each taking a box of ten bottles with them.

The next day at the hospital they arrive early to go over details and then did their usual rounds and as prearranged, met in Dr. Warren's office at noon. This was the best time for them to take the bottles of champagne down on the back, freight elevator without a bunch of peering eyes. At that time most of the staff would be in the lounge having lunch and only a few would be on the floor and the remainder, would be in patient rooms.

They cautiously went out of Dr. Warren's office, carrying their boxes, keeping an eye out behind them for anyone watching. There was no one. They made it to the elevator and when the doors opened, they quickly climbed inside. Soon they were in the subbasement.

The previous evening, before turning in for the night, Dr. Warren had made a call to Nurse Bond, informing her to have everyone, including the maintenance staff and security all in the kitchen of the facility. He stressed that there was to be an important announcement that concerned everyone. Nurse Hood said she would take care of it.

As they entered the facility, Nurse Hood met them, assuring Dr. Warren that the residents of the facility were all gathered in the kitchen.

When they entered, Dr. Warren did a mental count of the faces in the room and was pleased. They were all there and the count was less than 30 individuals.

Smiling, he moved over to the far side of the room so that he and the other two doctors could stand behind the island and face the group. They placed the boxes on the counter and then Dr. Warren addressed them.

"We have good news for you. We have confidence that the pandemic is over and that it is safe for you to return home and be with your family and friends. We have appreciated your dedication and support during this period and wracked our brains for a way to show our appreciation. We hope this demonstrates how much we admire each and every one of you."

With a nod toward the kitchen staff, they came over to the island and Dr. Henderson asked them to get out champagne glasses. When the glasses were lined up on the counter, the doctors began opening the boxes and pulling out the bottles of champagne. The kitchen staff helped to open the bottles and fill the glasses, while the doctors played host, handing a glass to each one of them and asking that they wait until all had been served so they could toast the moment together.

As they imagined, the staff was ecstatic to learn they were going home and announcing this just before the arrival of the glasses of champagne did not give them time to think about it. So, the doctors, standing at a viewing point of all the employees, raised their glasses for the toast and watched carefully as each one of them took a sip.

It is excellent champagne. Sonya enjoys the feel of the bubbles, like crystalline pearls on her palate, exploding with acidulous flavors that stand out against a rich, smooth background of ripe fruit and exotic wood.

Sara Brown had never had a glass of expensive wine or champagne, but she is quite sure this fell in that category. She could smell the fragrance of flowers as she brings the glass to her lips and when her ever expressive friend Veronica leans in and whispers, "The bubbles bounce around my mouth like the music of a symphony orchestra bounces around my head." Sara turns with a puzzled expression to see Veronica's smile. Veronica tries to explain. "You know what I mean; the music seems to enter your head from all angles…"

Even Mrs. Eduardo who does not drink except for the wine at communion is enjoying the champagne, her pleasure visible on her face.

The results are flawless. One instant the group are high fiving over the joy of hearing they are going home, and after a sip of congratulatory champagne, quiet ascends over the room.

Next comes the hard part. First, each of the doctors goes from body to body testing to make sure they are indeed dead. They are.

Outside the side door is a refrigerator truck. Each of the doctors came dressed in their infectious disease clothing in tow. Now, they hurriedly began putting the attire on. They knew that if by chance anyone saw them, they would not be able to identify them. Since what they were about to do was not normally part of their jobs, it is important to be camouflaged. Knowing this was something they had to do quickly and alone, they were sure to cover every precise detail. What they were doing was too bizarre to put into words, but they knew there was no other choice to be made.

Now, before they begin to place the bodies in the bags, they do another count to make sure this is everybody. "They are all here. The staff, the maintenance, and the security. Every person is accounted for."

It amazes the doctors how smoothly it is all going. Never have they done anything like this before, or do they plan on having to do it ever again, but it is reassuring to know if they put their heads together, there is nothing they cannot accomplish.

During that last meeting, the doctors thought of everything. Once the decision was unanimous, they discussed how it would be accomplished. Of course the method came first and then they went on to planning it down to the last detail, from having the head nurse gather all the employees, to even where to stand so that they could visually watch the employees as they shared the 'good news'.

They had Dr. Henderson go over the computer records for the facility and make sure there were enough cadaver bags in the facility and finding there were, they next double checked the records of each employee in the facility to verify the count as well as their weight so they knew what they were up against. Then, they checked on the count and location of the gurneys in the facility. Doing this helped to determine what they needed to accomplish the transfer and spend less time looking for the elements to carry it out.

Next it was necessary to get a large refrigerator truck situated in the space between the main hospital and the annex and that was simpler than they could have realized. All it took was Dr. Henderson, dressed in his infectious disease outfit to approach one of the drivers in the parking area and explain that they needed to move some highly contagious COVID-19 patients.

Now, their timing was right as it was during the busiest time for the drivers so when the driver on duty, Edward Flint was approached, he said, "Sorry, doc, but we are too busy to get on that right now. You will have to transport them to the morgue, and we will get them later."

"No can do. They are still contagious."

"So, what do you want me to do about that."

"Tell you what. Can you show me how to drive one of these rigs and I will do it?"

"What? Are you crazy?"

"No, just have to take care of this immediately."

Dr. Henderson had been convincing, and the driver took him to an empty semi and gave him a quick lesson on how to maneuver the truck and work all the gears. Before parting, the driver gave him the keys.

Dr. Henderson had waited until the man was out of sight and then driven the semi to the loading spot they had chosen, which was next to the freight elevator that went down to the subbasement area. There it sat ready for their cargo. They worried that someone would see it, but no one did.

Dr. Henderson and Dr. Evans push gurneys to the exit with each employee encased in one of the cadaver bags designed to stop the spread of the Covid-19 virus, so they were integrated 5-layer rubberized body bags.

They work in unison. The bodies are heavy, and it takes two of them to get one body into a bag, position it so that they can pull up the zipper and then move to the next.

They worked nonstop, placing each body into a cadaver bag, and then lifting it onto a gurney and wheeling it out the side delivery entrance to the facility which faced the freight elevator. It took them, close to ten hours to get the bodies out and remove any evidence of what had taken place.

When they were done, they left the facility. As planned no calls were to be made at the hospital so each left their departments and returned home to make their assigned calls. Dr. Franklin Henderson called the mortician and arranged for the truck to be taken and the bodies cremated.

Dr. Timothy Evans contacted the contractor who had been paid well to set up the facility and gave him a figure of what he would be given if he could take the facility apart in a week.

Dr. Warren was to tie up any loose ends. The families were contacted, and he explained what had to happen. They met with no disagreements. Unfortunately, they could not reach Dr. McKenna's family, but she had on file that in the case of her demise she wanted her body cremated. In normal times they would have to get the okay from the family, but this was not normal times. They went forward with the plan.

In practice the system works perfectly smooth with the bodies being transported and cremated. Even the contractor dismantling the facility in record time was handled efficiently and if anyone were to come down to the sub-basement, they would not know that the facility ever existed.

For the doctors if this action were to go smoothly, they must believe in their motive power. They could not let human passion and sentiment enter the picture.

Chapter 59

For Elise, the new reality hit her smack in the face. People walking around with masks, shortage of staples on the shelves and the fact that there is no way they can return home; at least for the present time as the third wave of the coronavirus put everything at a standstill once again. Thanks to the generosity of Bai, they have a place to stay as long as they need, but for both Matthew and Elise there is an urgency to get home.

"Dad, do you think it is like this at home?"

"Yes. It was quite bad in Europe during the first wave and from talking with your mother, it was the same there. She said she had fortunately stocked up on most essentials…you know how she is…but food she had to search for. She told me that one day when she went to Wegmans, they had no meat of any kind. Lucky for her she likes those impossible burgers…" He said, his voice trailing off, not concealing his worry.

Several times they tried to reach Sonya and now it seems the phone is off, or the battery needs charging. Where is she?

Sensing his concern, Elise said, "Dad, it is time. Go on, call the hospital."

"You are right. We have been trying so long; she will understand us doing this." He turns to face his daughter and as if to reassure himself he says, "It's not 'normal' times, it is drastic times, and we need to hear she is okay." He dials her work number.

It rings several times and finally the line is open.

"Good morning

"Good morning," Tina responds. "Who am I speaking with?" He recognizes her voice.

"Is this Tina, Dr. Tina Williams," he asks, but before she can answer he continues saying. "Tina, it is me, Matthew McKenna. I have been trying for months to reach Sonya and have not had any luck. I know you are busy there, but you know I am not one to bother her at work. Only, I need to hear her voice, to know she is okay."

There is a long pause. Tina is torn. When she had heard what had happened, she had a hard time accepting it.

She had noticed Sonya was no longer on the floor. She had tried to call her at home and been unable to reach her.

Tina leaned her cheek against the phone searching for the words to tell her husband. She had refused to say the words because to say it would make it real. Sonya and she had gone to medical school together. Later they would share the birth of their children and even the marriage to their husbands. Tears filled her eyes and rolled down her cheeks as she stood holding the phone, emotions taking her over.

"A minute," Tina said, trying not to have her feelings heard in her voice.

She took her free hand and wiped the tears from her cheeks and then reached in her pocket trying to find a Kleenex. When her hand closed over one, she pulled it out and carefully put the phone down on the desk. She pulled down her mask and blew her nose. A sob escaped her lips as she tried to control herself and as she had done before, she calmed herself by thinking, what if Sonya was not dead. She had not seen her body, so there was a chance she was still alive.

"Tina, are you still there."

Tina came alert and takes a deep breath and clears her throat before bringing the phone to her ear.

"Yes, Matthew, I am here. I just got a little distracted. Listen, I have not seen Sonya in a while, but as soon as I do, I will tell her to call you."

"Thanks, Tina. I appreciate it."

The line was disconnected, and Tina still held the phone to her ear. How could she give him the worse news he would ever receive? What if she was right and Sonya was not dead?

It was not a lie, Tina told herself. She had not lied to her best friend's husband. She really did not know for sure.

Chapter 60

"This is awful. I had no idea it was this bad."

"I forgot. You last saw Wuhan when it was overflowing with people going every which way. This is the new Wuhan, the city that will be forever known as the place where the coronavirus is thought to have originated."

Elise takes in the empty streets as Bai tells her that during the first wave of COVID-19 they were under lockdown for more than 50 days."

"I hate to say it, but I guess in a way I was lucky I was so sick and did not know how bad it was."

Neither Bai or her father responds to this as Bai maneuvers his SUV easily down Jianghan Street, a famous commercial walking Street that is now bare of pedestrians and traffic. Finally, her father breaks the silence.

"I was in Europe when it hit. I do not have to imagine what it was like, I lived it. In the first week of the quarantine people were caught by surprise."

"I cannot speak for the US, except from what Sonya shared with me, but in Europe it was awful. Everything was in short supply and the city was on lockdown. Italy was like a ghost town during that first wave and then after beating back COVID-19 in the spring, most of Europe began seeing a resurgence. Spain reported close to 10,000 cases a day, more than it had at the height of the outbreak in the spring.

France reported thousands of cases a day and in Germany, numbers were low, but rising steadily. They are calling for, how did they say it, renewed vigilance. It is the same as a total lockdown, but nicely said. I had to drive here...drive here from Europe as there was no other way to get out of the city."

Being a writer, Matthew is wordy, and he has done his research. He pauses, recalling his trip, then continued. "I have to say though that few disputes rose to the initial challenge of a lockdown. In Bergamo, a hotspot in Italy's Lombardy region, crematoria were so overburdened in March that army trucks had to transport the dead to other cities—that opened people's eyes. But by the end of May, Lombardy registered zero COVID-19 deaths for the first time. By early July, the European Union and the United Kingdom together averaged fewer than 5000 new cases per day, whereas the United States and Brazil which have roughly the same population recorded 50,000 and 40,000, respectively."

Matthew is pensive, feeling a need to let it all out. "The rising case numbers today are not quite comparable to the peak in April, but the increase shows that Europe relaxed measures too early and too much and that sent out the wrong message. What they should have done was emulate New Zealand by stopping community transmission completely and zealously guarding against reintroductions."

Matthew looks at his daughter and smiles.

"I do not envy the powers that be. People's willingness to stay alert and remember new rules wanes quickly. As people return to work infections rise and young people partying does not help at all, nor does reopening schools across the continent. Basically, people want their life back to normal and will not tolerate isolation without a fight."

"So, Dad, what happened during the second wave."

"As in the spring, every country has its own strategies for controlling the pandemic. Belgium has one of the strictest face mask policies, for instance, but crossing the Dutch border to shop in Maastricht they can take off their masks. Even within countries, the rules can change. Germany went from a mandatory 14-day quarantine for people arriving from countries considered risky to voluntary tests at the airport and other entry points, with no quarantine for those who tested negative. In my opinion they needed to define one central policy in Europe."

"But" Bai adds, "are not we better prepared during this third wave."

"Yes, you are right. Face masks were not available or even recommended in the beginning but have become ubiquitous in most countries. The emphasis on hand hygiene is clearly being followed along with the ban on almost any outdoor activity, including jogging. People are asked to focus on indoor activities. We have learned outdoor hospitality is generally fine, nonessential shops are fine if people wear face coverings. Even public transport does not seem that risky with all the methods of sanitation in place."

"We have seen a massive change in the social structure and interactions of populations from the start of the pandemic and they say that the conditions that spread the virus then will not necessarily be the same ones that are creating the risk now. They think that more-targeted measures probably will not be enough to keep the virus from resurging and we will reach a point where stricter measures must be taken but it will not be complete lockdowns. Believe it or not, right now, that is the case. People are encouraged to work from home and large gatherings are banned but shops and restaurants are staying open as well as schools…not as it used to be but getting close to some semblance of normal."

"You said that it is probably different in the United States."

"That is what Sonya tells…told me," he quickly changes the word not understanding why he does it."

"Compared with the United States, Europe has one advantage as control measures are not nearly as controversial. Protests against masks and social distancing broke out but they represented a small minority of the population. In the United States, openly fighting against the mandatory restrictions was more prominent."

"I am sure you felt it here, too."

"Yes," Bai interjects. "It was just before the Lunar New Year, and people were on holiday. And then came word of the coronavirus quarantine. I was in shock at first but calmed when friends said the media and the government were saying the virus was no big deal."

"Yes, same where I was," Matthew added. "Then the authorities announced that nobody could leave the city, and public transportation was cancelled. That was all in the first week. And knowing that my wife was in New York and my daughter in Wuhan, I started freaking out."

"Your mother's a doctor?" Bai asked Elise.

"Yes. She works at one of the biggest hospitals in Rochester and they are one of the best, so I am sure she is safe." She paused, then added, "You are probably thinking New York City; which dad says is the epicenter of the virus in the United States?"

"Yes…"

"We live in Rochester, New York which is in Upstate New York, about four hundred miles from New York City."

"So, Matthew, you embarked on your trip across the country to get here. How was that?

"That trip would have been just as difficult under other circumstances, but COVID-19 did not help. If it had not been for a friend who had some pull, I would have never made it. He was able to get my papers in order, map out my trip and provide the necessary details for timing at certain border crossings. It was long, strenuous, and unexciting, to say the least, but it was my reason for making the trip that made it all bearable. I had to get to Wuhan, I had to find Elise. So, I handled the stress and frustration knowing that it was necessary for me to get here, but it was eye opening to say the least."

"When Italy issued quarantine orders on 11 municipalities in the northern part of the country, I thought I was doomed. That order halted train travel and with airlines already grounded it seemed impossible to get to Wuhan. That quarantine also meant I faced the possibility of being stopped and forced back, or worse, quarantined, but my friend was able to route me so that I was not on the best roads for travel at times and when I was on main thoroughfares, they would have enough traffic so that I would blend in. In any case, it worked. From driving, to hotels, to having the right money at the right location, he planned every little detail, and I followed his instructions to the letter. And here I am."

"So, what do you need to know to drive through Europe," dad.

Matthew considers his daughter's questions and then shares some of what he learned.

"In France and Italy, highway tolls are collected based on distance traveled, much like in Pennsylvania or New York. Germany has no tolls for cars. Austria and the Czech Republic, however, work on flat-rate, time-based vignettes, or stickers that you must pull over and buy at the border. You can get a sticker for one week, 10 days, one month, or one year. There are some digital vignette-reader gateways over the autobahns, but you might be forgiven for thinking that they really do not care. A small example, however: If you are caught on an Austrian autobahn without a vignette, it will run you €400–€4,000, or, roughly speaking, $530–$5,300. If you are a foreigner, of course, they'll just take your car until you figure out where that five grand is coming from."

"Yet, under different circumstances, Italy is probably the most fun country to drive through, period. With its winding roads through rolling hills, but they have a speed monitoring system to keep you in line. First, you see velocità controllata warning signs; then come the eye-level radar "kiosks" that also read and record your license plate. If your plate's registered as arriving "too soon" by successive radar stations, the software marks you as too fast. The longer you keep this up, the heftier the fine gets, and it can run into thousands so being mindful I had to stay within the speed limits. In Germany there are stretches of the Autobahn where there is no speed limits and if you are not careful, you are dead. I cannot tell you how I appreciate the rear-view mirror. And I learned how to stick my arm out the window with my palm down, patting the air softly until I could safely move right. Seeing the puzzled expressions Matthew laughed and added, "It is the international "slow down, you bastard" hand signal.'

"Something else my friend shared with me on my travel days. Sunday was the best days for travel on the Autobahn as European truckers are forced to travel under, or at, the equivalent of 60 mph. This causes heavy congestion in the right lane, where the trucks run. Another interesting point is that especially on Sundays there seems to be a 90/10

Rule with truckers. Ninety of the truckers are off the road in Central and Western Europe, 10 percent are on the road."

"Along with travel time, there were important things to remember when I had to pull off and find my hotel for the night. You must read the fine print when parking in town. As a foreigner you are a third-class citizen, automotively speaking. They will tow your car for the slightest parking infraction. Traffic authorities in Berlin, for example, have only recently begun to consider displaying English on their almost universal ticket machines which means that if I cannot understand what it says, I need to ask someone since there is no excuse for running over the time limit. If you do you might be fined from $10–$40, depending on the length of the offense."

Bai nodded in agreement.

"Well, I do not want to accept it." Elise said. "I do not want to be forced to stay here when I need to get home. I do not want to be locked up like an animal and not able to go for a walk if I want to."

"Get used to it baby, because you do not have a choice."

After all that talking, they finally found a place where they could pick up some clothes for Elise and get some food to take home.

Chapter 61

Matthew used his time in Wuhan to research and write. He wrote how they had to adapt to meal planning and working with neighbors to get food and supplies delivered.

He wrote how fortunate he was that he could work remotely and how others were learning to do the same and he wrote what he knew about the disease itself, the people changing their life's to fit the situation and the deaths and illness around them. Mostly he wrote about how everyone thought that we, as a society, were too advance to even mimic what had happened during the 1918 virus. Boy were they wrong!

As the third wave took hold in Wuhan, Matthew continued to check on the spread of COVID-19. The days in quarantine turned into weeks and weeks into months as they kept contacting the airlines and train service to see if they can get home. Each time they were told there was nothing they could do for them.

At first, they were forced to remain in the house with only one person allowed to go out and shop. If it had not been for the size of Bai's house, they would have gone stare crazy.

Bai had a home gym so they all managed to get some exercise and with little to occupy her time, Elise was becoming quite the cook and when she was not cooking or exercising, she was calling the airlines to see if they had found her luggage. There was no telling where the luggage had gone. Had it made it all the way to Rochester, New York or was it waylaid somewhere along the route. She had spent quite a sum on clothes for the trip. She knew it was silly but, in her defense, this was a big thing to her, and she had wanted to look successful. Worse than the clothes was the loss of her shoes and all her skin and haircare products. When she did get back to her apartment, she would need to buy everything. "Oh," she thought. "Thank goodness for Amazon."

After several months of calling and checking on the luggage, she finally gave up.

They were like a family now. Bai was not only a friend of Elise's, but also of her father. Elise could tell he liked Bai as he treated him like the son he never had. This was good because Elise found she more than liked this attractive and obviously remarkably successful man. She appreciated that he had inherited money and this place, but still held down a job. But she was soon to be shocked by the extent of his wealth.

One day as they were all together, sitting at the dining room table, Elise asked as politely as she could. "Bai, you do not have to answer, but I was wondering about…about all this," she said her arms spreading out to take in the area.

Bai had just taken in a mouthful of food and raised a finger as he finished chewing. He then picks up his glass and takes a short drink to wash it down.

"I am sorry," Elise says, sensing his hesitation has more to do with not wanting to talk about it.

"No, it is okay. He pauses. "Let me start at the beginning." He takes a sip of wine. "I think I told you I was just a baby when my mother died. It has always been my father and me and he passed in 2017." His eyes mist as he continues. "He was everything to me. We had the kind of relationship that I witness you have, Elise and Matthew. We were son and father, but also best friends."

He takes another sip of wine. "My father owned businesses. He was a lawyer by trade, but later in life he switched to buying companies, including the travel agency."

Elise interrupts him. "You mean the agency here, you own it?"

Bai smiles. "Yes, and several others across Europe. That is why I was so interested in hearing about your father's trip. I find listening to people has made my agency great."

"I do not know what to say. Why didn't you tell me?"

"Well, you did not ask, and I did not want to sound like I was bragging."

Elise nods. "So, go on."

"Well, my dad Ma Zhao is the cofounder of e-commerce giant Alibaba."

Elise lifts her shoulders acknowledging she knows nothing about Alibaba. But her dad does. "The company, in less than 20 years of inception was listed on the New York Stock Exchange with a record setting IPO that raised $25 billion."

"That is right, Matthew. He also had stakes in several other firms and financial institutions."

Bai starts to stop there but decides to tell them everything. He loves these two as family and they have a right to know all there is about him.

"My mother was the daughter of one of the richest pig breeders and inherited her fortune when her father passed on, and her mother and her brother died in a plane crash. Her fortune was somewhere around $14 billion."

Elise realizes her mouth is hanging open and she quickly closes it. She opens it again to say, "I did not know. I had no clue."

"I know you did not Elise. I was going to tell you, but I never saw the right time. You, I admire because you did tell me about your family."

Bai wanted to tell Elise he loved her and wanted to marry her, but again he held off. What he had told them both was overwhelming, and they needed time to process before he sprung that on them.

Bai spent his time making sure they were comfortable. As the days passed, the relationship between the three of them only got better and Bai knew it had nothing to do with his money.

Chapter 62

The announcement is made that the quarantine is over, and they can go out as long as they wear a mask and adhered to social distancing.

It is the same everywhere and not just in Wuhan. The quarantines had lifted. That evening, after dinner, Bai asked Elise if she wanted to go for a walk the following day. He asked her father if he would like to join them, but he declined.

Over the many months they had spent together, out of respect for her father, they had not been intimate, but had shared a few passionate kisses when they got the chance and with a house the size of his, the chance came frequently.

They had been given space by her father, who spent a lot of time writing and trying to reach her mother, but it was not the same. They would be able to meander about at will and she was ready to take in different scenery.

They started out early the next morning, planning to find a place to grab a bite to eat and just take freedom all in. Winter was over and the weather was warming quickly, giving a sense that 2021 was going to be a better year than the last.

Bai and Elise were back to the way it had been when they were touring. There was an ease of talking about non-essentials and sharing the beauty around them as they smelt freshly cut grass and flowers blooming. When they tired of walking, they returned home.

"Hi kids. Have a nice walk."

"We did, dad. We are going to drive up to East Lake and wanted you to join us. You have not seen it, have you?"

"No, I have not...yes, if you do not mind, I would love to join you."

They were heading toward the door when the cook came in the front room. "Wait a second, Bai, I will fix you a picnic basket to take with you. Just give me a minute."

"Sure, Changchang. That would be nice."

"So, tell me about East Lake," Matthew said.

"It is one of the largest sites in Huazhong District. It is also the largest "City Lake" in China and there is lots to see and enjoy. It will be wonderful to have a picnic there."

With Bai doing his guide thing, they visited the Ting Tao, Moshan, Luo Yan Island and stood admiring the Museum of Hubei Province. Though they could not go in, they admired the Moshan temple, all the time listening to Bai's history of the area.

When they were hungry, they found a lovely park with seating and while Matthew and Bai went to get the picnic basket, Elise stood looking across the area, thinking, wondering and hoping that Bai would pop the question. She had no doubt he felt the same and that he wanted to be with her, only he had not asked her to marry him.

The food was fantastic. Changchang had packed all the best that Wuhan had to offer, including a bottle of wine.

When they finished, they climbed back in the SUV and Matthew asked if they could stop at the liquor store.

There was a mischievous smile on his face when he returned, with his purchase concealed.

"So, dad, whatcha got there."

"A surprise my dear." That was all he said as he leaned back enjoying the ride back to Bai's.

Elise could not remember ever being so happy. They pulled into the drive and while her dad went inside, they took a walk around the estate, then joined him in the front room. When they entered, Matthew was smiling. "Guess what. I can arrange airline seats by the end of the week."

While Elise did not know what to say or whether it was time to express her personal feelings, Bai did.

What Bai hears is he has only a few more days to be with Elise. Feeling four sets of eyes on him he attempts a smile. "That is wonderful, Matthew."

He meant those words; he really did because that is what they had wanted. Bai excused himself, "I will give you a few minutes," and without waiting for a response he hurried upstairs to his bedroom. There he went into his closet and moved his clothes aside so that he could open a hidden door. It swung open to reveal a safe.

None of his movements were planned as he quickly entered the combination and then, taking a deep breath, reached inside to pull out a small velvet box. He turned it over and over in his hands before finally relocking the safe and closing the entrance. He took the time to readjust the clothing before carrying the box to his dresser.

Bai's shoulders rose as he took in a deep breath before slowly opening the velvet box to display its treasure. He had not looked at the ring for some time and just like the day his mother had given it to him to place on the finger of the woman he planned to marry, its beauty left him speechless.

The Emerald & Trapezoid Triple Diamond Engagement Ring set in white gold was flawless. There was the emerald cut 2 carat diamond in the center and two 1 carat emerald cut diamonds on either side. He loved the ring and he hoped that Elise would too. He stood admiring it for some time and when he heard voices calling him from downstairs, he tucked it safely in his pocket and hurried down to join his guest.

That night they cooked dinner together. It had been decided to make a fully American meal for Bai and he was game. He had enjoyed a bit of American cuisine, but never a full meal so they were determined to include all the frills.

The dinner consists of a main entrée of barbecued chicken on the grill, prepared by Matthew. They put Bai in charge of preparing rice that he is to later add beans and a special sauce that Matthew will prepare. Elise is on the salad. She is busily making a Caesar salad from scratch. She had to get the recipe off the internet, but she was putting the ingredients together with a twist of her own.

There is a lot of rushing back and forth, forgetting an ingredient, and going back to the cabinet or refrigerator to find it as they chat amongst themselves. Matthew tells the two about the first time Sonya, his wife cooked for him. "Do not get me wrong, she is not great, but a good cook now, but she had little time to get anything done those days…sort of like now." He pauses and then in a cheery voice adds. "She tried to make steaks and a salad… that was it."

"I do not think you told me this story before."

"I probably did not. But anyway, what we ended up trying to eat, and I mean trying, was the toughest steaks I have ever attempted to chew, flavorless as she did not even season them"

"Oh no, I can relate to that. The first time I tried to cook meat it was dry and tasteless."

"Bai, when did you cook," Elise says teasing, "I thought Changchang has always been with the family."

"She has Elise, but that does not mean we never cooked our own meals. We did not do it often, but we had our time in the kitchen." Bai pauses. "Sorry, Matthew, please continue."

"Thank you, Bai," he says with a grimace at his daughter. "So, with the steak she prepared a salad..." He looks over at his daughter.

"Come on dad, I can cook, and I definitely can make a salad." He watches as she dramatically pushes the plunger on the lettuce spinner.

"Anyway, she put together a simple lettuce, tomatoes and cucumber salad. She even purchased a loaf of garlic bread." Turning toward his daughter adds, "You know the type that comes in a foil bag and you put it under the broiler to toast and melt the cheese." Elise nods.

"She stuck the bread under the boiler and proceeded to make the salad. She did not spin the lettuce or even dry it off after she rinsed it. The knife she cut the tomatoes with was dull, so they squished extra juice on the lettuce. The cucumbers did not have a fighting chance and they were fine." Bai and Elise are laughing as he continues.

"Well, she forgot about the bread until the smoke started billowing out of the oven and I thought we would have to call the fire department..." His voice drags out on the last word as his mind goes back to that day."

Elise looks over at her father. "Dad, dad are you all right."

He snaps out of it, nodding while sentimental tears fall on his cheeks. Sorry kids. Let's get with it.

They finish the meal preparations and to make the conversation light, Bai talks about the places he took Elise during her travel guide tour.

Everything looked good and the scent of the barbecue chicken filled the air. Since Elise finished her salad early, she helped Bai with the final preparations of his rice and bean dish, explaining that her mother had made this for them often. "Sometimes we ate just the beans and rice for dinner."

Bai liked this feel of knowing these intimate details about her family and wanted to hear more.

"Let us set up dinner on the deck and enjoy the garden."

"Wonderful. Help me get everything out there."

The men gather dishes, napkins and eating utensils, while Elise goes to the grocery bag and pulls out the crusty rolls. She found a tray in the drawer next to the stove and put the bread, condiments and three glasses of water on it to carry out to the deck.

"Where did you find that?" Bai asks.

"My, if you are not familiar with your own kitchen, how do you expect me to believe you cook," she laughs.

"Give me that..." he says with humor over his shoulder as he heads back in the house to get the food and bring it out. When he returns Elise and Matthew remove the dishes and Bai places the empty tray on the cutting board next to the grill. They are ready to eat.

The meal is perfection as they enjoy their cooking. "I think I can get use to American cooking," Bai says between mouthfuls of food.

"I am glad," Elise replies shyly.

With the meal over, the three work together to clean up and put the leftovers in the fridge. When everything is back in order, they head back out to the deck. Matthew pauses and turns back to get the champagne he purchased earlier.

"Oh, dad, you sentimental old man. Your surprise is champagne to toast our wonderful host." Matthew winks at her.

Bai brings out a wine bucket with ice to keep the champagne cool. Matthew takes a white kitchen towel that Bai has also brought him and begins to open the bottle. Carefully he removes the wire casing, pointing the bottle away from them. Bai is at the ready, taking the wire casing so that Matthew has his hands free. He lays the towel over his right palm and then grabs the end of the bottle, encasing the cork as he pulls. It pops out and comparatively little of the liquid bubbles out.

Elise, who has been lighting candles on the deck, pauses and claps her hands. Her father bows.

Getting into the mood, Bai turns on the outside twinkling lights that are everywhere. Strands run across the deck's pergola top, stretching out to the trees, fence, and outbuildings. In one instance the area becomes a wonderland.

"Oh, my Bai, it is magical." Elise says as they toast each other with expensive fluted champagne glasses.

From the first sip, Matthew is glad he has splurged as this is indeed awesome champagne. Bai goes to the ice bucket and removes the towel. He looks over at Matthew and smiles. "Ace of Spades by Armand De Brignac." This is superb Matthew."

"Well thank you Bai. I am no connoisseur, but from the many book signing events I learned that this was number one among champagnes. I figure tonight deserves nothing but the best that the world can offer."

As if ingenuous, that is the perfect cue for Bai as he turns to Matthew and says, "Matthew, can I see you for a minute in the kitchen?"

Elise strolls around the garden enjoying the beauty of the estate and does not see her father and Bai enter the house. Finally, she turns and heads back to the deck. She strolls, hesitates, staring first at one and then the other. "What is going on guys," she asks seeing a strange look on their faces.

Lights twinkled behind her and in front of her as she regains her composure and steps up on the deck where her father and Bai stand poised with the lights glittering around them.

Bai's hands are clenched in his pockets, one pocket being the one that holds a small, velvet ring box. Now is the perfect time to propose—he knows it, he has seen it many times in movies and read it in books. But now it is real, and he wonders about the details behind the proposal scene. Does he just pull out the ring and say, "Will you marry me?" or, wait for Elise to say something first. There are so many questions left unanswered for Bai and not knowing the answer has his heart hammering in his chest, but the biggest unanswered question is will Elise say yes?

"Come on guys, you are scaring me…"

Bai steps forward and when he is right in front of her, he drops down on one knee, reaches into his pocket and pulls out a small velvet box. He looks up at her and when her eyes meet his, he opens the lid. "Elise McKenna, will you marry me?"

Elise is stunned into silence at both the contents of the box and the man who holds it. No way could this be any more perfect an evening. The ring is the most beautiful thing she has ever seen and the man holding it is the love of her life.

Bai is still on his knee and he feels his body sway. The delay in her response has all kinds of doubts running through his head. Has he misread her feelings? Does she not want to marry him? Could she have a serious boyfriend back in the States that her father is unaware of. It is all possible.

Finally, Elise finds her voice. Breathlessly she says, "Yes, oh yes Bai."

He stands up quickly and moves closer to Elise. He draws her into his arms, kissing her deeply before stepping back to take the ring out of the box and carefully sliding it on her finger.

Elise cannot stop staring at it and when her father comes over to give her a hug, she holds out her hand so he can get a good look. "Wow, that is some ring," he said as he releases his daughter and turns to hug Bai.

"Son, I could not ask for a better husband for my daughter or for a better son. Welcome to the family."

While in the house, Bai and Matthew not only discussed the proposal, but also the plans for going to the States. Now they share them with Elise who is all smiles, sipping her Champagne and taking peeks at her ring that fits perfectly.

"Are you listening to us Elise," Bai says as his new fiancé stares at her ring and seems to be miles away."

"What? Yes, I am listening. We are all leaving for the States as soon as possible," Elise says.

"No, you and your father need to get back as soon as possible to find your mother and I need to take care of a few things here before I join you."

Elise pouts. "Bai, I understand, just do not take too long…please."

"Well kids, it is time for me to turn in. I am tired and I need my sleep." Matthew kisses the top of his daughter's head and pats Bai on the shoulders. "Just so you know it, I am the happiest guy in the world right now. Ah, that is after Bai of course." He turns and leaves them alone.

They sit on the deck discussing the arrangements for the next day. There was so much to do, and it would take time away from them being together. But Elise assured Bai she understands. That night they spend in Bai's room.

The next few days, Bai is gone most of the time tying up loose ends and the last night that the McKenna's will be in Wuhan, Elise asks, "What about your house, your family, your job?"

"Well, my bride to be, I have made arrangements so that I will be able to work anywhere and I have no family left to say goodbye to; it is more friends and business associates." Bai pauses and walks across the room to stare out the window. "I also have made arrangements for the care of the property which I plan to keep so that we have a place to stay should we come for a visit."

Bai turns around to look at Elise. "There are a few financial things I still need to deal with, but with this coronavirus it does not happen quickly. You can believe I will be there as soon as I can."

Chapter 63

On April 7, 2021, Matthew and Elise are taken to the airport by Bai. Elise is returning to America and though she is sad to leave, she is anxious to see her mother and share what she has done and seen in her homeland. As she prepares for her trip home, much of what she has is new since her lost luggage has never been found. She smiles thinking of all that use to seem so important to her, is no more than a memory now. She has changed in many ways. She no longer sees her career as more important than her personal life and she knows that what she wants to do is write, and not just travel guides.

Elise pauses in her packing, smiling. This city of 10 million has now become a part of her history as well as her mothers. She has seen its lakes and its extensive gardens, and throughout Hubei, China she has visited the ruins of the past that her great grandmother told her about. Elise sighs. If only she could tell her she has walked where she walked.

It is now spring, and the weather is starting to get comfortable again with temperatures reaching the low seventies. Elise removes a sweater out of her suitcase and puts it on before gathering her bags and heading downstairs to join her father and Bai. She might just need it, later. The only sad part today is leaving Bai, but that is temporary, she reminds herself.

When Elise is halfway down the stairs, she sees they are both waiting for her and each takes a bag to carry out to the car.

"Is that everything?"

"Yes, I think so. If not, you can bring it with you…or we can keep some things here for when we visit." Bai grins. "I like the sound of that."

"Me too."

Matthew interrupts, "Okay you love birds, Let us get the show on the road."

As usual, Elise offers the front seat to her father and climbs in the back. It was November of 2019 when she first left Rochester and now almost a year and a half has passed. It did not seem possible she has been gone so long.

This will be a trip she will remember for the rest of her days. Even the worse of it holds fond memories because she found Bai, the love of her life. Though she was ill and did not live through the first shutdown, she was there for the last. Seventy-six days of lockdown meant flights in and out were canceled. Train and bus routes were suspended. Highway entrances were blocked. The streets were empty, and people were ordered to stay in their homes as part of an unprecedented effort to contain the novel coronavirus. There were tough measures put in place — most people could not even go grocery shopping or bury their dead, but it seem to have worked. New coronavirus cases, which used to number in the thousands each day, slowed to a trickle.

But now Wuhan is starting to get back to normal and she is leaving. Elise can tell that as she gazes out the window. She can imagine people are visiting parks, markets, malls and on the roads, there are many more cars.

"It is nice to see things getting back to normal," Elise says.

It is her father who responds. "Yes, it is, but I have been reading a lot online that despite the enormous progress, many Wuhan residents remain hesitant and it is the same around the world. From what I have read about home, they have started sports, but no one can attend the games. I actually saw they have cutouts of people in the stadiums."

"No, you are kidding."

"That is what I read. And, Elise, that store you like to shop at in the mall is no more. Lots of stores, bars…just about everywhere have closed their doors for good."

"I know. I read that people go home early and there are few brave souls on the street at night."

"They are scared. We saw that when we went to the store. When we got close to some people, they took a step back." He paused. "They are afraid of contagion, especially now that contagions come from other countries."

"Well, from the internet I think we are going to see the same in the States. People eating outdoors instead of in restaurants and they wear masks like we are still seeing here. Wuhan is reopened, but there are still restrictions just like there are all over the world."

"To make this trip back home on cell phones we had to fill out a questionnaire asking if we have any possible symptoms of the coronavirus, or if we have been in close contact with someone who is sick. We were given a green QR code which means we are healthy and safe to travel. We could have been given an amber or red code that would restrict us from using the subway, going to a restaurant, or going to work, or getting on a plane. I am sure we are going to run into that again at layovers and at home."

Thoughts of the airport brings back the memory of how she had woken from a coma and found herself in a hospital. She was treated for COVID-19 and for a serious head injury from falling and hitting her head. When she finally was on the road to recovery and out of quarantine there was another problem. She had no idea who she was and neither did they. That is when she was taken to an on-site psychiatrist each day who tried to help her remember. Most days she tired easily and though she tried hard the sessions ended with her feeling frustrated and scared. Would she ever remember who she was?

Until a week before the arrival of her father and Bai, she was still unable to remember until that day when her doctor told her that he had good news. His eyebrows raise and he starts to speak more animatedly than he has before and he says, "I have received a call from a Mr. Matthew McKenna who has learned that his daughter Elise McKenna is at our hospital." He grins, his arms reaching out and says, "You are Elise McKenna from Rochester, New York," he states it as fact.

She grins back and feels excitement radiating out from her. She wants to bounce up and down on the ball of her feet like a giddy child dancing with joy, but just as soon as the feeling begins, it ends. Her brain stops working and there is zero thinking going on in her head.

Slowly her mind comes alive with the reality. She repeats the name, 'Elise McKenna' and she knows the doctor is right. That is her name.

From that point the doctors begin to brief her on all that had transpired to bring her to the hospital. They mentioned names and places and it helps her regain her memory. The doctor's final words to her are, "When your father arrives, I will bring him straightaway to you.

Elise feels the car slowing and sees they are at the airport. It is hard saying goodbye to this place and especially to Bai, but they only have a few minutes before she must board the plane with her father.

Their flight takes off early that morning from Wuhan to begin the trip to the States. Where it had taken her a day and a half to get to Wuhan, it now takes virtually three days to return as the coronavirus has lasting effects on the country.

Chapter 64

More than fifteen states are asking travelers to self-quarantine for 14 days as a joint effort to control the number of cases within their states. Connecticut, New York, and New Jersey governors require travelers from Alabama, Arkansas, Arizona, Florida, North Carolina, South Carolina, Utah, and Texas—known "hot spots" to self-quarantine for 14 days upon entering the area. That affected two of their layovers. Texas closing Dulles forces the pilot to obtain an alternate route. They run into the same problem in Newark.

At the first layover change in the States, Elise and Matthew anxiously listen to the news and hear Dr. Amesh Adalja say, "I think it is important to note that in the era of the pandemic, no activity is going to be risk-free, and everything is a nonzero risk. And each individual is going to have to think about what risk is tolerable to them and what risk is not."

As they enter the airport, Elise can smell the disinfectant everywhere. "Smell that?"

"Yes. They are all trying to keep areas as clean as possible, but you think they could find something that smelt better. They both laugh as they continue toward the check point.

There are signs everywhere listing the mask requirements and for social distancing. Thy read them and reread them at each of their layovers.

When they entered the airport, Matthew pointed out the plexiglass partitions at ticket and gate counters and as they get to the checkpoint, they see the same. There are acrylic barriers at the checkpoint where they must interact with airport personnel. They are asked to keep possession of their boarding pass, place it on the document scanner and then show the boarding pass to the officer for visual inspection.

They are directed to lower their mask for ID verification and again if the alarms at the security equipment, but aside from that, the mask becomes a permanent fixture throughout their travel.

Social distancing and wearing a face mask are rules and not suggestions and they are gently, but firmly told this will be enforced for theirs and their fellow passengers' safety.

Elise whispers to Matthew. "I feel like a criminal—don't you feel like a criminal?"

"Yes, but it is for our safety," and trying to make light of the situation, he adds, "Did you see the old 3-1-1 rule has changed. They are now allowing one oversized liquid hand sanitizer container in our carry-on bag."

"Ah, that explains it. I was wondering why there were so many of those on the belt. I thought they were free giveaways until the person in front grabbed hers and put it in her carryon."

A few passengers wear shoes that echo on the floors as they head toward their gate. The airport is like a ghost town compared to before COVID-19 hit. That bothers Matthew who is used to crowded airports and it gives him the shivers.

There was an extra step during check-in. They had to fill out a health declaration form when they checked in online or if they had not, they could do that at the airport. The form asks them to pledge that they will: wear a face covering while traveling; will not travel if they have symptoms of, have been diagnosed with or had exposure to COVID-19 in the past 14 days; and will check their temperature before flying to make sure they do not have a fever. It is all self-reported, of course, so passengers travel at their own risk and will say whatever they need to say to get on the airplane.

A constant is that mask use is a requirement at all airports but even in places with signs strategically placed some travelers ignore them. To really get away from people, he has Elise sit with him at an empty gate in each of the airports.

They watch as the passengers continue to arrive until the waiting area is full and they see there is plenty that has not changed. Passengers still crowd the gate when it is time to board. The passengers stand up before it is their turn, ignoring the gate agents telling them to keep their seats. "What idiots," Elise whispers to her dad. It is like they are afraid someone is going to take their assigned seats." Michael just nods, keeping his daughter close to his side and trying to avoid getting into a group of people.

"Excuse us," he says when he tries to make it to the gate and passengers seem intent on remaining in front of him. "They called us so please let us through."

Finally, he can push them to the front to board.

As soon as 10 people pass through, she pauses, holding back the rest who though irritated, stop and wait. This continues and Elise and Matthew watch in dismay.

But, as was the case pre-COVID-19, plenty of passengers continue to stand up and crowd the area waiting for their turn which slows the process even more as people who want to social-distance have to squeeze through to get to the gateway. Then they must have their temperature checked once more before boarding, slowing the process even more.

In first class there are as usual, few passengers. Elise peeks to the rear and knows that because of the size of the plane the passengers will be able to social distance, though crowded at the front of the gateway it would have seemed impossible.

When her dad and her are situated, they are handed what is labeled a 'Fly Well Pack'. It is a see-through bag and inside is a disposable face mask, and several of those hand-wipes. Elise takes one out and reads, "Use one for your hands and the other for surfaces."

Matthew reads the small print. "The wipes are alcohol-free and last for up to 24 hours and, according to the packet, protects against 99.99% of germs."

While passengers fill the aisle waiting to enter business class and coach, Elise entertains herself listening to their complaints.

"You wait and see, there are no mask police on the plane. Most passengers kept them on, but on my previous flight I encountered one nearby passenger flouting the mask requirement. She was in the row across from me and the mask hung off one of her ears the entire flight while she read a book. The only time she put it on was when a flight attendant approached and again when we were preparing to land."

"I hear you. On trips to the restroom, I saw passengers without them, too."

It pleases Elise to know others feel a need to have everyone follow the rules and as they board the plane each person who passes has on their mask…at least for the time being.

Once the plane is loaded and ready for departure, she pays attention to the flight attendant who begins her welcome-aboard greeting, followed by the usual script about in-flight service.

"Shortly after takeoff, we will offer complimentary soft drinks," she says, pauses and adds, ""Oh, just kidding," catching herself and giving the COVID-19 version of the food-and-drink service announcement.

"Sorry, I go into autopilot sometimes." Elise likes her accent. Having spent so much time in China she finds it comforting. "We are offering a limited service at this time of just a cup of water and a bag of snack mix. We are following regulations very diligently, but we look forward to hopefully offering you full service again soon."

During the preflight safety announcement, there is another change to the script when the oxygen-mask tutorial begins. "You will remove your protective face covering," the flight attendant begins, with emphasis on the word 'remove', "then place the yellow cup over your nose and mouth."

Elise peeks at her father and sees he is resting. In some ways, flying has changed dramatically, with face masks a must, little-to-no in-flight service, and passengers warily eyeing each other, especially when someone sneezes, clears their throat or pushes their face mask down to their chin or neck. Except for one barking dog and a crying baby, this is the quietest flight she is ever been on. She falls asleep.

With limited in-flight service, the flight attendants are not traversing the aisles and thus not actively looking for scofflaws. Announcements about keeping masks on are made on a few of their flights but not all. In addition, passengers get reminders when they check in for their flight.

At one point during a layover Elise watches as an older couple plop down, right next to a woman working on her laptop in a row of four seats. The woman looks up and starts to say something, then stops. She immediately moves down to the end of the row. At least they are all wearing masks.

On the lighter side was those searching for food. Each time they land, the airports are empty of the usual hustle and bustle of passengers. But we realize the downside to this. Few or no places to grab food or a cocktail.

However, signs are posted telling passengers where they might find something open. Anxiety builds as stomachs growl and a man toting cups of beer to his gate is stopped by other passengers asking where he bought it.

Confused, the man cannot think what to say.

"Come on man, where?"

He finally finds his voice and tells them, then steps back, careful not to spill as they take off down the aisle.

Elise has prayed that at one of the layovers she would be able to grab some of Barrio Café's famous guacamole, but it, like most restaurants, is closed. The more they move about the airports as they get closer to home, they notice social distancing is largely ignored in the gate area and mask use is spotty.

Exiting the plane is a social-distancing nightmare: The flight attendant had a final announcement for passengers: "Please maintain social distancing while exiting the aircraft." Lucky for them they are in first class and do not have to deal with the fact that as one passenger says, "Ha-ha ha… No one is doing it!"

Another passenger says, "I can't believe the flight attendant said, "Please do not all squish into that aisle that way." Her partner responds, "Yeah, I think she had, had it and didn't care how she said it."

Elise's father has helped her relax through the constant delays and rerouting. They are both glad now that Bai had insisted that they fly first class all the way, even though first class is much different this time. In fact, it is not much different from coach in that they have social distancing in effect that leaves the center seat empty except if traveling with family.

She did miss the fancy meal, but at least they had a snack bag with bottled water and were told they could have another if they wished.

Elise spent the night tossing and turning, unable to sleep. The pared down meal served to them in first class was not enough to satisfy, but they did not complain, especially after the second night of flight caused by the redirection of the plane. There was nothing anyone could do, but grin and bear it.

But finally, they land in the States in New York City-- not Rochester. At first Elise had thought it was over, and this would be the last time they would have to get on a plane, but they are still over 400 miles from home.

She had made it through customs before, but this was different. They face a new dilemma as in batches they are taken to the U.S. Quarantine Station, staffed with quarantine medical and public health officers from CDC.

Here it is explained that they are separated from healthy people until they are each tested and if no one test positive or shows symptoms they will be released and sent on their way. They are told that they may be contacted once they arrive home and that they must adhere to a 14-day quarantine at their residence.

Elise looks at her dad and he smiles. "Don't worry Elise. It'll be fine." They move along and take a seat while the rest of the passengers go through the same process of a cheek swap and temperature check. Elise prays.

Finally, they are told they are clear to go and they board their last flight. Neither Elise or her dad are aware of how empty the planes had become during the first and second wave of the coronavirus. What they are seeing now, for most who have flown during those first two waves, is something more like 'normal'.

Along with the other passengers that are on their way to Rochester, they waste no time getting on the plane and soon they are in the air. Matthew starts making calls to find someone to pick them up at the airport. He reaches Dr. Williams; Sonya's friend and she agrees to come to their rescue.

With their feet finally on the ground, Elise, and Matthew hurry along with the other passengers as they make their way to baggage collection, hoping that their bags are there. They stand at a distance, but in view of the conveyor belt. "That is mine," Elise says and begins the process of pushing through the crowd that is not adhering to social distancing. Matthew helps her get her bag and right behind it comes Mathew's. "Thank you, Jesus. Thank you," Elise whispers.

Quickly they grab the bags and squeeze back through the crowd.

Chapter 65

Tina is waiting at the curb and toots her horn before climbing out of her car so they can see her. She has been mulling over in her mind what to say to them and she only hopes they wait until she delivers them at home before she has to say anything.

As they head down the expressway toward home, Elise feels as though they are in the world all alone. No traffic blocks their progress and when Elise glances at the opposite lanes beyond the divider, it is the same. It is like the whole world has disappeared and she has entered the twilight zone.

While Dr. Williams chats with her father, her mind runs rampant over all that has happened to her since she left the States and now what used to be familiar to her is as different as it had been in Wuhan. It makes her uncomfortable and she cannot shake the feeling that more change is about to come.

"Elise, what do you think?" Tina asked.

Elise had not been paying attention. "What, Dr. William. I am sorry, I was just looking at how empty of cars the expressway is." She adds, "What did you ask me."

"Your dad mentioned you had lost your cell phone and you had to pick one up in China."

"Oh, yes, my friend took me to a store to get one. There was so few choices, what with this coronavirus, however they did have that gorgeous Xiaomi Mi Mix 2S. Bai, that is my friends name, said it was not available in the United States yet." Elise has purposely not called him her fiancé as she did not want to get into that discussion now.

"Hmm…Yes, I have heard of it. Xiaomi unveiled a new version of the Mi MIX 2, in March of 2018. How is it? The real question is, though, does it work on your carrier's network?"

"It does, and it has 64GB of storage and 6GB of RAM." Elise pauses as she searches through the new purse, purchased in China. "Ah, here it is."

Tina hears paper being unfolded in the back seat and soon Elise's voice rings out, clearly reading. Tina smiles.

"The Xiaomi 2S is powered by the Qualcomm Snapdragon 845, it features the same 5.99 inches (152 mm)

1080p IPS LCD display found on the Mi MIX 2, a new dual 12 MP camera, Qi wireless charging, and is pre-loaded with Android 8.0 Oreo." Elise stops, and leaning her arms on the back of the front seat adds, "I am not sure of what all that means, but it does work on my Spectrum network which is all I care about. I am sure you understand how it is when you see something that is new and have the added pleasure of knowing that not everyone can get it, well, your interest peaks."

"Can I ask what it costs?"

"Sure." There is the sounds of her searching in her purse. Elise finds the receipt. "It costs at 3,299 yuan, which translates to a little less than $530. That's not bad considering some phones today costs over a thousand."

"I agree, that is not bad at all. I might just check into getting one. I am due a new phone."

Elise sits back and continues to stare out the window. They had exited the thruway and were going down residential streets on their way to her parents' home. The pandemic caused sickness, death, and social shutdowns worldwide, but it really hit home seeing the changes in a place so familiar to her.

As they drive toward home, Elise sees a man up ahead crossing an empty street and she can make out that he is wearing a face mask.

Her head is on a swivel as she stares in disbelief. "Residents are still facing confinement and being asked to practice social distancing," Dr. Williams says.

"You will find it is quiet and like this in most cases, especially since the third wave hit. Before that, people were getting anxious and started trying to take back the freedom they were used to. They ignored masks and social distancing and then, the third wave of the coronavirus hit. They got it then. They began staying indoors and only coming out when necessary."

When they finally pulled up into the driveway of her parents' home in Irondequoit, Elise felt an overwhelming sense of despondency. This is not what she had expected. Coming home meant going to the groceries and picking up something special for dinner or giving her friend Melissa a call and telling her all about her trip over a glass of wine. Or just going to work and handing in her travel log on Wuhan…At that thought Elise let out a wail that scared Dr. William who was turning into her father's driveway. She hit the brakes hard, Elise felt herself being thrown forward so fast it felt like her seatbelt was going to cut her in half.

Her father put out his hand and braced himself from the force and they both turned around to face the back seat.

Elise sat there trying to catch her breath, then sensing she was being stared at, she sucked in her lower lip before she said, "Sorry guys."

"What happened?" her father said in a loud worried voice.

Feeling stupid, she almost whispered. "I just realized that I lost my laptop and my phone. "Tears started to run down her cheeks.

"Are you hurt?" Dr. Williams said, unloosing her seat belt and starting to open the door.

"No, I am fine." Trying to find the right words, she paused. "It is just that my whole write up for my job was on that laptop. I had videos and pictures on my phone that were irreplaceable."

"If your phone is lost or stolen, the loss of photos may not be your biggest problem. Did you check with your carrier to have the phone locked so no one could use it?"

"No. I did not think of that."

"Don't worry," her dad added. We can call your carrier and handle that. They may be able to restore all or most of your information, including your photos."

"Maybe if I had done it earlier. I do not think after all this time they will still have a backup of my phone."

"You never know."

Dr. Williams got out of the car and they followed, getting their luggage, and carrying it into the house. Once inside, Dr. Williams paused. "Do you need help or want me to stay?"

"Oh, no, thank you Tina, you have been a big help. Just, if you hear anything about Sonya, will you call us?" Up until now the changes in the area had held their attention, allowing Tina to hold off sharing information about Sonya.

Tina stood there now trying to decide what and how much she should say to them, knowing it would be wrong to stay quiet much longer. Finally, she said, "I will stay a while longer. I am sure the food in the refrigerator is too old to eat and thawing something from the freezer will take time. What is available is food delivery by just about all stores."

Elise and Matthew gazed at her, both wondering why she would say that. It was a weird thing to state, but then, Tina had said they had been on overload at the hospital.

"Great. Let's order a pizza…ah; if that is all right with everyone. I have not had a pizza in…" Elise paused as it hit her how long she has actually been gone. "In over a year."

No one responds to that. Instead, Matthew takes out his phone, presses his Two Ton Tony app. It only takes a few minutes and having lived with two women for so long, he knows what to order without asking. He orders a fully loaded veggie pizza.

That done, he picks up his luggage and Elise's and moves them over near the stairway. Then, while Elise and Dr. Williams sit in the living room, he goes to find a bottle of wine and some glasses.

"Listen Elise, I know this has been a lot to process, but it will all turn out okay."

"Thanks Dr. Williams." She contemplates, "I am being selfish thinking about my personal problems. What is more important is that my mother is missing. Am I right, Dr. William? You have not seen her, and you do not know where she is, either…am I right?"

Dr. Williams wanted to wait until they had eaten and had a glass of wine to calm them, just give them a chance to enjoy their homecoming before she told them. It was just conjecture, nothing she could prove or did she herself fully believe. Yet she was quite sure something bad had happened to her friend.

Tina looks at Elise's face, crunched into worry as she waits for an answer while in the kitchen, they can hear Matthew. He is busy opening cabinets, searching for snack food to go with the wine.

Matthew finds some unopened crackers on one of the shelves and puts them on the counter. "Cheese and crackers," he whispers as he goes to the refrigerator, smiling as he makes his way over to the fridge.

Smiling he opens the refrigerator. The putrid stench of decaying vegetables mingled with the scent of rotting meat, obviously removed from the freezer, and sat on the fridge shelf to thaw assaults his nostrils. Matthew raises his arm and blocks his nose with the back of his hand as he bravely opens the deli tray, adding yet another offensive odor to the air. Quickly he closes the fridge and backs away moving across the kitchen and takes a few deep breaths to chase away the feeling of fluttering wings of birds rising in his stomach. He continues to take deep breaths until he feels he is back in control.

It takes longer to check his emotions as he realizes that it is more than the smell of rotting food that has him feeling faint, it is the thought of what this means. Sonya has not been here in a long, long time.

Matthew puts the crackers in the little handled wicker serving basket that Sonya had purchased on one of their trips to Mexico. He had thought it impractical at the time, but when they dined outside and she could carry the appetizers and drinks easily because of the handle, he later praised her on the purchase. He shakes his head, trying to remove the memory that brings tears to his eyes.

With the crackers in the basket, the wine bottle opener tucked into his pocket and carrying the two bottles of wine by the necks he makes his way back into the living room.

It is just when Lisa can find no more excuses to keep from sharing what she knows with Elise that Matthew returns. Her expression speaks words as she sighs seeing him standing in the doorway.

Elise rushes over to help him put his bounty on the coffee table. She notices he has crackers, but no cheese.

"I will get us some cheese to go with the crackers." She says.

"Elise, stop. Ah, Elise, you do not want to open the fridge…"

She looks at her father, then over at Lisa with a puzzled expression. "Why not," she asks innocently.

461

"The smell in there is enough to knock you off your feet is why not."

It should not have been funny, but the way he says it, demonstrating how it threw him back and he plugs his nose mimicking closing the fridge again, has them roaring with laughter.

This takes away the tenseness of the moment and Matthew glances over at Lisa, letting her know he has some idea that there is something she has been holding back. Lisa nods in response.

Luckily, the doorbell rings at that moment.

Elise gets up and starts toward the door. "Wait, Elise," Tina says. Elise stops and turns around. For an instant she thinks she sees a look of terror on Lisa's face and surprise is plastered all over her dads. They are in stunned silence observing Lisa putting on her mask, going over to the door and looking through the peephole. She then, moves her body so that the two cannot see what she is doing as she puts on the chain lock before opening the door. "Yes," she says softly.

"Pizza delivery from Two Ton Tony's," the visitor says. While Dr. Williams fiddles with the chain, Matthew comes up behind her and takes out his wallet. He pulls out a twenty and hands it to the delivery man who hands Dr. Williams the pizza as he reaches in his pocket for the change. "No, you keep it," Matthew says.

"Thank you, sir…. madam."

The man had barely made it down the steps when Dr. Williams shuts the door and locks it. This time she puts the chain in place.

Matthew is giving her a puzzled look, but Tina pretends not to see it as she heads back in the living room. "The pizza's here," she cheerfully announces.

They are hungry, hungrier than they thought as Matthew opens the pizza and is happy to see there are napkins and paper plates with the delivery. Each takes a plate and napkin and before they return to their seat, have already taken a bite.

Silence prevails as they eat. Each grabs another slice when they finish their first one. Since leaving Wuhan, Matthew and Elise have not had a proper meal and this is more food than they have had in days. It is only natural for them to concentrate on eating now as the silence lingers in the air. For Lisa, it gives her time to relax before she must share what she knows about Sonya.

"How about that glass of wine?"

"Ah, I am so full I could vomit. I think I ate to fast," Elise says. "Can you pour me a glass of the red wine, dad."

Tina speaks up, "If it is not too much trouble, I will take white, please."

Elise stands, wiping her hands as she heads to the kitchen.

"Where are you going Elise?" Matthew ask.

"Just going to get us some glasses. Unless we plan on drinking directly from the bottle, that is." That forces a smile and Elise goes into the kitchen.

She wrinkles her nose, the smell still lingering in the air from her father's exploration of the fridge. When Elise opens the curio cabinet near the back door, she sees a spider web above it. The hairs stand up on the back of her neck as worry sets in. Her mother has not been home in some time. She needs to know what is happening and she needs to know it now. Taking the time to give the glasses a good rinsing, she dries them with a paper towel and then hurriedly she takes them with her to the living room.

"Okay, enough stalling. Dr. Williams, please tell us where my mother is."

Tina stands and takes a glass from Elise. She carries it over to Matthew who pours the white wine into it. He can read the anguish on her face, but he, like Elise, cannot hold out any longer. No matter what it is, they must know.

"Please, Tina, tell us what you know." Tina stalls, trying to find the right words. She watches as Matthew fills Elise's glass and then his own.

Matthew tries to manage a reassuring smile for his daughter and then turns to face Tina.

Tina picks up her napkin to wipe her mouth before she begins. She needs to control herself if she wants to help them through the facts of what she knows for sure and that is all she tells them.

Chapter 66

"First I want to say that this is all here say, what I am about to share with you, and I have no proof." They nod.

"Well, some time back Sonya mentioned to me that something was happening on our floor. We were working with the worse cases of COVID-19 and our patients tended to not make it, so it was not surprising when they passed. But Sonya had either seen something or knew something that I did not, because she was becoming paranoid, so much so that when I asked her what was wrong she said she did not want to get me involved, but that I needed to be careful."

"That scared me, but she would not tell me anything no matter how many times I told her it would make her feel better if she shared it with me."

"It was like that for months. I would see a patient missing and immediately know they had died and had been taken off the floor. She would have a patient disappear and she would be immediately suspicious. So, it was no wonder that Dr. Warren started assigning Sonya's patients to Dr. Henderson. He walked your mother off the floor and took her to his office. That was the last time I saw her."

"What?"

"Hold on. Let me finish while I have the nerve to continue."

Elise looked at her father with a perplexed expression wondering why Dr. Williams would make such a statement…while she had the nerve…but they leaned back and let her continue.

"So, after that episode, I called Sonya on her cell and at home, trying to reach her, but I never did. I even approached Dr. Warren and asked where Sonya was. You know what he said, he said she had a nervous breakdown and they had taken her to where she could get help."

Tina walked across the room and took a Kleenex out of the holder and then turned back around. She sat down wiping her eyes.

"I am sorry. I will be fine." In a few minutes she continued.

"I thought at first that sounded reasonable. She had been acting strange and was feeling the pressure of the ward. I was too, but I believed she had reached her limit. So, I let it go. I think it was maybe a couple of months before I went back to Dr. Warren and asked where Sonya was and his exact words were, he could not share that with me. He should not have even told me anything about her medical condition at all. Again, I had to agree with him. It was a personal matter and as such it was not to be shared with other employees. They could only share it with family and, lucky for him, family was not available."

"Oh, Tina, I am so sorry."

"No, I am not telling you this to make either of you feel guilty. I am just trying to share everything I know or think I know at this point."

Dr. William took a deep breath and then continued.

"It was a few months after that initial conversation that I received a call from a Tempest Delong."

She could see the forehead lines appear on Elise and her father as they tried to not interrupt.

"I did not know this woman, Tempest, but she explained that she was a friend of Sara Brown. That name did not ring a bell with me until she explained that Sara was the head nurse at the testing center for the coronavirus."

"That rang a bell with me. I remembered a situation where there was a rumor that new patients were coming in via helicopters and some of the staff on our floor offered to help, but Dr. Warren was adamant that they had it covered. He said that the patients were accompanied by the medical staff from the clinic and they could take care of it."

"Sounds reasonable, doesn't it," Dr. Warren said, not expecting an answer.

"Anyway, they did handle it, except one patient, who we later learned to be an Andrew Matthews, broke free and was retrieved by another doctor along with a Veronica Peters"

"Veronica was a friend of one of the staff on our floor—Linda, and she recognized her immediately. It was this nurse assistant Linda who knew Veronica and who told us that the patient was derange. When she offered her assistance, Linda had been shooed away."

The patient slipped into a room when a nurse came out and immediately after the pursuers followed, and Linda had watched through the window of the room."

Tina had to stop. She took a sip of her wine and then looked them directly in the face. "This nurse's assistant said that the patient was blue, and he tried to bite them as they struggled to get him back in the stairwell and off the floor."

That was the other thing. They could have taken them all on the elevator to another floor with the patients, but they had with them a ban of security, the staff from the facility and the patients all hustling down the back stairwell and using the freight elevator."

Again, Tina paused to take a sip of her wine and when Elise started to talk, she raised a finger in her direction to silence her. She continued.

"It was then I remember Sonya had asked me about that stairwell. She wanted to know where it went as it was never used by anyone. If you wanted to take the stairs, you used the ones at the other end of the hallway next to the elevators. We were told they were the safer ones. Well, if that were the case, why would they take, I think, around ten deranged patients down on a freight elevator. Yes, they were acting like raging lunatics, but it was a freight elevator."

Tina sighs. She lifts her glass of wine and takes a sip, keeping her eyes down. "Sonya did not return, and Tempest said that Sara was missing as well as her whole staff from the Test Center. She was worried and wondered if I could help her find Sara."

"So, that is what we have been trying to do, except in checking we realized that Dr. Warren and Dr. Henderson were the contacts for the Test Center, and we did not dare approach them. Anyway, they would make up something that sounded logical. So, we managed, in checking with the nurses and other staff to come up with the names of the nine people who had been assigned to the Test Center, along with Sara Brown. We were shocked at what we learned."

"Shocked, what did you learn." Matthew spoke, his concern apparent in his voice.

"We learned that this Sara Brown and each one of the staff were without close friends or family. People might know of them but were not able to tell us anything about them that would help. Most had not noticed they were missing."

"So, Dr. William..." Tina interrupted Elise. "Please call me Tina."

"So, Tina, what do you think was going on."

"Well, and it is only my opinion, when they set up that test center, one of the criteria must have been that they pick individuals to work there that did not have a lot of contacts so if something went wrong, they would not be missed."

"Why would they do that."

"Again, just my observation. I would say that they were testing vaccines for the coronavirus that were not approved. Maybe something that one of the doctors was conjuring up and wanted to keep it secret. Or they just were afraid with all that was going on, they did not want anyone in the facility who might be sharing with a family member or friend."

"I think something unexpected and unexplained happened. It might have all started out innocently, but then..."

"Do you have any idea what it was that freaked out the test subjects?"

"No, not at all, but I am beginning to think that where they were taken is where Sonya is. I think there is something in the basement of the hospital and somehow Sonya got wind of it and those in charge found out she knew."

"What would it matter if she did. She is a doctor, and she works there?"

"Knowing our boss, Dr. Warren and that pain in the butt, Dr. Henderson who was assigned Sonya's patients, I would not put it pass them to be doing something; like trying to develop a vaccine for the coronavirus. I noticed how many patients were disappearing off our floor, but I thought they died. We were working with the critical cases so that was not so preposterous an assumption. But now..."

They were all silent, thinking about what Tina had said.

"So, do you think Sonya is in the basement of the hospital?"

"Maybe. One of the nurses on our floor had mentioned that she had seen men bringing equipment on the service elevator. Then again, because of the situation we were in with the coronavirus, she just thought they were setting up some isolation units or something. You see with the circumstance as it is, no one would question that."

"So, we need to get into that basement and see what is there." Matthew said.

"I agree, but I do not think it should be us alone. We need to alert some high authority to go with us but first we need to know what to say to them. We do not want to have them wave us off as crazy. After all, Dr. Warren and Dr. Henderson are extraordinarily successful doctors and well thought of in the community."

The three sat back deliberating. Matthew spoke first. "I think I have it. I have a contact on the police force who we use, meaning my editor and myself, to get security when I am putting on a book reading in questionable places. I could contact him."

"And say what?"

"Say that I need him to check something out for me. He is more than just a contact; over the years we have become friends. We have gone out for drinks and talked about our families so if I told him my wife was missing and asked him to check the hospital he would. I would just tell him that the last time she was seen was going down that back stairwell that leads down to the basement."

Tina nodded, thinking that would work. "But he needs clearance to get on the floor and then get to the basement."

"He'll come up with something, I am sure. I will contact him in the morning. Right now, we should all get some sleep." Matthew turned to Tina. "You should stay here. You can sleep in the guest room. It is awfully late. Call your husband and tell him you are here so he will not worry."

"That is a good idea." Tina got up and they could hear her talking to her husband. When she returns, she says, "Show me my sleeping quarters."

Elise gets up and walks with Tina to the guest room. "There is a bathroom in here and there is a pair of pajamas and a robe in the closet."

"I'd ask if you were expecting me, but I know you were not."

Elise laughs silently. "You know my mother. She is always ready for everything. She keeps the necessities in the spare room just in case. You will find everything you need in the bathroom as well."

Tina smiles and hugs Elise. "It is so good to see you, and it is a relief to have help in finding Sonya. I have been so worried."

Elise manages to smile back while her insides are flip flopping, and she has all she can do to not break down and bawl. What helps her remain stoic is that as much stress as she and her father have been under, Tina has shouldered so much more. She is her mother's best friend.

That night in the confines of the bedroom that he shares with Sonya, Matthew breaks down. He allows himself to stop fighting against the tension in his chest and shoulders that built from worrying what has happened to his beloved wife. His eyes mist and he does not choke back the sobs that he has wanted to release for so long. He must be strong in front of Elise and Tina even though his heart is breaking. He had known Sonya was missing. He knows that if Tina knew more, she would have told them. There is still hope that she is being held in the basement, or somewhere else.

Elise shows Tina to the spare bedroom and at the doorway, she tries to swallow the lump in her throat as she turns to say, "You are family Tina. Sleep well." Elise knows that none of them will.

Chapter 67

Something that Dr. Warren did not know was that there were cameras in the subbasement that were not a part of his facility. When the hospital added on the new wing, they decided to add surveillance cameras throughout, including the basement and subbasement areas. This was something that had not been done when the hospital was originally built as it was believed unnecessary. But the company in charge of installing the security for the building had updated the old equipment throughout and suggested it would not be a bad idea to continue it all the way to the subbasement. It turned out to be a good idea.

Thaddeus Hutchinson of the FBI was assigned the job of being the lead on the hospital investigation. It was not an assignment he would normally take, but he knew Stan Peters and if Stan believed there was something going on, then he did too. Stan had called asking for their help on several cases and Thaddeus knew him to be an excellent Sheriff on the Rochester force. He was always one of the first on the scene, and one of the first to pursue a suspect. He liked the guy and when he said there was something going on, he trusted his instincts.

Stan Peters was contacted by Matthew McKenna, who told him his wife was missing. Matthew and Stan had gone to college together but did not become friends until later. It happened one day at a book signing when Stan had come to check him out. He was not sure at first this was the same Matthew he knew, but once he saw him there was no doubt, he was one and the same. He had walked up to the table for his autograph and said, "Ah, I knew him well." Matt had looked up, not recognizing him.

"Excuse me?"

"You are the same Matthew McKenna that when to the U of R, aren't you?"

"Yes, I went to the U of R."

"Well, my name is Stan…" Matt interrupts him.

"Peters. Stan Peters, you old dog you."

After that meeting, they went out for drinks and found out that they lived just a few blocks from each other. They would get together as often as they could either alone or with their wives. He was someone that Matt could depend on and when he asked for his help in finding Sonya, he did not hold back any details of what was known and what they suspected. He had Stan speak with Lisa and supplied him with contacts to check into the situation. Stan didn't hesitate to call in the FBI.

The FBI began their investigation immediately after Stan contacted them. SSA Thaddeus Hutchinson was the head of the department and set about informing his team. There was SSA Barnaby Watkins, the best tech in the business. If anyone could get his hands on what they needed, from the hospital site, SSA Watkins would. He was asked to tap into their computers at the hospital and the private ones for the doctors in question. Then, see if he could get a map of the premises, both hospital and private as well as any surveillance tapes covering the premises.

Next, he took SSA Jennifer Steward, the team's Communication Liaison and SSA Charles Hunt with him to the McKenna house. He would have SSA Hunt listen as he interviewed Matthew, especially since SSA Hunt told him he was an admirer of Matthew McKenna's books. When Thaddeus had stared at him questionably, he added, "Don't tell me you didn't know Matthew McKenna was a world renown author, Thad." Thaddeus had given Charles a pensive stare as an answer.

SSA Jennifer Steward would interview Dr. Williams as she has the skills and patience to work both from a professional and personal level. Because of how close Dr. Williams was to Dr. McKenna, it would be necessary to handle the conversation with finesse and not cause the doctor any more stress. Thaddeus could tell she was extremely anxious and had said she should have done something, or at the least, believed her friend. She needed to be assured she had acted appropriately.

From that meeting they gathered not only contacts, but information concerning the hospital, how it ran, and the general layout. When they left the residence, they had several leads to follow.

Knowing that if they kicked off the investigation outside the hospital, they would get the soundest leads, they began by contacting Tempest DeLong, the best friend of Sara Brown. This assignment was given to SSA Pamela Brewster and SSA Morgan James. Those two were close in age to Tempest and would be able to talk her language.

It was through her that they were educated on the incident at the Test Clinic and how she had obtained the position. She seemed a wealth of information up until the disappearance of the patients and the staff.

"That day," Tempest DeLong said, "I was there, watching it all go down. Sara had called me to tell me not to come to the clinic because there had been an incident. She said she would call me later and fill me in. Since I was just a block away, I started to turn around and that is when I saw those black helicopters landing on the top of her building. I pulled over to the side of the road and like we all do these days, took out my cell and started videotaping the scene. It was not until I heard the staff screaming and crying did, I realize that this was bad, unbelievably bad"

"What did you do then Miss DeLong."

"What do you think. I hauled ass. I did not want to join them. I know I should have called someone, but I was afraid so I kept quiet, hoping I would hear from Sara."

Of course, the last question asked of Miss DeLong was what she had done with the video. She pulled out her phone and, in a few minutes, had the video running on her cell. That, along with the surveillance camera tapes would give them a full picture of the situation. They would have the inside of the clinic and tape of what happened after they were taken off site.

They also learned from Tempest that she had wanted to be part of the staff at the test clinic but had been turned down. She later learned that it was because of her answers to the question, 'do you have any family who you are close to and see frequently'. She had answered 'yes'. Later when she had asked why she had not been hired, they said that it was easier to work with individuals who had no contact with family since if they became infected, might spread the disease to them. Tempest looked at Special Agent James, "Sounds like a reasonable question, huh." He nodded.

"I thought so too at first, so I did not protest. When Sara was hired though, that is when I knew I had been shafted by answering just that one question. I had more experience than she, and her assistant Veronica Peters had none. If this were a test clinic, would not you want the most experienced and the most trained in that capacity. Well that would be me."

That is when I knew there was something strange about the clinic and I, being a super snoop would go often for lunch so I could get a look around. Nothing raised red flags until that day, but I think it was a front for testing unauthorized vaccines.

"Why do you say that Miss DeLong."

"I say that because I saw a vial that did not have the usual label with the name of the manufacturer on it." The Agent started to say something. "No, wait, I have worked in test facilities before. The bottles must be labeled so that they give the proper medication to the right test subject. If they did not have labels you would not know who got what."

She was right of course. That and her ideal of the hires having no family or friends would be checked out, but he was sure that was going to be proved right as well.

"Did Sara not pick her own staff."

"No. Maybe the interviewer did. I do not know." Tempest was shaking her head and then started crying. "It is my fault is not it. I should have said something sooner. Maybe if I had, Sara and the rest of them would be alive. I am so sorry."

Morgan let Tempest cry it out while he got her a glass of water. When she finally lifted her head, he handed her a Kleenex and she wiped her nose, then using the back of her hand, brushed the tears away before taking a drink of water.

SSA Brewster soothed her by saying, "Miss DeLong, none of this is your fault. There is nothing you could have done and if they had found you out, I am sure you would not be sitting here filling me in on what happened."

That made Tempest feel better. She reached out her hand for her phone and Morgan said, "Can you send that video to my phone. He handed her the number and watched as she forwarded it to his phone. When he received it, he checked to make sure it worked. It did. Morgan then turned to Pamela and she read his expression. They both got up to leave.

"Listen, Miss, I think it will be best if you do not mention any of this to anyone, including your family. We do not want anything to happen to you."

"No problem. That is why I kept it to myself in the first place."

When Pamela and Morgan filled him in, SSA Hutchinson was confident, this was the break they needed. It was all he could do to calm himself so after drinking two cups of black coffee, he began getting everything ready for the morning meeting. He, as well as his men had been at it all day and needed a good night's sleep before they viewed the videos.

Thaddeus went to the FBI tech man. "Barnaby, I have a job for you."

"What boss."

"There is a video on this phone and these," he said showing him the tapes. If you can make copies and then see if you can put them in a sequence so that they run in one continuous flow, I would appreciate it."

Barnaby gave him a smirk. "I can do anything. I am the God of this technology."

Thaddeus laughed. "I know that. That is why I came to you. Start with the cell video. The tapes are all dated." He paused. "Oh, and Barnaby?"

"Yes boss."

"Thanks. Do you think you can have it for me in the morning?"

For a second there was a surprised expression on Barnaby's face. That was short order. But then he was the Master of Technology.

"No problem...no problem at a-l-l." The last word spread out for a minute while Barnaby was no longer in the real world, but instead was already working on the video.

Thaddeus was used to this dismissal as it was Barnaby's way. He enjoyed what he did and when something came his way, he was all into it.

Chapter 68

At home, Thaddeus goes through the evening only half present; something Audrey, his wife, has accused him of on many occasions. He cannot help it, as he feels his consciousness ebbing away. With dinner over and Audrey cleaning up after their meal that he cannot remember tasting, his eyes grow heavy. He remembers moving to the couch and sitting down, but all else is blank until he wakes to the gentle tapping on his shoulder. With strenuous effort he opens his eyes.

"Come up to bed, sweetie," she says. Thaddeus wipes his hands over his eyes and forces them open. From the shadows in the room he realizes it is late. He looks up at his wife. "How long have I been asleep?"

"I could say forever, but it is been only a couple hours. You need to go to bed."

Thaddeus stands slowly and heads for the stairs. He stops and turns back around to face his wife. "Aren't you coming."

"No, not right now. I want to read for a bit and then I will be up."

Thaddeus nods his head and leaning heavily on the railing he makes his way upstairs. Somehow, he gets through the nighttime regimen and climbs into bed. The last thing he remembers is arranging his head on his pillow.

The next morning, he wakes slowly with his wife's face inches from his, shaking his body by pushing on his chest and stomach.

"I'm awake, I am awake."

"I swear, it gets harder and harder to get you up, my man."

"I know. I am sorry." He stares up into her beautiful blue eyes. "What time is it?"

"It is after eight."

Like a bullet he is fully conscious. "Oh, no, I am going to be late."

"I have got the coffee going and I will put it in your travel mug and take your briefcase and put them near the door. Is there anything else you need?"

"No...yes, a kiss."

Audrey smiles and accepts his quick kiss before he disappears in the bathroom.

She grins, hearing the electric toothbrush and the shower being turned on simultaneously. "The man is showering and brushing his teeth…. who does that?" She is still grinning as she goes downstairs.

In fifteen minutes, tops, Thaddeus makes an appearance. "How do I look."

"Same as usual."

He blows her a kiss and says, "Wish me luck."

"Luck."

His shoes echoed on the tiled floor of the lobby of FBI headquarters. Special Agent Thaddeus Hutchinson flashes his badge as he lowers his mask before making his way to the elevator and once the door closes, he pats his hair into place and adjust the strap around his neck so that his badge displays properly. He takes long, slow, deep breaths gently disengaging his mind from distracting thoughts and sensations. When the doors of the elevator open, he steps out, feeling refreshed and heads to his office.

When he opens the door to his department, he is met with darkness and silence. It is comforting and familiar to him as he easily makes his way down the aisle. At the stairs leading to his office, he pauses, tips his head to the left and then to the right before taking the stairs two at a time

Thaddeus stops in front of his office door, as his nonconscious visual system monitoring the environment causes the hairs on the back of his neck to rise. One hand rest on the door handle and the other pauses in the process of retrieving the key. He is about to unlock his office door when an eerie feeling comes over him. He senses he is being watched.

Slowly he moves his hand from the handle and places it on the stock of his gun before slowly turning around.

His eyes span the area, taking in the light emanating from computer screens displaying wallpaper with the FBI insignia. Nothing…he sees nothing. Keeping his hand on his gun, he looks to his left and his eyes adjust making out a shadowy figure in the darkness. He draws his weapon.

"Whoa boss. Did not mean to creep up on you."

"Barnaby? What the…"

"Sorry. You said you wanted the video first thing. I heard you come in."

Thaddeus relaxes. "I am sorry. Did not mean to pull a gun on you."

"I understand. From what I saw when transferring the video and tapes, these are scary times. Wow."

Barnaby wants to ask about what he saw but knows better. "I have set it up for viewing on the screen in the conference room." He pauses then asks, "What time do you want me there."

"Join us at 8. That will give everyone a chance to have a cup of coffee before we begin."

"Boss, can I tell you something."

"Sure, what is it."

"That video is like a horror movie. I would wait until their cups are empty before we start the show."

Thaddeus laughs. "When has it been any other way, my friend."

Thaddeus turns and unlocks his office. He steps inside and turns on the light. While lifting the window blinds that shield him from the bullpen below, he watches Barnaby as he returns to his office.

Checking is watch he sees he has a half hour before the group arrives, so he puts it to good use organizing his materials for the presentation.

He is in the process of mentally arranging what he will say when he hears a light rap on his door. He looks up to see Jennifer Steward, his team's Communication Liaison standing in the doorway. Her long blond hair glistens in the light from his office. He smiles thinking of how her features gives the appearance of one who can be swayed, but the media and local police agencies soon find out that is not the case. Thaddeus believes that before she had a family she was a fierce adversary but now being a mother she has the added skill of patience and that helps to unruffle any feathers and have the local police willing to accept their assistance in their investigations.

Jennifer walks over to his desk and sits a cup of coffee in front of him. He gives her a grateful smile as he takes a sip. "Thanks Jennifer. Can you gather the team and have them set up in the conference room?"

"Yes, sir, no problem."

"Oh, and Jennifer, make sure they bring their reports on the test center case." Jennifer nods then turns, closing his door behind her.

Thaddeus Hutchinson knows his team sees him as a workaholic. He is. They also think he is too serious and needs to learn how to let loose and enjoy life. That is also true. But they respect and trust him and that is what he needs to run the team.

As Thaddeus made his way to the conference room, he sees SSA Charles Hunt sitting at his desk, involved in something on the screen. Charles is young, innocent, but mentally smarter than all of them put together. His wayward hair and baby face make it hard for him to be taken seriously by anyone, except this staff who depend on him to come up with solutions where none can be seen.

SSA Barnaby Watkins is already on his way to the conference room. He is the best tech analyst and communications liaison in the FBI, even the world as far as Thaddeus is concerned. His dirty blonde hair is long and shaggy and his beard spotty in places, but his technical intelligence makes up for what he lacks in appearance. He rarely joins them in the field physically, but he is with them mentally, relaying information and filling in what they need checked out.

Thaddeus walks down the open hallway to the stairs, he can see SSA Jennifer Steward on her way to the conference room.

Right behind her comes SSA Pamela Brewster. One of the major strengths of the staff who usually plays within the bounds of the FBI, but at times she can become extremely agitated and make the wrong choice. But this feisty dark-haired beauty is a good agent. She has the insight necessary and the will to take whatever steps necessary to get the unsub behind bars.

Right beside her is SSA Morgan James with his charming smile and white teeth, he brightens anyone's day. Because of Pamela's personality, it has always been best to partner her with Morgan who sees life from all angles and can calm Pamela down because she trust him. Morgan is confident and assertive. Growing up in a racially mixed environment has peaked his ability to handle people. Of course, his extreme good looks helps.

Finally, SSA David Monihan arrives. He spends a few seconds shedding his jacket and looking over phone messages, then, seeing Thaddeus walks with him to the conference room.

David was the one Thaddeus had the hardest time being the boss to. He is several years Thaddeus's senior and had been one of the founders of the unit. His dark Italian good looks and suave manner add class to the unit, but more so his knowledge of the workings of the FBI steer the group in the right direction every time.

That is his unit, and he is proud of each of them. David and Thaddeus walk in together and see the team seated at the round oak table that allows them to have their notepads and personal effects in front of them and have a good view of the screen on the far wall. It is next to the screen that Thaddeus stands, waiting for everyone's attention.

"Good morning everyone. We have a lot to go over this morning and we are going to start with videos of the areas involved in this investigation. The first is of the Test Clinic set up a short distance from the hospital. It was where the so call episode happened. We now know that this site was not an authorized COVID-19 vaccine testing clinic and we are pretty sure it has something to do with Dr. Griffin Warren who is the head of the coronavirus extremely contagious ward at the hospital, and his colleague, Dr Randall Henderson.

On the screen appears pictures of the two men in question.

"I am sure there are others involved, but those two are the main ones. We will see the video of the Test Center first." He has Morgan and Pamela fill them in before they run the video.

Thaddeus nods at Barnaby and he starts the video. This group has seen the worse of the worse during their years with the unit, but nothing has prepared them for this. At first, they appear curious, but their expressions change to shock and disbelief as the scene unfolds.

It is like a sci-fi movie with blue people acting like deranged animals. Thaddeus points out Sara Brown, "She was the lead nurse at the test clinic."

All eyes focus on her attempts to manage the test subjects that are blue and unresponsive. When one swings out at her, she yells, "Come on people, let's get out of here."

She only needs to say it once as her team quickly leaves the room with her following behind them. They stand in the hallway and Sara locks the door.

Someone says, "I do not think they even know how to open the door." Sara responds, "Maybe not, but let's not take any chances."

The team watch as Sara tries to remain calm as she places a call for help. They cannot tell from her end of the conversation who she has called but in minutes of making the call, help arrives.

They watch the coordinated efforts of the security as if this has all been practiced ahead of time. Two security officers take the staff out of camera range. "There is a stairwell that leads to the roof through that entrance," Thaddeus says.

One of the two remaining in the hallway says something into a radio on his shoulder, but they cannot make out what he says. It is apparent later when ten other security personnel arrive and join the other two at the door to the room where the test subjects have been sequestered. "Got the syringes he asks?"

Soon each of them has a syringe and from their actions it seems this is not the first time they have done this. Could this have happened elsewhere, Thaddeus wonders.

One of the security men takes the lead and nods at the others as he opens the door. When the door opens the test subjects do not pay them any attention; at first, then suddenly one reacts stumbling forward and the men spring into action. They move swiftly each holding on to one after the other and inserting a needle into their arms and before they can move to the next, the other is showing signs of sedation. They continue until every one of the test subjects has been sedated.

The next scene shows the roof where there are two large helicopters waiting. At the window of one they can barely make out a face and assume it is one of the staff. Then one by one the security bring up the test subjects, supporting them under their arms and getting them into the other helicopter. When the last one is in, security climbs in and shuts the door.

"Stop the video, please Barnaby."

Barnaby stops the video and waits.

"Whoa, that is shocking," David said.

"It is so farfetched it looks fake," pipes in Jennifer.

"I can assure you it is not. The first part of the tape was the surveillance cameras inside the building. The last was a video that Sara Brown's friend Tempest DeLong, shot with her phone when she arrived to meet up with Sara."

"So, why are they, you know, blue," asks Pamela as she looks over at Charles.

"I cannot answer that without more input, but I would say there was something wrong with the vaccine they administered that turned them blue."

Morgan laughs and says, "You think!"

"Barnaby, you can play the rest of the tape."

Barnaby starts it again.

"You are looking at the coronavirus wing where Dr. Sonya McKenna and her friend, Dr. Tina Williams work. They report to Dr. Griffin Warren."

Since Morgan and Pam had gone to the site, they add particulars to the remaining scenes. "You can see the ward is where the most contagious patients are kept, those who are seriously ill."

"From what we learned talking with the doctors it was not uncommon to have patients missing on the floor. It was assumed they had either died or gotten better and were moved out of the ward."

At that point Thaddeus resumed.

"Now you can see them arriving to the floor with the test clinic staff and clients. We do not have footage on their arrival, but we assume they landed on the roof of the hospital so as not to draw attention."

Thaddeus pauses and takes a sip of his coffee before continuing. "Look closely. They are using the freight elevator and stairs at the far end of the floor to transport them. See how some of the guards stand in front, blocking the view of the patients as they try to move them off the floor."

"Pause it there, Barnaby."

Thaddeus moves closer to the screen and points.

"I know it's hard to tell with all the medical gear on, but I believe that is Dr. Warren, watching them and when the last person exits the floor, he follows. The other man following him, we believe is Dr. Henderson."

Barnaby does something at his station and the badge on each of the doctors is clear. They are Dr. Warren and Dr. Henderson.

"Thanks Barnaby."

"Can you stop it again Barnaby," Morgan ask.

"Sure, no problem."

The image on the screen freezes. "I just want to add that from this point on we do not have any visual since there are no cameras on this back staircase, but there is one on the freight elevator. Which is why these two doctors did not think there would be any cameras, especially in the subbasement. What you are about to see, we have sped up so that we can get to the point we need." Morgan breaks off. "Okay Barnaby, start the video, please."

The video begins again and as Morgan requested earlier, it moves in quick time passing over the arrival of the test subjects and their staff and slows when the two doctors appear. "Okay guys, look closely now." The team leans in as Morgan says, "that is a mirrored building in the subbasement. We managed to get our hands-on tapes inside this building. It was huge and not only contained an area for patients, but offices, bedrooms, and a fully equipped kitchen. It was like a hotel or home environment at the far end of the structure. It was obvious that it had been designed to house everyone who worked there and that they were living right there on the premises.

Pam speaks next. "Okay, this gray-haired woman is Lottie Bond. From what we have learned, she was the head nurse of the facility." She then pointed out the maintenance and the staff that handled the housekeeping and cooking.

"Stop there Barnaby."

"See those bolts. From a blueprint we found they were used like a pully system to suspend the patients in layer from the ceiling. They were suspended on cots that could be raised and lowered. It, we believe was a way to fit a lot of patients in the room. We think that originally there were close to a hundred patients before the 10 from the test clinic arrived."

She nods at Barnaby and he starts the video again. They watch patients being removed and assumed they have died and then see new patients being brought in. At first it was only Nurse Bond handling all the care of the patients, with Dr. Warren making an appearance now and then.

Pam explains that they think they had high tech computers doing most of the care and reporting on the patients.

Pam turns to Charles. "What do you make of them using mirrors."

"Mirrors create the illusion of depth and space so they can really help make a small room feel bigger. So, mirrors are also great for narrow spots such as hallways. But in this case, I think the mirrors were used to confuse the patients and anyone else who entered the facility. Or maybe it was the only materials that could reflect light enough to make the environment feel less like a basement."

Thaddeus nods in agreement with what Charles has shared. "Keep your eyes on the video, team."

They all turn back and witness the moment that Dr. Sonya McKenna, made her initial discovery of the facility and later is shown talking and being escorted around the facility by Nurse Bond. They watch as Dr. McKenna leaves.

Next, they see Dr. Warren come for one of his visits to the facility. They hear him talking with Nurse Bond who informs him that the new hire had just left the premises.

"What did you say?"

"The new hire was here. A doctor Weston."

It is apparent by his expression that Dr. Warren is shocked by her announcement.

Pam says, "I think Dr. McKenna used the alias, Dr. Weston."

"Okay Barnaby speed up." Barnaby does so.

"Okay stop here," says Thaddeus. This is a few days later, he explains. They watch as Dr. Warren goes into Dr.

McKenna's office. What they say is not heard, but from the expressions the team can guess it is not good.

It is hard to keep focus as they see Dr. McKenna struggling to get away from her boss when she sees the syringe in his hand. She is no match for him as he sticks the needle in her arm, then waits until it takes effect. With her sedated he manages to move her down the hall to the back staircase and leaning her against the wall, he opens the door and drags her through the entrance with him.

The final scenes were of Sara Brown and her staff, along with their clients being taken to the facility. The balance of the tape was sped up again and they witnessed Nurse Bond now being assisted with Sara Brown and her staff, along with Dr. McKenna.

When the tape stopped, disgust, apathy, and disbelief was seen on the faces of the team.

"There is one more set of tapes," Barnaby informed them and all eyes returned to the screen, watching as the construction workers tore down the structure, thinking they had gotten every piece of debris, but there was a few shards of the mirror left behind and that was what Morgan passed around the room now.

Thaddeus stood. "Okay, team, we have a lot to do, but we were lucky to get these videos. No one knows we have them as no one knew they were there at the hospital; except of course for the ones on the upper floor and the engineers who built the hospital. But that is years ago, and I am hoping that none of them are still around."

He pauses and looks at his team. "By now Dr. Warren and Dr. Henderson know we have...or at least someone does...the tapes from the mirrored menagerie so we need to be cautious "

Barnaby adds, "Do not forget the tech at the hospital who got us the stored information of the building of the facility and several other tapes."

"Barnaby, how do you read him."

Barnaby is thoughtful for a moment. "I think he wants to keep it on the down low, but…"

Thaddeus is quiet, thinking then speaks. "Let us play it cautious and say it will leak out that we have the tapes and know about the facility."

They have no reason to have tapes in the subbasement, but I am glad they were there." Morgan says.

"As for the tape of the test center evacuation, the only one who knows we have that is Ms. Tempest DeLong, who shot the video on her cell."

"Can we count on her keeping quiet."

Morgan does not hesitate. "Yes. She is a close friend of Sara's and wants to know what happened to her. From what she saw, she is afraid for her life so she will keep quiet."

It is at that moment, Jennifer's cell rings. All eyes are on her as she listens to the caller. They cannot read her expression, so they wait patiently for the call to end. "Okay, thank you. I will let the team know."

"What is it Jennifer," Thaddeus asks.

"That was the local police calling. It seems there was a fire at the Test Clinic, and everything was ruined."

The team smiles. They had been smart to act quickly.

Thaddeus asks David what he has discovered on the regulation of vaccine testing. David stands and pulls a chart out of his briefcase that he pins on the story board for all to see.

"Well, the U.S. Food and Drug Administration's Center for Biologics Evaluation and Research is responsible for regulating vaccines in the United States. What happens is a sponsor of a new vaccine product follows a multi-step approval process, which typically includes an Investigational New Drug application, pre-licensure vaccine clinical trials, a Biologics License Application known as a BLA, inspection of the manufacturing facility, a presentation of findings to FDA's Vaccines and Related Biological Products Advisory Committee and usability testing of product labeling."

"I am taking it that none of that was done?" Thaddeus says.

"You've got that right." David continues.

"After approving a vaccine, the FDA continues to oversee its production to ensure continuing safety. Monitoring of the vaccine and of production activities, including periodic facility inspections, must continue as long as the manufacturer holds a license for the vaccine product."

"FDA can require a manufacturer submit the results of their own tests for potency, safety, and purity for each vaccine lot. They can require each manufacturer to submit samples of each vaccine lot for testing."

He finished saying, "None of this is on record for this test facility."

"Are you sure, David." Thaddeus asks.

"Positive. They have no records of the clinic or any reports on any vaccine they were testing."

Thaddeus then sums it all up. "We need to find that staff and if not already dead, the patients that arrived at the hospital from the test center. The clinic staff was in hysterics, stumbling along the roof and being shuttled into a separate helicopter from the patients. We know they were all taken to the subbasement facility and if the lighting was not playing a trick on us, the test subjects restrained and their skin blue. They were acting manic."

"We also learned from Dr. Tina Williams, Dr. Sonya McKenna's friend, that Sonya was convinced something was going on and she decided to find out what it was. We also know that because her family was out of the country and unable to get back in time to raise alarms, they were able to seize her and it had gone smoothly."

"Oh, yes," Jennifer adds. "We interviewed all the doctors and nurses throughout the hospital to get a handle on what they knew or saw. We also picked up syringes from the test clinic and medical containers which we sent to be tested by the CDC. We initiated paperwork to find out who each member of the clinic staff and the test subjects were so that we can talk with them, but so far we have nothing except what we already know." She looks at her comrades. "We planned on going back to the clinic for one last check, but that is not possible anymore."

At that moment, Jennifer's cell tings and she looks at it. "Ah, she says. They just sent a picture of the test clinic...it is in rubbles...Barnaby, can you turn on the television."

> A 3-Alarm fire in an abandon building near the RGH was engulfed in flames. Several local fire departments fought the blaze, but the building was destroyed. They searched the rubble and found that no occupants were trapped or injured. As of the time of this writing the fire remains under investigation.

Barnaby is already in the process of connecting to the cell and soon a picture of what remains of the building is on the screen. The staff checks it out after listening to the broadcast.

At this point Thaddeus gives out assignments. "Jennifer and I will talk with Dr Griffin Warren. David and Charles will meet with Dr. Timothy Evans who may or may not be involved."

"Who is that again?"

"That is the doctor that had checked one of Dr. McKenna's patient and found he had been misdiagnosed. What we are thinking is that this was a plan to discredit Dr. McKenna."

"Pamela and James sit down with Dr Randall Henderson."

"What are we aiming for," asked Pam.

"It is time we make them aware of what evidence we have, and the videos show their involvement. Then they will hopefully tell us what happened to all these people."

Charles, the youngest member on the team speaks up. "Nothing about what we have learned is normal. In my opinion that is a test clinic unofficially set up to test vaccines for the coronavirus that have not been approved for testing in any form and I bet these doctors went straight for human subjects."

"I think you are right, Charles...I think you are right."

Chapter 69

Over at WHO headquarters the same conversation is underway. Edward Krauss says. "What a mess. There was a fair amount of fear and panic at the clinic. I think this site was involved in illegal vaccine testing; not sanctioned by us. From the panic on the faces of Miss Sara Brown and her staff, I do not think they were aware that they were doing anything illegal."

Everyone seated at the meeting of CDC nod in agreement. "So, what now."

"We leave it in the hands of the FBI and the local authorities, and we supply all data and information we can to help them get to the bottom of this situation."

Nearing the end of the third wave of the pandemic, things were settling down, but not every state or country was back to normal. Now as the investigation gets underway, the FBI is careful to wear masks, gloves, and visors to make sure they are not spreading the disease as they investigate the matter.

What the staff uncover is enough to get a confession from Dr Griffin Warren, Dr. Timothy Evans, and Dr Randall Henderson. They confess their involvement and explain what they intended to do at the test clinic and at the facility in the subbasement.

It is Dr. Warren who tells the FBI that all the patients died. He stresses that the 'pulley system' had been his idea. It allowed them to handle a lot of patients with limited staff. He seems to be proud of how efficient and upscale the facility was and shows only remorse that it had to be destroyed.

In his words the first patients sent to the facility were dying by the time they were taken down to the new facility. The vaccine he developed could not help them, but he admittedly had noticed changes in their brain activity which he did not share with the other doctors until later.

They removed the patients from the critical ill facilities and told the families they had died at the hospital of COVID-19 and were contagious. When they did die, they had them cremated, since they already had the approval of their families. Their decision was accepted. After all, they were the doctors. The cremation allowed Dr. Warren to keep his drug a secret and for the others, it meant the facility could be protected.

It was then that the group met and decided to set up the test clinic and see if they could find the right combination of drugs to cure COVID-19. The prestige of being the first to find a cure was what drove them forward only Dr. Warren did not use the approved drugs. Instead he made his own and used it on the test subjects just as he did with the earlier patients. When the test subjects were reported as being dangerous and had turned blue, Dr. Warren was only slightly shocked.

The other doctors working with him were scared. The test subjects were violent and test reports coming from the facility revealed something had affected their brains. In the end they all died.

David is not buying it. "You are telling us that all them died. Why?"

"Do not know."

While Dr. Warren is being interrogated, in another room they are talking with the other doctors. SSA Brewster asks Dr. Henderson. "What happened to the staff from the test Center. They were taken down to the facility with the patients.

"Ah...eventually they were infected."

"How, how did that happen when the patients were chained up."

"I do not like the use of the word; chained."

"Do I care...be honest here."

"So, what about the original staff in the facility. Let us see now, there was Nurse Bond, maintenance and housing staff...what happened to them?" SSA James ask Dr. Henderson.

"They were infected and died."

SSA James drops the folder hard on the top of the desk. He stands and taking the folder, leaves the interrogation room.

He finds the rest of them standing there, just as annoyed. "I am not buying it. They are not being totally honest."

"What do you mean."

"I think that the patients did die. That much is true, but I do not think the staff all were infected with the coronavirus and died too.

"I agree with Morgan. "They could not let them live to tell what they had seen."

"Okay, try the weakest link. I think Dr. Evans might just tell the truth."

Thaddeus decides to handle this while the team views him through the one-way mirror.

"Okay, Dr. Evans, you will be going away for a long time. We know you were a part of this cover up and we know that the test center was illegal. The only way to help yourself now is to tell the truth. Where is the staff from the test center and the facility? And where is Dr. Sonya McKenna."

They can see the shock register on his face at the mention of Sonya, but he manages to pull himself together before he speaks.

"You are wrong. You have the tapes. Does it show anywhere on there that we murdered the staff."

SSA Hunt joins Thaddeus in the interrogation room. "Your right. We cannot prove that you got rid of the staff, but I think I know." He whispers in SSA Hutchinson's ear and leaves the room.

In a bit, the other doctors are brought into the room occupied by Dr. Evans. Once they are all seated, Thaddeus continues.

"Here is what I think. You poisoned the staff. I cannot prove it right now, but we have checked each of your residences and taken anything questionable to the lab. It is just a matter of time before we find out the truth."

There are concerned expressions on the doctors' faces.

"So, what happens now," Dr. Warren asks.

"It is not up to us. We are turning all of you in along with all the information we have, to the local police. Hopefully, they will get justice and closure for the families."

SSA Hutchinson pauses, "Oh, wait, you made sure there were not any families to get involved where the staff was concerned, but you had not expected Dr. McKenna to get involved. She has family."

Chapter 70

Now came the moment that SSA Steward hated most. She had to meet with the family of Dr. Sonya McKenna. She asked Pamela to come with her for moral support and Pam agrees.

As they drive to the McKenna residence, they are silent, needing those few moments of sanity before facing the McKennas. When Jennifer had called to tell them, they would like to come over and talk, she could hear it in his voice they had an idea that it was not good news. Mr. McKenna had asked if it was all right if Dr. Tina Williams joined them. They had told them it was fine.

When they pull into the driveway, they are impressed by the house. A lot can be learned about a family just by their home. From the window treatments, the color of the door and the gardens around the front porch, Jennifer feels the love and care the family takes in their environment. When they open the car doors and start up the walk, they let the back of their hands touch giving moral support.

On the porch, Jennifer reaches out and presses the doorbell and in seconds the door opens, and they are ushered into a warm milieu. Matthew excuses himself to reach out and close the door behind them.

"Welcome, my name is Matthew McKenna, Sonya's husband."

Pamela smiles, shyly. "Yes, I know you. I know your books. I have read all of them. You are a great writer."

"Thank you," he says questioningly.

"Sorry, I am SSA Pamela Brewster of the FBI. This," she says turning to Jennifer, "Is SSA Jennifer Steward."

"Hello. We were expecting Agent Hutchinson. Please come into the family room. My daughter and Dr. Williams are waiting for us."

They follow Matthew into the family room, and he introduces his daughter, Elise and Sonya's friend, Dr. Tina Williams. They recognize each of them by the pictures they had on the story board at the FBI. Elise McKenna sits on the sofa, hugging the arm rest. They know that Sonya was part Chinese and her father, African American and Elise seems to have taken the best of both races. She is quite stunning.

On the other side of the room, seated in an overstuffed lounge chair is Dr. Tina Williams. She seems restless as she waits to hear about her friend.

"Please, have a seat. Can we get you something to drink?"

"No, we are fine," Jennifer says as they walk over to take a seat in two side chairs that face the occupants of the room. Once seated, Jennifer begins.

"I do not know how much you've been told, but we wanted to come and tell you what we know to be true."

Jennifer begins telling them all of what happened at the hospital, as it pertained to Sonya McKenna. They did not share any facts concerning the test clinic but verified that most of what they had heard from Dr. Williams was true.

"Your mother, wife and friend she began," looking at each person in the room, Dr. McKenna had thought something suspicions was happening to the patients at the hospital and had investigated the matter. What she had found was a mirrored facility in the sub-basement of the hospital and using the alias of Dr. Weston was able to take a tour of the place with Nurse Lottie Bond who ran the facility. In any case, Nurse Bond informed Dr. Griffin Warren of the visitor who claimed to be sent to work at the facility. She had no reason to doubt that, as she had asked Dr. Warren to send her help."

"Dr. Warren did some checking and found out that Dr. Weston was really Dr. McKenna. He waited for the opportune time and he sedated her and took her down to the facility. They kept her there, along with others but when they realized they had to get rid of the facility, it meant they had to cover their tracks. The patients, we believe all died of the coronavirus or the unapproved vaccine they had administer, but the staff, we believe from evidence found in the debris were poisoned."

Though they try hard to cover it up, the family is disturbed by her words. Elise hangs tightly to the arm of the chair and Matthew turns his body slightly away from them.

"Dr. McKenna was trying to save lives and in the end her life was taken. She was a hero and though I know that it is hard to accept her being murdered for what she believed in, find comfort in knowing she could not turn her back on people being used in that way."

Jennifer paused and gave them time to absorb what she shared and then asked, "Do you want to ask us any questions?"

There is silence and then Matthew coughs, to remove the lump from this throat and speaks. "I just want to thank you for being open and honest with us. We had heard most of it, but now we know what the truth is. We thank you for that."

Jennifer can hear Elise sobbing and watches as Dr. Williams gets up, with tears on her cheeks that she wipes on the back of her hand as she goes over to comfort Elise.

Pamela hands Matthew her card and one of Jennifer's. "You can call us any time. Right now, the case is in the hands of your law enforcement officers and rest assure all the parties have been arrested and will go to prison for the rest of their life."

"We cannot thank you enough, Agent Steward and Agent Brewster. Let me show you to the door."

Matthew sees them to the door, then goes into the kitchen. There he leans on the counter, letting the tears flow. It is now true. Sonya is not coming back. She is dead. She is dead. He breaks into uncontrollable sobs as he continues to lean on the counter for support.

Chapter 71

As long as he has been doing this job, he still cannot get over how cruel people can be to one another. But this is one of the worse investigations he has faced. Murderers killing people and unbalanced people turning on their spouse and families has been what he has dealt with.

It is sad, it is frustrating that they are called in after the local authorities have no luck in solving the case and must leave once the people responsible are in custody. But that is their job, and it has been rewarding up until now.

These are doctors, healers, not murderers. Thaddeus Hutchinson stands, trying to focus his mind on having another successful conclusion to a case. Yet, the satisfaction does not come

He does not want to admit why he cannot enjoy solving the case, so he gets up and walks to the window of his office.

SSA David Monihan is having the same thoughts. He tries to fake listening to the younger members of the team chatting about this and the other, but he has not quite gotten to that point where he can put the matter behind him. He is not that versatile anymore. These days after he has fixed an elaborate meal for himself and his wife and they have had wine with the dinner and a stiff drink after, he is able to let it go and face another day. Only he is not so sure it is going to happen that easily this time. He stands, thinking he needs to go home, but he looks up and sees Thaddeus gazing down at the team. He has the same expression on his face as David envisions, he has on his. He goes up to join him.

"Hey, Thaddeus, want a drink." Thaddeus looks down at David's hand and sees he has a bottle of bourbon.

Managing a weak smile of thanks with a nod he turns and goes over to his credenza to retrieve two glasses that he takes over to his desk. He watches as David pours them each a glass and sits in one of the side chairs. Thaddeus sits in the other one and they toast each other.

A comfortable silence remains as they enjoy the bourbon, then David speaks.

"We have been at this a long time, but I think, like me you are trying to make sense of this one. Thaddeus you know as well as I do, there is no sense to be made."

"I know that David, but it is doctors who have committed murder...willingly. I can accept the desperate need to try and stop this pandemic by finding a cure. That I can understand, but they went too far when they murdered the staff. That was pure adulterated murder."

David takes another sip of his bourbon as he tries to find the words needed to make them both feel better.

"Think of it this way. It was an act of human nature to try and cover up what they had done. They were not acting as doctors, but as humans." He pauses and takes another sip of bourbon. "Our team, us, faced what might have been an impossible case and solved it. We put all the pieces together and those responsible will never see the light of day again. That is a win."

Thaddeus stares at David. "You're right. Yes, it is. They are where they belong and cannot hurt again. Thanks David."

"You are welcome."

Summary

There is a false confidence level in the advancements made in disease control so that this pandemic took everyone by surprise. We have Flu vaccines produced and updated yearly, and yearly vaccinations are offered. There are antiviral drugs in existence that treat flu illness, and in the event of virus exposure, can be used for prevention, as well. Importantly, many different antibiotics are now available that can be used to treat secondary bacterial infections.

And this happens all over the world through the World Health Organization. WHO has a Global Influenza Surveillance and Response System that monitors changes in seasonal flu viruses, as well as monitors the emergence of new in human flu viruses. It is a group effort between the

United States, Australia, China, Japan, and the United Kingdom. The united laboratory testing and flu surveillance around the world was established to focus on pandemic preparedness efforts but COVID-19 hid behind a veil of pneumonia before it was recognized for what it is.

In 2019, the world population was 7.6 billion people. COVID-19 overwhelmed health care infrastructure, both in the United States and across the world. Hospitals and doctors' offices struggled to meet demand from the number of patients requiring care. The event called for significant increases in the manufacture, distribution and supply of medications, products, and life-saving medical equipment, such as mechanical ventilators.

The biggest challenge is the time required to manufacture a new vaccine against COVID-19 which could take months to test and then once the proper vaccine was found, the challenge faced was to inoculate those 7.6 billion people.

All these issues show that more work needs to be done, both here in the United States and internationally, to prepare for the next pandemic. It is not if there will be one, but when.

In the case of COVID-19 the search for a cure went on for almost two years as scientists continued to sequence the gene and microbiologist tried to replicate the virus for testing.

Experiments were desperately conducted in secret and openly to understand the virus. They picked it apart but instead of a cure they did learn that it was the unique combination of all the coronavirus genes together that made it so particularly dangerous.

It was the old saying, desperate times, call for desperate measures that lead to the unauthorized testing of vaccines on human subjects.

While all this was happening, we as a people dealt with ruined relationships when one partner was afraid to go out beyond the doors of the home. Whether or not we were infected we wanted to visit friends and family. We wanted to attend weddings and funerals.

Eventually we gave in and the government followed suit allowing schools, businesses, and restaurants to open and sports events to begin again. From that first and second wave, we did not learn our lesson and found ourselves facing a third wave with anew social distancing, masks, deaths, and disparity when all we wanted was our lives back.

About The Author

Juanita Tischendorf has published over ten books of fiction and non-fiction, with most settled in Upstate, New York where she lives with her husband Mark. Her life experiences helped fine-tune her writing skills. She is a business school graduate and has completed writing courses at the University of Washington and has participated in several master classes on writing. She writes from her heart using strong, believable characters.